A Dragon So Savage

A Wrath and Revenge Novel

First edition

Line editing by Enchanted Edits

Proofread by Muse & Margins

Covert Art by INK Book Designs

Interior Character Illustrations by Lia Ramirez

Map created by K. Christine

Contents

Warning

A Dragon So Savage is a dark romantic fantasy. It contains some topics that may be upsetting to some readers. Your mental health is more important than consuming this story. Please note the following content, and read with caution:

- Explicit language

- Trauma

- Secrets and betrayal

- Descriptive on-page sexual activity

- Mentioned nudity (there are dragon shifters, so they are nude after each shift)

- Violence, blood, torture, and gore

- Death (parental, child, various characters)

- Psychological abuse

- Sexual violence (not explicit)

- Panic attacks/ anxiety

Pronunciation Guide

A lot of readers probably wonder where or how authors come up with the names in their books. For me, I used names of: Orcas, different items around me smashed together, names of characters from my favorite TV shows, and pets I've had in my life.

T'naka: Tuh-naw-kuh

Takae: Tuh-Kie

Cimmerian: Si-meer-ee-uhn

Caligness: Kuh-lig-nuss

Santavarre: San-tuh-var

Raeganarde: Ray-guhn-narde

Stygian: Stig-ee-uhn

Aquasailies: Ah-kwuh-say-lees

Menticide: Men-tuh-side

Florauna: Flor-aw-nuh

Brythos: Bri-thos

Anamnesis: An-uhm-nee-sis

Asahi: Ah-sah-hee

Akira: Ah-kee-rah

Godival: Guh-dy-vuhl

Valkara: Val-kuh-ruh

Orcalorne: Or-kuh-lorn

Monsteralafe: Mon-stair-uh-layf

Kuma: Koo-muh

Vizcaya: Viz-kay-yuh

Ivalea: I-veil-ee-ah

Amalia: Ah-mahl-ee-ah

Drakar: Dray-car

Zynth: Zinth

CALIGNESS

CIMMERIAN

GODIVAL MOUNTAINS

DIVAL WOODS

FORGOTTON PASSAGE

SANTAVARRE

THE LA

TORRAVER

LANDS OF STYGIAN

BARREN LANDS

ANAMNESIS CAVE

JASAILIES

RAEGANARDE

This book is dedicated to all who can't sleep at night, whose minds are constantly churning an endless waterfall of thoughts, ideas, and fears. To those that suffer in silence, fighting battles no one else can see. Battles you feel you have to face alone.

You aren't alone.

Prologue
Fifteen Years Earlier

"Please, Mother, just one more story!" Mother's stories were always filled with magical creatures, my dreams would feature flying dragons and fae creatures who liked to trick humans. They always made me laugh!

"Okay, Amalia, but you must go to bed after!" She cuddled in closer after grabbing the worn, leather-bound book. I placed a hand over her large tummy—my sisters said it was a baby boy, but I'd rather have another sister.

"Girls! Would you like to listen to the Kingdom End Chronicles?" my mother shouted. Squeals and feet pattering against wood sounded before my sisters barreled into bed with us.

Ivalea and Vizcaya argued over who would get to be closest to Mother, while Monet and I sat quietly, tucked under the covers. "Okay, girls, calm down. Viz— Ivalea! No pulling hair!" Mother sighed then winced, grabbing hold of her tummy.

"You okay, Mama?" Monet asked, face sullen with worry.

"I'm fine, your sibling is just moving around a lot, won't be long now until we meet the little girl or boy." Mother ran her hand along Monet's cheek, then tapped me on the nose. Vizcaya and Ivalea finally settled down, and Mother began reading.

"Long ago in the world of Caligness, magic hummed in every tree and stone all across the lands. You could feel it in the breeze as it skirted across your skin, you could taste it in the water, see it shimmer in your dreams." She wiggled her fingers down like she was mimicking rainfall. We all giggled as she continued. "Dragons, humans, and fae lived in kingdoms stretched across Caligness, each having their own sacred lands to call home. For centuries, they lived in harmony, but all good things must come to an end."

"No, Mother, they can stay happy forever! Like us!" Ivalea said.

"Oh, honey, how I wish that were true." Mother kissed her forehead with another little wince as she shifted back to read on.

"Humans grew hungry—"

"For samiches?" Monet exclaimed excitedly.

Mother chuckled. "No, sweetie, not for sandwiches, for *more.*" We all looked at each other. What else could there be?

"Humans saw how the dragons had glittering crystals, pristine healing waters, mountains that reached the skies. Fae had lush forests, festivals, and most importantly, magic. Humans had drained their lakes, hunted their wildlife until there was nothing left, and destroyed their forests to build homes. They wanted more land, but they didn't want to share. Do you know what their leader said?" Mother asked. My sisters and I looked at each other, then turned our heads back and forth to say no. "Why share what we can just take?"

"B–but you tell us taking isn't nice! I always have to share." Vizcaya crossed her arms with a huff.

"You're right, *taking* isn't nice," Mother said. "So one night, when the moon was barely a whisper, humans followed their leader into the Forgotten Forest where the fae kingdom's border lay. Their leader was cunning; he had created devices that *tick, tick, ticked.* The humans planted them into homes of the fae while they were sleeping, then ran back into the darkness of the forest. When they were safe and hidden, they made those devices explode. *BOOM!*"

"Noo Mama, I don't like this story!" Monet sniffled as she ducked her head under the covers.

"It's okay, Mon-Mon, it's not real, it's only a story." I tried to comfort my sister so Mother wouldn't stop reading.

"Yeah, Monet, don't be such a baby," Ivalea retorted.

Mother shot her a stern look. "Do we need to stop for the night? Seems like you girls need some sleep."

"No!" we all yelled in unison.

Mother pressed on the side of her tummy, her face flinching. "Okay, we will finish this one, then we *all* need to get some sleep. Mama included." She propped the book on her tummy and started reading again.

"*BOOM!* Flames shot to the sky, devouring the homes and gardens the fae cherished. Not a scream was heard, but the fae never truly die. They are one with the magic throughout the lands. Their souls lifted and intertwined with the wind, the rustling of the leaves telling them where the culprits were. The souls swarmed the humans. *'Balance will demand a reckoning for every life stolen,'* they hissed in anger." Mother made the sound of a snake when she said the last part, and we all giggled.

I shifted to face my mother and asked, "Why are humans so mean?" It made me sad what they had done.

She brushed a strand of my hair out of my face. "Oh, honey, not all humans are mean or bad. Some would sacrifice everything to do what is right. Even if it means sacrificing themselves."

"I want to be a good human!" I said cheerfully.

"Oh, sweet girl, you are one of the best," My mother crooned. "You all are my sweet girls."

"Oh my dragons! What about the dragon's mother?" I asked. They were my favorite!

Mother laughed. "Oh my dragons? I kinda like that phrase, it can be our little inside joke." She winked at me. "Okay, the dragons. The dragons, great beasts that kept to themselves, now stirred. The act against the fae was an act against all the other kingdoms. The humans had started the Kingdom End War. The war was deadly, with losses of every species. Humans planted explosives in the dragons' nests, annihilating their hatchlings and unhatched eggs. The skies were nothing more than smoke and wails. One dragon, white as snow, named Takae, called for the end of humans, demanding their deaths for what had been done. However, the Shadow Dragon Kiako disagreed, for not all humans had attacked. He believed the innocent should be spared."

"I love the Shadow Dragon!" I said excitedly. "He's nice."

"It takes great strength to have compassion during tragedy," Mother said. "The three fae rulers were torn on what was right. They all agreed they couldn't spare any more losses. The Shadow Dragon proposed a plan." Mother's eyes went wide. "He said, *'We take to the skies and leave the humans to survive on their own.'* And so they struck a pact, with the dragon's abilities and the fae's magic, they would carve the lands and take them skyward. The Water Dragons flew over the boundaries, spraying waterfalls of aquamarine onto the soil, creating deep rivulets which turned into roaring rivers. Next, the male Florauna Dragons would loaf on the ground and use their boulder-like tail to pound into the land, causing the weakened soil under the newly created rivers to fracture into deep faults miles below the surface. Once the fractures were made, the fae from Calicon and Aerial Dragons used a combined effort of magic and wind to separate the loosened large masses of land

and defy all odds by moving the masses upward. The air itself trembled from the sheer power, It was a slow and exhausting task that took its toll on many.

"Once the masses were past the surface level, the braver fae of Orcalorne were to ride atop the Shadow Dragons as they transported the masses above the highest clouds. The dragons cast cloud-like shadows beneath them. To humans, it would simply look as if a murderous storm was blowing in. Once above the layers of clouds, the fae imbued all nine land masses to keep them idle in the sky and cast a visual spell to hide the bottoms from human sight."

We were all transfixed on Mother as she told us the story. She was breathing heavily, talking was too much for her. "Is that the end of the story, Mother?" I whispered. "Are you okay?"

"Oh yes, Amalia, I'm fine. Just a little tired. It's not quite the end, little one. We're almost there." She sucked in a breath and finished the story. "Below, the lands had shifted, unlike what they were before. Humans would try and venture past their border but suddenly feel the urge to turn and run. The lands of Caligness were theirs now, but they couldn't get to them."

"What about the white dragon, Mama?" Monet asked.

"Takae was angry. He swore revenge on the leader who took his family. Grief took over, and he vowed to return from the skies when he could end the humans forever. The Menticide Dragons never forget."

Mother shifted uncomfortably, and we all moved to give her space. "Okay, girls, time for bed." She winced once more as she lifted from the bed.

"Mother?"

"Yes, sweet girl?"

"What if the mean dragon comes back?" I said, unable to shake the feeling that the mean dragon would be under my bed and take me.

"Well, that's what your daddy is for. He will always protect you. When you look up at the sky, remember it holds more than stars."

"It holds dragons!" I shouted.

Mother laughed and looked at me. "And as for the mean dragon, even smothered fires can come back burning brighter than before, but you are surrounded by people who would sacrifice themselves to save you. Those who care about you are your water against the flames."

I rubbed my eyes and pulled the covers up to my chin. "I'll be your water, too, Mother," I said sleepily.

Chapter 1

An invisible gaze had stalked me since morning. I could feel it in the pricks along my neck that raced down between my shoulder blades, sending shivers down my spine. The kind of sensation that made you turn around in anxiety-ridden panic, even without a sound to startle you. As I stood within my field, the goosebumps stretched over my skin. Petals of vibrant colors filled my vision as I warily looked around to find the source of my unease. There was nothing in sight but the endless fields of flowers that lay at the bottom of the Godival Mountains. Even they knew something wasn't quite right. They seemed to alert me in the way they all were in a synchronized flinch from some creeping wrongness, their stalks seeming to cower away from an invisible threat.

I took a few tentative skips into the field while glancing around. Thin, delicate, pink and yellow silky tendrils brushed against my bare legs as I traversed through the flowers. When I was a few paces in, I closed my eyes, threw my arms out into the air beside me, and let my body soak in the warmth of the sun. The rays beamed down while I took a deep breath and twirled around, taking small steps between each movement to travel farther into the space. A large shadow rippled over the field so quickly, I almost believed I had imagined it.

I turned my gaze upward, brows pulling together, narrowing my eyes. The sky looked unnatural. I tilted my head and moved a trembling hand to shield my eyes from the blinding light of the sun. Millions of tiny, fiery-golden, crystal-looking flakes fell in a light rain, landing on my skin like soft kisses before absorbing into me. *What the hell...?*

Dizziness washed over me like a rogue wave. I staggered, arms dropping limp, vision swimming with flecks of the beauty that had rained down on me. I started to sway slightly, suddenly lightheaded. *That'll teach you to twirl too much at twenty-three years old*. Logic hissed at me that something much worse was happening.

"Amalia!" a distorted voice called out, slicing through my confusion. Twisting, I attempted to look at who would be in my field. I'd rarely seen anyone visit the fields like I did. I liked to think they were mine alone. You'd have a higher chance of finding a fairytale creature like a dragon before seeing another person.

One heartbeat was all the time it took. I was slipping away. I could feel it. I became weightless before I could fully turn my head. The ground vanished, no longer beneath my feet. Every limb felt like clouds. *Was I floating or falling?* A jolt of electricity surged through my body, lightning struck within my veins, setting my nerves aflame. The field blurred into a kaleidoscope of colors. Then I was nothing at all as darkness sank over me.

A rush of heat swarmed around me as the beats in my chest quickened to an unnatural rhythm. I watched as a young woman walked past me, like I wasn't even there. Dirt climbing up and staining her calves. She stopped just a few feet away from where I was, a haze taking over my vision, making it hard to see as my eyes began to water. A harsh, heated wind picked up as debris flew all around. The woman turned back, a stone expression locked in place. She was looking past me, through me, to something or someone else. It was so hard to see her clearly. I tried to rub my eyes, though my hands never reached my face. Squinting, I strained to see her. I tried to focus. Her face, down to her clothes and arms, were also caked in a thick film of grime. What had she gone through? I couldn't speak, no matter how hard I tried, my vocal cords feeling as if they'd been singed like a log left to burn throughout the night. The woman took a few steps toward my position, raising her hand toward what was beyond me. Frustration bubbled to the surface as my vision prevented me from seeing clearly, no matter how hard I struggled to focus on the one standing before me. It was as if she were choosing what to show me. Her skin began to glisten the closer she neared, making me think she may have been wet if she wasn't covered in dirt... wait. That wasn't dirt. It... It was blood.

Coating her entire form. The woman choked back a sob, her outstretched arm snatching back to cover her mouth, eyes squeezing shut like she couldn't bear whatever emotion consumed her. After a few seconds, her eyes snapped open, a look of determination in them before both arms extended, reaching like she was summoning something to come to her. Heat radiated below me, but my gaze didn't leave the woman. I watched helplessly as fire flowed from either side of where I stood, heading toward each of her arms. A soundless but painful scream burned my throat; she didn't hear me. My legs attempted and failed to lurch toward her. I didn't move—my feet felt like they were locked in place with shackles. I couldn't save her. She didn't see me. The fire reached her hands, and as the flames licked at her skin, she tilted her head up to the sky, her body arching. A strangled sound filled the air as she cried out an apology that got swallowed by the sound of death; whoever the cry was for could never have heard it. Before I could blink, the flames devoured her blood-coated body. I fought against the invisible chains holding me in place. I thrashed my fists against the walls I couldn't see stopping me from intervening. The fire erased her existence, turning her into nothing but ash swirling in the night wind. The world around me trembled from a bellow so powerful I felt it in my bones, infecting me with the emotions behind the horror-stricken sound. Heartbreak, anger, and disbelief ricocheted through me until a shockwave made my vision go black.

I gasped for breath as air refused to fill my lungs, which felt as though they were constricting, like a snake wrapping around its prey. I tried to open my eyes, but they didn't budge. Stuck in a slumbering state by some invisible vise, I tried to stir, but my limbs weren't moving either, as if they were no longer attached to my body. *Move. Scream. Twitch. Anything! What is happening to me?* Fear made my heart frantically hammer against my chest.

Something firm and warm cradled my head, providing me with a moment of serenity. Reminding me of when one lies in a lover's lap. Only one other person knew I visited here—Story, my best friend. I'd known her since I was a toddler, and we'd been inseparable since. Our families let us go off on whatever adventure we found, never asking questions, just letting us run freely. This wasn't her lap. This lap felt strong, and where hers was bony and delicate, this felt thick and muscular, radiating a warmth around me. I felt... safe. *Too safe.*

A burst of unease scorched me. My stomach dropped as the recollection that I had been feeling someone watching me all day resurfaced. The hand that was caressing me could easily be the hand that would end me. The hand of the one who had been watching, waiting. *Were they waiting for this moment?* Not only could I not see them, I couldn't move to defend myself, not that I really knew how. I tried to twitch a finger, nothing. My mind was screaming at my body to listen to my commands, *move, open your eyes, run.* But my limbs simply interpreted those as suggestions that they had no intention of taking.

I felt a rough hand gently caressing my face, slowly, carefully, then the caress moved up my cheek until their fingers ran tenderly through my hair. As much as reason tried to tell me I should be afraid, my pulse slowed, matching the rhythm of the caress. I tried to open my eyes again, they fluttered ever so slightly before a voice murmured, "I'm sorry,"—unfamiliar, yet so intimate, as if I knew them—"for what they've done."

My head rose, weightless once more for only a moment, before the ground I had come to memorize welcomed me like a friend. The sharp blades of grass tickled my ears, I wished they could whisper to me everything that was happening. Help me understand. The slight buzzing of wings of what I could only assume was a bee collecting pollen from a flower above me brought my thoughts back to the moment. *Breathe. Just breathe.*

Footsteps led away from me toward where I knew a small group of trees lay, just before the end of the trail I had taken to get to the field. Silence surrounded me. *Breathe.* I tried again to wiggle my fingers, willing them to do something, anything. I was rewarded with the slightest flicker of movement, but it was enough. A burst of adrenaline spread through my veins, boosting my confidence and encouraging me to try to open my eyes again. Blurry splotches of blue seeped through the slit my eyes created. I took a few deep breaths, trying to calm my racing heart. It was no longer thrumming out of fear, but hope.

Footsteps sounded again—closer now. *The stranger was back.* I didn't attempt to move my body, opting for limpness, as I felt my head being lifted again, a bit more forcefully than before. I tried to pry my eyes open one last time; bright sun brutally attacked, piercing my eyeballs with a white-hot pain. I jerked my head away from the onslaught, fright filled me as an automatic groan escaped my lips, giving away I was conscious.

"Amalia?" The voice said—clearer now, soaked with confusion and another emotion I couldn't quite place. "Gods—you're awake?" they said breathlessly. I slowly turned my head in the direction of the voice. My movements felt forced and sluggish. I realized, as his face became less blurred, that I knew this man. His features were coming into focus. I saw his eyes first, which were so strikingly light blue they looked icy. Resembling the waters surrounding the glaciers of Raeganarde, an abandoned winter kingdom in the Forgotten Lands. I could make out details of his features, like his strong jawline and full lips that were partially parted, framed by laugh lines; his straight and narrow nose that turned just slightly to the sky at the end; and his light blonde hair that reflected the sun, a color that bordered on almost white.

I still felt a dizzying sensation, the world around me spinning like a never-ending dance. But *him*? Lane, he filled my vision, grounding me.

"L—Lane," I coughed out, my throat burning as I spoke. "Wha—What happened? Did I pass out?" Some small part of me knew I hadn't. I—No, my soul felt... different.

His jaw flexed as his eyes raked over me, tilting me to sit up before he said, "I'm not sure passing out is the correct phrase." A cautious smile lifted his cheeks. "You survived, let's focus on that for a second. Can you stand?"

Survived?

My brain started spinning, and I felt as though I were going to slip back into oblivion for a second time.

"Woah, hey, Amalia, easy. You're okay," Lane said as I felt my body fall back.

Tingles ran through my body, sending warning bells; something wasn't right. *I wasn't right.* Lane caught me before I fell. "What happened to me?" Rubbing my head, I tried to make sense of the fact that I'd gone from being in my field to waking up practically paralyzed.

I sat up slowly with the support from Lane's hand still on my back. As I got upright and took in a breath, I smelled the blazing stars around me. Their faint scent of vanilla soothed my anxiety as it filled my nostrils. With a steadying breath, I moved to my knees, then lifted my right leg while pushing off with my left. Lane followed my movements like we were one person, then shifted his body effortlessly so I could lean against him.

"We can stay like this for a moment. Try to get used to the feeling, and then you can attempt to take a few steps." He must have seen the doubt in my facial expression, because he immediately responded with, "Don't worry, I will be right here. I'm not going anywhere."

I slid my left foot forward. My heart lurched watching the withered plants beneath me rip easily from the soil, not able to lift my weight off the ground. "I don't think I can," I whispered, more to myself than anything.

"You can." His voice was rough. "What you just went through is something humans were not meant to survive." Calloused palms came up to cup my face briefly before returning to hold me. My body was already swaying without the support like a sapling trying to stay upright during a vicious summer storm. "Try again, but focus on lifting your foot." My brows pulled together as his words registered in my groggy mind.

Lane started to turn me, so we were facing the trail back to our village, still about fifty feet away from where we were. With some assistance, we started toward the trail, me clinging to his brawny bicep as I tried to take small steps.

"What exactly did I survive?" I asked, voice trembling from the effort to speak, looking over at him while still paying attention to my steps. One misstep or above-ground root and I'd be a goner.

Lane looked at me with uncertainty swirling in his eyes. "I don't know," he said blankly. The words were hollow, his attention quickly skirting away from me.

Didn't he say that humans were not meant to survive what happened to me? How would he know that, if he didn't know what happened...

I quickly realized I had to relax my face as it ached from the sharpened stare I sent his way. My thoughts had always had a way of showing all over my face. His jaw clenched as he noticed my skepticism...

"You don't know?" I asked, distrust lacing the question.

He just stared ahead.

"But you just—"

"Listen, I don't know what happened." His eyes began to darken. "I saw the villagers in the market on my way to the field, and they were all on the ground, none of them got up."

Everything stopped for just a moment. "What do you mean, didn't get up, Lane?" With each labored breath I took, I felt them quicken and become more shallow. My lungs felt like knives were slicing into them.

"They were dead, Amalia."

I gasped for a breath that my lungs refused to take in. "Ev—everyone's dead? My family? Story?" My chest began to tighten. The weight of everything felt like a boulder weighing me down. "I-I-I c-can't b-b-breathe," I said, clawing at my throat. I stumbled as my mind spiraled. My sisters, my brother, and Father. Were they also gone?

"Hey, hey, Amalia, I'm here, I've got you." Lane braced my back against his chest, his taut form wrapping around me like a blanket as my knees buckled. He crossed my arms over my chest and held me tight as I fought to take in a full breath.

"How are they gone? What happened!" I screeched. The sudden grief was too much.

"Just calm down, Amalia. You're still here."

"CALM DOWN? Lane!" I shouted through the struggle. "You just said everyone in the village is dead, and you're telling *ME*, who just woke up with no control of her body, to calm down? Are you insane?" I was practically gasp-screaming at him, everything was a fight, I was battling myself to walk, to talk. I looked at the trail ahead, and I no longer wanted to walk toward it. I looked back at my field and the mountains, back where everything had always been good and peaceful. It had always been a sanctuary for me.

"I could be wrong. I hope I'm wrong, but if not, you need to be prepared," Lane said, his voice held a hint of regret.

A nod was all I could manage while struggling for air as I stared blankly at a tree ahead. Numbness overtook the shock. "I woke up, though." A small ember of hope ignited. "So they could all be waking up now as well. Right?" My instincts knew the answer, but I couldn't help but want to be wrong.

Lane's silence doused that ember quickly, and I faced the trail. The branches that interlaced together overhead created a shaded path of gloom, the leaves falling in slow motion from the limbs high above my head, like the trees were crying over the loss.

After a few minutes of us shuffling down the path in silence, I asked, "So, if what happened affected *everyone*, as you say. How are you alive?" The more we walked, the more time I had to think. I was able to grasp that I'd almost died. I needed answers as to why. Answers I felt he had, but would he share them?

He shrugged his shoulders. "I wish I knew. It may be the same reason you are."

"Why were you headed to the field?" He had been in Cimmerian for a while now, and I had never seen him visit it on his own.

"I see someone has some of their energy back." He glanced at me with a crooked smile that lifted his right cheek. "Well, I've been wanting to talk with you all day, but I just couldn't find the right time. Then I noticed you heading here, so when I finished helping your father, I headed this way."

"Talk?" I echoed the word.

"Yes. Talk."

Clearly, I had to pry this out of him. I was the one struggling to function, yet he couldn't carry this conversation. "Abouuuuutt?" I said, dragging out the word in hopes he would be less mysterious.

"Amalia, this is not the time for this conversation. At all." I could tell by his tone that was meant to end this conversation, but I wasn't one to leave things be.

"Hello?" I waved an arm out weakly. "Are you forgetting I'm moving at a snail's pace?" My foot snagged on a barely visible root, causing me to stumble before Lane's hand darted out, steadying me. "Thank you," I said quickly before continuing, "Unless you'd like to carry me, I think we have some time." My breath came out in pants from the exertion of trying to hold a conversation, but I needed this distraction.

The realization was sharp and hit me quickly, those feelings of being watched. It had been *him* lurking, waiting to supposedly have a conversation.

"I promise it can wait. We should really discuss what the plans are for when we reach the village if everyone..." his sentence trailed off as he rubbed the back of his neck.

"Is dead," I finished for him, my face deadpan.

"Amalia."

"Well," I continued, even though each word was a struggle, "the first thing I will be doing is having a mental breakdown, because that will mean the death of everyone I love." My voice went up an octave like it was just another cheerful conversation between us.

Silence and pressure suffocated the space, and Lane's eyes roamed over me. Studying me. "You don't need to do that," he said, bringing us to a stop.

"Do what?"

"Brush what could be waiting for us off with jokes, like it's not affecting you."

I'm not sure if it was the fact he saw through me so easily or that his words made everything I was trying to shove deep within me rush to the surface. "I don't know what you want from me, Lane. This is the only way I can handle what is going on. The sky shimmered, then I woke up with no control of my own body, then you tell me everyone I know is probably dead. If I don't find a way to deal with it, I will crumble. This is how I deal with it."

"Shimmered?" His eyebrow went up. *That's what he took from my outburst?*

"Yes," I said, slightly annoyed, "it looked like the sky was raining diamonds or something. I know it sounds crazy, but that's what I saw."

"Did you see anything before? What about after, do you remember anything?"

He asked the questions so quickly, my mind went blank. I thought for a moment, trying to recall anything else. What could I say to him to explain? "I don't really remember. I suppose I felt as if I was falling asleep while still awake. Which, I know, sounds equally weird, but honestly, that's exactly what it felt like. My body was going to sleep, but my mind was still active and trying to register what was going on around me." One memory burned in my mind. The woman—I didn't recognize her, but I'd felt a connection with her. I didn't know if it was a nightmare, but I couldn't allow myself to speak about it. There were already enough unknowns for us to handle. This one could wait. My hair brushed my shoulders in a sweeping motion as I shook my head back and forth, trying to clear the vision of the flames consuming her away and refocus on the conversation.

Lane was silent, the still, quiet air making me writhe. I threw my hands up before they collapsed against my thighs and blurted, "I sound crazy, don't I?"

Lane jumped back from my sudden outburst like I had been hiding behind a corner and pounced on him. "No, you sound alive, and confused. I just don't have the words to say. I'm sorry that it happened to you, and I wish I knew why it didn't happen to me." He paused for a moment, his mouth twisting up ever so slightly before adding, "And I can't believe I missed the raining glitter." He shot me a sidelong glance; I retaliated with a hit to his shoulder that wouldn't bruise a newborn baby. The attempt at easing my small spiral didn't go unnoticed.

"Shut up," I said, running my hands through my tangled waves of burnt apricot. "It was rather beautiful before it made me pass out." I shot him my own smile. This time he let me make the joke without any comment. My heart was heavy despite the mask I was hiding behind, "Maybe there are others alive, and we will find out more once we get back. They could have seen something different, heard something."

"Yeah," Lane replied solemnly as he scratched the back of his neck. "Maybe."

We walked the rest of the trail in eerie silence. Even the few songbirds perched on tree limbs were mute. I had never known them to not have a song to share. I couldn't help but feel the underlying warning there, like they were waiting for us to see what they already had. A large, rotting oak tree that had fallen long ago lay ahead. The mushrooms growing in waves along the sides of it had become a marker for me to gauge where I was along the trail. I knew we were about thirty feet from a bend that led into the main courtyard of our village. Every weekend, markets took place in the mornings. If I had my mind right, the courtyard should have been full of people and life.

A rush of chills ran down my spine, and I slowed to a stop, casting a glance behind us.

"Are you okay?" Lane asked, putting his hand out for me.

Staring into the empty space where I could have sworn I saw shadows moving between the trees, I looked at the branches, which were unmoving. I uttered quietly, "I'm fine, I thought I saw... a shadow."

Lane's face became serious, "We are on a trail, there are shadows everywhere." His words pulled my attention to him. His striking blue eyes deepened, shapes resembling shards sharpening around his pupils. A deep blue rim outlined the outer edge, the color of aqua filling the middle.

After a few moments, he looked at me and said, "Why are you staring at me?" The words came out defensive.

"I... I'm sorry, it's just your eyes." How had I never seen them like this before?

"I've been told I can thank my father for them." There was a hint of malice in his voice as he spoke, making me wonder why it would be something he loathed. He had been banished to live in Cimmerian almost a year ago, I could imagine that would cause resentment between father and son. A part of me wished to reach out and soothe him.

"Can you walk with me?" I held out my hand to him, so he knew I didn't just mean by my side. We both needed to be closer, for entirely different reasons. Him for the internal battle I brought attention to, and me for what we were undoubtedly about to see.

He looked down at my hand as his jaw clenched; he had never had to think about this before. "Of course." He slipped his rigid fingers with my trembling ones, and we moved forward.

We took thirty steps together, each one silent. No sounds other than the crunching of fallen leaves and twigs snapping under our feet, before we reached the clearing where it opened into the courtyard.

Silence.

It was like we'd reached a void. There should have been chatter, kids playing, music from the old men sitting and playing banjos in rocking chairs by the jerky cart.

There was nothing.

My feet hit cobblestone, and I took in the scene that awaited in front of me, sending my world into darkness.

Bodies.

So many bodies strewn haphazardly over the ground. There was no blood, there were no visible wounds, it was as if they'd all fallen asleep where they were. Sleeping, as I had explained I felt my body doing not too long ago in the field. I stood there and watched for the rise and fall of chests for seconds, minutes, but nothing. My heart felt as though it was about to pound out of my chest, each beat as powerful as an earthquake. Why was mine still beating and not theirs? I couldn't help but scan the faces for my family. Terrified I may see my brother, his infantry uniform torn while he lay on the ground. My sisters, grouped together because they never left each other's side. They weren't wanderers like me.

I dropped Lane's hand and tried to speak my fear, but a sob I didn't know had built in my swollen throat escaped instead. I threw my hands over my mouth to stifle it and dropped to my knees. A sharp pain greeted me as vulnerable skin met rough stone. I lifted my hands from my mouth just an inch to utter the choked words, "I don't understand."

Beside me, Lane didn't say a word; he just started moving into the courtyard. He kneeled beside the Glendar twins, one boy and one girl, about seven years old. Their small fists still clutching Claudia's hand-stitched lambs—the ones she'd slipped them after their father's fury over a few escaped pigs. I remembered her mischievous wink and words that day: *"Every adorable troublemaker deserves a soft place to lay their head."* Lane placed a finger under each of their small, innocent noses, checking for a breath. When his head fell and shoulders drooped, I knew they were gone.

I peered at the entire courtyard then, at all the people I had grown up around, all the people I'd just seen full of happiness a few hours ago. Leonard and Grewton, sitting in the rocking chairs with jerky lying on the ground beneath the hands that lay limp on the armrests. Claudia lay over her market table, coins spread out on the wood as if she had been handing someone their change just moments ago. The twins, and the ladies of the morning group who drank chamomile tea and sang morning tunes for all who passed by.

The ladies were always dressed in the most exquisite silk gowns, showcasing their curves with vibrant oranges and pinks. They all lay on the cobblestone ground; it was too dirty for their dresses to be on it. I got up and scrambled to the twins first, trying to pick them up off the ground. "We have to get them off the ground, Lane. It's filthy, their father will be furious."

"Mal, please," he pleaded with me. I was spiraling, I knew I was. Yet I still ran over to the ladies of the morning. Using my feet, I scooted their dresses together so less fabric was strung out across the ground. I felt tears burning trails along my cheeks, I couldn't stop. I needed to help them. I needed to fix this.

"Amalia." Lane's voice was a muffled whisper now, like he was speaking underwater, and I was already adjusting the twins' weight in my arms, smoothing their brown hair to the side.

I headed to pick up the jerky Grewton had dropped. *"Ain't nothing here goes to waste under my watch, in my day we'd be beaten to a pulp for so much as a crumb left untouched,"* I could hear his raspy voice lecturing us. I tried to place it back in his hand, but the jerky would just fall back onto the cobblestone. I shoved the piece forcefully under his sleeve, lodging it between the arm of the chair and his lifeless arm, determined to make this scene right.

I was trying my hardest to bend down to get another fallen piece while holding the twins, but they were so heavy, and I was still weak. I fell to the side and slammed my right shoulder against the cobblestone, pain ricocheting through my bones. The twins fell to the ground, their heads making an audible *crack* as they hit stone and lolled to the side. Everything I had shoved down broke free, ruptured. I was wailing, I knew I was, even though I couldn't hear a thing besides a loud ringing. My breaths were coming in quick succession. Tears were taking over my vision. I grabbed the twins, cradling them in my arms and rocking back and forth, repeatedly asking through a shattered voice, "Why, why, why!"

Looking around, I saw Leonard's banjo with its snapped cord. Everything became a watery blur, and I couldn't focus. I felt my own threads snapping one by one. There were just so many bodies. No, they weren't just bodies... I knew... I'd known them. I'd grown up with some of them, had been influenced and molded by others. I'd seen them all just earlier this morning, bustling about trying to prepare for the market to open. Now this would be my last memory of them. Lifeless on the cobblestone.

Lane dropped beside me as the air around me shifted. His arms locked around my body, becoming my only anchor. His body was tense as it supported mine. His chin rested on my shoulder as he pulled me against him. Guilt swallowed me as I listened to his heartbeat. Why did we survive when everyone else was dead?

Chapter 2

How much time went by with Lane holding me as I wept uncontrollably? Minutes? An hour? He didn't complain, he just held me, knowing there were no words that could be said.

Then my memory struck like a cornered snake, making me recoil from his comfort.

"You've seen this." I got to my feet quickly. "You saw all of this, and what?" I said as another sob bubbled up, throwing my hands out to the twins that had fallen from my grasp before motioning to the bodies around us. "Just left them?" My emotions needed an outlet, and he was the only one here who could receive them.

Lane jerked back as if I were that cornered snake, and he had been the one to get bitten. "You think I did this or something?" he snapped.

"I didn't say that, but how could you walk through this courtyard and see what lies around us and LEAVE?"

"I went toward the only heartbeat I heard!" Lane surged to his feet.

Silence.

"Wha—?"

"I mean, that I had to know if you were alive. *You* were who I wanted to try and save." He motioned to the people lying in the courtyard. "I don't know these people like I know you. I just wanted to get to *you*."

His words felt like a confession, and I whispered, "Me?" I looked up to meet his eyes, the shards of deep blue had returned.

"Yes!" he yelled as he ran his hands through his hair, clearly frustrated with me. "I saw what happened to these people, and despite what you may think right now, I did try. I checked as many as I could, but I didn't feel anything from them." A bitter laugh escaped him. "I didn't see the shimmering sky, I saw death. *Felt* it."

I wish I could swallow my accusation, stop it from having left my mouth.

"I—I—"

"Don't," he said, swinging a glare in my direction. Piercing me like a blade. His eyes flickered. "Whether it was the right thing to do or not, I do not regret choosing you." He sighed, rubbing his face.

Above us, birds flew from the woods, squawking as they passed over, rushing to some unknown place. Lane tracked their path, jaw hardening as he watched.

Lane was a new face in Cimmerian, but was still very well known, being that he was one of King Tatum's sons. Lane had an older brother—Knox, I believed his name to be. Lane, however, had been widely known as the king's favorite up until about a year ago, when he had been banished from Santavarre to live in Cimmerian.

Many legends stemmed from Santavarre. Before my mother died, she'd read me storybooks that explained how the lands were made from dragons and fae, that's why Cimmerian was the only kingdom left with human life. When the dragons and fae left, the lands became tainted, haunted. Now, Cimmerian was the last kingdom with soil healthy enough to sustain human life. Everywhere else we called the Forgotten Lands, unlivable places which held unnatural creatures, so the stories say. Even though they were stories, they held great power over everyone in Cimmerian; no one dared to go past the field, and only a few chose to venture to Santavarre.

Lane broke me out of my thoughts. "Listen, you don't need to say anything, I won't let you think the worst of me without knowing the reasons behind my actions," he said as he started walking away.

"Wait—"I tried to stand, but my knees buckled. "Where are you going?" I quickly asked, trying once more to stand.

"I'm going to check for survivors. You're welcome to join, unless you think one person can do anything here." He threw his hand out to gesture at the bodies lying around the courtyard before continuing toward the village houses, clearly a jab at the statement I had made.

I owed him an apology. I knew I did, but after that, I didn't want to give it to him. I went to take a step and stumbled, but I caught myself on something fleshy that moved as I grabbed it. I looked over to see that I was gripping Grewton's hand, and the weight of my body had made the rocking chair rock backward. Its creaking sound sent goosebumps over my arms. I took a sharp inhale and yanked my hand back, clutching it to my chest. I peered at the old man once more, taking in what would likely be the vision of him

I'd always remember, sorrow filling my soul. I glanced behind me at Claudia's table and grabbed a handful of crocheted blankets, the scent of citrus wafting up from them. I draped two over Grewton and Leonard, one over both of the twins, then the rest over the bodies I passed as I made my way toward Lane, who, even irritated, was waiting for me.

It may not have been much, but it was better than them lying dead in the open as if no one had ever cared about them. Before leaving the courtyard in our wake, I spanned the lifeless forms for the blonde, silky strands of Story's hair. She wouldn't have been around the market, she hated crowds. She and Ivalea had become close during the time Lane and I spent together. They could be together. She would most likely be within the woods behind her cottage. Lane had built us a hidden fort tucked away behind some discarded debris. She'd often wait there, gossiping with Ivalea until he and I finished our duties. I clung to that knowledge as we walked.

We followed the narrow cobblestone walkway. Along this main path, there were little cobblestone alleys that veered to the left and right, each lined with stone cottages. The village pathways were in different states of disrepair; some had deep potholes, others had vines that grew from the ground and wound upward along the stone, weaving around house rails. The birds favored the vines because they bore fruit during spring. The villagers, on the other hand, hated them because of the razor-sharp thorns protruding up and down the stems. *I suppose that won't be bothering too many people now.*

"Should we go check the fort for Story?" I asked Lane as I wiped a few drying tears from my cheeks. I'd asked to cut the silence more than anything. I was too numb to truly worry about where we were going, even though I desperately wanted my best friend.

"I thought you would want to check on your family," he said, stopping and turning to me with caution in his eyes.

I didn't know if I wanted to go, if I wanted to see whatever may have been waiting. If I could handle it. "You really think that they may be alive?"

"You're alive, I'm alive, we cannot be the only two that survived," he said, even though as we walked, we were passing corpses draped over porches and lying at the bottom of stone steps. Not as many as the courtyard held, but enough to smother any hope I had in my heart.

We'd passed six alleys now along the main path, three on either side, which meant at the next one we needed to turn left, and five buildings down would tell me if I no longer had a family. My steps slowed as I fought the urge to run back to my field and pretend none of this was happening. Lane silently put out his hand for me. A small gesture from the canopy trail to show I wasn't alone.

I took his outstretched hand, inhaled, and then we walked.

We stood in front of my house, unmoving. With how fried my nerves were, I wouldn't have thought I was breathing if I wasn't still standing upright.

"I don't think I can do it." I took a step back from the wooden door that held the fate of what my future would look like. "This isn't like the courtyard; this will destroy me."

"Would never knowing be more peaceful?" he asked quietly.

Silence surrounded us as I gave his question considerable thought. Could I live with not knowing, now that we were there? No, I didn't believe I could. It would always haunt me, the what-ifs. What life would I be living, though, after seeing my family lifeless in a home that held so many memories? Could I do that? There really was no easy way out with these choices. "Well..." I said. "I don't know what the right decision is." What I kept to myself was, *I don't know what will hurt less.* I had never been skilled in handling emotions. I tended to shove them to the depths of my soul, where they could stay hidden, where I didn't have to face them. I'd let them silently fester until I could let them out in my field, away from anyone who could witness it. I wasn't sure I could do that now.

"There would never be a good time or right time for this. You are not alone, though. I am here with you and will be as we walk into the house." His hand rubbed the small of my back. "Who all should be inside?"

"I'm not sure," I said as I bit my lower lip. "My family is kind of all over the place, if you haven't noticed from the time you've spent with them. Maybe my sisters? Possibly my father."

"Your brother?" he asked, stepping up to the doorknob.

Although anxiety and fear had fueled the worry I would see him in the courtyard, I had known he wouldn't be here. "He left on Monday to join the field forces. His training started this week." There was a tunnel within the woods that had been created over a hundred years ago, now the field forces used it to get to their training grounds in Raeganarde, an old kingdom, now part of the Forgotten Lands. Nobody in Cimmerian knew the location of the tunnel entrance except the general and captain of the field forces; all new recruits had to be blindfolded until they entered it. It was used in the Kingdom End War our storybooks were inspired by. There had been a pang of jealousy watching my brother leave, knowing he'd get to see another kingdom. He got to leave Cimmerian.

"Would you like me to go in first?" Lane asked, bringing me back to the moment.

I looked at his hand grasping the knob. I brushed my hands over the blue fabric of my dress and readied myself to enter the house. My father would have been outside at this time, but there were no signs of anyone outside or between the rows of houses that I could see from where we stood. As I looked around us, all the buildings looked to be crumbling, like I had never noticed how battered the village was before now. I could almost feel the quakes causing the cracks in the stone as I braced myself to step inside.

I nodded my head at Lane, who twisted the knob and let the door swing open as I took a step into the entryway. I swore I could hear the whispers, *"Do you think he's ever kissed anyone?"* Monet would say.

"Of course he has. The real question would be, has he ever pleasured a woman?" Ivalea, always the one to make things inappropriate. Squeals and laughter filled my ears, but they weren't real, just ghosts of a memory.

Lane shifted behind me, causing the floorboards to groan, his hand braced the door-frame so hard that his knuckles were white. I moved up to stand in front of him, confused by his reaction. He had been around my family a lot this past year, but I always figured he'd never *really* allowed himself to be attached. My hand closed over his as I tried to understand. As our hands touched, I felt an electric charge race up my arm. A flash of the courtyard spread over my vision, everyone falling to the ground one after the other, and it made me gasp as shivers ran down the length of my body, heating it up. "What the hell was that?" I said, breathless.

"What was what?" Lane looked concerned and went to touch me, but I immediately pulled back, jarred from what had just happened.

"You didn't feel that—"

"That what?" he asked with that brow raised again.

I shook my hands in the air, trying to rid myself of the feeling, and tilted my head from side to side, hearing the small pops that released the pressure. "Nothing, I think I'm just losing it a little."

As I moved away from Lane and through the house, dread filled my bones. Not only was I thinking about what just happened, but I didn't see anyone yet, and that made me more nervous than if they had all been laid out in front of me. I headed right, toward the two bedrooms my sisters and I shared. As I reached the first door on the left, I noticed it hung ajar, and I could faintly make out a pair of fuzzy teal slippers sticking out from beneath the bedskirt on the ground. *My* slippers Viz had stolen because she claimed they complemented her skin tone better. I pushed the door fully open and quietly called out, "Vizcaya?" The slippers didn't move, and my heart lurched. I stepped farther into the room, glancing behind me to see Lane standing in the living area, his attention focused on me. "Vizcaya... are you alright?" Still nothing. I reached the foot of the bed we shared. The mint green comforter and matching pillows still lay askew as if we'd both just gotten up for the day. As I stared at the slippers, my heartbeat quickened, beating through my chest. *What should I do?*

My foot lashed out before I could think of a more logical reaction. The slipper, which was *not* attached to a body, went flying, making a light *thwack* as it made contact with the wall.

"You really showed that slipper who's in charge, Amalia." I could hear the smirk on Lane's face through his amused tone.

"You know, you could check the other rooms if you wanted to do something more useful than watching what I'm doing," I bit back. "You realize where we are right now, right? You realize that only happened because it wasn't attached to my dead sister's body!" A thunderstorm was raging inside me, and I was losing the battle of keeping it contained.

Silence answered, Lane leaned his tall, toned body against the doorframe, and I finally took his presence in. His maroon tunic clung to every ripple on his abdomen, and he wore dark navy trousers as his right foot, which was currently hidden away in midnight black boots, crossed over the left. My gaze lingered as I noticed his strong and defined arms were crossed, his right hand subtly rubbing his left bicep in uncertainty as he caught my attentiveness. "I know that, Amalia, I'm sorry. What I said was stupid." His head tilted. "Forgive me."

An awkward silence washed over us before I brushed past him and moved to the second bedroom without giving my own apology or accepting his. It must have been the confidence from finding Vizcaya's and my room empty, but I strode into the next without a thought. One of my many ongoing poor decisions for the day, the first being going to the field alone.

The breeze of the open window brushed over my skin, sending a chill over my exposed collarbone. The room was filled with the fresh scent of the blood orange tree my father had planted right outside Ivalea, Monet, and Lillian's bedroom.

Then my eyes landed on their large bed, which had always devoured them. That was where I found my answer as to what had happened to my family. Cuddled together on the bed were three of my sisters. They were under the muted pink comforter that had been their only comfort during so many illnesses we'd all endured during the winter months here. Each tucked in close to one another under the covers like spoons in a drawer, except for Monet, who was in the middle.

Always so defiant. She lay on top of the comforter, her black hair sprawled across the pink pillowcase like the ink she'd used to draw. She had always been warm, no matter how cold the house was. Vizcaya lay on the left, and Lillian on the right. Monet was holding onto our scrapbook that we'd been working on since we were children. We'd never been a wealthy family, and like most in the village, we had always had to make our own ways to pass the time. It contained our favorite memories together, pictures, sketches, spilled secrets of crushes or things we had done that we'd never want our father to know of. Whatever had been put in the book was never to be spoken of aloud in front of anyone but us.

They must have been relaxing and adding to it while I'd been in my field. It was laid open on Monet's lap to a blank page, but they all looked as though they had fallen asleep before they could start. After the scene in the courtyard, I knew they had not. I glanced over my shoulder, but no longer saw Lane in the hallway by the other bedroom. I walked toward my sisters, and when I reached the bed, I sat on the corner, not wanting to disturb them. They were all so beautiful, even then.

Vizcaya was thirty and the oldest of my sisters. Her straight, shoulder-length, dirty-blonde hair always looked like it had a constant shine to it, even on the most overcast days. Her round face had been gently kissed by the sun. That sun-kissed flush I was always jealous of had drained from her cheeks. The only sign anything was wrong. She had always been able to attract the attention of the village boys with her thicker hourglass curves. She could have married and left this dreadful cottage but stayed to care for her younger siblings after our mother's death. *Now look at her.* My chest tightened as the air became thick and hard to breathe, my mind screaming at me to leave, but my heart refusing to allow me to.

Lillian, the second oldest, had often been mistaken for Vizcaya's twin. At twenty-seven, she lay there with her blue eyes shut, a natural beauty who had never worn an ounce of makeup. She had hair resembling Vizcaya's with her dirty-blonde, slightly wavy locks falling just past her shoulders. Her hands were around Monet's arm. She was always looking after everyone. She'd wiped everyone's tears when Father became too harsh and never allowed herself to shed her own. What would she do at that moment? If she were me? Lillian would have been better suited for this, been more sure in her path and decisions. Now, she was free from ever having to carry anyone else's burdens again.

Monet was the youngest of us. She was only eighteen, just five years younger than myself. Striking with her freckled features. Monet had dark, wavy, charcoal black hair that reached down to her backside. She was the opposite of us all and was petite with nonexistent curves. Her pale skin on her oval face was a stark contrast to her dark hair and brown eyes.

My knees struck the floorboards as I slipped off the bed, and the truth coiled through me—they were really gone. I saw each of them and could picture the moments we'd shared. Each memory played like a movie with them speaking and moving, but death had taken them, and now all they were, were memories. There would never be more. There would never be the possibility of seeing Monet chase after the baker's son. I'd never hear Lillian and Vizcaya laughing quietly at their own inside jokes.

"Ivalea?" My whisper was heard by no one. She was not there. I looked around the small room at the lifeless walls, painted an ash gray color, for any sign of her. I stood to view the other side of the bed but saw nothing. That familiar swell of hope filled my chest. I looked at my sisters, putting my hand on Vizcaya's leg. "May your souls be forever filled with joy as you start the rest of your lives in eternal rest within the Elysian Islands," I whispered to them, a tear welling up but not flowing. My throat swelled as I said the words, "I'm sorry I survived. I'm sorry for leaving. I should have stayed." Getting to my feet, I squared my shoulders. "I should have died with you." I gave each of my sisters a kiss on their forehead before walking to the door. The tear finally escaped and ran down my left cheek, leaving a glistening trail of grief in its wake.

The door groaned as I rested my hand against the old wood, turning and taking one last look at my siblings. My fingers traced a notch in the doorframe as my gaze lingered. Somewhere deep in my mind, I was thankful, thankful that I knew from my experience in the field that what happened to them was peaceful. Still, I could feel that a soul-deep numbness had taken over. I gave the doorway a shaky pat as I walked out of the room, shutting the door behind me. The click echoed through me, a finality clicking into place.

"Lane?"

The eerie silence of the house answered instead. My father's door was already open, inviting me to find what lay inside. Brantley and my father had shared this room. They'd go over what Brantley could expect during training. My father had retired from the forces due to a disability over ten years ago, so he had been more than proud of Brantley for following in his footsteps. We were all sure Brantley was just doing it to learn how to score himself a damsel in distress.

I peered in, much more cautious now. The room was empty except for a few half-written letters in my father's handwriting. Pain sliced through me as I spotted the words *love you to the moon and back, bud*. Words Brantley would most likely never see. *Don't let yourself feel it, Amalia*, I told myself as I felt the weight of loss crippling me.

"Laaannee?" I yelled out, my voice raw with the unshed emotion I was keeping locked away. Still, only silence greeted me. I used to seek the silence; I feared I may never be able to appreciate it again.

I stepped out of the house and checked to see if he was waiting for me on the steps. "Lane, where are you?" I shouted, panic lacing my voice. *Could he succumb to the shimmer this late? Is he gone too?* I heard a noise on the right side of the house where my sisters' bedroom window was.

I quickly raced down the steps and ran around the house. *Smack!* I slammed into Lane's chest. He grabbed both of my arms just beneath my shoulders and said, "Hey, slow down, I'm right here."

"I was calling for you. Why didn't you answer?" My voice fractured. "I thought—" Not able to finish my sentence, I looked up to meet his eyes. They looked stricken with concern. Not at my fear, but like he was struggling to tell me something. "Wha... what's wrong?"

"I figured you would need some space and decided to go outside to see if I could find anyone else who made it. I passed by and thought you might want an orange from your father's tree..." His words trailed off as his eyes shifted to the side.

"What aren't you saying?" His eyes gave away his secret, and I needed to know what he was keeping from me.

"I found your father, Amalia."

My heart stuttered in my chest. Still grasping my arms, he slightly pushed me back, causing me to take a few stumbling steps.

"You don't have to go over there. He is lying on the ground by the tree. I can bring him in—"

I wrenched free from his grasp. "I want to see him," I said. My voice was thick, my throat swelling from the pent-up emotions.

"Amalia—"

"I want. To see. Him." I forced my chin up and wiped all traces of weakness from my face. "If I handled finding my sisters' bodies." *I could handle this.*

Lane sighed but dropped his hands and stepped to the side as he looked at the ground. Letting me make my choice, even if he didn't agree.

I moved around him and saw my father lying under the blood orange tree. The glossy evergreen leaves, peppered with fragrant white blooms, looked alive and healthy while my father's body lay limp below. I walked until I was at his side. He was wearing his tattered cardigan, which had more holes than I could count. It was his favorite piece of clothing, even if it was only held together by worn strings. It was then that I saw he still had a slightly reddish, ripe fruit in his hand, showing he had been picking the oranges when the shimmer had rained down. I wondered if he had even noticed it. He often enjoyed picking fruit from the tree and tossing it into my sisters' room for them. *Was that what he was about to do?* I knelt down and laid my right hand on his shoulder. My hand slid down his outstretched arm to where the orange was. His skin was still warm, tricking my mind into thinking he wasn't actually dead. "Thank you for picking me an orange, Daddy," I said to him. "You always knew they were my favorite after being in the field." I couldn't help but tell myself he had been picking this orange for me. He had been hard to get to know, never allowing people to see the soft side of him. Times like this, picking fruit for his daughters, he showed those softer parts. Just like my sisters, I kissed his temple. My lips lingered, not wanting to do this, not wanting this to be a goodbye he wouldn't ever know happened. I got to my feet, my legs shaking slightly, and stared up at the white flowers that watched over him. "I hope you'll have a tree in your eternal rest, and I hope it has the perfect orange waiting for me when I see you again."

A slight, cool breeze flowed through the air, lifting a few strands of my hair and sending the sweet smells of the blooms swirling around us. My chest had a boulder resting on it, my throat burned as I could feel it closing in on itself, and the tree became hard to make out as my eyesight blurred from unshed tears. I tried to control the pain from my heart breaking into pieces. I felt the cracks forming and heard the sounds of it fracturing open.

Lane's hand found my shoulder. I let it stay, but held my head high. I needed to show strength. Hardening my jaw, I locked onto one single flower as I worked on getting my breathing even once again. Focusing on the ways the petals curled and overlapped one another, I forced the moisture in my eyes away.

"I'm fine, Lane, you don't need to hover," I said sharply. My voice shuddered like the blossoms during a storm, but my resolve made sure it didn't break.

"It's okay if you're not. How can you be?"

I said nothing as I kept my eyes trained on the flower, noticing there weren't even bees buzzing around the blooms. I turned to him, face like stone, and repeated, "I'm fine."

"You can cry, Amalia. Please don't act strong for my sake."

"If I cry these tears," I said, pointing up at my face, my fingers hovering by my eyes, where a traitorous tear slipped past my defenses, "then that means this is real." My hand dropped to my side, and I stepped toward Lane. "It becomes a fact." My hands ran down my face while I exhaled. "If I keep them tucked away beneath the surface... then... then it's as if"—I looked back at my father—"this was just a dream. I only need to wait, Lane. I'll wait until some distant time in the future when I wake up and can see them again." A small smile crossed my face as a frown deepened on his. He simply nodded to me.

Lane came toward me, "Amalia—"

"No!" I growled, spinning back toward the cottage. I was drowning in sorrow, I needed this to not be my reality, if only for a moment.

"I'd like to grab some things from inside, and then I'd like to leave Cimmerian. We need to find out if your family is gone." Story was still missing, Ivalea. I couldn't keep hoping anyone else was alive when the truth was right in front of me. We needed to leave before something else happened. Before we were claimed with everyone else.

"My family?" Lane's brows turned down toward his nose, looking confused.

"I assume you'll want to go home, do you not?" Would he leave me here?

"Right. I would, but..." He shifted his weight from one foot to the other. "My father banished me here, if he survived... I don't believe he'd welcome me back," he said quickly.

"Well, there's only one way to find out, and right now this is the last area we should stay in if something is killing everyone."

I didn't wait for him to respond as I headed back into the house. Underneath my bed was an old, brown leather pack I often used to collect things when I snuck away to explore the woods around Cimmerian. I packed it with a few clothes, feminine products, my toothbrush, and other items I felt I may need. I strode into my father's room and grabbed one of his old black and gray field force packs and filled it with food, a blanket, and a few of my brother's old clothes. Lane walked into the room just as I was stuffing a pair of rolled trousers into the pack.

"What are you doing?" he asked.

"Packing you some items, unless you wanted to stop at your cottage before we leave?"

"Um, no, that's okay, this will be fine, thank you." He grabbed the pack from me and went to the bathroom to find any unused items my father or brother may have had extras of. I grabbed one of the letters and shoved it into my pack. There was only one more thing I wanted to take.

I entered my sisters' room again, my eyes going straight to the book. I let a sad smile spread across my face as I walked in and gently took it from Monet. I held it to my chest, tightly pressing my lips together until they tingled to keep a sob from escaping. I hurried out of the room and met Lane in the kitchen area. He was adding two cups and a glass container of tea bags into my father's... his pack.

"Are you ready?" I asked.

Lane startled, almost dropping the container onto the floor. "Eternal dragons, Amalia, you almost gave me a heart attack!"

"I'm sorry, but we should go." I made my way to the front door when he called my name. I turned toward him but did not walk even one step back.

"Your family, do you want to—"

"No," I said matter-of-factly.

"Amalia, it won't take much ti—"

"I said NO!" I shouted, feeling all the emotions I'd been keeping at bay rush up to the surface in an instant. I inhaled sharply.

"My sisters are sleeping in their beds, and my father is napping below his favorite tree. That is how they should stay. We are not burying them."

The deep, shattering emotions that threatened to erupt out of me gave me the power to decide in that moment that instead of breaking down, I would lift my chin and walk with strong, sure-footed steps out of the house that had molded me, for the last time. Knowing I'd never be able to step on these floorboards again, never being able to look at these walls, dreaming of how I would decorate if only we had the means. I would never have to live with ghosts and memories always reminding me of this day, breaking the crafted illusion I'd made for myself.

I made my way down the steps and made sure to avoid seeing the tree again. I waited at the end of the alley for Lane. Ivalea plagued my mind, could I really leave Cimmerian without finding her, without finding Story? Should I go with Lane or try to find my way to Raeganarde? Could I handle seeing them? My hope for finding anyone alive was nonexistent now. I didn't need to confirm that knowledge with the vision of them unmoving and shadowed by death, souls already within the Elysian Islands, a realm for the afterlife. I could make peace with knowing wherever they may lie, the heart of who they were would be worry-free in Elysian.

After a few minutes, Lane was standing next to me. No words were exchanged. I'd always wanted to leave this village one day. Leave behind the struggles of a poor family, explore the beauty this world had to offer, learn more about the myths I'd grown up learning that explained how this land was created. Most of all, I had always wanted to visit Santavarre. Now, here we were, leaving behind everything I'd known and heading toward a place I never thought I'd see.

Chapter 3

With our packs readied and nothing left in that town but the dead, we started our three-day trek through the Forgotten Pass to Santavarre.

Lane led the way as we walked in silence, his irritation bubbling like a boiling pot of water. Unsure of what to say or do, I just followed a few paces behind him. I had made the mistake of asking why we were walking instead of using the horse and carriage at the blacksmith's shop, to which Lane had grudgingly reminded me *I* was the one who had rushed us out of Cimmerian. Now we'd get to walk two days south, followed by one day changing direction to the west to get to the king's castle. I'd only seen pictures and heard stories about where King Tatum lived. I'd heard that the land his castle sat on was surrounded by water, except for one section that led into the main entrance, which housed eight guards—two on either side of the entry door and four that were stationed in the two watchtowers above. A few villagers had spoken about it in the market one morning, which led to me rushing to the Lagrange bookshop to see if any old history books had an illustration of the capital, but the pictures I'd seen showed no water.

"Is it true that your home is surrounded by water?" I asked before I realized words were spewing out of my mouth.

Lane froze mid-stride. "I'm sorry?" The question clearly caught him off guard. The sound of his boots crunching the debris along the path picked up again.

"King Tatum's castle... your home, I've heard villagers who say they've gone to him for requests mention that it's surrounded by water. I've looked up illustrations in our history books, though, and there isn't water. Sooooo... I'm curious, is there actually water surrounding it?"

"That's what has been rattling around in your head?"

"I mean, it's one of many things in my head, but it's the only thing I thought you could actually help answer."

His head tilted, with an eyebrow raised as if to say, "Excuse me?"

A few moments went by, and I was starting to think he had chosen to ignore me, then he said, "Yes, it is surrounded by water. The castle sits on one of only three sacred great lakes in this realm."

"Seriously? Why do our history books not show that then?"

"It is something my father does not particularly want people to know or remember."

"Why?"

"Well, if you were a king, would you prefer if people planned to attack by water and breached your castle, or would you rather they plan to attack by land and then watch as that plan falters the moment they realize they have to cross the lake?"

"I suppose that's never crossed my mind before."

"Yeah, well, my father is known for being quite powerful when it comes to the mind," he said, glancing my way. I hurried my steps so I was in line with him, not able to fully match his long strides.

"What happens if the shimmer has affected everywhere else and not just Cimmerian?" I pressed Lane.

"The shimmer?" he repeated.

A proud smile crossed my lips. "Yeah, that's what I'm calling it. Do you have a better name for it?"

He shrugged. "I guess not, but it's a deceiving name."

"How so?" I asked, thinking back to how beautiful it had looked... before it almost killed me and I collapsed, of course.

"Well, when you hear the word shimmer, you would think of beauty. It would make any human run toward it, not away from it. There's power in names. Words often act like a compass steering people in specific directions."

"Fair enough," I said, scrunching my face in thought. "Okay, fine, we will call it the death shimmer. That way, people know it's both deadly and beautiful."

An hour or so passed, I could see Lane's throat work on words he decided not to speak while my mind raced with flashes of the day. The silence between us felt strange. The past year that we'd known one another, it had been effortless to speak. We had often ended up being chided for neglecting our chores. We'd be sitting on the ground, rakes thrown to the side, debating some absurd topic instead. Silence was never good after tragedy. It just left you the opportunity to relive moments and think of all the things you should have done differently. Or worse, the things that could have been happening if not for the tragedy.

What would I be doing if the death shimmer had never occurred? I definitely wouldn't have been walking to King Tatum's castle with his banished son. Maybe Story and I would have been finding ways to reach the mountains. We'd never gotten far, usually only halfway through the field before we'd both get a sense that we should turn around and leave.

"What's going on in that head of yours?" Lane looked back at me over his shoulder. "Plotting something?"

"What?"

"Your face is so incredibly scrunched right now, I fear it'll never go back to normal. That usually means you're deep in thought."

"My face is not scrunched," I said in protest, but realized I was getting a headache from scrunching my face too hard. Relaxing, I felt instant relief at the change in tension.

"What do you think you'd be doing right now if things were different?" I asked.

"Well, it's got to be around three by now, maybe four?" he said, looking up at the sky. "I think I would have been in my cottage reading."

"That was a rather boring answer," I said, expecting him to reply with an act a bit more rugged than reading.

"Oh, I'm sorry my answer did not live up to your expectations," he said dryly.

"Vizcaya and Ivalea used to say they always pictured you chopping wood in the back of your cottage," I said with a shrug of my shoulders. "Chopping wood with an axe is much more enticing than being tucked away in your cottage reading."

"Do you not like reading?" he asked.

"I love reading!" I said defensively.

"As do I, I can escape into any world and become alternate versions of myself or versions I could never imagine myself to be." I stared at him momentarily, stunned at how honest he was being. "I find reading to be much more exciting than chopping wood would be. Although I suppose your sisters imagined me doing it differently than I do." He winked at me after that, and I felt my face flush, because they'd definitely written some interesting visions. Vizcaya often had him shirtless... Ivalea, on the other hand... he usually wore nothing, and she'd had a way of using VERY descriptive terms in those entries.

I thought about the fact that I had those very entries on my back, tucked away in the leather pack.

"I have also been thinking about my family, the people in the village."

Lane kept quiet, waiting for me to continue.

"I know I snapped at you, and I'm sorry."

"Snapped at me, which time?" Lane rebutted mockingly.

I appreciated his attempt at keeping the mood light. "All of them I guess, but more specifically when you mentioned we should bury my family... maybe you were right." I felt lighter as the confession left my heart.

"I can't help but think of them now, how I just left them there to rot." A small sob threatened to escape as I choked on the last words. "I rushed us out of there so fast, all because I didn't want to face what had happened."

Lane stopped walking ahead of me and turned to face me. I closed the few steps that had separated us and came to a halt about a foot in front of him with my head down, not feeling like I could make eye contact without breaking.

In a gentle voice, he said, "Amalia, I'm going to say something that is meant to ease your pain."

"Meant?" I asked softly, noting the keyword.

"Yes, meant. I know it will not be easy to hear, no matter how I say it."

"Okay," I said, almost inaudibly.

"You did not leave your family to simply rot. You wanted to preserve them in a memory that wasn't filled with thoughts of death. They would be rotting away whether they were in the ground or above it."

I had been feeling uplifted until his last few words. I understood why he'd said it was meant to ease with the inflection it probably wouldn't. He must have noticed the change in my expression, because he put his hands on my shoulders and pulled me against his chest. His arms wrapped tight around me in a hug, breaking the shield I had been struggling to keep around me.

Lips quivering and tears filling my eyes, I said, "Yeah, I just wish I had given them a proper burial. What if I do happen to go back to the village? I would have to see the bones of who they used to be." I was so angry and emotional I had just wanted out of the village, away from the bodies that would now forever haunt me. Thinking clearly, I realized how my actions didn't truly help me. I'd just created a more traumatic moment for myself in the future.

Lane unwrapped his arms to cup my cheek and slowly rubbed his thumb over my skin.

"I won't allow that image to ever be burned into your mind."

"You don't really have a choice now, thanks to me, do you?" I said, lifting my right hand to rest on his wrist. Even though the moment he said it, I did feel a change. The pain of it wasn't searing, I felt relief. His words, his *touch,* comforted me, showing how the smallest show of support can make a difference when you let it in.

He gave me a small, lighthearted smirk and said, "You underestimate my abilities." He dropped his hand but laced the fingers that were resting on his wrist with his and gently pulled me to continue walking. "Come, we need to cover as much ground as we can and find a place to camp. This path is not safe at night."

"What do you mean, not safe? Everyone is dead, who's going to hurt us?"

"Humans are not the only thing you should fear, Amalia." His tone was serious, which made me believe I should trust his words. I had never left my village other than to go to my field, or a few hundred yards into the forest, but always with Story or Lane. I truly did not know what to expect, nor had I ever heard whispers between villagers about what they'd seen beyond our border. I'd read about the myths, sure, but what was really out there, I had no idea.

We walked another few hours, my legs felt numb from the exertion. Lane finally spotted an area he deemed worthy of camp. He dropped his pack off his right shoulder, down onto a bare stretch of land backed by a line of deep evergreen trees with long, needle-like leaves. We didn't have much except the blankets I'd packed, food, and a few changes of clothes, so there wasn't much to do. So I thought.

Lane moved with precision as he started gathering sticks and pine straw from the ground.

"I didn't bring anything to start a fire with," I said hesitantly, not wanting to dampen his momentum. He simply looked up and smiled at me as if that was an adorable thing to say. Awkwardly, I stood watching him, looking around to see if I could help in collecting things we somehow would burn without a fire starter of any kind. I bent to my right and plucked a fistful of grass.

Lane strode over holding an armful of material. I extended my hand out, offering him the green blades like he was one of the horses I should have remembered to take, and said, "Here, we can add this to it."

Lane's shoulders stiffened with the force he used to stifle his laughter, the laugh lines that framed his mouth gave away his amusement at my attempt to help.

"What?" I said sternly, my outstretched hand quickly tiring as it stayed between us. I made a motion with my hand, shoving it toward him to say, "*Here, take it.*" Lane adjusted the sticks so they were under his arm, then gently brushed the blades of grass out of my hand. I watched them slowly sway to the ground and pursed my lips together.

"You're scrunching your face again," he said.

"That was rude," I said, crossing my arms. "I was trying to help you."

"I know, and it was appreciated, but grass would last half a second in a fire. We need something more substantial." He lifted his armful of sticks to get the point across. "It's okay, though, I can handle the fire if you wouldn't mind setting up the blankets and something to eat."

"At least it would be half a second of warmth," I mumbled under my breath as I stomped away toward where Lane had dropped his pack on the ground. I heard him let out a low chuckle as he walked to drop the pile on the ground. I kneeled down at his pack, opening it to grab the blankets and food. I grabbed one blanket out of the pack, which uncovered a loaf of bread Lane must have put in, and shuffled down farther searching for the second blanket. All I saw were clothes and a few other food items. This couldn't be right.

I dumped the contents of the pack onto the ground. There were no extra blankets. I let out an exasperated grunt and put my head in my hands, rubbing at my eyes. Lane wasn't within my eyesight; he must have gone deeper into the trees in search of timber for the fire. I took the *only* blanket and shook it out, then laid it on the ground near where Lane had dropped his pile of twigs. "I doubt twigs would last very long," I grumbled, now irritated about the grass rejection and the fact I'd only packed one blanket. Another necessity I left behind in my haste. I kneeled and broke apart the loaf of bread, crumbs dropping onto my dress from the dryness of the loaf.

Staring into the tree line, waiting for Lane to return, I noticed shadows pulsing like a heartbeat between the tall pines. The sight brought me to my feet, my eyes narrowing on the spot.

A twig snapped.

Lane emerged from the tree line with a huge grin plastered on his face. I looked back at where I had seen the shadows, but there was nothing there.

"Follow me," he said, his eyebrows pulling together before he waved his hand, gesturing for me to hurry. He started sprinting back toward the trees, and I trailed behind him. Our pace became a light jog that consisted of him pushing through the branches and me narrowly avoiding getting decapitated by all of them once he passed.

"Could you maybe try and *not* hit me with every branch, please?" I asked.

He looked back at me, still smiling. "It'll be worth it, I promise." He picked up his pace, and I had to sprint to keep up with him.

"I... do not... enjoy... this moment... sir," I said, panting between words.

"I've seen you in your field, you'll be fine," he retorted.

"That's frolicking." I wheezed. "I'm a frolicker, not a run—" *Bam!* I slammed into Lane's back, falling backward with a thud, then flung myself onto my back with my arms outstretched over the ground as if I was about to make a snow dragon. I closed my eyes and tried to catch my breath.

I really hated running.

Chapter 4

"Amalia, what are you doing?" Lane was standing over me with both hands on his hips, using one hand to rake through his hair.

"I was trying to tell you before I face planted into your back that I'm not a runner." I pushed up to my elbows and chucked a small pinecone at him. The chuckle that came from him warmed a newly frozen part of me.

"Whatever it is, better be good. Because I practically died," I said, instantly regretting the words given the events that had unfolded that day. Lane must have seen the change in my expression. He scooped me up underneath my arms and stood me up right before stepping to the side. "Oh, it is."

That's when I saw it.

A little pond tucked away into the trees, hidden from anyone who may be passing through. The water was glistening even though it was shaded from the surrounding evergreens. It had a slight rippling effect, subtle movements dancing across its surface in tandem with the rays of sunlight.

"It's gorgeous." I gasped, holding a hand to my mouth. "I've never seen a pond this beautiful anywhere in Cimmerian." I walked toward the edge of the water in complete awe. All along the shoreline were little yellow flowers mixed in with lush, green, ankle-high grass, rocks with squishy green moss growing on the sides closest to the water, and white mushrooms that resembled little puffs of cotton sprinkled the area.

"It's not a pond, Amalia."

"It's not? What is it then? A puddle?" I asked sarcastically, rolling my eyes.

"It's called a spring." He walked and stood on my left side while placing his palm along my lower back. "Look closer." He pointed to a spot in the middle, where the surface was shifting.

"You see how the water is rippling there?"

I looked closely, nodding my head. "Yes, it looks as if someone is underwater blowing bubbles."

He snorted. "Exactly, that is the spring. There is an opening in the ground where the water is continuously flowing from."

I stared at it, watching how the ripples created multiple reflections of myself. I couldn't help but picture them as versions that still had a family, a life without some unexplainable tragedy.

"Do you want to go in?"

"I'm sorry, what?" I said, snapping my attention to him. "Go in?"

"Yes, as in submerge yourself in the water you seem so fascinated with. Do you know how to swim?" He reached down, trailing his fingers through the water.

"OF COURSE I KNOW HOW TO SWIM!" I shouted at him, effectively ruining the tranquil space.

Lane threw his hands up in defense. "I'm sorry, I was just asking! It's not like there are any bodies of water in the village."

He had a valid point, there wasn't. Which was a big reason I'd assumed this was a pond. We had multiple wells we used for water, but nothing like this. He was also right about me not knowing how to swim, but I was sure as hell not going to tell him that.

There was said to be a coastline past the mountains where your toes would disappear into the soft embrace of the sand. Lane had told me one day when we were lying in the field looking up at the clouds, trying to find animals or objects within them, that he had swum in the waters there. I didn't believe him. No one had ever gone that far. He'd explained it so vividly, though, I couldn't question him for long. He said the waters were rough, breaking in waves, making loud, thundering claps. His favorite thing about it was the saltiness of it, the way it coated your skin, filled the air. He'd spoken like he'd been transported back in time, reliving the memory, and it made me want to visit it one day.

Before I could say anything, Lane was lifting his shirt over his head. This time, I really did think I was about to die. We had spent a lot of time together, but there was never a moment when I'd seen him shirtless. My sisters and I definitely had our fantasies, some of which were tucked away in my pack. He turned to throw his tunic on the ground next to the closest rock, every one of his muscles going rigid, and I quickly admired the taut, sun-kissed muscles that flexed with each movement he made. He glanced over at me, and I quickly found a mushroom. I fought to act like I had been staring at it the whole time.

I bent down, a few waves of hair falling to conceal my face, and gave it a few soft boops to really seal in the act. I chanced a look at him, tucking a few strands behind my ear. He was standing with his arms crossed over his golden chest, grinning at me.

"Can I help you?" I asked, lifting my chin and asserting a confidence I did not have, crossing my own arms to mimic his posture.

"Funny, I was just going to ask you the same thing." He let his hands drop down, his biceps flexing as he started unzipping his trousers.

"WHAT is happening right now?" I stammered out, manically looking for my emotional support mushroom.

"Well, I'm not going to get my trousers wet, and if you'd stop acting like the vegetation is the most exciting thing you've ever seen, you'd notice I have briefs on."

"Who matches their underwear to their tunic?" I asked in judgment, trying to change the subject. His briefs were tight-fitting and showed the outline of his seemingly large appendage.

"I do. Who notices something like that?"

"I do," I countered, fighting the spreading smile.

"Mhmmm," was all he responded with before he jumped into the spring. Water erupted up from where his body went in, hitting me with an icy spray. The shock of the water's temperature caused me to gasp as I stumbled backward. I wiped the water from my face and watched as it settled back down. Lane flicked his darkened blonde hair to the side when he came up for a breath. Smiling up at me, he swam to the edge of the spring. Lush grass was flattened as he rested his elbows on the edge with his head tilted to the side. "Aren't you coming in?" His cheerful tone didn't match the challenge in his eyes.

"It's freezing," I countered. He looked so collected when I knew that water felt like a block of ice straight from Raeganarde.

"I can keep you warm. Come on, it's really not bad once you're in. You just have to get used to it." He stayed in the same position along the edge, patiently waiting for me. I was having an internal battle trying to decide if risking my life was worth him not finding out I'd lied about being able to swim.

I decided it was.

I walked to the edge and peered into the water. "How deep is it?" I asked.

"You're scrunching your face again."

"How. Deep. Is. It," I repeated, glaring at him.

"Well, I seem to have forgotten my measuring tape, so why don't you just come in and see for yourself?" he countered.

Prick.

"Well, *Lane*," I drew his name out for emphasis, "I'm asking because I'd like to eaasseee myself in instead of jumping straight in like some kind of Water Dragon."

"What do you know of Water Dragons?" he asked as he tilted his head in the opposite direction like a dog hearing its favorite word. I'd clearly intrigued him.

I fumbled with the hem of my dress. How comfortable was I with taking it off? "Just what my mother used to read to me. They were creatures believed to have existed hundreds of years ago. They vanished, and when they did, the lands changed." I lifted the fabric over my head in one swoop before tossing it to the side. "I remember thinking Water Dragons were the most beautiful. The drawings of their scales were a mixture of aqua and shimmering teals." I bent down, taking my shoes off.

"Do you believe they existed?" he questioned, pushing himself away from the edge. His body parted through the water effortlessly. *I could do this*. I dipped my toes into the water and quickly yanked them out at the ice-cold bite that greeted them. Lane's chuckle reached me as he flipped from his back to his stomach, using one arm, followed by the other, to propel himself through the liquid ice.

"Let's go, Mal!" Lane shouted from the opposite edge of the spring. It wasn't far, maybe only twenty-five feet away, but to me it looked unending. I eased my body into a sitting position by the water. I bit back a yelp as, inch by inch, my feet sank further until the water was over my knees.

Lane swam back to where I was seated. "Are you going to answer me?"

"What was the question again?" The water was numbing my skin, tingles taking over, and the reality of the poor decision I was making clouded my thoughts.

"Do you believe Water Dragons existed?" he repeated as he treaded water.

"Oh. Well, I don't think so. I think if they did, there would be more evidence than our storybooks. Plus, if they did exist and were these magnificent creatures like the myths claim, how would they just disappear?" I started to move my legs back and forth in the water. Lane was right, you did get used to it after a while. "None of the books I've read ever say how, just that they did." I looked at him. "Do you believe they existed?"

Lane closed the distance between us and reached his hands out, placing them on either side of my body. He was so close I could feel his chest brush against my legs. I silently thanked myself for shaving my legs that morning before leaving for my field.

"I do," he said. "I believe all stories stem from some kind of truth. The descriptions portrayed in the myths can't just be imagination."

I watched him as he spoke, just mere feet away from my face.

"Look at the Godival Mountains," he said, using one of my favorite places as an example. "Could those have been created by anything but a mythical creature?"

"I think people often mistake natural wonders for some greater power. Not realizing the fact we exist at all is a miracle in itself. Can't there be things that don't have an explanation?" I said, moving my feet slightly, just barely grazing his skin.

"There can, but I still believe creatures such as the Water Dragons exist." He moved his hands to my calves and met my gaze. His eyes had darkened into the dark blue shards I'd noticed forming many times today. My skin felt like an inferno even with the icy water cooling me, and I shifted forward slightly.

"Slide in and I'll hold onto you," Lane said, coaxing me into the spring. I envisioned how sliding into the water with him so close would go. It had been an emotional day, a traumatic day, and I was still attracted to him in this moment despite it all.

This was not smart.

I slid down into the frigid water, his hands skated my ribs as he steadied me. I couldn't tell anymore if I was breathless from the temperature of the water or the temperature of his hands as they traced up my body.

I stayed still like an upright plank as I frantically searched for anything to focus on besides his face that was now only inches from mine—not because I was uncomfortable, but because I feared I'd feel his body and completely lose it.

"You need to relax," Lane said, his laugh stirring the water around us.

"I am relaxed," I barked.

"Yeah, I can see that." His eyes rolled as he adjusted his hold on me. "Wrap your legs around me."

"Wrap my what around where?" I choked.

"Your legs. Around my waist."

"It's okay, you can just let me go. I'm pretty used to the water now," I said through chattering teeth. The last thing I needed to do was wrap my legs around him.

"Are you sure? You look pretty unacclimated to me." He eyed me warily, not believing a word I said.

"Yes. I'm sure. I've got this. Thank you, Your Highness, but I'm not a damsel in distress."

Lane released me with a lifted brow and pushed himself back into the middle of the spring. Instantly, my breath was stolen as my head went under water, and I kicked my legs to get above water, my knee striking a sharp stone. I reached the surface and sucked in a gulp of air. Lane called my name, but I went under before I could utter a word. A small part of me recalled distorted images of Lane using his arms to swim to the other side. My arms and legs flailed dramatically until I reached the surface again. Water invaded my lungs, making it nearly impossible to stay above the surface.

"Amalia!" I could tell he was closer this time. A rough, gurgled version of "I'm fine" spewed out while I flopped around trying to grasp at the edge.

I felt Lane's hands wrap around my waist and haul me up to him. Instinctively, I wrapped my legs around him while my right arm hooked around his neck.

"So, what were you saying about not being a damsel in distress?" he teased as I fought for air.

"Shut up," I rasped.

He brought me over to the edge of the spring and lifted me out of the water like I weighed nothing. The grass was a welcome feeling, and I spread my fingers through the sharp blades.

"My question about you not being able to swim was pretty spot on, wasn't it?" he asked, raising that eyebrow again. "I knew you were lying, but I didn't think you'd go as far as you did with it."

Face turned down in a scowl, I crossed my arms over my chest and said nothing before moving to stand on shaking legs. Lane watched me with a hardened gaze, his jaw rolling. It took me a moment to realize I was standing before him soaking wet, undergarments clinging to my body.

"Oh my dragons!" I shrieked, turning to grab my dress. I heard the splashes of displaced water as he pulled himself out of the spring. He sauntered over to me and took the dress from my hands. He put his curved finger under my chin and lifted it so that I was looking at him.

"You do not have to be embarrassed in front of me, for anything, Amalia." I gulped and nodded slightly, not able to speak from the adrenaline currently coursing through my veins. He dropped his hand and motioned for me to lift my arms, draping the dress over me before he grabbed his clothes. "Let's eat and get a fire going. I think we've had enough water play for today."

"I think we've had enough of everything for today," I replied.

"Good point."

We walked back to the site. Lane set his clothes down next to the blanket and walked over to the pile of debris he'd collected to make a fire.

"You know, you could put your clothes back on," I said.

"Why, so they can be wet and cold like yours?"

I looked down at myself to see my dress soaked at the shoulders where my hair lay.

"I can only imagine the sight I was in the water." I cringed just replaying it in my head. I was never going to live this down.

"Well, if you can imagine a fish flopping around on land, that pretty much sums up how you looked, only in the water."

The glare I sent his way while he tended to his debris pile would have made him burst into flames. He was too busy rubbing sticks together to notice it wasn't just sparks he created. Flames erupted before him, eating up the twigs and branches he had piled up like a starved animal. Lane fell back. "What the fuck!"

"What?!" I shouted over the crackling of the fire. "Isn't that what's supposed to happen when you start a fire?" I expected his hair to have singed strands by his reaction, but he seemed unscathed.

"That was not normal." His forehead was traced with wrinkles. He looked somewhere between utterly shocked and confused.

"Maybe you're just better than you think," I chided. I received a blank expression, as if it were the blade of grass fiasco all over again. He scratched the back of his head, throwing a few thicker pieces of timber onto the flames.

"Yeah, maybe."

The sun had set, and the last remaining sliver of light was quickly fading. "I'm going to go behind the trees and freshen up. There's a piece of bread set out for you here on the blanket." I pointed to where both of our portions still lay. I wasn't sure if he'd heard me, because he didn't move from his spot by the fire, still scratching his head. I walked to the tree line, glancing back at Lane before finding a tree I thought could give me some privacy. I peered around the tree to make sure he couldn't see me, then I stopped breathing.

Lane chose this opportunity to change out of his wet briefs. He was facing away from where I currently stood, so all I could see were the fire-lit muscles of his back flexing as he removed his briefs and laid them by the fire to dry. My eyes betrayed my logic and traveled down to where his bare cheeks were exposed. They tightened with each lift of his legs, every bit of him carved to perfection. I inhaled sharply. He was glistening from the spring water, his golden hair now deepened from being wet, every muscle defined and exposed. He leaned forward to get the fresh clothes he warmed by the flames, and I suddenly went lightheaded. What had been tucked away in his briefs was now out and hanging, his cock was visible in the flickering flames as he bent to retrieve his clothes.

Lane's demeanor changed like a predator who was being stalked. He turned toward where I stood so fast I lurched backward, stumbling until my ass met the fallen pine straw with a squeal. My hands covered my face as I thought to myself what an imbecile I was. As I slid my hands down, Lane was there, leaning against one of the tall pines.

Oh shit.

"What are you doing?!" I shouted.

"What am I doing?" he questioned slowly. "I apologize, I could have sworn I just caught you staring at me from afar. Then I heard you yelp and rushed over." He crouched down to my level.

"I wasn't *staring* at you," I snapped, noticing he'd thrown his trousers back on.

"Mhm," he said with a raised eyebrow. "I suppose both things can be true. So what were you doing, Amalia?"

"Nothing, I was making sure you couldn't see me."

Lane let out a deep laugh as he turned and commented, "I guess I should have made sure *you* couldn't see *me*."

I hated him.

I had never allowed myself to think of Lane in any capacity other than a friend. He was a prince, even if banished. There could never be a future between us. There had always been an attraction, of course, but that's all it could be. He'd always been nice to me, my whole family, training with Brantley before he left for Raeganarde. Working on repairs with my father, acting as if he didn't see my sisters ogling him every second. He and I? It had never been flirtatious. There had never been tension. It was such a natural friendship.

He was always meant to return to Santavarre, and I would always be in Cimmerian. Why I was acting like a feral cat in heat right now was beyond me. Maybe my body was trying to compensate for the heartbreak. Maybe I had always felt like this but never allowed it to rise to the surface, and now with everything else I was harboring, I didn't have the energy to hold it back.

Yeah... I was going with that.

Once I saw Lane was back at the fire, I finished freshening up and headed back to our little site. I felt Lane's gaze on me; I crossed my arms over my chest where I knew my nipples had hardened from the cold wetness seeping from my hair. I wasn't naive enough to think he wouldn't notice. What I was unsure of, was what would happen next. Would he show the same lack of restraint I had?

The fire popped as Lane placed a few thicker logs onto the fire. My stomach growled, a reminder I hadn't had time to eat anything since the death shimmer. I flopped on the blanket and inhaled the bread within minutes.

Lane's brows furrowed as he looked at me. He'd seen me scarf food down before, so I didn't know why he seemed so put off about it now.

"You're bleeding," he said. The fire cracked, and a few embers flew from the makeshift pit and floated down to the ground.

I had forgotten about hitting my knee while fighting for my life in the spring. It wasn't a large wound; I likely wouldn't have given it another thought.

"It's nothing, just a scratch. What got you banished?" The question flew from my mouth before I could even finish my last thought. I could feel Lane's gaze burning a hole through me more than the flickering, heated flames could. I may have gone too far with my question. I stayed silent, allowing him to decide where this conversation would go. If he didn't answer, I would accept it and move on. In all the time he'd spent in Cimmerian, he had never opened up about what brought him there.

A few minutes passed without so much as a sniffle in the air, and I was about to break the palpable tension before he finally spoke.

"Why?" he whispered while poking a stick into the fire. As he stoked the flames, I felt the walls being built between us.

"I'm sorry, I know it's personal. You've never spoken about it since arriving. Now it feels rather important to know since I'll be at your side while we face your father—if he's alive. You returning and how he reacts will affect me, too." I gave him a light shoulder shove to break the tension. "Right now, you're the only person I know that's alive." I cleared my throat before continuing, "I figured I should know what we are getting into."

He swallowed. "Don't apologize, I should have told you and your family the moment you were chosen to be my babysitters." His mouth turned up, and I could breathe a little easier. After everything, the last thing I needed to do was drive a wedge between us. I didn't think I could survive solitude in a world consumed by death.

"What do you know of my father?" he asked.

"Um... not much, honestly. I've heard whispers that he has been in power far longer than the last twenty years, which is when our books say he came to take reign. I've heard he is filled with more hostility than any human before." I thought for a moment. "Although men who've returned to our village said he was nothing but kind and healed their heartbreak or traumas. That must take a kind man to do, no?"

Lane let out a dry, humorless laugh as he tossed the stick into the fire and stood up.

"I got banished for disagreeing with a decision my father made."

"Banished for a simple disagreement?" I couldn't believe that.

"I wouldn't say it was simple." Lane ran his hands through his hair, a tell for when he was feeling anxious.

"Okay... What was the disagreement?"

With one hand still tangled in his hair and the other perched on his left hip, he looked up at the sky before speaking.

"My father believes in blind loyalty among family. You are to follow each other no matter what. My decision to disagree with him meant I did not respect him. It meant, in his eyes, that I was turning my back on my family. He banished me to prove that I needed him. I needed to learn to fall in line."

"What did he want you to agree with?"

"A plan he had based on revenge. I thought it should be done quickly, he wanted an elaborate scheme."

I could tell he wasn't going to elaborate further about this. Even though my curiosity was not satiated, I let it go.

"Oh, well, what about your brother?"

He lowered his head to where his chin almost touched his chest. A wicked smile moved over his features, turning his charming laugh lines into something almost sinister. "My brother, my dashing brother." He moved so that he was standing facing me.

"He was allowed to stay. Father would rather he be somewhere in sight. Our mother, understandably, had a sweet spot when it came to Knox. She has always protected him fiercely against our father."

"You sound as though you dislike him?"

"We have never been close. My father and Knox have never seen eye to eye. I believe my father sees right through the charming facade he puts on. It only worsened when our mother passed on. My father once told me he believed Knox to be..." A rustle in the woods stopped Lane from continuing as our attention snapped to the spot behind us, where we could still see the sway of a few lower branches. I looked back at Lane, and he held a finger over his mouth, signaling for there to be silence between us. I held my breath for added measure as Lane took a few small steps toward the swaying limbs. The sun was barely casting light as it disappeared below the horizon. The low visibility made the situation more unnerving.

My heart thumped so erratically it surely was trying to escape my chest. Lane was about ten feet away from the source of the noise when something jumped out from the shadowy spaces the trees created. Lane jumped back as a little brown squirrel ran past him and straight toward me.

"Hey!" Lane shouted as the little critter hurdled toward where I was sitting on the blanket. It quickly darted to where the pack was and grabbed hold of the remaining loaf of bread.

"Get it, Amalia!" Lane was stumbling over himself as he tried to catch up to the squirrel. I burst into a fit of laughter as I watched the scene unfold. The squirrel was trying to drag a loaf much longer than itself while Lane tried to catch it.

"This isn't funny!" he shouted, stumbling over himself and narrowly missing the squirrel once more. It very well may have been the most hilarious thing I had ever seen. Lane leaped toward the squirrel in a final attempt. He grabbed hold of the bread while the squirrel scurried back into the wooded area. Not without the mouthful it had been clinging on with. He dropped his head to the ground, his arms still outstretched from his leap. I was still laughing, completely useless, unable to help in any way.

Brushing himself off, Lane collapsed on the blanket as I tried to stifle the last few giggles escaping.

"Next time I'm letting it take the bread." He chucked the loaf of bread at me before dropping his hands on the ground above his head.

"I guess we will need to be more careful with our food," I said, still smiling. I grabbed the loaf and tucked it into the pack, then secured it tightly.

"I think it's time we try to get some sleep. I'm going to throw some more wood on the fire, so it burns through most of the night. We can use the packs as pillows, so no more vermin try to steal anything. Can you grab the blankets?"

Right, sleep.

We fixed the blanket and used our packs as pillows. I hadn't had the chance to divulge that there was only a single blanket for the two of us.

"Um, funny thing I forgot to mention earlier..." I awkwardly stammered out, nervously rubbing my arms.

"What is that?" He extended a hand out to grab a blanket from me.

"I somehow accidentally managed to only pack one blanket."

"Somehow accidentally?" he repeated.

"Yeah, I think I was just in shock and panic was controlling me, and I just... rush-packed, not really thinking, so now here we are with only one blanket," I spit out quickly.

"I see." And there those charming laugh lines were again, proving that he wasn't upset by this at all. Just highly amused.

"I'm sorry, if you want to use it alone. I get it, I'm perfectly fine being close to the fire."

"You're not going to sleep without a blanket while I have one. We can both go without while we use this one as a pad, it's fine. As long as you don't try any funny business."

"Me!" It came out high-pitched and squeaky. "I would not try anything, Lane."

"Well, you sure didn't mind sneaking peeks earlier tonight, so I can't be too sure what you're capable of. Here I thought you were just innocent little Amalia." He nudged me, and I felt my face go stark red. Luckily, night had claimed the sky, and all we had was the light from the fire and stars above.

"I was NOT sneaking peeks! I told you what I was doing, then was shocked to see you had gone straight nude in the open. How was I supposed to know what you were doing? At least I had the decency to find privacy."

"Decency, huh? More like you found a place to spy." His eyebrow lifted again.

I let out an exasperated growl. "Whatever. I'm going to sleep, goodnight."

"Night, Mal," he said. I could hear the humor in his tone and rolled over.

I lay there silently, listening to the crackling and popping of the fire burning. After what felt like a lifetime, I dared to glance back at Lane, who seemed to already be asleep. How nice it must have been to drift away so easily. Lying there with the world now quiet and no distractions from Lane or new wonders I was seeing for the first time, I was left alone with my mind. I shifted to lie on my back. A smile spread across my face as I recalled the squirrel wreaking havoc. The small glimmer was overcome with a sudden strike of grief as images of that morning stabbed through my heart. My smile vanished, replaced with a quivering frown.

The first plunge of the invisible knife was the guilt of how I'd left my family, and thoughts of Ivalea, who hadn't been there. Would my brother's body be preserved in the wintery lands where he was supposed to be training? Story, my best friend, I never even looked for her. Did she know that? Did she see me walk away from wherever her soul chose to rest?

The second slice was the people and children who had lost their lives without the opportunity to tell anyone goodbye.

The deepest puncture, why I'd survived. *What* I'd survived, and would it happen again?

I could feel my throat seizing up like it had been hours before. With no adrenaline to use or plan to focus on, I couldn't so easily stop the flood from overtaking me. I felt the hot tears create rivers down my cheeks. I tried to grieve silently as I stifled the sobs threatening to burst from me. I didn't know how long this went on, but I felt Lane's hand rest upon my shoulder, letting me know he was there if I needed him. I didn't turn to him. I couldn't use him for comfort when I felt so confused and overwhelmed. I needed to come to terms with my new reality on my own. I couldn't rely on him to fix me. Eventually, I succumbed to exhaustion and drifted to sleep.

Chapter 5

Consciousness came quickly, like I'd been flung from a nightmare. A cold sweat coated my body, my eyes swollen from the emotion I'd let out before falling asleep. Still dazed, I sat upright on my elbows and looked around. The fire had dwindled, leaving only glowing orange embers. Beside me, Lane shivered, his shoulders trembling slightly. Rubbing my eyes, I decided to gather more firewood. I would need to find thicker pieces like Lane had found earlier. Rising as quietly as possible to avoid disturbing him, I started toward the woods, retracing the path to the spring. At the woods' edge, I scanned the route; darkness swallowed everything, I would need to be careful not to get lost.

My bare feet moved along the cool soil, leaves crunching beneath my weight every few steps. I took a deep breath and savored the moment, how calming the outside air was. Even in darkness, I felt such a strong sense of peace that took away any fears that should naturally surface when alone in the woods. I reached out in front of me, feeling for gaps within the branches we'd created earlier. My toes grazed something dry in the soil as I shuffled my feet searching for kindling. I kneeled and picked up a brittle twig. It would burn just as long as the grass I'd tried to contribute. I kept it anyway, not wanting the twig to feel unwanted, and continued walking along. That had always been a quirk of mine. Lane would often tease me for it, always chastising me for giving emotions to inanimate objects. One morning he'd dropped a broom inside one of the taverns we cleaned and immediately went into theatrics about how we had to rush it to the clinic to be seen. He'd annoyed me so much that day. Ahead, the trees thinned, becoming silhouettes in the darkness illuminated by the crescent moon above. The spring shouldn't be much farther.

The pale moonlight glimmered over the water, and a light, calming trickle filled my ears as the water moved up from the spring. I closed my eyes, tilting my head up to the stars, and clung to the sound that eased my mind. Those violent thoughts and images that threatened to destroy me were quieted—even if only slightly. I kneeled down, shifting the gathered limbs to one hand, and skimmed my fingers along the water, swirling it around. A rustling in front of me snapped my focus to the dark void beyond the spring. A smile stretched across my face as I thought of the squirrel that had Lane head diving to the ground over some bread. I peered toward the noise.

"Come here, little thief." I repeatedly clicked my tongue to try and coax it out to me. It seemed to be working, as the darkness shifted. My pulse quickened as I understood with terrifying clarity I was not coaxing a cute little squirrel out to me. The form unfurled into something tall and misshapen. The hairs along my arms rose, the back of my neck tingled with a warning. I sucked in a breath that I didn't dare let out as my mind screamed Lane's words back to me: *"Humans are not the only thing you should fear, Amalia."*

My heart beat faster, and I couldn't tear my eyes from the figure. I knew I had to move, though. Whatever it was, it knew exactly where I kneeled because of my idiotic clicking noises. I looked sideways without moving my head, trying to appear as anything but prey, even though my instincts begged me to run. Three feet away, maybe four, was the rock where we'd tossed our clothes. I inched sideways toward it, shifting my feet, careful not to make a sound.

Placing my hands against the rough stone, I swore under my breath. Time froze the moment I heard the audible *snap* of the forgotten twigs breaking under my weight against the rock's surface. My head swiveled to where the figure was, its arms pulled and wrenched in outlandish directions. The right arm was crooked and jutted at a vicious angle behind the body. Its left shot upward as if reaching for the night sky, but the forearm was pointed directly toward where I was hiding, its hand dangling toward the ground. The creature's bones had to be broken—there was no other explanation. My breaths were shallow, my heart slammed against my chest, my entire body tingling with anticipation of what was to come, urging me to *MOVE.*

I couldn't move. I was paralyzed. My father had always said I would have the fight instinct instead of flight, but right then, I was clearly freezing as if I were a fawn separated from its mother. My legs trembled as the figure took a staggered step closer, aiding me in seeing what looked to be liquid running down its bumpy length; this was truly unlike any animal I had ever seen. The moonlit spring served as the only barrier between us. Its two legs made bile rise up my throat. The right foot faced forward, but the shinbone speared through its flesh like the snapped twigs beneath me. Its left foot was twisted completely around and seemed broken at the knee from the way the calf jutted out to the side. In my panic, I tried to rationalize what I was seeing. This had to be a human. A severely injured one... but what other explanation was there? Could there be catastrophic effects from the shimmer that weren't just death? Could this happen to me or Lane?

"He... Hello?" I choked out.

The creature fractured at the waist, a wet, splintering crunch, until all of its limbs were touching the ground in various deformed angles. My feet slipped as I stumbled back at the sudden movement, throwing one hand over my mouth to drown out the sounds of my panicked breathing. Tears burned my eyes, my chest heaved with pure terror, and tremors took over my body. Legs going numb, I looked back where I had entered the clearing.

Would I be able to make it back?

A wave of dread washed over me as goosebumps prickled the back of my neck. I'd taken my eyes off the creature. I whipped my head back to the spot where it had been. Nothing occupied the space. I slammed my eyes closed. *This can't be real, this can't be real.* A wet, clicking taunt sounded, chilling my bones. *It's trying to coax me to it, like I was doing. It's mimicking me.*

My eyes snapped open, searching the darkness. I urged my legs to cooperate and move. A shaky breath escaped as the clicking came again, slow and thick. Unsettling me straight down to my core. It repeated the sinister chant, signaling it was in front of me, and I tracked the shadows that didn't belong. The creature lurked forward. Cracks and pops filled the quiet space, its bones breaking and splintering as it closed in on me.

"I... I... I can help you, if you've been affected by the shimmer... It affected me, too. I... I... just need to go get my friend..." The words struggled to escape my mouth as my body convulsed in fear. I desperately wished for Lane to rush through the woods and tell me this was all just a nightmare.

Tisk tisk tisk tisk.

The sound it produced echoed around me, taunting me. *Tisk tisk tisk tisk.* The form moved into the moonlight, now only a mere six feet away from me. The smell of decay caused my knees to buckle. I may have almost died less than twenty-four hours before, but going against a creature such as that would not be something I could survive.

I took in the gruesome sight as it shifted to straighten its body. Growths covered the entirety of its form; they were fleshy and smooth, ranging in size. Some were the length of my thumb, others as large as my fist. There were hundreds covering the naked body. It produced a new sound, like a creaky door from my old home. A terror-filled whimper escaped me as the figure finished uncurling, revealing the head, hairless and pale. Inky veins coursed through its skin. A small, single slit lay horizontally where a nose would have been, mucus dripping from the opening. The rest of the head was covered in the near-translucent growths, just like the rest of its body. It was heaving, its shoulders moving up and down like someone trying to catch their breath after a long run. *Tisk tisk tisk tisk.* It clicked as if it had a tongue, but there wasn't a mouth moving that I could see. My gaze tracked down its nightmarish figure, still trying to decipher what exactly I was seeing. It was evident this was no human. My sights landed on a curved stinger. It looked like a hardened ivory tusk in the way it curved up toward its torso with a needle-like point.

"I don't want any trouble, I was just looking for firewood," I said on a shaky exhale, trying to reason with it.

It cocked its head sideways and a bone jutted out from its veiny neck, not yet penetrating its skin. A low rumble vibrated from the creature, and I noticed the bumps along its body shaking with the vibration, secreting a liquid that oozed instead of running down the unseemly flesh.

Red.

They were secreting blood.

A scream tore from me before I could stifle it, and at the high-pitched sound, the creature erupted into a grotesque monster. The fleshy growths peeled open to reveal eyes.

Hundreds of eyes cracked open simultaneously, each one a piercing, luminescent red, the thick blood that leaked from them reflecting the tears that had been flowing down my cheeks. *Crack. Crack. Crack.* Every bone snapped into place with a crunch that made me flinch as it grew to tower over me, then its body began to vibrate again, emitting a higher-pitched scream, mirroring what had come from me. My hands flew to my ears, and I crouched down trying to get away from the noise.

Then it lunged.

Black claws emerged from the tips of its fingers, and the mouth I hadn't seen before was now open. The jaw of the creature, hanging lower than any human's could go, held rows and rows of sharp, serrated teeth. Inky saliva dripped from them, ready to consume me as its next meal.

"What the fuck!" I screamed as I took a step back, feeling the bite of something cold.

It only took a second, my foot disappeared into the water, and I fell back as the creature—which was just inches from me—snapped its jaws shut where my head had been only a heartbeat before. Its claws, swiping through the air trying to snatch what its monstrous jaws couldn't, hit their target. I felt them rip through my dress, my abdomen exploding in a white-hot pain before I disappeared into the frigid water.

Under the water, I could see the muddled outline of the creature as it slashed at the surface. It couldn't swim, but neither could I. I let the spring consume me, even though my lungs begged for air. No thrashing or fighting. What waited for me was worse than drowning. If I was going to die, I would pick how I went. It wasn't going to be getting torn apart by whatever that creature was! My choice was stolen as my theory was proven false. The creature plunged into the spring, scenting my blood clouding the once-glittering blue waters, then locked in on me. Gliding through the chilled depths straight toward me.

Now it was time to fight.

I tried to kick, pull, swim my way to the surface, but I went nowhere. Panic took over, and I became frantic in my movements. The creature seemed like it thrived on my terror with how its behavior became more erratic, the more my fear consumed me. Its claws gripped my sides, and its teeth barreled for my face. I balled my fist and threw what strength I could into a strike underneath its chin, snapping its mouth closed. I tried to push against its chest with my other hand, but my fingers sank into the closed eye sockets covering its body. The need to breathe crippled me, bubbles burst from my lips as I gagged. I needed to get to the surface. I needed to get away.

Claws impaled my thigh while others struck my ribcage as the creature jerked me toward its body. I looked down and saw the curved member had gone through my stomach. Agony forced my mouth into a scream, which dissolved as I took in a mouthful of water, inhaling it, my lungs burning from the foreign substance. I felt myself losing control of my body when I started to drift into numbness. My body convulsed, sending fresh blood swirling around the nightmare and me. The creature's head snapped sideways the moment my blood reached it. Its jaw unhinged before snapping down on my right shoulder. I should have been screaming from the pain, it was excruciating, but I was no longer capable of reacting. Relief found me as my consciousness slipped away.

Something entered the water; the creature removed its teeth from my flesh, and its curved length ripped out of me. Above, moonlight glinted off of something new descending toward me, something made of onyx that made the nightmare fear the shadows it hid within. Blackness took over as I drifted down in what had become my icy tomb.

Chapter 6

"You fucking owe me, Tatum. The fact that you even had the audacity to insist I waste my energy on a human is revolting."

The voice speaking was commanding but smooth, like honey laced with broken glass. Every inch of my body was overwhelmed with anguish, pain that seeped so deep into my bones, there was no possibility of relief.

A human? As if she were not one?

"I always owe you."

Lane. I'd know his warm, husky voice anywhere. Usually clear and strong, it was now strangled with frustration. I heard shifting in the room and the crackles of a fire burning. I strained to open my eyes, suddenly taken back to my field, where I had felt this same struggle to move. Dread washed over me at the thought of not having control of my body again.

The angelic voice laughed as Lane said, "Just make sure she's healed."

"Or what, you'll beg me harder?" The words came out slow and languid.

My eyes slowly opened, and I forced myself to keep from shooting daggers at her.

My gaze darted to the side, scanning my surroundings through blurry vision until I saw two figures standing to the left of me. I saw a tall, serpentine woman who had her index finger hooked under Lane's chin. Her mouth, just inches from his, caught my attention as she looked into his eyes. "Why do you care what happens to her?"

Anger ignited through every vein as... What was this acidic feeling? Was this jealousy?

The flames in the hearth now danced up the stone walls. He pushed her hand from his chin, then turned in my direction. I snapped my eyes shut again and feigned sleep.

"You need to leave, Blaire," Lane advised.

She scoffed. "I need to leave?" A hint of defiance in her tone, as if him telling her to leave was the last thing she'd expected him to say.

"Now," he responded flatly. A twitch threatened to turn my lips up into a smile. *It was definitely jealousy I felt.*

The air was thick. "I'm sure your father would like to hear about this." Then the room shook with her exit as she slammed the door behind her.

Seconds ticked by. "You can stop pretending to sleep now, Amalia."

Shit.

I didn't move, thinking maybe he was just testing me. His sigh rumbled right into my bones. I felt the mattress dip near my ankles as he sat.

"For future reference, if you're going to act like you're sleeping, then you probably shouldn't cause noticeable incidents or stare at the people you're faking for." His words were filled with subdued amusement.

I cracked one eye open and saw him leaning against the bedpost, arms crossed.

"What do you mean, noticeable incidents?" I asked, using my fingers to quote his words before adding, "You seemed... rather occupied."

"I was. However, you can always interrupt." His face transformed from amused to haunted before he asked, "You didn't notice, did you?"

"Notice what?" I asked.

"You don't look like you're feeling well, are you okay?" He shifted closer and ran the back of his hand down my cheek. The memories invaded in a brutal onslaught. The monster lunging for me, jagged teeth, blood and ice surrounding me as I dipped farther into the water, losing the fight. How was I here?

"H... how did I get here?" I bolted upright. "How a... am I alive?" I stuttered out before blinding, intense pain penetrated every nerve. I writhed in the bed, my head cocking back, unable to process the unrelenting assault from within. The bed creaked and groaned as I moved furiously.

"Blaire! Get the fuck in here, now!" Lane roared into the open room as he cradled my face in his palm. His other hand brushed the hair back from my eyes as he whispered, "It's going to be okay, just hang on."

I heard the door burst open as the air in the room turned chilled. My body calmed on the bed, the agony coming and going like waves. I could almost see them as Lane continued to comfort me.

"I thought you said you healed her?!" he snarled.

"I said I made sure she lived. I didn't say shit about ensuring she'd be pain free." My eyes opened as she laughed before saying, "Looks like she's experiencing exactly what she deserves." Her gaze slithered to me.

Screw her.

Within seconds, Lane had the woman—Blaire—by the throat, pinning her against the bedpost. My eyes went wide. She had one hand over the wrist that had her in a hold. There was no fear, just a challenge in her eyes while her lips curled in a sneer. Daring him to do something.

"Oh, Laney boy," she purred, "you know I like it rough."

Lane ripped his hand away before he said, "Blaire, either heal her fully, or you can spend time with Dr. Folsom again. He'll *really* show you what rough is."

A flicker of fear showed as her confidence waned. "Fine," was all she said, but the smile that had died showed there was much more tucked behind that one word. Her back straightened as she turned to face me. If looks could kill, I would have died instantaneously. Her red eyes, so much like the creature, dripped with ferocity as she stepped toward me.

She was stunning with her platinum blonde hair and streaks of red framing her diamond-shaped face. I watched her ruby lips move as a devilish smile spread across her face.

"I'm going to enjoy this," she said to me before she placed both hands on my abdomen.

"AHHHHHHHH!" A guttural scream ripped from me, the blinding pain too much to bear. I no longer cared about her features or the eyes only fit for nightmares. The last thing I heard was Blaire's laughter spiraling into the darkness with me.

I woke up alone inside the same bedchamber I had before. No Lane, no Blaire, or creature wanting to rip me apart. I went to sit up, bracing for pain as I threw the soft covers off, but shock rippled through me.

"What the hell?" I scrambled up, running my hands over my bare stomach, not believing that the only things I saw were scars. Although a bit tender, the raised, pink marks were no longer painful.

How was this possible? My heartbeat was all I could hear. What had Lane yelled at that wretched woman? *I thought you said you healed her.*

"Healed me?" The words came out in a whisper. That wasn't possible. Had I been dreaming then, or was I dreaming now? I couldn't have been, this wasn't my house, this definitely wasn't my bed. My heart was now racing as my mind spun out of control. I tried to move, to leave this room, find answers, but my feet couldn't match the pace the rest of my body was moving. My hands and knees caught the wooden floorboards with a loud *thud*. *Breathe in, Amalia.* I inhaled deeply. *Now exhale.* I listened to the words my father used to speak to me to quell the panic attacks that would wash over me.

Heavy footsteps closed in on me as I raised my head up. I saw black boots similar to Lane's, but these met stark black trousers fashioned with a black leather belt, a sword holster hanging on the right side. My gaze continued up to a tucked-in, white tunic and black vest, large, tanned arms crossed at a broad chest, before I reached a bewildered gaze taking me in.

"Hi," I squeaked, waving one hand awkwardly in the air before dropping it to my side. My hand met flesh.

The mystery man's brow arched, his gaze flicked from where my hand dropped, then lazily up to my face. "Hello, Amalia," he said in a dark voice.

My brows furrowed. "You know my name?"

"I do," he drawled with a nod of his head while his eyes passed over my body once more. "Do you usually greet people like that?"

"Like wh—" I looked down and felt my heart stop. I was naked. Fully nude.

"Oh my dragons!" I shrieked as I ran straight back to the bed and threw the covers over my entire body, including my head.

"I'm SO sorry. I honestly did not realize!" The words came out muffled from how close I clutched the covers to me, overcome with complete embarrassment, I was sure the redness on my face could be seen through them. "Ohhhhh, I wish I had never made it out of that spring. Creepy bleeding eye monster, please come kill me now," I moaned.

"You certainly do not need to apologize for that." The man chuckled as I continued to try and disappear.

"What's going on here?" I peeked out, seeing Lane standing next to the man. He stood a few inches shorter.

Intense, crackling energy burst between them. I heard what sounded like a low growl, but I wasn't sure who it was emanating from.

"Amalia was just waking up," the man said, his jaw clenching.

So, he didn't plan to tell Lane that I'd just given him the entire Amalia show. I didn't mean to, of course. I had been so distracted with how I was alive, how I'd been healed, I didn't even think twice about the state of undress I was in.

"I... I would get up to properly greet you"—the man's mouth tilted up as I spoke—"but um, it seems I have no clothes on," I said with an edge as I glared at Lane, making it clear I would like information on why this was the case.

"Leave us," Lane said while keeping his eyes locked on mine.

The man leaned his head down in my direction. "Dark temptress."

He lifted his head, making eye contact with me before winking and turning to the door as Lane barked, "Dark what?"

At that, he turned slightly toward Lane. "Just a little joke between us." He gave a quick, lopsided grin. "Ask her about the cute wave she does." Then he left the room.

I didn't know him, but I would kill him.

"What did he mean by dark temptress?"

"I don't even know who he is. The better question right now, Lane, is why am I naked?" My voice rose to a high pitch on the last word.

"I thought you'd be out for much longer." He glided over to the bed and sat on the edge next to me. I went to repeat my question, but he continued on his own. "Blaire is the one who stripped you. I left the room, I swear to you." He ran his hands through his hair as he said, "You were torn to shreds, Amalia. Your stomach, your thigh, your shoulder..."

Mindlessly I reached up to place a hand on my shoulder, flinching, as I recalled the teeth ripping into my flesh.

"The orbichor did so much damage, I thought you were gone." He took the hand I had placed on my once-torn shoulder, and his fingers closed around mine as he looked into my eyes. His gaze grew intense, spearing into me as he worked on the words, "Blaire has the ability to heal." He paused long enough for me to mouth the beginning of a question before he continued. "There's a lot you're going to learn about the world outside of your village. For right now, I want you to know you are safe. Everything else can be discussed later. Blaire brought you a change of clothes while you were sleeping. Yours were... well, ruined." He stood, releasing my hand. "I'll step out. You wash up, and then we can walk the grounds if you'd like. The bathroom is just to your right through that door," he said, pointing. "I'll be outside the main door whenever you're ready."

In five long strides, he was out of the room without another word.

So many questions made a permanent residence in my brain. Lane's footsteps retreated like there was no time for me to understand. "Wait!" I yelled after him. "What do you mean, she has the ability to heal? Where are we? What's an orbichor?"

If he heard me, he let silence answer instead. *Later* would likely never actually come for me to ask them again.

It was a spacious room, its size larger than my entire home back in the village. The bed I was in was placed against the back wall, which looked straight at the main door. There was a fireplace on the left that had a deep navy, velvet loveseat facing toward it, and a small bedside table next to me with only a ring stain on it from whatever had rested there. The bathroom Lane had spoken of was off to the right of the main door.

I hopped out of bed. It didn't so much as creak with the absence of my weight. A stark contrast to the sounds it made while I had been writhing in it. I clutched the fabric of the top sheet, pulling it tight around my body before walking across the room. Lane said I was safe, but how could I be safe or comfortable? I didn't know where I was, or who was in this place. Were we in Santavarre already? How did we get here so quickly? Thoughts continued to flood in as I entered the bathroom, and my mouth gaped open. It was smaller than the bedroom but still larger than one person needed. The copper tub drew my attention. It had to be at least eight feet long with plants that spread around the outer edge and up the walls. The leaves variegated with colors of deep greens, whites, and pinks. There was something hanging from the ceiling—a large, matching copper square shape with tiny holes covering the surface.

"I hope those don't end up being eyes..." I muttered to myself, staring at the object suspiciously. I went to the vanity where I found the clothes Blaire had brought in and a robe, running my fingers over the material and feeling its plush textures. It was so much softer than anything I had seen woven in Cimmerian. I looked around for how to fill the tub. In Cimmerian, we'd had a hand-cranked system located outside that we would use to fill buckets, which we'd have to carry indoors to fill our bathing tub. Our bathroom consisted of rags and a waste pit we relieved ourselves in. Only the wealthier cottages on the outskirts had the pleasure of running water inside their homes. I never had the chance to see what the system looked like.

I located two copper nozzles and turned the one on the right. Water cascaded from the ceiling like a steady rainfall. I placed my hand under the fall of water and felt the frigidity before yanking my hand back, thoughts of the icy spring coming back to me. I took a few tentative steps back as my eyes wandered to the second nozzle, and I reached over to turn it. Nothing happened.

"Well, that was uneventful."

I peered over my shoulder at where the clothes lay, wondering about where my pack had gone, when I caught a glimpse of my reflection in the mirror just behind them. My eyes widened until I resembled an owl, the kind that would perch in the animal barn from time to time. Tears welled up, threatening to cascade down my cheeks as I saw the wreckage that was me. My normally wavy, strawberry blonde hair was matted to the scalp, my right shoulder, although healed, was a canvas painted with dried blood and scars. I stifled a cry, mindful of Lane just outside. I inhaled deeply, then allowed myself to look further. My abdomen was crusted with a deep, rusty red, and four jagged slash marks marred my skin, surrounded by different hues of dark blues and purples. My hand moved over the marks on my skin. My skin was actually smooth, as if the marks were painted on and hadn't almost been the death of me.

I couldn't stand to look at myself any longer, I needed to get cleaned up. I placed a shaky hand into the stream, expecting a chill, when I felt warmth spread over my palm. A laugh escaped me, and I hurriedly hopped into the bathing tub, standing under the warm droplets falling furiously around me. It was invigorating! I spread my arms and tipped my head back, relishing the feel. I made quick work using the lavender scented soap to clean myself, taking extra care around where the marks were, just to be safe. My hair took some time as I tried to massage the soap into the mats and ease them loose. Once finished, I wrapped the robe around me and forced my feet to step out of the tub, not wanting to leave the heated water.

The clothes Blaire had gotten for me were... different than what I would have typically worn. I supposed anything was better than nothing. I slipped on the black trousers, which hugged my body, followed by the top. It had thin straps, maybe an inch thick, and the fabric reached the middle of my torso, leaving me feeling a bit insecure. I wouldn't have said I was overweight, but I definitely had a few what I liked to call "pudge packs" to lose... and they just so happened to be on display in this outfit. I made the decision to throw the robe over the clothes before leaving the bathing chamber. I made my way across the room to the main doors and expected to see Lane when I opened them, but I didn't.

I cracked the door open and saw no one at first. I stuck my head out more when a striking caramel-skinned man popped into view.

"Well, hey there!" He was leaning against the corridor wall, smiling at me as if we were longtime friends. A cascade of lush curls caught my attention as they fell in dark tendrils softening the sharp lines of his face.

"Uh... hello..." I looked around him, not seeing Lane anywhere.

"The name's Bash, it's a pleasure to meet you, Amalia." He stuck his hand out. "Lane was summoned by his father, so he asked me to escort you to get some food." His hand dropped, and his face pulled in as he looked at me. "If I may say, I think he was expecting you to be dressed for this."

"I'm starting to get weirded out that everyone seems to know my name, and yet I'm surrounded by strangers who are either in my room or waiting outside." I opened the door a little more and took a step out, clasping my hands together in front of me. "I have clothes underneath the robe. I would much rather look like this than walk around in only what Blaire left."

"I'm not so sure Lane would approve of that decision," Bash said, cocking his head to the side.

"Good thing he doesn't have a say over what I do or what I wear. Last time I checked, that was solely up to me." I crossed my arms, my left foot jutting out to the side.

A perfectly straight and pearly white set of teeth lit up his face as he smiled.

"We are going to be good friends." He bent his arm, an invitation for me to lock mine with his, then motioned down the long corridor with his other.

He didn't feel like a threat, but how did I know I could trust this man? He was dressed in black pants similar to the man who had been in my room earlier, and a black, loose-fitting, long-sleeved tunic that was tucked into the waistband of his pants. His hair was short in the back, light brown, with longer strands hanging to frame his face. Stubble lined his jaw and upper lip, giving him a more rugged look.

"I'm a patient man, take your time," he said in a cool tone. I met his stark green eyes and couldn't help but feel a flutter in my stomach as I weaved my hand in his arm before we walked.

Chapter 7

Bash and I had been walking through the castle for what felt like a lifetime. I shouldn't complain, it was truly inspiring. The corridor walls were decorated with paintings of mythical creatures, dragons soaring through sunset skies, and fairies dueling in lush forests. Plants were thriving in giant concrete vases as tall as I stood. The walls themselves were most memorable even without the decorations, white stone with glittering golden gems and swirls throughout the face. With the sun shining through windows from the opposite side, it created a dazzling, scintillating effect.

"What kind of stone is this? I've never seen anything like it." I dropped Bash's arm and walked to place my hand on the cool stone. As I ran my fingers over the shimmering gems, the color was so familiar. I dropped my hand and looked back at Bash, who wasn't paying any mind to me. He was speaking with an older female I hadn't noticed was even around.

Interest piqued, I silently joined them.

"Amalia, this is Orzelle. Orzelle, Amalia." Bash didn't let a second go by when I returned to his side before introducing us.

"A pleasure," Orzelle said, shooting her eyes over me before slightly bowing. Her tone implied she felt anything but pleasure, the way she drew the words out, each one dripping with bitterness.

"Oh, um, you don't need to do that. A handshake is fine!" I stretched my hand out to her and quickly felt the awkwardness seep into the air as she just stared at my palm. Repulsion showed along her weathered features as her eyes narrowed and her lips pursed. She took a tentative step back, her nose wrinkling as she jutted it up in the air.

"Bowing is a sign of respect and custom for the people that live in and near the castle," Bash informed me by whispering into my ear, amusement painted all over his face.

"I apologize," I said, taking a slight bow as well.

"Well, I must be going." Orzelle turned to Bash as her face transitioned to serious, her stare hardening. "Do not forget what I said." With that, she continued down the hall.

"Did I offend her?" I asked.

"Another simply existing too closely will offend her. She just had a message for me. I will warn you, if you can, steer clear of her." He held his arm out for me again, and I took it more quickly than before, feeling a bit tense at his words.

As if he could read me, he said, "Not because she's dangerous... well... not really. It is just that she likes to report *everything* to King Tatum. She's a good fly on the wall. Sometimes you won't even realize she's around. Listening."

"Hmm. I was just thinking to myself before I came over that I hadn't even seen her in this section and poof! I walk away for two seconds, and you guys are speaking."

Bash looked down at me with that charming, boyish smile again. "Someone sounds jealous."

"Get over yourself!" I squeaked, flabbergasted. "I don't even know you, how on Elysian could I be jealous?!"

"Ohhhhh and easy to rile up. Yes, this is going to be a great friendship. I will add that she was probably a bit frazzled about you walking around the castle in a bathrobe." His laugh echoed off the walls.

I yanked my arm back from his, not wanting to entertain his smug remarks any longer. Fighting the urge to look down at myself, I stared straight ahead and refused to give him the satisfaction of seeing me squirm. As we neared the end of the corridor, it opened up to a covered outside area. There was a fire pit burning with cushioned seats surrounding it. As we approached, I noticed the man from my room earlier was sitting with his boot propped up against the pit. He was just staring into the flames when we walked up. Bash cleared his throat.

The man briefly looked up, then back at the flames before quickly shooting his gaze to me.

"Amalia," he said, keeping eye contact.

"Man, I still don't know," I replied with a nod of my head.

Bash nudged me, knocking me off balance just enough to make me have to catch myself. "Have a seat." I shot him a glare and took a seat opposite both men.

"I'm starting to think there won't be a time when I see you in clothes," he exclaimed as he sat back in his seat, positioning his hands behind his head.

"Wait, what?" Bash questioned, sitting forward in his seat, resting his elbows on his knees. "What do you mean?"

"Oh, you haven't heard?" The man's eyebrows shot up as he placed a hand over his heart, acting like he was stunned. "She just tried to seduce me earlier when I went to check on her. She was standing before me completely naked."

Bash bellowed out a laugh, slapping his knee. A swift pang of pain sliced through my chest as a memory of my father doing the same gesture entered my mind.

"WHAT?" he yelled. "Here I thought she had the hots for me, being all jealous of Orzelle and I."

What on Caligness was happening right now?

"First of all!" My voice was high as I tried to raise it above theirs. "I did not try to seduce you. I don't even know WHO you are." I pointed my finger at the nameless man so he would know I was directing those words at him. "I haven't a clue as to what your name is! And I surely am not jealous of anyone! I don't know either of you!"

"And yet, you're already in love with us." Bash sighed and leaned back, glancing at the other man. "So, are we flipping a coin or sharing?" He wiggled his eyebrows for effect.

"Oh my gods! You two are seriously deranged!" I could feel my face flush with a shade of pink, and it was not from the heat of the small fire. "Can you just be quiet, please, or tell me when Lane will be back?"

"King Tatum is a very busy man, so you don't have to worry about Lane being away too long with him during the day. Is there a reason you're in a robe, Amalia? Did Laney boy not get you basic necessities like clothing?" The mystery man leaned forward, his elbows resting on his knees, mimicking Bash's movements, waiting for my response as he rolled his jaw.

I glanced at Bash and then back before I said, "I have clothes underneath it, but I wasn't comfortable with what Blaire picked for me. I feel better in this, but I would like to find actual clothes, or my pack, if either of you could assist me with that before Lane returns."

"I told her that the pretty boy wouldn't approve," Bash said.

My eyes snapped to him. "And I told you he doesn't have a say... but I would like to avoid having to explain this a third time."

"Bash, go fetch her pack for her, please." The man motioned to the castle with his head. A nod of acknowledgment was all he received from Bash before he got up and left.

"Wait, my pack is actually here?" Tears pricked my eyes. I hadn't let myself think about it being gone. The confirmation it was here sent a rush of emotions through me.

Lashes fluttering to quell the moisture, I said, "Does he usually follow your orders without question?" He got up and sauntered over to the seat directly next to me, and my heart forgot to beat for a moment. "I wouldn't think friendships would last very long if I treated them that way."

"Bash follows my *orders,* as you call them, because he is my best friend. Even more than that, he is kind, and compassionate, and will do anything to ensure the beautiful guests in this castle are comfortable. Which, you stated, you are not."

I could feel his eyes on me, my chest heaving like an electric current was tethered between us. Being this close to him and not delirious from nearly dying, I noticed his eyes. So unique and divergent looking. They were a striking deep purple with a black rim lining the outer section of his irises. I wasn't sure what came over me, but I reached my hand out toward his face. Feeling as though I needed to bring him closer, dive into them, be completely overcome with wonder.

That is, until he caught my wrist. My skin tingled at his touch as the flames in the pit grew more intense.

Those lavender eyes cast a sideways glance at the pit before locking onto me. "Has no one ever taught you it's impolite to touch someone without permission?"

"I—I." I couldn't form a sentence.

He raised an eyebrow at me. "Yes? Dragon got your tongue, dark temptress?"

I narrowed my eyes. All he did was chuckle in response, which sent me over the edge. I wasn't sure if it was from leftover fatigue from the attack, the death of my family, or the fact that my entire world was gone forever, but I snapped.

"I think it's interesting that you boys are able to joke and play and do whatever it is that you're doing right now when everyone in Cimmerian died. People dropped dead after fucking diamond dust fell from the sky." My hands flew up into the air. "They will never laugh or joke again." My voice started cracking, and I felt the unshed tears threatening to break free. "No one is left to mourn them, to know they even left this life. So you keep thinking that you're cute, keep acting as if there's no care in the world."

I could feel my face burning with heat from the anger and grief boiling inside me as I continued to hold his gaze. His facial expression never changed, he still held a smirk while watching me. Only his eyes shifted, taking me in.

"You are left." He released my wrist. "You have gone through a lot in a short time, I understand how overwhelmed you must be feeling. However, the way we act does not directly reflect what we are feeling." He leaned his large frame back into the seat. "You may see us joking around, but that does not mean we don't care about or aren't concerned with what happened to Cimmerian." He shifted slightly. "I have a feeling you may understand that more than most."

"How many people are in the castle?" I asked, needing to shift the concentration away from me.

He took a considerable pause before speaking, likely thinking his attempt at finding common ground between us would affect me. "A hundred and three beings are living within the castle, about twenty others are just beyond the moat." He picked up a poker that was leaning against the fire pit and started adjusting the wood to enhance the flames currently reduced to a low smolder.

"They all survived like I did?"

"No human survived like you did." His attention to the fire halted as he looked at me. His eyes seemed to try and tell me something.

"How am I here?" I muttered. He was more forthcoming with information than Lane, and I needed answers.

His knuckles turned white as his grip on the poker tightened. "You were brought here after the attack."

Brought here? Did Lane carry me? "But how? We were still at least two days away." I was dying in that spring. *I felt it.* I wouldn't have lasted two full days. There's no way Lane could have carried me here in time.

"Alright, I got her some clothing." Bash came jogging down toward us, waving a bundle of fabrics in one hand. "They should make you feel more comfortable, although I must admit, I'm liking the robe." An acknowledging smile pulled at my cheeks while I silently urged the man to answer, but he didn't.

"Thank you, Bash." I got up and retrieved the clothes from him, clutching them to my chest. The man moved to stand with us as well. "You can go back to your chambers to change. I can inform Lane to find you there."

"What were you just about to say?" I tried once more to get answers. "Before this one interrupted our conversation." I jerked my head in Bash's direction, which made him throw his hands up in a confused surrender.

"Hey!" We all turned to see Lane now making his way over from inside the corridor.

"Fucking dragons," I muttered to myself, thoroughly annoyed now that the man and I had been interrupted twice. "What's your name?" I leaned into him, asking the question in a hushed tone.

Looking down at me, that grin returned before he stated, "I think I like you not knowing." *Of course he does.*

The air quickly grew thick with tension as Lane reached us. Bash and the man next to me visibly tensed, locking down their jaws, all traces of their teasing gone. Crossing their arms over their puffed out chests, they stood taller than moments before.

Lane's gaze cut between us, brows furrowing in an instant. Mystery man stepped in front of me like he needed to shield me, and spoke.

"Blaire's choice of clothes was not suitable. She was just heading up to her chambers to change into what Bash was able to find for her."

I sidestepped him so I could face Lane, his fists clenching at his sides.

"Can you walk me back?" I addressed Lane with a soft smile as I nodded for us to head away from this weird standoff that had the air crackling.

Lane took a few steps backward, clasping his hand in mine but not taking his eyes off the man. Neither wanting to back down from the other.

"Of course, let's go. I need to speak with you in private." We didn't speak again until he shut the door to my bedchamber and we were alone.

I let out a long breath and shook out my arms that were tingling with anxiety. "I'll be right back, I'm going to change out of this," I said, pulling at the plush robe.

In the bathing chamber, I looked at the clothes Bash had retrieved for me and smiled. Stripping the robe off, I placed it on the side of the tub, then slipped on the undergarments. It made me laugh thinking of how awkward they must have been for him to get. He had placed them in between the pants and shirt to hide them from view. Next, I pulled on the plain white chemise that was definitely too large for me, so I tucked the bottom into the denim trousers that, to my surprise, hugged my soft curves perfectly. I waited a few seconds before leaving, nervous about what he needed to speak to me in private about.

Lane was seated on the bed as I exited, one leg draped over the other, waiting for me. He patted the bed beside him twice, gesturing for me to come sit with him.

I couldn't sit with how my mind raced with the possibilities of what he might say. So I paced instead while asking, "What did you need to talk to me about?"

Those glacier eyes tracked me as I went back and forth in front of him. "My father wants to throw a masquerade in celebration of you and I."

My pacing stopped. "... Why?"

Lane's stare sharpened, like I'd slapped him across the face. "You and I are the only known survivors of a tragedy. He wants to celebrate our strength and resilience."

"Oh..." The thought about a party being held because I hadn't died along with everyone in Cimmerian didn't sit well in my gut. *How am I supposed to celebrate that?*

"It's an honor, Amalia. One you deserve after all you've been through."

"No, no, I think it's very kind." My pacing resumed as my words stumbled while trying not to offend him again. "I just... I don't know, it feels a little odd... celebrating while knowing how many lie dead back home. Plus, the man with Bash said over a hundred people live here. If they survived, shouldn't we celebrate everyone's survival?" Looking down, I intertwined my fingers to keep from fiddling. "This feels more like a celebration of their death. It just doesn't feel right to me." I dropped my arms and turned to him, hoping he understood.

"You cannot cease to live and experience this world simply because others left it. As for who survived here, the shimmer, as you call it, didn't need to fall here. They did not experience what Cimmerian did." Lane placed a hand on my knee before he stood. "He would like it to be in a week's time. You will enjoy it. I'll be with you the entire time if you need someone to lean on."

I flashed a weak smile as he started for the door. "Wait! What should I do?"

He paused mid-step. "What do you mean?" he said with a half-turn toward me.

"Um... Should I help any staff? Do *you* need help with anything? I can't just stay in this room forever."

He reached the door, pulling it open. "Try and get some rest for now. You don't need to do anything, Amalia. You can just be."

"Just be?" How was I supposed to do that in a place I don't know? Did he forget this was *his* home, not mine?

"Yes. You are free from chores to get done, or people to please and care for. It's time to care for yourself, which starts with rest." He walked a few steps through the door before retreating and turning to me one last time. "As for the man downstairs, I'd recommend you stay away from him."

Chapter 8

Five days of silence so weighted I felt like I'd been buried went by. I was rotting away like my family.

Day one, I'd done nothing of importance, no one came to show me around or ask for assistance with duties, and although I should have enjoyed that after what had happened, all it did was leave me with my mind. I counted the wooden floorboards, soaked in the bath, lay in bed and traced the textures on the ceiling.

Day two, I'd thrown the little bedside table, causing one of the legs to break and tumble under the bed. I had retrieved it and found Bash had hidden my pack there, tucked away safe. I'd felt my soul crack looking through my sisters' and my book, and screamed until my lungs gave out. I'd replayed the moment I found my family more times than I could count. Seeing every detail over and over again. Relived the attack, swearing It was happening all over again as I broke open the scars from clawing at my flesh during a panic-induced fit.

Day three, Lane graced me with his presence. He had brought me food instead of the whispering maids that usually dropped the plates just inside the door with sidelong glances before quickly leaving. I could hear them once he left, disgusted that the *prince* was serving me food. I was nothing here, just some Cimmerian girl Lane pitied. No one cared that we had an entire year of friendship, or that we had lived through something traumatic together.

By day five I was making the bed, preparing to go find the dining area to eat breakfast around other people. I craved human interaction, and I wasn't staying in this room like a caged animal. Stepping outside the door, I peeked down the corridor to my left to make sure no one was there. I slipped out and quietly made my way weaving down the halls, down a flight of stairs. Determination to find my way made my situational awareness slip, and I collided with a hard body.

"Whoa, little survivor, you must be on quite the mission to run into me that hard. That actually hurt a little," Bash said as he rubbed his abdomen where I had collided into him.

"I'm so sorry, Bash! I was trying to figure out which way I should go next, I didn't even see you there." Two women walked by, pulling my attention. Were their ears... pointed?

"Where are you heading?" Bash's question snapped my focus away from the women, who were now scurrying off, untucking their hair so it fell over their ears.

"I wanted to find the dining area so I could have some breakfast."

"Did Lane not bring you any this morning?" Concern filled his features.

I sighed. "I'm tired of being alone, I need to be around people and not left alone for days on end inside a room."

"He is not going to be happy about that." Tisking at me, a smile spread across his face.

"I haven't been happy being left to replay the nightmares of this past week in my mind, so I think he will have to get over it." His smile faded slightly as he took my words in, then he lifted up a bent arm for me to take. "What are you doing?" I asked, confused.

"It's your lucky day. I'm going to escort you to the dining hall, where we will eat breakfast together."

I couldn't stop the warm smile that spread over my face no matter how tightly I tried to press my lips together. *Damn, he is growing on me.* We made our way silently, Bash looking ahead even though I could see him casting subtle glances at me every now and then, while we walked through the beautiful architecture, the vaulted corridors, and the fantasy-inspired artwork that made this castle awe-inspiring.

Instantly I was overcome with mouth-watering smells that swirled through the air. I took a deep breath, inhaling the savory aromas. Sprinting to the door up ahead, I heard Bash chuckle behind me. Entering the dining hall, I saw a table that was easily eight or nine feet long, full of platters, each containing a different type of food: muffins, eggs still steaming, bacon, sausages still glistening with grease, fruit, and more. I rushed to the end of the table where I saw an open seat.

"The food isn't going anywhere," Bash said, amusement etched into every word.

"I'm sorry, I just want to dig in!" I said as he pulled the chair out for me. "I've never seen so much food in one place." Quickly taking a seat, I went to grab a plate and stuff it full with at least one of everything when a solemn woman took the plate before I could. "Hey! I was about to use that."

"Allow me, ma'am. Just tell me your selections, it would be my pleasure to serve you this morning," she said in a quiet tone, her eyes downcast.

"Oh." An uncomfortable feeling washed over me at what she would think if I said what I wanted... which was truly everything. Snickers and shushes sounded behind the woman.

"You should be able to tell just by looking at her. She more than likely would eat every last scrap on this table."

Blaire. That angelic but venomous voice was one I remembered well.

Barging in solely focused on the smells, I hadn't noticed the others lingering in the room. I looked up at the woman, who was still waiting for my reply, holding my plate as it trembled in her grasp. She looked just as uncomfortable as I felt, her body shifting from one foot to the other. At that moment, I chose not to care what any of these people thought. Fuck them all. Especially Blaire.

"She's absolutely right! I would love to try a little of everything, but start me off with whatever are your favorites, please." I tried to fill my words with as much joy and appreciation as I could. "I've survived worse than a stomachache, so don't be shy!" Flashing a cool smile in Blaire's direction, I made sure she wouldn't gain the satisfaction of feeling triumphant in tearing me down.

Blaire scoffed. "Yeah, thanks to me. It's best if you remember that." Her sharp words were followed quickly by an eye roll before she shifted her focus to a short, beefy man next to her.

Bash chose the seat closest to me on my right. "Always looking to pick a fight," he said before I could come up with a retort.

Another worker, a man this time, carried over a plate of meat and set it in front of Bash. "Does he not care what you'd like?" I asked.

"I'm sure he doesn't care one bit. But I am a creature of habit, and Leonard knows I request nothing but bacon and sausage in the mornings." He started shoveling the protein into his mouth.

I scanned the table for the woman who was preparing my food. I found her on the far left, grabbing a muffin and adding it to the plate she had wedged between an arm and her hip. My ears filled with the sounds of my stomach growling and Bash chewing. Growing more irritated by the second as the sounds grated my nerves, I watched as the woman studied the plate with an approving nod just before heading in my direction. She neared where Blaire and the stubby man were seated, his chair angled so he could face Blaire, his leg inching slowly out to the side. Blaire started to chuckle, throwing a hand over her mouth and turning her head.

No, he can't be about to do what I think he's going to do.

Sure enough, as soon as the woman reached his side, his leg jutted out, causing her to pitch forward. The plate of food fell and exploded into shards of porcelain on the ground. Her knees cracked against the floor and a small, pain-filled whimper escaped her as Blaire and the man howled with laughter. I was on my feet before I could think about what I was doing.

Who does something so cruel? Why?

I rushed to the woman and grabbed her hands. "Are you alright?" She flinched, her eyes stayed down, but I could still sense the tears she was fighting. "Let me help you," I said softer and started grabbing for the food when a boot came crashing down, smashing the muffin I was reaching for deeper into the floorboards. Pulling my hand to my chest, I stared up, eyes wide, and saw Blaire standing over us. A look of hatred was plastered on her face. I was beginning to think her sour expression was permanent, especially around me.

"What do you think you're doing?" she spat down at us.

The woman beside me cowered lower, clearly too afraid to speak, so I did. "Well, before your dick of a friend here"—I pointed my finger to where I assumed the stack of lard was still sitting—"tripped this woman for no reason, I was patiently waiting to try this food. Now, however, I am helping her clean it up, since clearly you two are not. You seem to only be capable of making everyone's lives worse."

"Hey!" the man barked as crumbs flew from his mouth. One of Blaire's eyebrows raised before she sank down to my level, the woman beside me recoiling, getting as close to the wall as she could. "Watch it, human." Her eyes looked me up and down as I stayed kneeled. "I am the reason you are alive right now."

"Do you expect me to thank you?" I tilted my head. "How is that even possible?"

"Let's not pretend you healed her out of the kindness of your heart, Blaire." Bash leaned against the table behind her, arms crossed, just out of her view. "You did it out of fear. So back off."

She took a deep breath and rolled her jaw before slowly coming to a full stand. "Oh Bash, how cute of you to play watchdog to the new little pet." She twirled to face him.

He replied with a simple smirk that didn't meet his glaring emerald eyes. "You of all people should respect a survivor."

His words struck something in her. She stumbled back like it was a physical blow before she motioned to the man. "Let's go, Kuma, it's getting a bit dull here."

He slumped farther into the chair like a child when they didn't get their way. "I wanted to watch her pick it up. It's the best part!" The man, Kuma, was short and stocky with a bright blue streak of hair that raced from his forehead to the nape of his neck, shaved on both sides of the streak. His face, strong and resilient, was formed with a hefty, square jawline, broad cheekbones, and a narrow chin. Everything about his facial features would have you second-guessing how you spoke to him, yet the rest of his body was lackadaisical and sluggish, as if he didn't need to worry about appearance or watch his back. Based on his personality so far, I found that hard to believe.

"Now," Blaire bit out. Kuma followed as he rolled out of the chair, clearly not pleased about missing the aftermath of what he'd caused. I resumed helping the woman once they exited.

"What's your name?" I asked.

Her chocolate eyes snapped up to mine, stunned. "M-my name?"

"Yes, I'd like to be able to properly address you. Mine is Amalia." I grabbed a few pieces of broken bacon bits with one hand and placed them on the mound of mutilated muffins I'd been trying to hand-sweep into a neat pile.

"My name is Asahi," she whispered.

"Asahi, that's a very beautiful name. I wanted to apologize for how you were treated. I hope you know you didn't deserve that." Even the drunkards who wreaked havoc in the early morning hours in Cimmerian had been treated better than this.

Her hands stilled. "Why are you being so kind? It is my place to be at the service of guests in any manner they see fit. It is my duty."

A chill ran down my spine at her words, a sickening twist in my stomach at the thought that anyone believed they deserved this treatment just because of the job they held. "Whether you are meant to serve or not, it is never okay to be treated the way you just were. If they were decent humans, they'd appreciate you and your service, not use you for entertainment that is practically abuse." She looked at Bash with an unspoken question. He hadn't moved from his position against the table. He gave her a small shake of his head before I slowly said, "Anyways, I just wanted to apologize, and let you know I was really looking forward to trying your favorites."

Asahi took what I'd collected from me. "Thank you for your compassion. I'll get you a fresh plate, ma'am."

"Oh no, that's not necessary. I don't mind getting it. You have enough to deal with."

I headed to the table to grab a new plate and heard Asahi let out a noise before Bash interrupted. "She has a strong will, Asahi, best to let her do it. How about you bring us some tea when you come back?" Bash's footsteps echoed in the near-empty room.

"Yes, sir." With that, her petite frame hurried out of the room.

"Have a seat, Amalia, after you get your food."

I quickly gathered a new plateful and sat in my previous seat. He didn't speak, so I began to eat. Everything was delicious, so much flavor packed into every bite. I hadn't realized how uninspiring our food in Cimmerian was until eating at the castle. Saltiness from the bacon, bursts of sweetness from the sugar-topped blueberry muffin, I truly was tasting the Elysian Islands.

"The celebration is tomorrow."

I paused mid-chew at Bash's sudden statement. "Yeeesss?"

"I don't think you should go." His tone was serious, filled with an undercurrent of warning.

I swallowed hard and looked over at him. His face was void of any humor, sending a tremor down my spine.

"I'd love to hear why," I said as I set my silverware down a bit too hard. A feeling of being unwanted trickled into my thoughts.

"King Tatum will be present, and I don't believe his reasoning for throwing this celebration is genuine." He turned his body so that he was fully facing me. There was an emotion I couldn't quite place hidden beneath his features. It made me believe his words, even though I wasn't sure what was fueling his confession.

"I-I have to go, though. Lane said it was specifically being thrown because we were the only survivors of—of whatever happened. How do I just not attend?"

Dread washed over me and goosebumps pimpled my skin as he whispered, "I'm not sure, Amalia. Fake a sickness if you have to, but if you must attend, never be alone with him."

Chapter 9

Bash's words still ricocheted through my mind as I lay in bed that night. *Never be alone with him.*

What was I supposed to do with that piece of advice? How was I supposed to ensure I wasn't left alone with the king? A gentle knock on my door disrupted my spiraling thoughts; however, I only shifted my head in the direction of the door, not wanting to get up out of the cloud-like comfort this bed offered. Asahi poked her head through the now-cracked door with a worried look on her face, her eyebrows creasing together.

"Hey, Asahi. Everything okay?"

"Sorry to disturb you, ma'am. I was told to bring the dress for tomorrow's celebration to you, right away. I hope I didn't wake you," she said in almost a whisper.

"No, no, come in, please." I gestured for her to come over as I sat up in bed, watching as she gracefully slipped the large dress through the door before shutting it.

"Where would you like it, ma'am?"

"Please, call me Amalia. Can you bring it over here? I'm too comfy to move." I giggled, patting the bed, urging her to join me. It would be nice to spend time with another woman, one preferably not named Blaire. Asahi walked over, her body petite and frail with pale skin, as if she never spent time outside. Her hair was a glossy black with smooth, straight strands that swayed with every step she took. She sat on the bed, laying the dress between us.

"Prince Lane insisted it was made with fabric in your favorite color," she said, unzipping the protective bag the dress was in. My heart warmed at the thought of him putting in the effort, washing away the resentment I had felt since being left alone for so long. The gown shined. Metallic teal fabric with a sheer layer of glittering fabric over it to make it look like it was covered in stars. I sometimes used to lie in my field, looking up at the stars. I wondered if he knew, if it was an intentional detail.

Diamonds laced the sweetheart neckline and waist area. There were two elbow-length gloves included that had been created in the same style as the dress, the sparkle noticeable even in the darkened room.

"Should I tell Prince Lane that you approve?" Asahi asked as I ran my hand down the length of the material.

"You can tell him it's perfect." My voice cracked. "Just perfect." I couldn't help but stare at the garments. I had never owned anything this beautiful in my life. My sisters would have shrieked with joy clutching the fabric to their bodies as they twirled around the room if they could have seen the dress. Asahi smiled at me softly, lingering for a brief moment before zipping the protective bag back up before walking to the bathing chamber door where she hung it for the morning.

"Have a restful night, ma'am." She bowed slightly before heading toward the door.

"Wait!"

She paused and faced me. "Did you need something else, ma'am?"

"Please, it's Amalia."

She nodded again. "Amalia."

"Stay, please. The silence here has been too loud. It would be nice to talk to someone." I pulled the sheet further up to my chest. She looked unsure of what to do. "If you need a better reason, I could always say that I am a lonely guest and it would be an appreciated service."

A bright smile graced her face, and we both laughed before she quickly came over and jumped in bed.

We talked for a few hours about what it had been like for both of us growing up. I told her about the day I'd found my family, stories from my childhood, and she told me about how she had also lost her family at a young age.

"I was young. A friend and I went out beyond our village, we had stayed out too late." Her hands trembled, but her voice was strong. "We could smell the charred flesh before the village was in sight." She told me how something came in the night and had massacred them while she was away. Most of her hometown had been burned to nothing but ash. That's what had forced her to live a life serving the castle's needs. She'd never found answers as to what had happened that night. "I think about it every day, why I was the one who survived. If I hadn't left—" Her words trailed off before she insisted on heading to bed.

As I snuggled into bed to sleep, I felt a connection to the words she had spoken. If there was ever a way for me to take her along with me and free her from this life with people like Kuma and Blaire, I would.

Chapter 10

Flames consumed buildings, and the screams of innocents filled the air, making me shudder. A man materialized carrying a small child, then he ran past where I stood. The child's ears were pointed, his green eyes shining in the smoke-filled village. I reached for them, to stop them, to ask what was going on. My hands never touched them as they faded into nothing. I frantically searched for anything familiar, but this place was a mystery. Faces I didn't know hung from burning structures, the bodies lighting a deadly path as their flesh bubbled from heat. The blood in my veins pulsed like it was being drawn in, like it recognized something here that I didn't. Suddenly, memories not belonging to me erupted in my vision—a ruby dragon, chained and bleeding, its tears being collected in a bottle. The memory dissolved into another, a woman whose ears came to a point being drained, not of blood, but a shimmering essence. Taking everything that made her whole. A pleading cry of help rang around me. I stumbled back, but I was consumed by the smoke. I grabbed at my closing throat, desperate for air, then came a laugh, low and rumbling.

I woke up in a cold sweat to someone incessantly knocking at my door.

"Come in!" I groaned, grabbing a pillow and placing it over my head. Lane strolled in with a large grin spread across his face, it faded the moment he looked at me.

Lane's voice sliced through the remaining fog left over from the dream. "Amalia." He rushed over to me. "What happened?"

I flinched as he pressed the back of his hand to my forehead. "Nothing, I just had a nightmare. I think your knocking may have woken me out of it." I waved him away and wiped off the sweat coating my skin.

"You're pale, are you sure it wasn't something else?" He placed the back of his hand against my forehead once more, then placed it on the side of my cheek, worry taking over his features.

"I'm fine, I just need to splash some water on my face. It just felt so real." I tried to give a smile to reassure him my words were true, but even that felt like it took too much energy. "What were you so happy about? You know, before you looked at me."

His face lit up with a child-like brightness. "I get to spend today with you, and of course, we have the ball tonight. I know I haven't been able to be with you this past week, and I've hated myself for bringing you here just to disappear once you were well."

"Then why did you?" I asked, not able to dull the sharpness of my words.

Lane looked away from me, focusing on the unlit hearth. "My father has kept me away, wanting to know every detail of what happened in the village, wanting to know if I'm ready to be the heir he wanted me to be before banishing me." A bitter laugh escaped him before he added, "I've been pleading with him to allow both of us to stay here, trying to protect you." He ran a hand through his hair. "It hasn't been easy. My father only sees others as one of two things: a weapon or a weakness."

"So I'm guessing he sees me as a weakness," I said, relatively offended yet unsurprised. I had arrived practically dead.

"We both know out there it isn't safe. You need him to allow you to stay here and have a safe place to live." Nothing he was saying to me was an answer to how his father felt.

I was too agitated to play this guessing game. "Lane, just tell me what he's decided."

"He wants to speak with you first." He looked at me like I was a flight risk and could run away at any minute.

I swung my feet over the bed. "Okay, well let me get dressed, and we can head there now." I threw the covers off and started toward the bathroom before Lane grabbed my hand, pulling me back.

"No, he wants to speak with you alone."

Never be alone with him.

Bash's words slithered into my head. "Wh-why do I have to be alone?"

"He wants to make sure our stories line up, that what happened is true. He believes you will censor what you say in my presence." Why would either of us change what had happened? Lane let go of my hand, and I took a step back.

Every nerve in my body was screaming at me not to agree with this meeting, but if I didn't, that meant I would have to face the creatures that lived in the woods. I would have to live in Cimmerian completely alone surrounded by corpses.

"Okay, when would he like to see me?"

"The celebration tonight. He will find you when he's ready for you," he said with a smile, but it didn't feel right. Why would he want to speak to me about what had happened in Cimmerian during a celebration dedicated to us surviving it?

"Okay. Yeah, it'll be fine," I agreed, even though my head was telling me the opposite.

"Yes, it will be fine, Amalia. The celebration won't extend late into the night, and once it starts to die down, you will go speak with him." Lane got up and stretched. "Now, how about we grab some breakfast? You can tell me about your week. We can take a walk before we have to part to get ready. I'll have Akira and Asahi come in to help you."

"That sounds wonderful," I said.

Breakfast was tasteless as Lane prepped me for meeting with his father.

"Don't speak unless spoken to, say sir after everything, thank him for his time." Lane went on, and as he did my nerves grew more stretched, ready to snap.

Lane snapped his fingers in the air. Asahi and two other women I didn't recognize hurried to pick up our dirty plates. "Are you ready to go to the gardens?" he asked.

The gardens sounded like the perfect escape. It may not be my field, but I needed the sun on my skin and the scent of flowers filling my senses.

Rose bushes were drenched in the rays of the sun as we walked the gravel path. A butterfly with wings a pearlescent blue fluttered over them, gliding with the gentle breeze. We made our way through the maze of petals and came upon a patch of tiger lilies. "These are my favorites!" I darted to the closest flower, stroking its soft, fiery petals and admiring the brown speckles that my father used to say resembled my own freckles.

Lane plucked one and placed it behind my ear, his thumb lingering only a moment as we looked at each other. I leaned into his touch and said, "This place feels different than

Cimmerian. I feel like I'm on the outside of some big secret the way everyone speaks in hushed tones and casts daggers my way."

"I have someplace I'd like to show you that might help, if you'd like to procrastinate getting ready," Lane said, dropping his hand away.

Nodding my head enthusiastically, he grabbed my hand and led me deeper into the garden. Ancient oak trees stretched tall, creating a shaded trail of interlocking branches, hanging moss stretching down to greet us. My pace slowed, and Lane wrapped his arm around me, squeezing gently. I looked up and gazed into his striking blue eyes. "You'll love it, I promise," he said, and a calmness washed over me.

When we arrived at a clearing, my steps faltered. I was stunned at the beauty that I saw. A small, emerald pond that was surrounded by hundreds of flowers of every color. Delphiniums towered over coneflowers, snapdragons, and salvias, bursting with vibrance. Oranges, pinks, and yellows mixing with purples, whites, and blues. Flowers that stood as tall as I did, while others stayed close to the comfort of the ground.

"This is incredible," I said as two hummingbirds danced around us before heading toward a stalky ruby flower.

"I know it doesn't compare to the fields in your village, but I hope that this small space can provide you with a place to heal and reconnect with who you were before your world ended and this one began."

Tears welled up in my eyes at his words, and I had to bite the inside of my cheek to focus on anything else besides letting them fall.

"I don't know what to say," I confessed.

"You don't need to say anything. I had our people grow the flowers from the journal you kept. The one where you'd draw the plants you saw. You deserve a place that you can retreat to, that isn't surrounded by four walls." He grabbed my hand and pulled me back under the oaks. "Now, let's head back and get ready. We don't want to be late to a party dedicated to us now, do we?" He smirked at me as I took a few more breaths.

Something didn't add up, another feeling skirting my spine, saying this wasn't right. It didn't make sense. "Wait." I pulled my hand away. "How did they grow them?"

He eyed me. "What do you mean?"

"I haven't been here that long—we haven't," I corrected. "How did they grow these flowers so quickly?"

Lane was in front of me in a blink, his hands cupping my face, judgment filling those peculiar eyes. "I show you something this beautiful, something special for *you*, and the first thing you want to do is question it?"

I tried to take a step back, but he held me in place. My mind whirled at the sudden shift between us. I just truly didn't understand. These flowers took weeks to bloom, and it had only been a week since Cimmerian, but I hadn't even thanked him. "I–I'm sorry Lane, I love it, thank you."

A warm smile spread across his face as a frown deepened on mine. "You're welcome, Amalia. Now, let's get back. This is a conversation for later."

As we got back to the castle and parted ways, my mind was still lost in the fog of what had happened. I slipped into my room and startled at the sight of two women standing in the middle, both hands clasped in front of them.

"Asahi." I breathed out. "You scared me, I didn't even register that it was you."

"Miss Amalia, I'd like to introduce you to my sister, Akira," Asahi said. She hadn't said anyone in her family had survived the fire, but I was glad to see she wasn't completely alone.

I stepped farther into the bedchamber and extended my hand out to shake Akira's, only she made no move to do the same until Asahi nudged her in the side. Eyes rolling, she extended hers out to me. Burn scars covered her hand, traveling up her arm. Traces could also be seen at her collarbone and kissing the start of her throat. "Uh, well, nice to meet you, Akira. Asahi has been amazing. It makes me happy to know she isn't alone."

"We were sent to serve you, ma'am, so what is it that we can assist you with?" Akira questioned, her voice monotone, lacking all emotion.

"Oh, well I've never had anyone help me prepare for a party before, so I'm not really sure what to ask of you ladies. I'm sure you need time to get ready as well."

Akira sent a confused look at her sister before saying, "Servants don't attend balls, we work them."

"Ma'am... Amalia, we are only to go to set out the refreshments and food, then we must leave until it is time to clean up," Asahi explained.

"This party is supposed to be in celebration of Lane and I, so I think that is enough for me to invite my own guests."

"She can't be serious," Akira stated to Asahi.

"Oh, I believe she is very serious," Asahi retorted. "Miss Amalia seems to go against the grain in everything she does."

"I *am* very serious, go get your dresses and then come back and we can help each other."

"Well, since we aren't allowed to attend, we do not have dresses."

"Akira!" Asahi hissed, elbowing her sister in the ribs.

Akira elbowed back. "What? Should we just wander about the halls and then come back in, in the same clothes we are now, and have this conversation in an hour?"

"You cannot speak to Miss Amalia in such a way, we are here to serve." Asahi looked afraid, and when she looked at me I could see the terror in her eyes. "Miss Amalia, please don't be angry. Akira isn't normally this... vocal." She shot her sister a glare. "It's just that you remind her of the fire that took our family."

I didn't understand how, but that wasn't information I should try and pry from them, especially in Asahi's frantic state. "I'd rather have friends than servants. I'm not important. Well," I amended, "I'm not royalty, and I would never complain to anyone about this. You don't need to be afraid."

Both sisters shifted uncomfortably. Akira tucked her hair behind one ear. I tried not to stare, but it was pointed, and I was sure I wasn't seeing things. A memory scratched at my brain, but it couldn't make it to the surface before she caught me staring and covered it. I threw open the armoire, exposing multiple dresses in black, red, and a deep navy. "Both of you pick a dress to wear while I go get mine on." Neither said anything, they both just looked at me with wide eyes, so I hurried off to the bathroom, leaning against the door as I closed it.

I reached up with a trembling hand and unzipped the bag, exposing the beautiful fabric. I pulled the dress out, pressing it against my body as I twirled around the large bathroom. I looked down at the shimmering fabric, tracing my hands over its silky surface. I couldn't help but think how desperately I wanted my sisters there to gush with me over it. I looked up into the wall-length mirror and caught the sorrow filling my features. Shaking my head and blinking rapidly, I shoved those feelings down. This was going to be a magical night. I needed to keep the armor around my heart; I couldn't shed anymore tears over something that couldn't be changed. People who would never come back.

Steeling myself, I stepped out of the bathroom and gasped as I took in Asahi and Akira. They looked otherworldly.

"You guys look—" I was at a loss for words. Akira had chosen the form-fitting, cardinal red dress that was meant to allure, with two cutouts on either side of her abdomen, and a hip-to-floor-length slit to show off the wearer's leg. She didn't shy away from how the fabric showed off her burns that licked farther down her body. Asahi had chosen the navy-blue option, which had a strip of fabric around the neck that widened at the chest before ruffling out at the waist into a puffy skirt that reached mid-thigh. Even with the dresses large bottom, her waist was accentuated in a way that immediately drew your eye.

"Absolutely stunning. I feel inadequate next to the two of you," I said, still in awe.

Akira threw her hands in the air. "That's it, I'm changing."

"Oh, stop it. You're gorgeous, embrace it! Also, get used to hearing it, because I have a feeling all you two will be hearing tonight are compliments." I laughed.

"Thank you, Amalia, but I really must insist we shouldn't go. It was nice putting on these dresses for a change instead of cleaning them, but servants don't attend these things." Asahi smoothed her hands down her dress, not able to contain the excitement on her face.

"Well, tonight you won't be servants. You're my friends, and I can't attend without my friends," I said, turning to the small mirror on the vanity.

"We aren't friends," Akira stated, causing Asahi to hiss another disapproval at her.

Her words stung, but I said, "Ah, we will be tonight, and I already consider you my friend whether you like it or not. Luckily, I'm a patient person, and I can wait until you inevitably love me and consider me a friend too." I slipped on the two elbow-length gloves that felt as if my hands and arms were wrapped in velvet. Twisting from side to side, I dissected how I looked. "I feel like it's missing something."

"Your mask!" Asahi chirped as she ran to the bathroom.

"And you'll need to do something with your hair."

I looked at Akira. "My sisters used to always braid my hair, but I never learned how to do it." I fumbled with a few locks before giving up and smoothing out the fabric of my dress instead.

Akira sighed. "Well, I suppose I could do it for you." Annoyance laced her words.

"Oh, well that's very... friendly of you," I said cheerfully.

"Do you want me to retract my offer?" Akira may have put on a tough front, but I thought there was a fresh, steaming cinnamon roll underneath.

"Nope. Shutting up now." I was not going to try and find it today.

Akira came over to me and started twisting my strawberry blonde locks together, starting from the top of my scalp and curving around to my left side into a single long braid. Asahi came back holding a silver metallic mask with teal stones that outlined the top then curved into an intricate design above the eyes, resembling swirling waves faced away from each other.

"That's an interesting design," I said, grimacing.

"It was made by one of our oldest mask makers," Asahi said with pride.

"Can they still see?" I asked, taking the mask and holding it like it could infect me with a deadly disease at any moment.

Asahi threw her hands on her hips as Akira tried to stifle a snort. "It is an honor to wear this, Miss Amalia." Akira's and my eyes met in the mirror as she finished my braid and we both burst out in a fit of laughter. Asahi quickly followed after, trying to hold onto her composure and failing.

A knock on the door froze our laughter as Lane walked in. Asahi and Akira both scooted behind me, clasping their hands in front of them and bowing their heads. Lane placed his hand on his chest and took a step back like he had been pushed. "I must say"—he ran a hand through his blonde hair—"you look enchanting, Amalia. I may not be able to survive the night."

A blush heated my cheeks. "Don't Akira and Asahi look gorgeous as well? I told them they're invited tonight as my guests. I'm sure there are plenty of other staff that can handle things. I need them with me tonight." His jaw ticked. He was clearly displeased, but he said nothing about it, and quickly hid it behind a toothy grin.

"You two will be turning many heads tonight." He bowed his head to them, making them grab each other's hands and squeeze slightly. His charm affected them just as he'd planned. "Shall we head to the main event, ladies?"

Squeals erupted behind me and they both surged by, each grabbing one of his arms. "I can't believe we are really allowed to go! Thank you, Prince Lane." Asahi beamed.

"I guess I had no part in this," I said, smirking at him and mouthing a *thank you.*

We reached the Grand Ballroom and could hear the violins playing soft melodies when two young boys ran up to Lane. "Hello, Prince Lane. We were told to walk you and Miss Amalia inside once you arrived!" one blonde-haired boy said.

"Yeah, yeah!" another with soft brown locks added excitedly. "We know it's a very important job, and we won't let you down, I swear it!"

Lane laughed, ruffling the boys' hair up. "I have an even *more* important task for the two of you."

The two boys' eyes widened at that, and they leaned in. "MORE important?" they said in unison.

"Oh yes," chided Lane. "You see, I have these two beautiful ladies here with me as well, and I think they're in need of escorts such as you fine young gentlemen."

The two boys whipped their heads to look at each other, then at Akira and Asahi. They held out their right hands and bowed slowly. "This is the cutest thing I have ever seen," I said. Akira scowled at me as the words came out.

The main doors were solid wood stained with a darkened hue and embellished with gold flakes. Lane held his arm out for me. "Oh, Demetri, Willard!"

"Yes, sir?" the young gentlemen said in unison as they escorted the sisters into the party.

"Be sure to give them your masks also." With that, both boys took their masks off and handed them to my friends. I laced my arm in his as he added, "They aren't required, but it's best to hide their identities since we didn't get approval for them to attend." Embarrassment crept up my body. "It's okay, they deserve a night of fun, we just don't need to draw my father's attention any more than we already are."

"I'm so sorry, I didn't think." There was still a current of tension between us after the gardens. He acted like there wasn't, and maybe it no longer plagued his mind, but I couldn't help but hold on to it.

As we passed through the doors, I was engulfed in laughter, music, and savory smells. The room was extravagant. Windows lined the back wall, letting the fading light from the sunset scatter onto the dance floor, painting the attendees in peach and orange hues. Dresses with feathers and frills swooshed around to the rhythm of the music playing. Men's masks were adorned with sharp spikes and dark tones. My eyes tried to follow the scent of roasted vegetables and braised meats. Just as I took a step toward the aromas, three thundering pounds echoed through the space, freezing everyone in place.

On the marbled stage in front of the band stood a tall, broad man with snowy hair, his face stern and unmoving as he surveyed the crowd, waiting for every voice to silence and notice his presence. Which didn't take long. He had his hands resting on top of a white cane with an iridescent orb on top. His shoulders were back and his head held high so that when he looked at the crowd, he was looking down at them.

"Your presence tonight honors the survivors of the Cimmerian tragedy." His voice was deep and husky, booming without the need for any enhancements.

"As most of you are already aware, my son returned with a survivor from a village about a three-day journey from here. The kingdom had been hit by an unknown aerial substance, causing near-instantaneous death as it rained upon the land."

Gasps and murmurs broke out as unease spread through the crowd like a wildfire. White gloves flying to cover painted lips, I saw what must have been the mother of the two young boys, Demetri and Willard, pull them close to her sides.

"Not to worry now, we are safe here in Santavarre. My scouts have been sent to Cimmerian and will return in a day's time with an update on the last human kingdom. For now, we celebrate Lane and Amalia tonight"—his golden staff pointed to where we stood—"the two sole survivors of this atrocious attack. I have nothing but hope that they will help us get to the bottom of this and ensure an event this catastrophic never happens again."

"Raise your glasses," he boomed, "and make room in the middle of the floor for Lane and Amalia, Defier of Death, to share a dance." The king's eyes locked on me.

"Of course, this is how he spins it," I heard Akira mumble under her breath as she and her sister came to stand beside me.

My stomach dropped. "A what?" I choked out.

Lane's palm waited upturned for me to take. "We are to perform the first dance as the survivors." Lane pulled me toward the center of the room as everyone around us shuffled out of the way. Looking back at Asahi, she gave me two thumbs up. Akira wiggled her fingers at me in a wave, then chugged her glass of champagne. As we walked, everyone else was still holding their glasses in the air, and the king had a merciless glare set on Akira.

Lane pried my hands from the death grip I had on his arm and twirled me away from him before spinning me back against his chest. My eyes met strangers', and I looked up at Lane, who was smiling down at me. "Breathe," he said into my ear before I twisted to face him, one hand moving down to my waist as his other held my hand. He guided me backward for three steps before we sidestepped two, he spun me, and we repeated the movements to the opposite side.

"Why is everyone still holding their glasses in the air?" I asked while trying to concentrate on the movements.

"They are not to drink until we finish our dance. It's supposed to be a show of respect."

Tripping over my own feet, I said, "Well, it's a little creepy."

"It'll be over soon," he promised as he spun, then dipped me low to the ground, my head hanging back before he slowly pulled me back against his body. Even wearing a mask covered in chocolate-colored diamonds, I could see his eyes flick from my chest to my mouth.

The sunset sky seemed to darken, casting an ominous, shadowy illusion around us. "You know, I don't think I got a chance to compliment you back," I said, taking in the sight of him as he stepped back, both of us spread apart from each other. His deep chestnut suit complimented his blonde hair, which was combed to the side. His blue eyes were vivid behind the mask he wore. It was covered in intricate diamond detailing of wings on either side above the eyebrows. The mask covered both of his bright eyes with a central, chocolate-colored diamond at the top. "You look very dashing tonight. This color suits you well." He pulled me close, and we swayed together. "My mother used to warn me about the princes in fairytales, they were always too charming."

"Careful, Amalia. Is that heat I see in your eyes?" He had a heated gaze set on me. I tripped under the attention, but he caught me and dipped me low once more as if it was meant to happen. "Ah, too stunned to speak now as well, hmm?" His breath caressed my skin.

"Oh my dragons, Lane, just take the compliment and calm yourself."

Lane's laugh came out like a purr as the music faded; this was more like the Lane I knew. Those around us took sips of their beverages before grabbing their own partners and beginning to dance themselves. Lane went tense against me as a voice cut through the noise.

"Why, Miss Amalia, how I have wanted to finally meet you."

I turned to come face to face with the king. Bash's words flashed through my mind: *Never be alone with him.* A chill skittered down my spine.

Chapter 11

"Leave us, Lane," King Tatum said in an uncompromising tone, making it clear it was not a request.

"Yes, sir." Without hesitation, Lane turned and disappeared into the crowd.

Through the sting of abandonment I said, "King Tatum." Then bowed my head and curtsied slightly before looking at him. "Thank you for ton—"

He raised his hand in the air, and I stopped talking. "I'd like to talk with you privately, Miss Amalia. I know you have no place to go and are hoping to stay here. Lane has made this point very clear. However, don't mistake my hospitality as an answer. I'm quite interested in why you were the only survivor in your village. I find it peculiar, to say the least."

Hairs raised on the back of my neck, and beads of anxiety-induced sweat formed along my forehead. "I would also like to know why I survived while my family, and the people I grew up around, all died. I would like nothing more than the answers to the millions of questions I have asked myself over and over since it happened. But I regret to say I don't believe I can give either of us the answers we want." I could hear the edge in my words, so I curtsied once more, hoping to show him I meant no disrespect.

The king's face turned predatory as he advanced toward me, causing me to take a step back in return. A smirk lifted one side of his face. "Shall we go somewhere private then?"

"Actually, I was hoping I could get a dance in." I spun around at the familiar gravelly voice.

"Your dance can wait," the king said as he placed a hand on my shoulder. Fear seized me as soon as his rough skin touched mine. I wasn't sure if it was from how he held himself or Bash's previous warning. Either way, I was thankful for the interruption.

The man's amethyst eyes nearly glowed with the challenge. "It really can't," he said as he held his hand out for me to take. It took only a second to make the decision to place my hand in his. "I suggest you let her go."

The silence was thick, and somewhere beyond us a glass shattered, followed by hushed voices and quick footsteps.

A rumble came from the king's throat, low and threatening. "You would do well to remember who it is you're in the presence of." Spit flew from his mouth. "I am your king."

The man smiled wide before gently tugging me to him, and the king released me. "As king, I know you wouldn't take a woman away from a party dedicated to her before it really started. Not with all these people waiting to meet her." He motioned his arm to the silent crowd watching, waiting.

The king's jaw hardened so much, I swore I could hear the cracking of teeth. "I expect you to come see me tomorrow, Amalia. I will send for you when I am ready. Unfortunately, I have some other business to attend to." His eyes flicked to the doors before he leaned in and added, "You *will* come alone."

"Yes, sir." My words came out feeble under his intense gaze. With that, he turned and strode away, shouting, "Dance!" to the eavesdropping crowd. I turned to the man, whose obsidian mask covered the left side of his face. The right side only covered just above his eyebrow, leaving most of his face visible. The mask was a dusty mix of black and gray, with scrollwork weaving up the sides. The middle of the mask was what drew my eyes, though—it was a bit haunting, a dragon's face with what appeared to be sunbeams behind it, with two violet eyes that glowed like his.

The man started swaying our bodies side to side. I cleared my throat. "I guess I owe you a thank you."

"You owe me nothing, little temptress." His thumb brushed my waist. "Consider it more entertainment than anything."

"What a hero," I said, fighting back a grin as I slipped my hands around his neck. "I could tell you guys seem to have a really great relationship." At that, he laughed, the sound reverberating through me.

"So, do you have a name?" I asked, since in every interaction I'd had with him, he had yet to introduce himself.

"I do indeed," was all he replied.

Rolling my eyes, I looked over my shoulder to where the band was playing a song with more beat than they had been. I felt a finger under my chin as the man tilted my focus back to him. My eyes fluttered. "Sorry."

"Don't be." A silence came between us as we continued to sway back and forth, not matching the rhythm of the song. Moving as if we had our own melody that only we could hear.

His gaze dropped to my mouth. "Knox," he said.

My heart started beating frantically. "Excuse me?"

"That's my name." His fingers flexed at my waist, and I might have stopped breathing.

"Oh, I'm Amalia."

"I know who you are," he said, chuckling.

"Right, I forgot." Nervous laughter escaped me. Why was I acting a fool right now?

I froze mid-sway. "Wait." It dawned on me who *he* was. "You're the other prince. You're Lane's brother, King Tatum's other son."

"He would never claim me as his son," Knox said, although it didn't sound like that claim hurt him in any way.

"Do you claim him as your father?" I asked, genuinely curious. I assumed I knew the answer based on their hostile interaction, but I had seen my own father and brother fight more often than not. They still had a great deal of love between them. He didn't answer the question, but he did change our steps, so we fell into the beat of the song.

I scanned the crowd, looking for Lane. His golden locks were bent close to Blaire over by the refreshments as she laughed at something he said.

"So, how are you holding up?" Knox asked, turning us so they were out of view.

"Oh, I'm fine I guess. You all have been really great in allowing me to stay this long, and healing me of course. Even though I still haven't been told how that is even possible."

"Right, do you want a moment to think of a real answer?" he whispered so only I could hear.

I stiffened. "What do you mean? I was healed days ago. I really am fine."

He dipped me so low my braid fell from my shoulder and brushed the flooring. "Try again." He lifted me effortlessly, but I felt the weight of his question against my lungs. "I'm not talking about how you are physically. I can't begin to imagine what goes on in that head of yours on a good day, let alone now."

"That's a little rude," I said. He waited as the stringed instruments played in the background.

I hadn't really had to think about how I was in any other aspect, because no one had asked. Everyone had just treated me as if I was fine because the mask I wore said I was. Which was okay, but it also forced me to act a certain way to keep up the facade. So I wasn't sure how to answer him without seeming weak or as if I were complaining after all they'd done for me... He seemed interested in the real answer, though.

"When my family would have late nights working, and I'd be home by myself, I would read. I would read as much as I could before falling asleep, because I could escape from the day, but also because I felt like I wasn't alone and could drift off in another world with people I'd come to know... But now, after everything, after all the loss, every time I close my eyes to sleep, I feel nothing but utterly alone. My mind replays everything on a loop, and it hurts more than I could have ever imagined. Then, when I wake up, I'm still alone until I run into someone, and then I have to exert energy trying to put on a brave face and act as if I'm okay. I'm only here because of you guys. Because of Lane, and as much as I don't want to admit it, Blaire. So I can't be anything but fine." I sighed. "But if acting okay is the price I have to pay to stay here, I'll happily do it."

"You can be whatever you need to be. Surviving shouldn't be a transaction, Amalia. Anyone who expects you to be fine after what you've gone through doesn't truly care about you. Only what you can offer them."

"I should have buried them," I blurted out. "I think about that the most. I left them there to rot. How could I have done that?" Voice breaking slightly, I blinked rapidly to try and hold back the tears that were threatening to well up. I didn't know this man, yet I felt the ability to speak the inner thoughts I'd fought to conceal. The confession tore from me like it begged to be heard by him. Even with this small admission, I could feel a weight lift off my heart, which I think was the real reason tears rose to the surface.

He didn't even flinch, yet I still felt the need to apologize. "I'm sorry, I don't know why I said all that to you, we don't even know each other."

His voice was low and sinking into me. "Maybe for the same reason you are still dancing with me even though the music has stopped."

Startled, I looked around. Mostly everyone was off the dance floor, no music to be heard. How had I become so unaware of what was going on around me? Knox took my hand, bowed, and placed a gentle kiss on the back of it. "Thank you for a lovely dance, little temptress." He turned on his heel and left before I could say another word.

Someone cleared their throat. "I was told to bring you a drink. Lane figured you might be thirsty after that longer-than-expected dance." That cruel yet angelic voice spoke behind me. "Guess you just think you can have them all."

"I don't know what you're talking about," I seethed.

"Well, let's see," she started as she held her hand up, counting on her fingers. "There's Bash, Lane, of course, and now the other brother, Knox."

"I think you should stop caring about me so much and focus on yourself. I don't know what your problem is, and right now I don't think I care." I grabbed the glass from her and downed the green concoction, something lime with a bitter aftertaste.

She sneered. "My problem is really your species in general. I'd hate you no matter who you were."

"My species? What does that even mean?" The constant confusion that bubbled up every time anyone here spoke was really starting to become infuriating. They all acted like there was some big secret, like we weren't all the same. They acted as if just because I survived the shimmer, I was suddenly less than, or tainted in some way. I could tell she wasn't going to elaborate by the way her jaw tightened, like she had spoken out of turn, her eyes flicking around the room in what I'd almost describe as slight panic. I chose to try and end this conversation civilly.

"Thanks for saving me, and for the drink. Turns out I *was* parched from dancing." I took the cherry out of the now-empty glass, biting it off the stem, which I then tossed in her general direction. I turned to find anyone else to be around but her.

"I bet you were," she said, drawing out the words. I didn't let it slow me down as I found Asahi and Akira. I needed to dance these feelings of confusion and hate out of my system with women I didn't want to strangle. I found them already by the dance floor, waiting for the band to start up again, looking radiant as they giggled and conversed with each other.

"Are you guys enjoying yourselves?" I said, sneaking up behind them.

"Oh Amalia, this is the best night we've had since being here. I don't know how to repay you." Asahi looked around the space with starstruck eyes.

"Thanks. For this. I guess," Akira muttered, shrugging one shoulder. Her almond eyes showed she was enjoying herself just as much as her sister. A tall, tawny-skinned gentleman approached in a silver suit, sleeves rolled up to his elbows. The fabric of his suit was adorned with an eccentric black embroidery racing down the front from his shoulders to waist, and he wore a silver mask that covered his face entirely, only showing his amber-colored eyes.

Bowing slightly with his hand held out to Akira, he said, "Would a stunning creature such as yourself care to make my night's wish come true by dancing with me?"

Akira's face blanched in what looked like disgust and confusion. "Stunning creature? Your night's wish?" she repeated sardonically.

"She'd love to, how kind of you to ask," I quickly interjected, shooting a glare at her before pushing her toward the man. I watched while trying to stifle a laugh as she awkwardly took the man's hand before squealing in disapproval as he dipped her in what I'm sure he thought would be a charming move, only to be met with a shove to the chest as she attempted to stomp away. The man grabbed her hand and spun her back to him, whispering something that immediately made a blush appear on her face.

"I know it's only been about thirty seconds, but I think my sister may have just met her match."

"I think you just might be right." We broke out into laughter just as the band produced a mellow tune. As we stood to appreciate the sound, it felt as if I were standing on a sandy shore, listening to the waves crashing against the bank. I had never seen or visited a beach, yet this music made me believe I was there. I didn't know the song they were playing, but it was so relaxing. "Want to dance with me?" I asked Asahi.

"Oh, I don't dance. I enjoy just observing."

Asahi's eyes jumped to something behind me, making me turn around to see Lane.

"That's good to hear. Maybe Miss Amalia would care to honor me with a dance instead?"

"Oh, yes, I'd love to." I took his arm as he led me to the dance floor, close to where Akira and the man swayed together, bodies tucked into one another.

"Are you enjoying yourself?" he whispered into my ear, sending a shiver down my neck.

"I am, it almost doesn't feel real." My vision was hazy like I was in a dream.

He breathed me in. "You look intoxicating tonight."

"Oh? Compared to my disheveled look every other moment?" An echoed laugh circled the words.

His lips tipped up on the right side of his mouth. "Well, your robe look the other day was a hard one to beat; however, I think you've done it."

"Listen, it was either a robe or clothes that made me look like an overfilled muffin. That beast of a woman knew she brought clothes that wouldn't fit."

"Hey, now." He lifted a hand to my chin and tipped my face up so that I had no choice but to look at him. "You would have looked perfect even with unbuttoned trousers and a backward chemise." I couldn't hold back the smile that escaped as I gave him a gentle fist to the shoulder. He pulled me close, and we fell into a comfortable silence, just feeling the soulful rhythm moving through the air. I even started to feel like I was swimming. The song came to end with a drawn-out solo from the harpist. Lane slowly dipped me back before swooping me to the left, anticipation building as he gently brought me up to meet him as the last note played.

"Did you ever think about what this would be like back home?" he said, breathing heavily.

"What?" I asked, equally breathless from the intimacy of how close we were.

"I always pictured what it would be like to dance with you as you twirled in your field." He took a step back. "You never thought about us?"

"I-I don't know, I never allowed myself to think about it. I was nobody, you're a prince. I am, quite literally, not in the same realm as you. If I learned anything growing up in Cimmerian, it's to not hope or dream for things you can never have."

"You could have had me." A sad smile formed, and he took my hand and slowly spun me around as he said, "You could have anything you want in life, no matter where you come from."

I wasn't sure if it was all the spinning or what his words did to me, but I became lightheaded, nausea causing me to stumble out of his grasp.

"Amalia!" I heard my name come out in a gasp as Asahi lurched for me. Lane quickly righted me before she reached to assist.

"I think I've done enough spinning for one night," I said, leaning against him for support. "I should probably head back to my bedchamber."

"I'll take her back." Asahi didn't hesitate to help me, grabbing my arm, shifting my weight from Lane to herself.

"We both will," Lane retorted, not releasing me fully to her. Her grip on me tightened.

Just as we started to head out, we heard Akira yelling at her newfound friend. I couldn't make out much except for a few explicit words followed by a very firm "I'd never sleep with a neanderthal like you."

"Oh dear…" Looking back at her sister, I could tell Asahi felt torn on what to do. They were supposed to be keeping a low profile.

"Go ahead. I'm fine, really," I assured her.

"Are you sure?" Relief flooded her features. Her eyes glanced quickly at Lane before settling on me.

"Positive. This was just a lot—I'll be fine after I rest. Come see me in the morning."

"Of course." She helped adjust me in Lane's arms before squeezing my hand and hurrying over to her sister.

We made our way down the long corridors, weaving between passed-out bodies and drunken couples who couldn't wait to find privacy before ripping each other's clothes off and doing, well… many impressive acts. Even though I wasn't feeling well, I couldn't deny that the sight built a tension in the air between the god-like man currently being my savior and I. *Focus on anything else.* I tried to look up at the ceiling instead and immediately felt the ground disappear beneath me as if I were falling. Then I was in Lane's arms, my head resting on his shoulder, my hand against his chest. *This is not how I intended to distract myself.* "I'm sorry," I slurred, even though it came out more of a whimper.

"Shhh… selfishly, I was hoping I'd need to carry you anyways."

"Hmm."

I must have dozed off, because the next thing I felt was the comfort of my bed and the weight of the comforter being placed over me. I felt a dip in the mattress next to me, and Lane took my hand into his, tracing small circles with his thumb, soothing me. I could feel myself drifting off again and gave his hand a small, appreciative squeeze before letting sleep take me from a pretty magical night.

Chapter 12

Screams and pained groans filled the silence of the night, piercing my ears and shaking my core. Frantically, I looked around for the source, desperate to save those who were crying out with what sounded like all the strength they had left... but there was nothing around me but clouds of smoke. My heart started to race as panic seeped in. The ground beneath me shook in unison with a loud thumping, similar to a large beast walking. I spun, trying to see through the smoke, when a rush of heat swarmed around me, burning my lungs. I ran. I ran until the smoke started to clear and I could make out the shadows of forms clashing together. People were fighting, swords striking against each other, slashing through flesh and bone. Blood, sweat, and ash coated everyone before me. As I went to take a step toward the chaos, an enormous, scaled tail slammed into the ground just mere feet from me, causing debris to fly at me, hitting my body. Shock rippled through me as my eyes tracked up the tail to the entirety of what was before me. A beast, a monster, that had only been seen in old fairytale books. A dragon.

Breath catching, I looked at where the tail had made impact and saw the bodies that were now crushed next to someone holding the end of a sword that was now lodged in their stomach. It was a man, I thought. One who felt familiar. A larger group of men were rushing toward the beast now with their weapons raised. The dragon inhaled deeply before stretching its long, dark neck out, brilliant purple flames igniting and aimed at the group who had now scattered or launched themselves to the sides. My hands flew over my mouth to stifle my yell. I didn't know who was good or bad. I didn't understand what was happening. The flames heated the night and consumed everything in sight, then they turned, heading toward... me. I felt the intense power as they flew in my direction. There was no time, I couldn't escape them. My eyes closed, fear swelling in my chest as I felt my skin burning, and burning, but not to the point of excruciating pain. Slowly opening my eyes, a myriad of colors overwhelmed me. Shades of deep blues, oranges, reds, and yellows I'd never seen surrounded me, barreling past me. Turning in the direction they were headed, I saw her.

The woman from my dream in the field, with her arms outstretched, beckoning the flames to her. They licked at her skin before devouring her, her body turning to ash and lifting away into the night. A ground-shattering bellow came from behind me, so powerful I could feel it like a physical blow. Cupping my ears and dropping to my knees, I kneeled before the giant beast, the source of the anguished roar. Had its power just been taken in the midst of a war? It let out one more sorrow-filled cry as its body slammed into the ground.

***

Bolting awake, heart beating erratically, I sat upright in bed trying to slow my breathing. This was the third nightmare I'd had that had shaken me to my very core, having felt so real it was as if it were a memory and not a dream. The back of my right hand was slick with sweat from my forehead. I threw the feathery covers off my body and headed to the bathing chamber to relieve myself. As I entered the room, sleep controlled my movements, making them sluggish. I removed my undergarments with a groan and sat down on the chamber pot. Relief took over as my head dropped, and my gaze landed on my lap, where bruises marred my skin in dark shades of violet and bluish black. *What the hell?* My hands ran over the marks, flashes of my dream came back to me—debris, burning chunks of rock flying at me. Striking me. I frantically searched the rest of my body and found no other marks until I made my way to the mirror, where I saw similar bruises marking my collarbone on both sides. Tracing them with a finger, I whispered, "Impossible." The marks were tender to the touch.

Could a dream hurt me?

A forceful knock on my door startled me out of my spiral, and I hurried to answer it. I took a breath to compose myself before grabbing the copper handle and pulling the large wooden door open slightly, expecting to see Asahi. Instead, I opened the door to eyes that resembled a grassy meadow. Bash stood stoically outside, but within an instant his demeanor faltered as his eyes scanned my face.

"What happened to you, Amalia?" His voice was on the edge of a growl.

My left hand shot up to rub my collarbone as my right nervously tucked a strand of hair behind my ear. "Oh, um, nothing. I just woke up and still feel a bit groggy, I shouldn't have drank so much last night."

His eyes followed the movements of my left hand, and I could pinpoint the moment he must have truly caught a glimpse of the marks by the hardening of his jaw and the way those cool green eyes darkened into a murderous glare.

"What the fuck is that?" Barging in through the door, he made his way into the middle of the expansive room, his head on a swivel, searching for the cause.

"It's just some bruises, Bash," I said, coming up behind him.

He whirled on me. "Bruises from what, Amalia!?" He shifted the collar of my night-gown to expose more of the marks, and the color drained from his face. *I don't remember changing. Did Asahi come and help me last night?*

"Mal..."

Shoving his hand away, I turned, trying not to memorize that look he had.

"I truly don't know—I woke up like this, but..." Trailing off, I wasn't even sure what to say. I had a dream and somehow what happened in it actually happened in real life as I slept? I would sound crazy. No one would believe me.

"But what!?" he exclaimed, an urgency in his tone, eyes wide.

"But... I did fall in the bath last night rather hard... I didn't think anything of it; however, when I woke up this morning and saw this... It must have been from that. I had too much to drink, and it's really rather embarrassing, and I'd appreciate it if you didn't say anything to anyone... I don't think I could live it down." The lie slipped so easily from my lips in an effort to give me more time to make sense of things.

His jaw stayed tense as he studied me, but he didn't press further. I think we both knew I was lying.

"So why were you outside of my door? Since when do you call me 'Mal'?"

Jaw rolling, he waited a few seconds before answering me.

"Since today." He straightened his posture, squaring his shoulders and putting that expressionless mask back on. "King Tatum has summoned you."

"Right." Inhaling, I turned toward my armoire. "I should get dressed then."

"Yes, you should, maybe something to cover the bruises from your fall." His voice fell flat on the last word. Telling me he did, in fact, know I was lying.

Looking back at him, I flashed a quick smile. "I'll just be a few minutes."

"I will wait outside the door, and escort you when you're ready." With a curt bow, he left the room. I wasn't used to seeing him like this, so formal. He was all seriousness today and it was unsettling.

I opened the doors to the armoire and peered at the clothes before me, all of which accentuated the chest, which didn't help with my current predicament. Shifting through the items, I came across one outfit that just might work. The black, sleeveless top showed off the shoulders, but it had a high neck which offered no visibility to what was on my skin. There was a gold dragon motif on the left breast, and the right shoulder was a tan color, giving the top some color contrast. Snatching the fabric, I quickly got dressed, slipping on the black, detached sleeves that reached the middle of my upper arm and hooking my thumbs through the holes. The top fit perfectly, the waist was cinched, and the material had been sewn tighter around the bust to flatter the body. I placed two black belts that had silver buckles around me to lay loosely in a crisscross fashion over the black, high-low skirt. I was worried as I slipped the skirt on, because the front rested at the middle of my thighs. However, both sides had longer pieces of black fabric that flowed beautifully with any movement, and a tan piece of fabric on the left side that was embellished with a black, lace-up feature, which should allow some coverage. I threw on a pair of black boots then hurried to the bathroom to ensure there were no marks showing.

I brushed my hair, threw it in an updo, and went to meet Bash at the door. Something caught my attention in the corner of my eye on the nightstand next to my bed. Walking over, I narrowed my eyes. It was a book. The silver hardcover had two black wings etched on it. I'd seen this book before, *Beauty and the Beast*. It was one of my favorites growing up and followed a young woman who sacrificed herself to save her father from a mythical beast, a dragon. Yet, even though the beast was nothing but terror and scales, she somehow fell in love. Seeing the beast's vulnerability and loneliness through his hardened armor.

I opened the cover to see a short, handwritten note that read, *To help you escape from what your mind won't let you forget.*

My chest heaved, I needed to sit. I didn't have to wonder who had left this for me. I had been a complete imbecile with Knox last night. I'd vomited words at him and he... he'd listened. Then went out of his way to drop this off for me? I wiped at my eyes and tucked the book underneath my pillow.

I yanked the door open, expecting Bash to be there. However, it wasn't just Bash at the door; Lane stood nose to nose with him, both of them puffing up their chests in a standoff.

"Hey Lane, are you here to escort me to your father instead?"

"Yes," "No," both men said in unison.

Lane spoke first, a smirk tilted one side of his face. "Where's my brother? Usually, you're up his ass. How about you go follow him like the good little bodyguard you try to be," he quipped, taking me by surprise at the sudden hostility.

"Woah, that was a bit ru—" I tried to say.

"He's gone on a little trip. Said he had to fix something you made a mess of. I'm guessing there are a few things we can blame you for." Bash then slammed his chest into Lane, knocking him off balance, causing him to stumble backward as he caught the wall and righted himself.

"Hey! What is happening right now?" I yelled, running between the two and holding my palms against their chests.

The air filled with the sound of Lane's throaty laughter, and slowly, I turned my head in his direction, overcome with complete confusion. I repeated my question with less panic laced into the words. "What is going on?" My head was bouncing between the two men. Lane sauntered over to me like he hadn't just been in a *whose dick is bigger* match.

"Oh, just having a little fun with Bashikins over here." He slapped a hand onto Bash's shoulder and shook him slightly before Bash forcefully threw Lane's hand off of him with a snarl. "So, when can we expect my brother to return?"

"He'll be back today. He left yesterday during the celebration." Bash looked at me and held his arm out for me to take. "Are you ready?" His whole body was shuddering with built-up tension.

"She will be escorted by me, the prince, in case you forgot," Lane countered, holding his own elbow out.

"You are not *my* prince," Bash said, his tone murderous.

Then there was me, in the middle, confused and growing agitated with how this morning had decided to go. I noticed Asahi walking down the corridor and made my decision. "Or," I said, slipping past them both, "I can walk with Asahi, since the two of you clearly"—I whipped my finger back and forth between them—"have something to work through." Worry bloomed at the thought of leaving them alone with each other, but I had bigger problems to deal with currently.

The king.

"Asahi!" I jogged to where she peeped back around the corner hearing her name.

"Amalia! Hi." She seemed distracted as I reached her. "Are you okay?" I asked.

Asahi surveyed the corridor before she moved closer, whispering, "I haven't been able to find Akira. She never showed up for her morning chores."

I reared back. "What do you mean? Weren't you together last night?" I may have been sick, but I remembered her going back for her sister.

"I was, but she insisted she wanted to stay with that man. I assumed she had stayed the night with him, but I haven't seen her since. I'm worried. She's strong-willed, but she would never leave me to cover her chores without asking." She inhaled sharply. Her gaze could have penetrated walls with how she scrutinized the length of the corridor like Akira was going to materialize if she looked hard enough. "How rude of me, you needed something, are you okay?" she asked.

"Oh, I was just going to meet the king. He summoned me. I was going to ask you to show me the way, but finding Akira is more important. I can find my way."

"Nonsense, we can keep our eyes peeled for her while I walk you." Her heart was the purest there ever was, I was sure of it.

With no sign of Akira, we traveled through the garden until we reached a section of the castle I hadn't seen before. The corridor was breathtaking, opulent, with a series of arched ceilings that were so high it was a wonder how they were built. The walls and ceiling were crafted with mosaic tiles that were reflective, showcasing how every ray of light danced across them. Our steps were soft as we walked the polished, pure white floors covered in the colors mirrored off the walls. Who knew a simple walk to what may be the third most stressful moment of my life could feel so ethereal?

We reached the summoning room, and I gave Asahi a tight hug, wishing her luck on locating Akira. I demanded an update as soon as she could. I watched her walk away until I could no longer see her and steeled myself. I expected there to be guards standing outside, but I was the only one standing in front of the sizable doors. Each side had a straight edge curving at the top, meeting in a sharp point. There was an almost translucent effect on what I'd first thought was glass—that wasn't what this material was, though. It was smooth to the touch, thin, and sparkled like a crystal. A white wooden design, curving in waves, covered a lot of the space in a swirling pattern.

Crreeaaaakkk. The doors opened on their own, and I stepped back, peering in once they stopped.

"Are you going to continue wasting my time, or are you going to enter?" a booming voice said. The king.

"I apologize, sir. I was helping look for someone," I said, dipping into a low curtsy, looking anywhere but at him.

"I didn't ask why you were late. It only matters that you are."

I stayed silent, still dipped in a curtsy, trying to remember Lane's advice.

"You may rise."

Standing straight and lifting my head, the room proved just as captivating as the hallway leading to it. Not an item in sight among the expansive room, except for the raised dais above me where a desk and throne-like chair sat, along with King Tatum. The desk and chair mimicked the gleaming mosaic appearance, making it hard to concentrate on the king's words. Silence filled the air as the king stared at me. All the muscles in my body started tensing as if it were bracing for an impact.

"Lane informs me that your village is no more, your family are nothing more than rotting corpses. Is this true?"

A blade had surely just been plunged into my gut. "I-I..." Words escaped me, mind reeling from the bluntness and carefree tone of his voice; light, as if he had asked how the weather was.

"Is this true!?" he bellowed, slapping his large palm against the pristine desk.

Tipping my chin up, I inhaled a deep breath, holding it for a few seconds before exhaling, shoving down the fear and locking it away. He let out a charming laugh. "I'm sorry, my dear, please tell me what happened."

"I cannot tell you *what* happened, I don't know. All I can say is I was alone in a field I cherished, then when I looked up at the sky, there were dazzling specks of stardust falling." That moment seemed like a lifetime ago now. "Then I was nothing, until I woke up in Lane's lap."

King Tatum let silence fill the space around us, so I continued, "When I woke up, it took a while for my body to function normally. Your son helped me back to Cimmerian, which is where..." A thick bubble lodged in my throat as flashes of lifeless faces filled my vision, the orange tree that would never be picked from or enjoyed again, the knitted lamb deteriorating alongside the twins. Clearing my throat, I went on, "Where everyone lay lifeless. Spread about the courtyard, like their bodies had just dropped with no intention. Lane came with me to my home, which is where we found my family. Passed as well. After that, we decided to make sure you were alive, only I was attacked by a horrendous creature."

"Yes, I heard about the orbichor attack. Lucky you are, surviving two great ordeals like that. You seem impossible to kill, my dear."

"I suppose I am." I returned his hardened stare and added, "Sir."

"I disagree with what you stated, though." He lifted a mounted tusk from beneath the desk. "The orbichor. They are anything but horrendous. Quite stunning creatures, they are powerful, ruthless, void of emotion, only acting on the instinct to survive and kill. One of my best creations."

Chills swept up my spine, and the back of my neck broke out in goosebumps.

"Your creations? Why would you ever create something so monstrous!" Did Lane know this? He'd warned me there were things in the woods, but he had never said that his father created what tried to kill me, and *that's* what we needed to be on the lookout for.

"Watch your mouth!" The king's chair fell backward, creating a loud cracking sound as it hit the marble flooring. The shift in the atmosphere was palpable as his body turned to exit the dais. He approached me, hands clasped behind his back, a scowl fixed on his face.

"The so-called monstrous creatures you fear, my dear, protect this castle and the surrounding woods. They are the reason those who choose to call Santavarre their home are safe." He was too close. My heart slammed against my chest.

King Tatum's jaw clenched as his icy stare burned holes into me. "Frankly, dear, I'm trying to understand why you think you deserve to live here? You could go back to your village and live a full life. Yet here you are, disrespecting me in my home."

"Sir, I mean no disresp—"

"Whether you mean it or not does not take away the fact I have been disrespected." Arrogance leaked from his pores.

"I didn't choose to come here. I was brought here by your son after a monster—and that is what it is, a monster—attacked me. Your son chose to ask you for sanctuary on my behalf. I did not. I could go back to Cimmerian, my home, clean up the streets of the now certainly rotting bodies of the ones I once called friends, neighbors, family. It would never be a full life, though. Reminders in every stone of what happened. You do not have to let me stay here, and I will not beg for anything. I will not be treated as though I have done something wrong. I am a grown woman and demand equal respect."

"You will demand nothing from me!" Wet flecks hit my face as his voice echoed off the walls, making my bones shudder. I refused to cower to this man. I had done nothing to him, yet everything about him screamed hatred. I could taste it in the air, feel it crawling up my back.

"You will pay for your family's actions. You will suffer for what has been done. You will not find peace in Santavarre. You will not find peace anywhere." Hot breath glided over my skin, making a few stray strands of my hair blow off my shoulders.

What is he talking about? "My family? They are dead. Gone. What could they have possibly done to you? They never left Cimmerian. No one ever really left Cimmerian." My voice cracked slightly. Cimmerian was the last place with life that we'd known of. The Forgotten Lands—the long-abandoned kingdoms—were uninhabitable, people who went scouting the lands barely ever returned.

The king's laugh was sinister, much like Lane's had been outside my bedroom earlier.

"You believe I am naive enough to think you do not know who I am, what your *bloodline* is responsible for." The king scoffed as he turned and took a few steps toward the dazzling platform, a stark contrast to the suffocating air choking me within these four walls.

I felt like I'd been thrust into another realm. "I swear to you, I don't know what you're talking about. Please—"

"I can smell your tainted blood!" he boomed. "What do you know of the Kingdom End War, my dear?"

I could already feel exhaustion looming. I couldn't keep up with his whirlwind of thoughts. "That is a fairytale, sir, a story told to kids about how dragons built the lands we call home."

"It is no wives' tale, girl. The Kingdom End War was real. I was there. I lived it."

The proclamation left me feeling bewildered. My face contorted in confusion as my mind tried to process what he'd just declared. What did he mean, he was there? He'd have to be over a hundred years old.

"Sir, you say you were there, you lived it, but according to the stories, the Kingdom End War was a hundred years ago, and while you look aged—" and he did, his hair was well-kempt and short, white with a darker gray streaked through. Though, even with the aged hair, he was nothing short of strong and commanding. His face was worn around the eyes, but his jaw was chiseled, with a well-groomed beard. His body protected behind armor that was made up of white and gold details, screaming power. There had been no encounters with this man where his expression wasn't stern and focused, exuding authority no matter who took up the same space as him "—you certainly are not a hundred years old."

He leaned against the platform and crossed his arms, clasping his hands together.

"Did your father ever speak of a man named Mikulec?"

Mind combing through the stories we had been told while we were growing up, I tried to recall that name. Only one instance came to mind, but it hadn't come from my father.

"My mother, when I was just a child, read us a story about the first settlers of Cimmerian. They had grown greedy. They wanted more land than they had."

His eyes fixated on me.

My hands were slick, my mouth parched. It was hard to recall exactly how this story had gone, it had been almost fifteen years since the last time I'd heard it, but I dug into the depths of my memories, grasping at what I could. "She said their greed led to terrible decisions, which ignited the Kingdom End War. I-I don't remember much other than that."

Annoyance poured from the king's features. "Mikulec was the leader of the first human settlement. He opted into a species land agreement with nine other leaders which split the land into ten kingdoms. After the human population boomed, Mikulec demanded the agreement be revised, allowing the humans a larger kingdom to sustain the growing population."

"But it was denied," I finished for him.

"Yes." The king nodded his head curtly. "The lands were split fairly, and it was the humans who could not control their population or ensure their lands stayed healthy. We, the leaders, refused to allow them to infect any of the surrounding kingdoms or take away from the ones who knew how to respect the lands."

Memories of my little sister flashed. "He burned a village," I said, my eyes tracking his movements.

King Tatum drifted to the back of the room behind the platform. I swiftly followed the movement when he glanced back at me. There was a large steel cauldron hanging just inches from the ground, supported by four thick, crystal-like chains bolted into the ceiling. As King Tatum ran his hand along the rim of the cauldron, he continued, "After the rejection, Mikulec became enraged. He went back to his kingdom and put together a plan to *take* more lands from a neighboring kingdom." His fingers stopped their slow tracing of the rim, and his eyes shot to mine. "You stand in the land he turned to ash, what is now known as Santavarre." If what he was saying was true, that meant other aspects of the story would be true as well... that couldn't be right. The pointed ears, the hushed voices in the corridors, women using their hair to hide their features... King Tatum went on, "The humans who followed Mikulec waited until the moon was at its highest, when the fae who inhabited what was once called Orcalorne were asleep. They died not even knowing they were under attack. An entire kingdom turned to ash, just so the land could be taken."

Tears formed in my eyes, threatening to drop as I took in the information. The actions of those who'd built the kingdom I lived in. I rubbed my arms as my mind sorted through his words and focused on one word: fae.

"What do you mean, the *fae* who inhabited Orcalorne?" I questioned, knowing It had been in the book, but I'd been so young I never truly understood.

King Tatum let out a deep breath as the fingers that were tracing the cauldron rim started to tap instead. "Do you truly sit here in front of me, child, and claim you know nothing?" His tone grew more impatient with every word until he was practically snarling at me. His fists slammed onto the large steel pot, an echo vibrating the space between us. As his fists made contact with the steel, a glimmer of... scales? ...rippled over his skin, the color resembling the walls around us. *I have to be losing my mind. This is just a dream. Another nightmare.* King Tatum stood straight and adjusted his armor.

"I apologize," he said, stretching out the words.

"I understand you believe I know whatever it is you know, but I don't. We had a small sanctuary for sacred writings where I would sneak off to, to read when I could. It was full of fairytales and myths, though. There was nothing about a Kingdom End War, there was nothing about anyone named Mikulec except for the children's book my mother read to us." My voice was a plea.

He clicked his tongue at me. "The fae were our allies, they possessed magical capabilities beyond what I'm sure you can comprehend and had a deep respect and connection with the world around them. Both flora and fauna, even to the rocks and minerals that made up the kingdoms, had a connection to the fae. They could tap into the energy of all things, speak to others through the mind. They were cunning, and while they liked to play tricks, their power was respected."

"Did they all perish that night? The night Mikulec attacked?"

"No, the souls that night sought revenge. The only attacker who survived that night was Mikulec. He fled the forest, leaving those who had followed him to die. The souls made their deaths known. Two other fae kingdoms, Calicon and Monsteralafe, felt the losses, and were shown the knowledge of the attack in their dreams. The next day, they retaliated. Sparking the Kingdom End War."

So much pain and destruction, so many lives taken because of the actions of one man.

"Are you fae?" I asked, hands trembling, wondering if that's why he was so angry with me, if it was just humans he hated. But could there really be magical beings? I thought back to the orbichor, how... out of this realm it was. There was no other explanation for its existence than magic. My mind refused to accept that the story I'd heard as a child was real.

"I am not," King Tatum said, tone low, his eyes turning to slits as he grabbed the cauldron with both hands. His features darkened, making me take a step back as my body screamed a warning.

"A-Are they still within these lands? What are you? How do more people not know about this? Why was it never talked about?" The questions poured out of me, unable to be contained. Most importantly—"Why am I being punished for the actions of another?"

"QUIET!" The guttural voice penetrated my skull. I slammed my eyes shut as my body vibrated from the shock. I could feel my body shrinking, even though I tried my best not to show fear. *He wasn't human.*

"The dragons stayed out of the war—humans were nothing more than a pest—until T'naka, the leader of Monsteralafe, came to us asking for assistance. We denied him, not wanting to risk our kind. Mikulec had other plans. He assumed we had allied with the fae and decided to attack first. Humans struck in the night over the next several days and invaded all of our lands. They targeted our nesting grounds first, killing our unborn and hatchlings, along with the females protecting the young. Your great-grandfather was Mikulec. He is responsible for the death of my mate and my daughters. You were never meant to live, but it seems you are now his last blood relative."

I could barely get a full breath in, my mind was spinning, and I felt like I needed to sit down. *Dragons are real, fae are real. Is anyone here human? Am I the last?*

"Don't worry, dear. You have an opportunity to make up for what he has done. You see, I am in need of a few items."

I couldn't speak, I didn't even think I was fully comprehending what I was hearing or what was happening. I felt frozen, numb. He was speaking to me about mythical creatures and magical beings, and a war that, apparently, my great-grandfather started. How I was to be held accountable for the deaths of all those lost due to Mikulec's decisions.

He spoke again. "I would love nothing more than to watch you die, child, let's make that very clear. I wish to end the infestation humans have become. Lucky for you, there are things I need in order to avenge what's been lost. You acquire them for me, and I will let you live."

"H–how do I know you'll keep your word? How do I trust you won't just kill me once I retrieve these so-called items?"

"You don't," he said matter-of-factly. "I will allow a select few of my choosing to accompany you to collect six dragon scales—one scale in every kingdom they used to rule over—along with three relics, one in each of the fae lands. Each item is concealed and protected. Use those who travel with you to retrieve them. Once you do, bring them to me."

Dragon scales, scales from actual dragons. I gulped. "What are they for?" I asked.

"That, you do not need to know. Bring them to me, or die. It is a simple choice."

Bring them to me or die. I stood there unmoving, not sure what I was supposed to do, if there was something else I should say.

King Tatum approached the desk and had a seat. Picking up a quill, he started writing something as if I were no longer there.

"Sir, why can't you retrieve them? Why do I need to do it? How do I know how to find the scales? I need more information if I'm going to live." My voice was a plea at this point. I was confused and desperate.

King Tatum raised his brows and lifted his eyes just enough to see me. "I do not care if you live. If you want to survive badly enough, you will figure it out. Now leave." He said the last words with force before his attention returned to his task.

I turned to leave and felt like I was floating. I didn't feel my body, I didn't recall telling my limbs to take one step and then another, I didn't remember the doors opening as I stepped through the works of art I once thought to be beautiful. Instead, my mind was circling around one sentence.

Bring them to me or die.

Chapter 13

I reached the open breezeway with pillars covered in vines that traveled so high, I couldn't see where they stopped. To the right was the walkway that led to the garden, to the left was the pathway to the floors of bedchambers, mine included. I didn't know what I needed right now—What would help me in this moment? I decided to shove everything I felt and everything I was thinking deep down into a vault hidden far below the surface of my skin and walked to the garden. Breaking down would solve nothing. Breaking down would only prove his thoughts of me, that I was a child, weak. It would prove that his words, his threats, affected me. My pace picked up until I was running. I shoved past faces but couldn't take in their features. *What were they? Fae, dragons?* My vision was blurring, but not from the speed I was traveling at. Tears threatened to spill over, and I couldn't be around anyone when they did. I needed to be strong. I couldn't let weakness win right now. I couldn't break.

"Amalia!"

Lane's voice shouted my name. *He's been lying to me, his father wants me dead, they aren't human. They aren't human.* I wasn't sure if he was one of the faceless bodies I'd passed or if he just happened to notice my canter through the vibrant colors and shapes that were a complete opposite to my mind doused in darkness.

"Amal—"

Lane's voice disappeared as I slammed into somebody, the force knocked me back onto my ass even though my hands flew out to catch the fall. And just like that... I shattered.

The tears that had threatened to pour, attacked with the force of a thunderstorm. Rivers of salty water flowed down my cheeks, down my neck, seeping into my clothing. Gasps echoed from my mouth as I tried to take in air but failed. I knew I was crying, wailing, but no sounds were coming out. I shifted my body to where my hands and knees were on the soil, my face down as I tried to calm myself. I slammed my eyes shut when I saw the ground darkening with each flow of tears that hit dry soil and continued fighting for a breath, clawing at the fabric around my neck. My heart felt like it was about to explode out of my chest with every bludgeoning thump. There would never be relief.

Arms wrapped around me, pulling me against warmth. A hand brushed back the damp strands of hair that stuck to my face, tucking them behind my ear. My eyes opened, expecting to see Lane holding me, but instead I was met with violet eyes lined by a black ring, and dark hair that fell longer in the front, framing his face. *Those eyes, they weren't human.*

I flailed, trying to escape his grasp. A scream tore through me, so raw it shredded my vocal cords. "Let me go!"

"What happened, Amalia?" His features were twisted in worry, his forehead wrinkling as his gaze turned restless, roaming over my face and body, looking for what had caused this reaction from me.

"Did I hurt you? I didn't even see you." His hand cupped my face, prompting me to look at him, but I still couldn't breathe, I couldn't think, and his touch broke me even more, the warmth of him holding me sending me further into a fit. I pushed against his flesh, so warm and human-like, yet I knew the truth. Nothing I knew was real.

"I-I-I can't," was all that I managed to say.

"You can't what? Hey, talk to me. Breathe... breathe with me." He shifted us so that he was on the ground, sitting in a crisscross position with me cradled in his lap. He took my face in his hand again and inhaled deeply, then held it until I mimicked the action. The inhale was rough, as I was still sniveling. He slowly blew out his breath, the warm air gliding over me, and I did the same before I felt my lip start to tremble again, the wave of heartache coming back in full force. "Y-you're not real." I gasped. Dots flecked my vision.

"Keep breathing, deep inhale and slow exhale, Amalia."

"I c-can't, Knox. I'm s-so tired!" Sobs broke free and he pulled me against his chest as he rocked us back and forth gently.

"Shhhhh. I've got you." He glided his hand over my hair, repeating the words.

"I-I lost m-my w-whole family. I-I lost the l-life I kn-ew, l-lost everyone that h-had a part in m-making me who I-I am." Sniffles and tears consumed me as I tried to speak. "I was attacked, and brought to a place I don't know, surrounded b-by people I don't know. I-I have tried to be strong, I have tried to adapt, b-but I can't do it anymore. I-I'm in so much pain." Everything I had shoved into the deepest vault had broken free. All the unprocessed emotions, everything I couldn't take, strangled me.

He cradled me. "You're safe to break, Amalia. I'm here. I won't let you drown." His hand glided from the top of my head down the length of my damp and knotted strawberry locks. I could feel my body relaxing even though my lower lip continued to tremble in waves, eyes welling in unison. I pulled myself into him, my tears soaking into his tunic.

"You haven't allowed yourself to process anything, to feel it, or face it. You aren't allowing yourself the chance to heal. You shove it all so far down that your soul can't take any more. You need to feel this, Amalia. Everything that is consuming you right now, feel it or let it go. You can't keep it. You don't deserve to torture yourself."

And just like that, as his words sank into me, I felt every inch of myself let go as I got the permission to let it out, as if I had been waiting for someone to notice my silent fight I'd tried so hard to conceal. For someone to see what I wouldn't even allow myself to acknowledge. I was in so much pain, held together by sheer will and stubbornness.

He saw me, though.

He'd weaved into my shadows and found a way to set me free, even just for a moment.

I confessed the thought that had plagued me since waking up in my field. "I don't think I was supposed to survive what happened to Cimmerian." Then I told him the truth of what had really hit me harder than everything I'd kept hidden. "King Tatum wants me dead."

Knox's hand abruptly came to a stop during the caress; I felt his entire form tense as his arms held me against him tighter. "What?"

Fast-paced footsteps reached us as Lane ran up to where we were seated on the ground. "What the hell is going on, Amalia?" he said, a little winded.

"What do you mean, Tatum wants you dead?" Knox asked, his finger lifting my chin so that I was looking at him. "What did he say to you?"

"What?" Lane exclaimed.

"Shut the fuck up, Lane," Knox snarled. "Amalia. What. Do. You. Mean."

"H-he summoned me. He told me I could either find certain items for him or die." Knox pulled back, searching my face. For what, I didn't know. Maybe gauging whether I was lying or not?

"I'm sure you misheard, Mal," Lane retorted, standing over us.

"I did NOT mishear or misunderstand him. He made it very clear. He told me about the Kingdom End War, that apparently dragons exist, and fae. And how my great-grand-father was the reason for so much death. He wants my death to avenge the family he lost." Anger at the assumption I must have heard incorrectly seeped into every word. My red-rimmed eyes, although puffy and swollen, were still throwing daggers in his direction. I didn't say that I suspected *they* were dragons. How could I when they looked so... human? What if the peo—beings here wanted to hurt me like King Tatum? What if he sent his monsters after me again? How was I expected to survive a journey in lands I didn't know with beings that had a hundred-year vendetta against me?

Both men stayed silent, so I used the moment to make a request. "I need to learn how to fight, or at least defend myself."

"Absolutely not, there's no need for that. There has to be some sort of misunderstand-ing. I'll talk to my father immediately. It will all be alright." Lane seemed so calm, he acted like I just didn't understand what was now at stake.

"No!" I snapped. "It will not *all* be alright. It's all wrong! I need to know how to protect myself if I'm going to ensure your father doesn't kill me." I was taking my anger for King Tatum out on Lane, but I couldn't help it. How had he not realized the hatred his father had for me? For the people who'd taken in his son when he'd banished him. A quick pang cut through me as I realized me taking my anger out on Lane was the exact same thing King Tatum was doing to me for what happened to his family. "I'm sorry." I took a deep breath. "I'm just angry." Lane couldn't have known, he would have told me.

"You have every right to defend yourself, every right to feel safe knowing you can handle what comes your way. Don't ever apologize for fighting for that right," Knox chimed in, his words were for me, but his cold stare was for Lane.

"I will be her safety. I will always be there to defend her."

"You are foolish to believe that," Knox said.

"Enough!" I shouted, my throat sore from my sobs. "I need sleep before I listen to any more bickering. I will not rely on anyone else to keep me alive."

I would not die at the king's hands.

Chapter 14

The next day, I headed down to the dining hall to grab something to eat. I'd never had dinner the previous night in the aftermath of the day's events. Knox had carried me to my bedchamber. He stayed, reading me the book he had left. There were so many times I wanted to ask him about what he was, if he was the beast in the book. Instead, I listened as he read, laughed as he tried to imitate the female's voice, and eventually drifted off. I'd missed dinner after that, and my stomach was giving me a harsh reminder this morning. As I neared the dining hall, voices drifted down the hall to me from inside.

"She's nothing but damaged goods that hides behind an average face and smart-ass mouth." A gruff laugh followed what sounded like Blaire speaking. "The only thing that has their interest piqued when it comes to her is whatever the king has planned for her." She snorted, and I heard a chair scoot across the floor as if someone had just pushed from the table. Did she know what the king had asked of me?

Another laugh filled the air, followed with, "Average face or not, I sure would like to use her at least once. Lane gets to have all the fun." I was sure that it was Kuma, Blaire's little shadow. I moved closer to the gap in the door to hear better.

A throat cleared behind me, breaking my concentration on the conversation. I was startled to see Knox and Bash leaning on opposite walls, arms crossed with one foot placed over the other. Both looking smug, their brows arched as they looked at me.

"So the dark temptress also acts as a little spy in her off time," Knox said to me, one corner of his mouth turning up.

"Why anyone would give a shit what either of those two have to say is beyond me," Bash tossed over his shoulder at Knox.

"Agreed," Knox replied.

"I wasn't purposely listening... I mean... not at first."

"Uh-huh," they said in unison.

I tucked a strand of hair behind my ear as I glanced at the door, my stomach letting out an obnoxious growl.

"Geeze Amalia, go inside and eat something before whatever monster that was escapes." Bash stood up straight and took a step back while putting both hands up in a mock attempt to show fear. I looked at his ears, they weren't pointed, they were round like mine. *Did that mean he was a dragon?*

I rolled my eyes. "I don't particularly want to deal with them. I'll just come back later." I started to walk down the corridor through the two men when an arm swooped down and caught my waist, stopping me.

"You'll eat now," Knox said, locking eyes with me for a few seconds longer than necessary before he headed toward the dining hall door.

"What are you doing, Knox!?" My shout came out more like a loud whisper.

"Let him have his fun." Bash shouldered me before following him. "We heard every word."

Knox barged through the door, and even behind Bash's muscular frame I was still able to see Blaire and Kuma jump from the sudden intrusion.

"Knox, what the hell, you scared the shit out of me," Blaire whined, placing a hand over her exposed chest. She was wearing a dangerously red sleeveless dress. Not only did it match the red streaks in her hair, it hugged every inch of her until the fabric ended mid-thigh. Even with the top of the dress wrapping around her neck, the gaping cutout that was meant to bring attention to the wearer's breasts showed plenty. If that didn't catch passersby's attention, the lengthy slit on the right side would, as it showed she'd decided to go commando today. Despite her revealing attire, Knox's eyes stayed homed in on her face, never gazing anywhere else, even though mine did.

"I don't really care. This will be said nice and slow so that I know both of you have time to soak in every word I'm about to say without any doubt of what I mean." He grabbed a chair and spun it around so that the back was facing away from him, then he sat, resting his arms on the top before continuing. Blaire and Kuma watched him, not uttering a word, and Bash propped himself against the doorframe. "I have zero intention of using Amalia for anything—"

"I never sa—" Blaire quickly tried to interject but was cut off just as fast.

"I heard. Every. Word. Secondly," he continued like there had been no interruption, "the only average, or let's be very honest with each other, less than average creatures on this land are the ones I have the unpleasant opportunity to be looking at right now, that seem to think talking about someone behind their back like cowards is acceptable."

Kuma's smirk vanished and Blaire looked like she was about to try and say something again, but Bash spoke this time. "Honey, I really wouldn't if I were you." She scrunched her face at him before returning her attention to Knox.

"Amalia is stronger than most I've known. She who, let me remind you, did not choose to be here, she who has lost everything she has ever known, she who came from a village that now only holds the rotting bodies of those she grew up with. She is extraordinary and has a strength neither of you could ever possess."

"You think she's the only one who's known loss? Pain? Get the fuck over yourself, Knox."

In one swift movement, he was up, and the chair he had just been in was across the room in a thousand jagged and splintered pieces. He moved slowly, creeping toward her until he was inches from her face. Everything about him was threatening. "Unlike you, Blaire, she doesn't use her pain as an excuse to be a bitch." Silence filled the space as Blaire lifted her chin.

Kuma's eyes bounced from her to Knox repeatedly. He made an "oooooo" sound as he shrank farther into the chair he was sitting in.

"The strength it takes for her to get up every single day with the weight she carries and still be a decent human being, is a strength you have proven you'll never be capable of." He looked back at me as he inhaled deeply, cracking his neck before exhaling and turning back to the two, who I was sure were wishing they'd never spoken so freely in this room. "You two, on the other hand, serve no purpose"—he glanced at Blaire—"anymore. And are lucky to be alive. If I catch you speaking about her in the manner you have been again, I will happily slice your bodies open, starting from those undeveloped brains inside your heads down to your feet, and watch your entrails flow out of you while you slowly have the life drained from you."

I didn't know if it was from the lack of sustenance or the threat coming from him, but the space grew colder as shadows filled the corners of the walls, darkening the room.

"Oh, that image is gonna make me vomit," Bash said, holding his stomach. "I'm a little squeamish," he added over his shoulder to me since I hadn't exactly walked in the room yet. Instead, I had chosen to stay behind Bash. I tried not to, but a slight smile lifted my cheeks.

I felt a presence behind me and turned to see Orzelle standing there with a blank face. "Miss Amalia." She did a slight bow that I returned.

"Orzelle? What is this?" Bash said, drawing the attention of the others. Blaire and Kuma took the opportunity to leave the room—I'd never thought Kuma could move as fast as he did. I felt Knox behind me even though he wasn't touching me. My body heated, the nape of my neck tingling with awareness.

"What's all this about?" All of our heads turned as Lane spoke. Walking up the corridor to stand with me, he placed his hand over my shoulder and pulled me close to him. My hand landed on his chest from the unexpected shift.

I looked over at Orzelle, scanned her features, and said, "It's the king, isn't it?"

With a swift nod of her head, she said only a few sentences. "You leave in three days' time. You are to collect the requested items and return here. There is to be a ceremony on the second day where those who are to go with you will be announced. The king has granted you four months to complete your task." She turned to leave without looking back or waiting for follow-up questions.

"I don't even know where he wants me to go!" I shouted as she walked away, not bothering to respond. My stomach let out a loud growl that made Lane take a step away and look down at me. "When's the last time you ate, Amalia?"

"I don't really remember... Maybe breakfast yesterday? So much happened, food wasn't really on my mind."

"C'mon, let's get you some food." He placed his arm around my shoulder and ushered me past both Bash and Knox. I flashed an apologetic smile before he ushered me to sit at the table, calling Asahi out.

"Yeah, because we weren't already in the middle of getting her to eat or anything." Bash was glaring at Lane as he walked to the table and seated himself, throwing one leg up onto the table and biting into an apple he'd grabbed.

"Clearly you didn't get very far with that one job," Lane said lazily, as Asahi walked in and placed a fresh cup of tea in front of me, scents of orange and bergamot filling my nostrils. Next thing I knew, an apple was whizzing past my head at Lane, who dodged it with a second to spare.

"What is with you guys!" my voice blared.

"Enough, everyone. We have bigger things to deal with. Amalia has three days to learn what she can to protect herself before we leave. We need to discuss when we can train.

Between the three of us, she should get enough experience for any small skirmishes we may encounter," Knox said, breaking the tension.

"She is not training with any of us. She won't need to. I will be there with her and will ensure she is safe. This isn't up for discussion."

Up for discussion? He acted as if he ruled over me.

"Here you go, Amalia. I hope everything is to your liking." Asahi set down a plate of mostly bacon, a few sausage links, and two eggs. My mouth started watering instantly as I thanked her.

"You know, there is an underground atheneum I believe may have some information that could help you greatly," she whispered to me as she acted as if she were refilling my tea. My eyes snapped to hers, and she gave me a small smile before standing upright.

"Meet me in my bedchambers tonight and we will go," I said in a soft voice before donning a mischievous grin. I wasn't sure who the bad influence was, her or me.

"Oh, wait!" I said as I grabbed her arm.

"Yes, Miss Amalia?"

I had been so distraught I never went to get an update. "Did you find Akira?"

She solemnly shook her head, sadness filling her chocolate eyes.

"If she wishes to train, then she will. Since when are you her keeper?" Knox said, distracting me. Asahi took the moment to leave the room, and I couldn't say I blamed her.

"Since I'm the one who saved her!" Lane's hands slammed against the table, causing me to jump and drop my forkful of eggs.

"YOU saved her?" Knox asked in a deadly tone, it leaked with disbelief as the air in the room grew chilled again.

The two men stared at each other, jaws tense. The shadows in the corners of the walls looked like they were swirling inward toward us. The fact either of them thought they controlled or had a say over what I could or couldn't do suffocated me. I felt trapped, like I was in one of the coffins my family should have been buried in.

The dining hall door swung open as a guard in white metal armor stepped in and came to a halt, stomping both feet together and placing his hands close to either side of his body.

"Prince Lane, your presence is requested by the king."

"Thank you, Torgan, please inform him I will be there shortly."

Torgan, the guard, stomped his right foot, using his left hand to thump a fist into his chest before turning on his heel and exiting the room.

"Looks like you're saved by your dearest dad," Knox said.

Lane ignored the comment and came over to me. "Make sure to eat all of that and to rest up. I'll come find you later, and we can talk more about everything after my meeting with my father." He placed a hand on the back of my head, slightly pulling my hair to tip my head back, and placed a kiss on my forehead, stunning me for a second before I could form words.

"Of course," I said as I watched him walk out of the room, leaving me confused with one moody man and one who felt the need to either pick a fight or make everyone laugh. We sat in silence as I finished my plate of food. I could feel their eyes on me the entire time. I was sure they wanted an explanation for the kiss, but I didn't have one. I was just as bewildered as they were.

"We need to start your training today," Knox said flatly.

"Lane seems to think it's not necessary." He was the reason I was there, the reason I'd survived the attack. He was my support after waking up when the shimmer fell. How could I not trust him? He knew these lands better than I did. Wouldn't he know if I did or did not need training for something his father was orchestrating? I felt the need to prepare myself in my soul, but he was all that was left of what I knew—how could I just disregard his thoughts? My guilt was mixing with what I wanted, and I couldn't decide what was right.

Knox looked like he didn't recognize me. "I don't believe that for a moment. If he does not arm you or train you to at least defend yourself, what is he really building you up to be? Besides good bait."

His words hit me like a physical blow, and it caused me to wince away from him. I put the unfinished bacon strip back on my plate and stood, ready to leave. "I don't know," I said honestly. "What I do know is, as of right now, I owe him everything. What kind of person would I be if I did the exact opposite of what he says after all he's done for me?"

"An intelligent person," Bash said as Knox's features turned impatient.

I rolled my eyes and headed for the door when Knox grabbed my wrist and spun me back to him. I braced my hand against his chest, momentarily breathless. I looked up at him, and his brows knitted together as he looked down at me.

"You know you need to train. Don't let your guilt, or loyalty to someone who doesn't deserve it, sway you from doing what you need to do to protect yourself. I don't believe for a second that one kiss on your forehead"—he brushed a thumb over the spot Lane had placed his lips—"changed your mind. What happened? Giving in like that isn't you. Yesterday you were adamant, and now today you're willing to risk your life?"

Knox saw too much of me. He challenged too much. "What is your problem with Lane? He is your brother, and yet you all act more like enemies than family." I snatched my hand away from his grasp and matched his hardened gaze, showing I could be just as stubborn. The truth was, I didn't know why I'd given in. It was automatic, yet no part of me *didn't* want to train.

Bash stretched his arms over his head, clasping his hands together and arching his back as he said, "Well, since we only have three days, there's definitely not enough time to get into the long list of reasons why Lane is an absolute shriveled dickhead."

I let out a gruff groan and stomped toward the door, only when I reached it, I couldn't seem to make my feet walk through the doorway. My brain took over, knowing even though these men may have been pricks, they spoke some semblance of truth. I tilted my head back and looked up at the ceiling, where a spider had made an intricate, nearly invisible web—even insects had the ability to defend themselves in some capacity... "Fine..." I said as I turned back to them. "Train me, then."

Smirks graced both of their faces as they glanced at each other before settling their sights on me.

"We do not tell Lane."

Chapter 15

My pace quickened as I followed Knox and Bash into the training fields behind the castle, which were a vast space of luscious green turf. You'd never know it was meant for battle training by how undisturbed the area was. "Are you guys sure this is the training ground?" Looking around for even one scuff in the dirt, I saw nothing but vibrant blades of ankle-high grass.

Bash took a seat in the grass before falling onto his back, crossing his arms behind his head. "You guys do your thing. I'm in need of a nap."

I rolled my eyes and looked at Knox. "Sooo, what do I do?"

"Defend yourself," he said before rushing me.

A scream escaped me as I dodged to the side and clutched my chest. "What the hell was that, Knox!"

"That," Bash said, opening one eye, "was not defending yourself." Then he closed it again to resume his nap.

"I don't know HOW to defend myself, hence why we're here!"

"I wanted to see what your reflex is before we started training," Knox said, placing his hands on his hips and smirking at me. My dragons, I hated that smirk. I just wanted to slap it right off his face.

"Okay, and?" I asked, as my heart started to calm.

"You have zero survival instincts. You're truly terrible, and we have a lot to do in very little time."

"Gee, don't try to sugarcoat it or anything." I crossed my arms over my chest defensively.

"Would you like to be alive, or sweet talked?" he countered.

"Both," I said, kicking my foot into the grass trying to mess up its annoying perfection, distracted. I didn't see or hear that Knox was hurtling toward me, noticing only as his body crashed into mine, taking me to the ground. A pained groan left me, and Knox braced himself on an elbow as he looked at me. "I stand corrected, you're utterly terrible," he said, followed by a few clicks of his tongue.

"Never take your eyes off your opponent," he said, getting up and holding out one of his hands for me to take. I grinned as a plan formed quickly in my mind. I spun my body, throwing my leg out and connecting with the back of his knee. He looked down at me, unphased, holding back a laugh as my smile faded.

"Lesson number two, fix your face, you told me what you were thinking before you even finished the thought."

I huffed, got up, and brushed myself off. "Can we please be serious? Teach me something. Don't just tackle me expecting me to do something grand. I won't."

Bash yelled from his place in the grass. "He just wanted an excuse to touch you."

My finger waved in his direction. "You hush it. Either help or actually take a nap, I don't need the commentary!"

"Yes ma'am," he retorted.

The next several hours, Knox was serious. He taught me skills like having proper stance, balance, and footwork, ensuring I understood the importance of having a solid foundation. He showed me by demonstrating with his body, then adjusting mine when I didn't copy his movements or stances exactly. He never spoke to me like I was incompetent. Instead, he spoke simply and clearly, explaining terms further when my face gave away my confusion, even when I didn't want to voice that I didn't understand. Once he felt I had the moves down, he recruited Bash for a little game of testing how well I'd paid attention and retained what I was taught. Knox and Bash stood about twenty-five feet from me.

"Get into a defensive stance!" Knox called out to me.

I did as he said, trying to remember how each body part needed to be adjusted. My feet moved so that they were shoulder-width apart, my left foot slightly behind my right at a forty-five-degree angle. I bent my knees slightly and focused on squaring up my hips and shoulders in relation to where Knox and Bash stood, looking far too eager for whatever they'd prepared.

"Okay!" I shouted, checking my feet once more. "I think I'm in it!" I looked up, and both men were gone. *This is not going to go well for me.* "Guys!" No answer from either one of them. I breathed in and out slowly, just like Knox had taught me. I remembered how his hand had stayed on my abdomen while the other was placed on my back as he'd coached me through a breathing exercise that was meant to calm my mind. All it did was speed up my heart.

A rock whizzed by my face then. "Did you just throw a fucking rock at me!?" I whirled around in the direction the rock had come from and saw a stick twirling through the air. I ducked, covering my head, my anger growing at the ridiculousness of this training session.

"I thought we were being serious here!" It was only my life that was at stake, why would I think they wouldn't mess around? Suddenly, the lush grass I'd admired hours earlier rushed up, growing rapidly before I could understand what was happening. The once vast field was now like an endless maze with no start and no end, blades taller than I stood surrounded me, cutting off all visibility. Soon after, I was hit in the shoulder with a hard-packed ball of dirt. Turning toward the way it had come from, I let out an exasperated scream, frustration overflowing from me. "Enough!" My throat burned with the words, and I threw my hands down before bending to pick up a small rock by my foot. I threw it with every ounce of strength I had before my eyes adjusted to the fact that the grass was no longer above me, giving me full sight of the rock hitting Bash in the forehead right between his eyes, knocking him on his ass.

"Fuck!" he shouted, throwing his hands to his face.

Knox threw his head back in a full-body laugh. "Why the hell did you release the grass, you idiot?" he said through his hysteria.

"That wasn't me!" Bash yelled back, stopping Knox's laughing fit.

"What?" he asked. Both men looked up at me, Bash still rubbing his head with a scowl. Blood trickled from the fresh wound.

"I'm so sorry! I just threw it, I didn't even know where you guys were!" Neither said anything, they just stared at me until the silence was broken by horns blaring from the watchtowers at either end of the castle.

"We will have to pick this up again later," Knox said to me as he helped Bash up off the ground.

"What is that?" I asked, but they were already running, joining a group of guards who were racing to the towers.

I watched the sun set through the window in my bedchamber. I ran up to my room right after the horns blared, hoping I would get a glimpse of whatever they were warning of, but I saw nothing. I heard no commotion. It must have been some sort of drill. I decided to bathe and change into a long tunic and loose-fitting, light trousers for bed, knowing Asahi would be there later that night for our secret outing to the atheneum. I decided to try and sleep a few hours before she arrived. Thoughts of Knox's hands on me entered my mind again, only this time Lane's face followed quickly after with a hurt expression weaved into his features.

"Screams and pained groans filled the silence of the night, piercing my ears and shaking my core. Frantically, I looked around for the source. The ground beneath me shook in unison with a loud thumping, similar to a large beast walking. I spun, trying to see through the smoke when a rush of heat swarmed around me, burning my lungs. I ran. I ran until the smoke started to clear and I could make out the shadows of forms clashing together. People were fighting, swords striking against each other, slashing through flesh and bone. Blood, sweat, and ash coating everyone before me. As I went to take a step toward the chaos, an enormous, black, scaled tail slammed into the ground just mere feet from me, causing debris to fly, hitting my body. Shock rippled through me as my eyes tracked up the tail to the entirety of what was before me. A beast, a monster, that had only been seen in old fairytale books. A dragon. "There isn't much time. You have to go. "

My eyes snapped open to Asahi shaking me gently, telling me to wake up. "I'm up, I'm up!" I pushed her arms away as I tried to get out of my initial sour mood from these recurring nightmares. I was starting to think it was time I told someone about them.

"I'm sorry, Amalia, but we don't have much time. The guards are switching their rotation, so we have to go. Now!"

I threw the blankets off me and decided not to bother with changing as we sprinted out of my bedchamber and down multiple staircases before we got to the servants' chambers. It was a large stone room with beds lined along the walls, no privacy or personalization. A few torches burned in their hangers in the front, middle, and back of the room. "This is where you sleep?" I asked her. She simply nodded her head, her gaze glancing to a perfectly made bed. "Akira's?"

"Yes," she said, before taking my hand and pulling me through the room to a door that led outside.

"This pathway leads to the greenhouse," she said. She looked haunted, her features sunken, the brightness no longer there.

"You're worried?" It was obvious, but what else was there to say?

"Something's not right, she isn't the first of us to disappear," she said in a hushed voice. She grabbed my hand and yanked me forward, then left. As we reached the greenhouse, her pace slowed, and we ducked behind a large, white, flowering bush that gave off a sweet scent as two guards passed by.

"I heard they caught some fae bitch and sent her off to Stygian prison."

"Ahh, I wish they would have let us have some fun with her first."

"You couldn't pay me my weight in gold to fuck a fae whore. I heard their pussies coat you with a binding spell or some shit. You're never quite right afterward."

"Where do you hear this horse shit?"

Both men laughed until they had to wipe their eyes, moving past our hiding spot.

"What's Stygian prison? And what fae did they find?" My curiosity piqued higher than the Godival Mountains stood.

"Shhh!" Asahi hushed me as her eyes darted around the open area. With no warning, she grabbed me again, dashing toward the greenhouse. When we reached the door, she opened it just enough for our bodies to slip in and slowly closed it, keeping an eye on the outside perimeter until the door clicked into place.

"Wha—"

"Shhh!"

I snapped my mouth closed and just watched as she moved a few stacks of pots off to the side and threw a rug off what seemed to be a wooden hatch. I made my way to stand next to her as she unlatched the lock and flipped the wooden hatch open, ushering me inside. I took one look down and saw nothing but blackness. "That's a hard no from me," I said, stepping back.

"Don't be such a baby," she whispered at me, though it sounded more like a shout.

"You go down first," I said. "There's no way I'm just walking into complete darkness first. You're the one that knows this place."

"Fine. But you need to close the hatch after us."

"Easy." I shot her a smile as I reached up to grab the handle.

I followed Asahi as she entered the dark tunnel that led, for all I knew, to our death, and made sure to close the hatch behind us. As soon as the hatch shut, lights flickered on, illuminating the walkway. We were descending wooden steps in a stone tunnel that, even with the lighting, looked like it'd never end.

"So what is Stygian prison?" I asked again to fill the silence and keep my mind off the creepy space we were occupying.

"A terrible, terrible place." I could hear the shudder in her voice.

"Can you give me a little more detail than that?"

"It's not too far from where you called home. It's located in the Lands of Stygian. The prison is used for torture. Gruesome acts. I've only seen one who was sent there ever return."

"Who gets sent there?"

"Anyone the king wants information from. Or deems a waste of resources."

I gulped as I thought about the fact he wanted me dead. Our deal never said I would live happily, just that I would live. What if he kept me in that prison, alive but tortured every single day? I'd rather just die.

"What do you think that fae woman did to deserve being sent there?"

"Just existed," she said plainly. I glanced at her before she said, "We are here." Her hand turned an antique-looking knob, which opened up to a large, expansive room. Books in a variety of conditions were stored from floor to ceiling, stacks lined up against walls with no shelves, and display cases with locks which held the oldest-looking books. The smell of the room had me immobile; it smelled like worn pages. A light orb floated in the center of the stone ceiling, shining over thousands of books. I walked forward and spun, taking it all in. Asahi rushed to the back left shelf and grabbed a green hardcover that was as thick as my palm was long. She brought it to me. "This book has information on every dragon and fae species in the surrounding ten kingdoms, information on the Kingdom End War and what happened to them all. This will be invaluable on your journey, Amalia, please use it. It holds the answers to everything you would want to know."

"Won't they notice it's missing?" I asked, the last thing I wanted was to give the king more reasons to hate me, or worse, send me to the Stygian prison.

"No one comes down here. It'll be fine, just promise you'll keep it with you always." She grabbed my hands, pleading with her eyes.

"I promise, Asahi." She gave me a hesitant smile. "How do you know of this place?"

Grief poured over her. "Akira. They had taken her books when we were brought here. She followed the guards who had them and watched as they took them here."

"You're fae, aren't you?" I asked her. I had never seen her ears, she always made sure her hair was down, but her eyes weren't wild and shifting like others I'd noticed.

"I am." Her smile didn't reach her eyes.

It was then that I knew why Akira felt the way she did. "Mikulec was the reason you lost your family, why Akira has those burns. It was your village that he attacked first."

Asahi came up to me and looked me in the eyes as she tucked her hair behind her ears for the first time since I'd met her. "I do not blame you." She brushed my arm. "Many of us do not blame you."

The way my heart swelled for this female. To show this kindness took the kind of strength Knox had spoken of. As much as I wanted it, I don't know that I had what she did. She went to leave the atheneum, but I stopped her once more.

"Wait, I have one more question." She faced me, looking intrigued. "What do you mean you were brought here? Didn't you come on your own?"

She shook her head. "We were taken from the Skyward Lands. It's where we lived after the war. King Tatum needed fae for... something, I'm still not sure what. He struck a deal with our leader, any who were orphaned or committed crimes in any way would be sent back to the lands of Caligness to serve King Tatum."

As I lay in bed thinking about what Asahi shared, I flipped through the pages of the history book. I came across an illustration of a dazzling white dragon, labeled with bold lettering as a Menticide Dragon. Said to have the ability to alter, erase, and dig into your thoughts or memories. A shudder ran through my body—a warning signaling that was enough for the night. I closed the book and slipped it into the bottom of my pillowcase. My thoughts circled around Akira and where she was at, what types of dragons walked these walls, and which ones I could really truly trust—if any at all.

Chapter 16

The grand room buzzed with more excitement and life than the survivors' ball. This crowd was bigger, more lively. I stepped around the room, wondering who these people really were. *What* they were. Could I even call them people? Last night I'd been restless, waking up every hour until I read through the book Asahi had given me in the atheneum some more. The pages were filled with knowledge on fae and dragons who could take human form, my mind felt like I was living in an alternate reality. No one I knew here was actually human. Asahi had given me the book, knowing it would open my eyes to what lurked in the castle. How had the people of Cimmerian never known?

A sleeveless, deep navy dress with a sweetheart neckline hugged my skin. The top was snug against my chest and waist, while the bottom flowed out delicately. There was a sheer fabric over the navy that glistened with silver stars and speckles. It was like I was wearing a piece of the night sky. Asahi helped with my hair, leaving most of it down in waves, with two thin braids wrapping around the top of my head to mimic a crown. She used some natural ink from the flowers in the garden to paint my lips a deep, almost black tone that shone with hints of purple, claiming it was a method the fae had used to enhance their features. She then lined my eyes and lashes with a dark liquid that made my hazel eyes shine brightly.

The band was playing a sensual and slow beat, coaxing out the couples among the room. They held their partners close, kisses being planted on lips and necks as they rocked back and forth to the tune. A whistle reached me through the music. As I turned, I saw Lane suited up in evening blacks with one arm folded behind him and the other placed over his heart. He eyed me up and down, taking in my appearance. A blush formed on my cheeks, and I felt the heat travel down my neck. Twirling, I asked, "What do you think?"

He let out an exhale before closing the distance between us to take my hand, which was gloved in silver fabric. "You are so incredibly beautiful, Amalia."

He used his right hand to tilt my chin up so I met his eyes, those icy blue irises that looked as if they were made with shards of broken glass.

"You never came back to see me," I blurted.

Lane's brows pulled together, and his lips thinned into a slit.

"You said you'd come back to me after your meeting with your father, but you never did," I explained.

His tilted head snapped up. "Right, I'm so sorry."

"What happened?" I asked. "I heard horns blaring, I figured that's what kept you. Knox and Bash ran off as soon as they sounded in the fields." I registered the slip too late.

"The training fields?" His voice was shadowed with irritation.

I cleared my throat. "Yeah, um, Bash was challenging Knox, and I had nothing else to do, so I watched," I lied, guilt tugging at my vocal cords until I remembered he had been lying to me since the day we met. He watched me for a moment before he spoke.

"Yes, it is what kept me. There was a prisoner who managed to escape. We found them running through the Forgotten Pass." The music ramped up in the background as those around us cheered, supporting the change. My heart wasn't in the music. My head raced with all the things I'd learned the past day or so. I couldn't act like it was all fine anymore.

I decided to ask him a question that could make this dance either be one that secured a bond between us or ruined it.

My pulse thrummed. "What does your father need the fae here for?"

Lane stopped dancing. "What did you just say?"

"You said there were things we would need to discuss at a later time. Later has yet to come. I shouldn't have put off confronting you about these things for so long, but I won't be kept in the dark." My head shook in frustration with myself and him for keeping this information from me. He'd been lying to me since he was banished to Cimmerian.

"Why does your father need the fae from the Skylands, and why did you never tell me about what you are?"

He took both of his hands and ran them down the lengths of my arms. The act didn't send shivers, it boiled my blood. I knew I wouldn't get all the answers I wanted tonight, but I was determined to make him talk.

"How do you tell someone you just met that you're a dragon, Amalia? How do you think the people in Cimmerian would have reacted? They would have murdered me that night. Like they did a hundred years ago when they murdered my mother, my sisters."

His mask broke and those shards sharpened as he spoke. He recovered after a breath and said, "Then as time went on, too much time had passed for me to say anything. It became easier to just conceal it."

I didn't know how I would have reacted, but everyone else would have revolted at the difference. He would have been seen as a threat simply because they would have been afraid. I swallowed hard, trying to dampen my dry throat as the tension between us thickened. "Do you blame me like your father does?"

Lane hesitated. "I don't want you to think I blame you for anything." His gaze burned into mine, and I relaxed as the weight of his words lifted that worry away.

"I—I heard she will be sent to Stygian prison... that they torture people there."

"Where did you hear that?" he said, trying to keep the bite out of his words.

"I heard some guards talking." He didn't need to know where or when I'd heard them talking. That would only make this exchange worse.

"Fucking guards never know when to keep their mouths shut." His hand raked through his hair once more. "This isn't the time to have this discussion, Amalia. How about I go and get us some drinks?"

I nodded in agreement and watched as he left the dance floor, before looking at the couples around me, still glued to each other even though the band was playing a more upbeat song. I scoffed at how little I'd learned. He just wouldn't explain anything to me, and the more I tried to push, the clearer it became that he wouldn't.

"I see the dark temptress decided to be among the stars tonight."

Knox. My stomach jumped at the sound of his low, gravelly voice. Not turning to see him, I just replied, "I figured I'd dress in the stars I'll be among once the king gets his way and kills me." I glanced to where Lane was being handed two drinks, then was whirled around as Knox pulled me to him. I inhaled sharply as surprise and shock sent a jolt through me.

He put a finger under my chin as he leaned in close. "The only stars you'll be among, are the ones you see from pure bliss."

My core tightened as his innuendo sank in. "That's a rather inappropriate thing to say to your brother's girl."

"Are you?" he said as he ran a finger down my neck, blocking out all possibility of producing a thought in my head.

"Hmm?" he coaxed.

"Am I what?" I said, breathless, chest heaving. My body reacted so intensely to his touch, his words.

"My brother's girl."

Why had I even said that? Lane had made it clear he would like that, even acted like it at times, but we hadn't actually sat down to discuss it. Why, then, did I get a rush at the thought of this man thinking his brother had a claim on me?

"Knox." Lane's voice was laced with distrust. "Can we help you?" he asked as he handed me a beautiful cocktail that had a shimmering, rose-colored liquid in it, topped with an orange slice and a bright red cherry. The citrus smell reached my nose before I even tipped the glass to my mouth, showing how fresh the fruit was.

"I was just letting Mal know how striking she looks tonight." He lifted my free hand, placing a gentle kiss on my knuckles before sending Lane a wink and walking toward the back of the room. My heart stuttered a bit at the thought of him leaving early again like before.

"Save a dance for me later?" I called out behind him.

Pausing in his tracks, he turned just enough to flash me a wicked smile. "Of course, little temptress." My face fell flat at the use of the nickname before I turned back to Lane, his face now full of hard lines and a murderous glare.

"Why does Knox keep calling you that?"

"Why does your brother do anything that he does?" I quickly retorted, taking a sip of my drink. The flavor mimicked the smell and hit my taste buds with bursts of fresh, sweet citrus. "This is amazing."

"Thank you, I requested it specifically for you." Lane's face turned up with a cheeky smirk. "I thought you'd prefer something sweet but also refreshing." He lifted his right hand, using his thumb to brush my cheek. "I wanted to make something that reminded me of you."

"That's very sweet of you." Warmth washed over me as the liquid contents settled in my stomach.

"Attention, everyone! Attention, please!" The room started to quiet as the king took the stage. His powerful tone demanded eyes be on him. I could hear groups in the back still murmuring to themselves in hushed voices, and apparently, so could King Tatum. "SILENCE!" he boomed, his voice echoing in the grand space, effectively silencing every being that stood inside it.

"Tonight is a very important night." King Tatum paused as he looked around the spacious room with a dark stare. The smell of perfumes and alcohol blending together made it feel suffocating as every person turned their bodies to face him. "Tonight, we will say farewell and good luck as our own leave the protection of Santavarre." I heard someone mutter, "*What protection?*" in the crowd. "To venture out on a quest that will help bring back what rightfully belongs in Santavarre, something that was stolen long ago!" Cheers erupted all around us, everyone raised their fists, pumping them in the air in response to Tatum's words. I was shoved left then right in the commotion, causing me to drop my glass. No one so much as flinched as the glass shattered and spread among heels and shiny black footwear. Lane wrapped his arm around my waist and protectively pulled me closer to him as the shouts grew more piercing, the movements more forceful.

"That is enough," King Tatum said more calmly as he gestured with his hands for the crowd to simmer.

They were all a few drinks in and hard to soothe. It took a few silent minutes for them to revert back to their quiet demeanor. All waited for King Tatum's next words, waiting for their opportunity to erupt in support again.

"I would like to honor those who will leave in just a day's time by having them come up to the stage, to look you all in the eyes and make an oath. An oath to put what is owed above all else. This, my family." King Tatum placed a hand over his heart in a weak attempt at proving his sincerity. "This is your time to thank them for their bravery."

A few men hooted, others whistled so loudly it would have broken my glass had I not dropped it. My head began to ache with a slight throb.

"Firstly, I would like to bring up someone who has not been here for very long, but without this person, this quest would not be happening. She is the key." His eyes landed on me. "Please show your appreciation for Amalia from Cimmerian." King Tatum used the hand that was just placed over his heart and extended it out to me. Heads turned to find me, freezing me in place.

I felt Lane's hand leave my body as I blinked a few times, seeing the king's outstretched hand pointing in my direction, the flood of people looking at me with stretched smiles. Some mixed with confusion. Lane nudged me forward, breaking me from my stone-like posture, and I began to weave between the crown until I reached the stage, walking up the three white stone steps lined with gold edging. I stood next to King Tatum. He threw one arm over my shoulder as the other struck into the air with a balled fist. With that one motion, the crowd became a deafening sea of shouts and cocktail glasses.

Tatum pulled me closer to him and whispered as his face was just mere inches from mine. "Should you fail, I will kill them all." The stench of decay and berries filled our shared breath, and goosebumps raced over my skin at his threat. As I looked at the faces smiling up at me, yelling praise and thanks, all I could picture was them being slaughtered. The waves of joy and hope turning into crests of blood and carnage. I refused to look at him, to give him the satisfaction of knowing how he'd affected me.

"Why would harming your own people affect me?"

King Tatum shook me as a laugh bellowed from his belly. "These are simply weapons, my dear. I can see inside your mind, your heart. You would not sacrifice these people to save yourself." My gaze stayed straight ahead against the back wall, not focusing on anyone or anything until I composed myself, turned my blood into steel, and became an immovable force.

That is, until my gaze found Knox's. His stance deadly, every muscle taut like he was ready to attack. Those lavender eyes were lethal, no longer carrying hints of the playfulness he'd shown while agreeing to save me a dance. He wasn't looking at me, though. His stony glare was solely on the king.

I startled as King Tatum bellowed his next words, breaking my concentration from Knox. "Next, I am proud to announce that my son, Lane, a member of the Menticide Horde, will be accompanying Amalia on her journey, ensuring her safety." My eyes darted to Lane, who was walking through the crowd using the same path I had just moments before. Men and women shook his hand as he neared the stage. The crowd slapped their hands across his shoulders and back with proud expressions on their faces. If these people hadn't come here by choice like Asahi had hinted, was this all just for show to stay in the king's good graces?

As Lane made his way to me, King Tatum used the brief moment to say a few last chilling words. "You would do well to heed my warning, child." I swallowed, keeping my eyes ahead and holding my breath. The taste of rotten fruit coated my tongue. I heard the king's faint laugh as he moved away, and Lane moved in, placing a kiss on the side of my temple. There was no doubt in my mind he would follow through with that promise. Only having had a couple interactions with the man, I knew deeply that he was not to be underestimated. He knew no mercy, only savagery.

My head started to swim a bit, as the anxiety of being in front of the crowd with a deranged king who wanted me dead whispering threats in my ear drained me. I leaned into Lane's side, and his hand squeezed my waist in response. It should have been a comforting gesture, but all I could feel right now were thousands of pins poking in and out of my skin.

"From the Mending Horde, Blaire Ravenake." King Tatum stretched both hands out to the left corner of the room, where Blaire stood next to the table lined with roasted ham, a variety of veggies, and side dishes.

"Blaire will be an asset to the team with her abilities to heal in case anyone"—the king's eyes shot to me as one side of his lips quirked up in a mischievous smirk—"were to become injured."

Loud smacks echoed in my ears. I tried to watch as she sauntered to the stage, but there was a pain shooting through my temple like the largest, most burly man here had just landed a severe blow to my head. King Tatum clapped his hands, causing me to flinch with each impact. An absence washed over me as Lane's hand left my side so he could join in on the applause. My hands lifted to cradle my head as I was assaulted from both sides, the sound becoming too much for me to bear.

Features on faces blurred, noses mixing into cheeks, objects and people tripling then becoming singular before multiplying again. The hands clapping and fisting in the air started to move in slow motion.

I heard screams that vibrated my insides, my stomach dropping like when I used to jump off the highest tree branches in an attempt to scare Story. Suddenly, I was looking at the gold, glimmering ceiling before it became a starless night sky.

Chapter 17

A pain so deep I could feel it in my bones awakened me, a soreness that affected every muscle and nerve, making it near impossible for me to move. While the inside of my body felt like daggers were piercing every cell, the outside was cradled by the soft caresses from the sheets and pillows of my bed. The differences were jarring.

"Hey, careful. You took a nasty fall last night." Knox's voice was hard, matching his furrowed and pained facial expression. His hands glided over me with a softness so gentle, only a hum of his energy reached me. He had the book from my pillowcase on his lap. My brain cleared from its sleepy fog, allowing panic to take over.

"How did you get that?" I shrieked.

He lifted it out of my reach as I lunged for it. "I was going to ask you the same thing."

I sat back and filtered through ways I could get him to hand it over. It wasn't needed. He handed the book to me and said, "I think it's important you learn about the hidden world. I would keep this safe if I were you; this book holds its own secrets."

I took the book from him and held it to my chest. "Thank you."

He shifted off the bed. "Oh, and tell Asahi she's not as discreet as she thinks. She can be seen even in the shadows." He winked at me. *How does he... wait!*

"I'm supposed to leave today!" I jolted up, trying to swipe the fallen strands of hair from my face, hands shaking as my eyes darted around the empty room. My muscles clenched from the sudden movement, sending another shockwave of crippling pain.

"Damn it, Amalia." The words were laced with frustration and concern. "Blaire is on her way up to heal you. She should have been here by now." His eyes shifted to the closed door across the room before settling on me. His gaze tracked from my face down my arms and over my collarbone. The areas that were exposed from the plush cocoon. My attention followed his, as he placed a hand gently along my collarbone where the forgotten bruises peppered my skin. I flinched slightly, squeezing my eyes shut at the sudden stab even a light touch brought.

"These aren't from the fall, are they? Who did this to you?" His fingers grazed the skin as he inspected me.

I batted his hand away and stepped back. "No one, I don't remember what happened."

His head tilted. "You lie, why?"

"No, I'm not." I lied again, but he would never believe me about the nightmares. He would think I was crazy.

Even concerned, he still tilted his mouth up. "I can hear your heart, Amalia. The way it skips each time you *think* about how to lie, then the way it beats faster once the lie slips from your lips." I sighed, knowing I would not win this.

"I–I've been having nightmares. They feel more like a memory." Knox placed his hand on mine before lowering us back to the bed. "I see the same scene I think, but sometimes there are slight changes. They feel so *real.*" I looked at him, expecting to see judgment. I only saw security. Everything about his calm demeanor urged me to continue. His full attention was on me. "There's always fire, destruction, horrors, but one in particular had debris flying around. When I woke up, all of these marks covered me. I know it sounds crazy, but—"

"You think the marks are from your nightmare?" he stated, not an ounce of mockery in his words.

"Is that crazy?"

He contemplated the question. "I don't think it's crazy after everything you've learned exists in this world. Even I don't know all the things possible. Dreams can be messages to those who take the time to listen. Maybe you are being told something."

He traced the marks with his thumb. "Until we figure it out, Blaire will fix this."

Absolutely not, the last time she'd healed me it hurt worse than the actual attack. It was like her name flipped a switch in me. "That bitch isn't touching me." Venom seeped out as I jerked away from him.

"That bitch," he emphasized the last word just as I had, "is the only one who can get you healthy enough for today." The bed creaked as his weight left the mattress. His back was turned to me as he paced with one hand resting on his hip and the other wiping down the front of his face in exasperation.

"I'm ready now." My nostrils flared wide, each breath coming in sharp and deliberate, a silent portrayal of my defiance. Knox turned then, his expression turning sharp and cold like the rough edges of stone. Both of us locked in an unspoken challenge.

"Amalia—"

"I have been through worse, Knox, and you and your brother need to stop treating me as if I'm incapable of doing anything. If I say I'm ready, I'm ready."

He bit his lower lip, drawing my attention as he nodded his head reluctantly, then walked out of the room without gracing me with a retort. A part of me, the rebellious, independent side, felt like I'd just won the silent battle raging between us. The other side felt a loss at his absence, making me regret the acidity I'd infused into my words.

I sat in the reading room that overlooked the gardenscape with the storybook Knox had left for me. I had wanted a reprieve for just a while after I readied my pack with all that I could. A few outfits from the wardrobe in my room, a handful of oat bars Asahi had spent most of the morning baking and wrapping, the book she had given me from the athenaeum, a bar of soap from my bathing chamber, along with a few other miscellaneous items. With anxiety running through every vein, I needed a small moment to sit in solitude, then Bash found me and decided he would bother me instead.

"What are you reading? A novel on how to survive the next few weeks?" I looked up from the current page. He wore a lopsided smirk, stretching his arms along the back of the lounge chair he sat in.

"Ha-ha, very funny." I attempted to kick him, but he lifted his legs out of the way with a chuckle. "It's actually a story about a woman who falls for a beast."

"Oh?" One of Bash's eyebrows lifted as he acted intrigued by the premise. "Do go on." His hand raised in my direction, motioning for me to continue.

"Well, if you must know—"

"I must." He adjusted his body back into the chair until he looked as comfortable as a swaddled newborn.

"The beast is actually a man who was cursed, and only the woman can save him."

Bash tipped his head back. "Let me guess, with true love's kiss?" He let out a heavy sigh. "So predictable."

"Actually, the only way she can save him is by stabbing him in the heart with a blackstone dagger while he's in his beast form." I hardened my face to portray complete seriousness.

Bash's head shot forward, his body following suit as he leaned in, interest pulsing in his features, causing me to laugh aloud.

The sound of doors swinging open interrupted my laughter. "We need to leave for Lake Aquasailies sooner rather than later," Knox exclaimed as he strode into the reading room.

"Speaking of someone who could use a stabbing," I muttered under my breath. Bash quickly moved to a standing position. A deep wave of unease washed over me at the mention of leaving. Knox glanced at me and said, "If I were stabbed, I would allow myself to be healed so I could be at my best when I inevitably go against whoever stabbed me."

Bash's eyes darted between us. "I can be ready in ten minutes," Bash said, voice more serious compared to the playful flirtation we had just engaged in. Knox simply nodded his head in Bash's direction before Bash hurried out of the room.

Clearly, we were still annoyed with each other. My chair screeched as it dragged across the wooden floor while I got up to leave. I turned to tuck my book into my pack when my body froze. The scent of amber and oak filled the air around me.

I'd grown to know that scent in such a short time, and it controlled me in a way that felt alarming. Knox was behind me.

"Going somewhere?"

His low, breathy voice penetrated my core, making goosebumps spread all over my limbs.

I turned to face him even as every inch of me screamed to run in the opposite direction. "I should go as well." I grabbed my pack and meant to walk past him, but my feet stayed where they were.

"What chapter are you on?" It dawned on me he was referring to the book he had left for me.

"Oh, um, twenty-five."

I cleared my throat as his thumb brushed the bottom of my jaw. "That's my favorite chapter," he said. "Where the tension is building, they both know they feel *something*, yet don't disclose it to the other."

"You've read it?" He'd read me pages from it, but I didn't think he had ever read the whole book.

"It was my mother's favorite; she had to have read that same copy over a thousand times." He had never mentioned her before; he was allowing me a glimpse into his life. I wondered, if the fae had been forced here, were he and the others forced as well?

"This is her copy?" I asked.

An onyx lock of his hair fell forward as he dipped his head in answer. "I thought you had to go?" he questioned.

"Oh, right." I maneuvered around him and hurried toward the exit. My body felt like energy was zapping through it.

"Tell my dearest *brother* I'll be out there soon," he called behind me. Too worried about him witnessing the flush on my face, I refrained from turning to respond. Instead, I lifted my hand, wiggling my fingers to show he'd been heard. A deep, rumbling laugh chased me, and I willed myself not to melt as I forced one foot in front of the other.

Chapter 18

Twenty minutes had passed, and we were all waiting in the training field behind the castle. A few sheep wandered about this time, keeping the length of the grass in check, otherwise it was barren of anything noteworthy. A deep moat bordered the land, ensuring no one could easily access the castle, and beyond that was an eerie, still, thick forest of deep and medium greens.

"Where the fuck is he?" Kuma complained as he sat leaning back on both hands with his legs sprawled out in the grass.

"Shut it, Kuma. He'll be here when he's here," Bash barked.

"Obviously." Blaire's eyes rolled so dramatically, I wasn't sure how they didn't fall out.

I started toward where Bash stood, eyes trained on the doors leading into the castle, when my foot caught on something and I stumbled forward. Bash caught me before I landed on the ground, and Kuma burst into wet, throaty laughter. "I really hate that guy," I seethed, righting myself.

"That makes two of us," Bash agreed, his eyes never leaving the castle.

I leaned in and whispered, "How long will it take for us to reach the lake on foot?" He grinned down at me but said nothing.

"... Great... good talk, then." Crossing my arms, annoyed, I looked over at the moat. With the water such a rich shade of blue, you could tell it was deep. A movement beyond the water caught my eye; squinting, I tried to catch sight of whatever had moved. All I saw were a few lower branches at the tree line that were swaying back and forth like something had just run through and disturbed them. The familiar dread I'd come to know well overtook me, and I felt a shudder release from my shoulders to my toes. Bash must have noticed, because in the next breath, he had his arm wrapped around me with a firm squeeze. I looked up to give him a reassuring smile that showed I was okay, but his attention wasn't on me... It was on that same spot in the tree line that I'd been looking at.

With another squeeze of his hand and a serious look exchanged between us, he validated that I was not just seeing things. Something or someone was there.

"Knox is here." Startled, I jumped and threw my hand to my chest—Lane.

Lane stepped up beside me, looking Bash up and down. "Get your hands off my girl."

Still eyeing the spot in the trees, Bash replied with, "I'm not what you should be worried about."

He let go of my shoulder and walked to meet Knox, who was throwing him a bag that was utterly stuffed to the brim.

"Your girl?" I repeated.

Lane shrugged. "You know what I mean."

"Mmmm no. I don't." I didn't like the claim he made or how he made it. We'd had no discussions on anything between us. Had there been attraction? Of course, but I wouldn't say that we were anything more than friends. "I'm not your girl. I'm not anyone's girl, I'm just trying to survive."

Kuma inserted himself into the conversation. "No one wants you anyways, human. I know I can barely stand to look at you." He nudged Blaire looking for validation. She did a mock applause for him as he went to speak again. "Hell, I can even smell you fro—"

"Listen up, fuckers, if we plan to make it to Lake Aquasailies by nightfall, we need to get a move on it. Lane, you and Bash lead the way and act as scouts for anything ahead. Kuma, you will follow behind them, monitoring the sides of our path. Blaire and I will take the rear." Knox stood tall and sure as he spoke to the others, voice never faltering or stumbling. He was clearly born to lead. No one challenged his words, and the best part, he managed to shut Kuma up.

"Amalia rides on me," Lane said, interrupting the brief.

"That's not fucking happening," Knox said without changing his demeanor or tone. *Wait... what?*

"I-I'm sorry." I spoke up, raising a finger in the air. "Did you say ride on?" The words seemed to come out as a whisper with how the two males were now speaking to each other.

"She's mine. She rides with me," growled Lane, voice now booming, chest puffed out. The anger radiating from him was palpable in the air. He proved he hadn't heard a word that had come out of my mouth. Knox stood, unphased at the outburst, his eyes darkened from lavender to violet as his attention zeroed in on Lane.

"Excuse me... but..." I squeaked out.

"Amalia belongs to no one but herself." Knox took a single step toward his brother. "If this is about your ego, *brother*," he emphasized the last word as if it pained him to say it, "then don't worry, we are still very aware of your heroic *claims* regarding her." Lane rushed in Knox's direction, closing the gap between them quickly, face red, moving with a speed only rage could produce. Bash stumbled back as he pushed his hand firmly into Lane's chest, stopping his attempt to reach Knox.

"Be smart now, Laney boy," Bash said. "You know that would be a bad idea."

Kuma got up to his feet, placing himself just behind Lane as Blaire stood in neutral territory between them. Arms crossed and a grin plastered on her face, she was loving this.

"If this is about her protection, which it must be, then rest assured she's far safer in the back with me than she would be in the front with you." Knox took another step until they were just inches from one another. "Would you really want her where the danger—should there be any—would be seen first?" He tilted his head to the side, giving Lane a lopsided smirk, showing off just one dimple. A clear challenge. "She is safest with the strongest, and that is not you."

I reached to place my hand on Lane's shoulder, hoping to calm him down. As I did, he vanished into a medley of colors. The trees beyond the moat were nothing but green blurs as I whipped through the air. The world around me whizzed by, but I saw in slow motion. The only thing I could do was focus my sight on where I had been just seconds before, where a dragon now stood.

The wind stole my gasp, and before my brain had time to react, *SLAM*, my body cracked against a thick, hard surface. Clawing at anything I could, I tried to find something to grasp. Except I was still moving.

"Oh my dragons!" I shrieked as I realized I was on an actual fucking dragon! My breath caught, and shock drowned out every other feeling. I was situated just above what seemed to be a shoulder, and the only things keeping me there were the midnight spikes I slid onto, which protruded from the scales, giving me something to perch on.

"What do I do, what do I do?" Flattening myself against the smooth, black scales, I reached out to hold the closest spike, planting my feet firmly against the ones below me. Within moments, the massive beast slammed into the ground directly in the face of another.

The dragon I was perched upon was darker than a moonless night, its scales shimmering with a faint, iridescent purple sheen in all the places touched by sunlight. Even with its two shadow-sculpted wings tucked inward toward its body, the beast was massive in every sense of the word. I felt thunder rumble from beneath me just before the dragon let out a ground-shaking bellow. I could see from its profile it was exposing lethal teeth. The second dragon cowered, just for a moment, before letting out its own call in return, lowering its head.

Trying to keep the terror out of my voice, I shouted, "Bash!" My voice cracked, chest heaving. I looked around as the two creatures stood against each other. "Little help? What do I do?" I yelled out again.

"You're okay, Amalia, stay calm. You're safe with Knox. Just hang on."

"Hang on!" My foot slipped off one of the midnight spikes, but I recovered quickly. The movement drew the attention of the dragon I was clinging to, and as its head shifted to look at me, the opposing one took its opportunity to clamp its jaws onto its neck.

"Stop distracting him and stay still."

"WHAT?!" I blurted. *I'm on Knox, I'm on Knox and he's a fucking dragon. I mean, I knew they were dragons, but, this is a real fucking dragon.*

"He's just having a little conversation with Lane about his shifting manners is all," Bash tossed back to me. "Since he could have killed you."

The dragon *was* Lane. I could tell with absolute certainty from the blue eyes lost in a sea of pure white, crystalline scales. I scanned every detail, over and over. His wings were smaller than Knox's, yet still large. They appeared transparent, except for where thousands of diamonds filled the space in sections. Each vein of the wings, from shoulder to tip, alternated from shimmering transparency to glittering diamonds. They acted as a shield, keeping the otherwise fragile skin protected where it was most vulnerable. The diamonds contorted into a solid weaving pattern, from the tips of the wings, down to his shoulders, then coated all four of his thick, powerful legs. The diamond shield coated his belly and chest until they spread over the head, just around the eyes, ending as they stretched the bridge of his nose like a war mask. Everything about his dragon form was intricate and mesmerizing. His head was adorned with sharp, porcelain-white horns that extended the length of his serpentine neck and grew larger, more rigid, and more spaced out as they arced down his body before forming into a deadly display of glass shards at the tip of his tail.

Snapping me out of my trance, the dragon I was clinging to—Knox—stomped his paw into the ground a second time, digging his claws into the soil. The power of the act made vibrations shake through me. "Baaaaashh?" Looking around, I couldn't seem to focus on anything or anyone as fear clouded my senses. "I don't think it's going well!"

"Yeah, well, Lane could have killed you, had Knox not shifted and caught you in time. That's not something I see him letting go easily."

Taking a breath, I shifted my weight to try and speak when I lost my footing. The world tilted as I slid down his scaled body. A cloud of darkness halted my plummet. Knox's muzzle broke my descent. I was perched upon the bridge of his nose. His garden of onyx horns made it apparent I was lucky he knew me. One mishap and I would have been a human skewer. Legs shaking, I kneeled, intent on speaking to him. *Can he even understand me while in dragon form?*

"Bash?"

"Yes?" He sounded annoyed. Probably because I wasn't doing a good job at not distracting him.

"If I say something to him, can he understand me, or does he only understand... growls...?"

Just as the question left my mouth, an exasperated huff came from below me, followed by the thump of his tail, sending patches of grass and dirt flying away from where it had made impact. My attention stayed on where wisps of shadows flowed around the tip of the tail.

"Did that answer your question?" Bash drawled from somewhere below, still hidden from my view.

I leaned over, meeting one slitted eye that glowed violet as I said, "I take it you understood that then?" He chuffed, and Bash could be heard chuckling.

"Okay, great... So I appreciate you saving me, and not impaling me with your spikes as you caught me. I just wanted to throw out that you caught me with your body, so... I'm already on you. Which makes this disagreement obsolete." I whispered, "You already won, how about we leave for Aquasailies?"

Knox adjusted his head until it was level with his black-horn-covered shoulders, giving me an easy path to take back to where I'd sat. I managed to stumble into a sitting position between two large, rigid horns, saddling myself in place. Lane let out a low, threatening rumble before taking to the sky, Knox biting at his tail as he lifted off.

"Was that necessary?"

We launched into the sky, wind roaring in my ears, whipping my hair into a tangled mess. My knuckles paled as I clung to the obsidian horn. Below, bodies transformed into scales and teeth, they had shifted into the magnificent creatures that used to fly in my mother's stories. An astonishing show of intimidation and beauty.

I could spot which one was Bash by the reckless way he flew. The color of their eyes all made sense as I admired Bash's emerald scales. He was so much more impressive than I could have imagined. His wings were a dark green. The vulnerable skin between the brownish wing veins was leaf-like in texture. Tangled branches with overgrown leaves decorated the top of his head, they fell down like hair along his neck, the tip of his tail a large, brown, boulder-like form. Sharpened sticks jutted from his scales instead of horns. He blended in with the landscape below, becoming nearly invisible to me. Bash made his way through the sky until he was level with Lane.

Kuma followed about five or six wingbeats behind, his aqua scales reflecting the colors of the sky. Blaire then leveled out on Knox's right side as we brought up the rear. *Just wonderful.*

We flew for hours over a thick forest that eventually thinned out, revealing a cerulean lake that the beasts circled back for, each taking passes and gulping mouthfuls as they glided over, the tips of their wings grazing the surface. On Knox's pass, he went lower, coating my skin in a cool mist before we reformed our positions in the sky.

I leaned back, trying to ease my aching muscles against a large horn directly behind me, while I stretched my arms out without falling to my death. A chuffing noise filled the air, followed by another, then another. I held onto the horn as I tried to peek at the two beasts. Blaire's long, deep red neck was turned toward Knox as she chuffed to him. *They're talking to each other.* I struggled to lean closer, but Blaire's bright red, luminous eyes flicked to me, snapping me back to my original position. That's when the giant rotten apple dipped below Knox, leveling out on his left before she veered upward and over him. She returned to soar on his right just before doing a flip. *Show off.* I rolled my eyes as she glanced back at me, clearly making sure I didn't miss the show.

"I have a message you can understand while as a dragon and a human," I said to her as she turned her massive head toward me.

I did the only thing I could think of.

I gave her a middle finger.

Smoke billowed from her nose, then I was tossed up and became momentarily airborne as Knox rolled his body. I slammed back between his horns with a bruising thud and yelled, "What was that, Knox!?" He turned his face made from nightmares and shadows to me and let out an exasperated huff as he blew black smoke out of his nostrils.

"There's no way you even saw that," I grumbled, rubbing my tailbone.

I awakened to a thundering quake as we all landed. It was nighttime, and I couldn't see anything but the glowing eyes surrounding me. One by one, the eyes shrank and disappeared as they all shifted back into their human forms. I stayed seated as Knox made no move to shift. I went to adjust but couldn't move. Black tendrils had wrapped around my waist, holding me in place.

When Bash appeared, Knox hunched into a loafing position, making it easier for me to dismount. I hesitated as the tendrils loosened and slipped away, and Bash extended a hand out. "Jump, Mal. I'll catch you, I promise." I could hear the smile in his voice.

"And if you miss?"

"Then Knox will probably eat me."

Chuckling, I hurled myself off Knox's back, which was virtually invisible in the night. Bash grunted from my impact into his body. "Oof, gods, woman!" He wrapped his arms around me, then set me down next to him.

"Sorry," I mumbled.

"And here I thought you'd stay up there all night long."

"Horns are terrible pillows," I retorted, shaking each limb to wake them up.

Bash motioned for us to head to where the others were gathered. With an elbow to my arm, he said, "Oh, really? I heard you were getting extremely comfortable between those horns of his."

Mortification filled my veins and stopped me dead in my tracks. "Wh-what are you talking about?"

Bash grabbed his stomach as a laugh blared from deep within him. "We can still communicate with each other while in our dragon forms. It's a mental connection mostly, but we can also understand the different chuffs and sounds others make as well. It's just not preferred." He tossed an arm around me as we resumed our walk toward the group. "I, for one, don't mind a lady who snores."

I slapped his hard stomach, and I glanced back to where those glowing lavender eyes tracked me.

"Why hasn't he shifted?"

Bash followed my gaze. "Nice change of subject." He sighed heavily before continuing. "He's a protective one, Knox. He's going to do a sweep around the area to make sure there's no threats lurking in the trees that surround the lake."

"What could possibly threaten a dragon?"

"You'd be surprised." He looked down at me, removing his arm before we reached the group, who were all setting up their bed rolls for the night.

"Although, I'm not sure he cares about any of these fuckers enough to do a sweep. I'm almost positive there's only one here he's worried about protecting."

"You?" Sarcasm dripped from the word as it left my mouth. He winked at me, then sauntered off. I heard Lane and Kuma's voices, Kuma's hand slashed through the air as he spoke until Lane spotted me approaching, giving Kuma a sideways glare, dismissing the conversation. Trepidation grew deep inside me. Why did I always feel as though I was being kept in the dark on a secret everyone else seemed to know? The question coiled around my throat as I watched Lane paint a smile on his face.

Chapter 19

"Amalia, I want to apologize to you." Lane's hand ran through his disheveled hair as he stumbled on his words. "I-I wasn't thinking when I shifted. I could have killed you. I-I don't know what came over me." The apology hung between us, these glimpses of the darker side of him were surfacing more frequently. His knees thudded against the cool ground beneath us. His hands clasped mine and he looked up at me, looking so vulnerable and submissive for the first time since I'd known him. "Please forgive me, Amalia."

My previous unease quieted at the sight, and my heart clenched in my chest as I looked in his shifting eyes, rimmed red with true pain and regret. My hand brushed a strand of hair that lay in the middle of his forehead lightly to the side.

"I'm just still trying to wrap my head around what you all are. How I never actually knew the world I have lived in. I don't blame you, Lane. I have a lot to learn when it comes to being around a group of dragon shifters. Mistakes and accidents are going to happen. I appreciate your apology, but it is not needed." My knees touched the ground in front of him, and I cupped his face in my hands. His forehead met mine. "You are more than forgiven."

"Let's get a fire going and make a plan for tomorrow." Lane's thumb ran over the side of my cheek as he got up and headed in the direction of the group.

"Wait!" I called after him. My voice sounded more timid than I'd anticipated. "What were you and Kuma discussing before?" Bash's laugh echoed in the background.

"We had a disagreement up in the air that needed to be addressed. It's nothing to concern yourself with, though." His features lifted in a smile as he motioned his head toward the others.

Sleeping mats of various fabrics and textures lay on the ground in a circle formation, Blaire lounging on her mat of fur that resembled a toasted slice of bread. Propped on one arm, she examined her nails, ignoring us approaching. Kuma was next to her, lying on his back with both hands resting on his chest, his attention on her. His eyes lingered on her with the only show of feeling I'd seen him express, even as she pretended everything around her didn't exist.

"Get a fire going. Now." Lane commanded. "We need to plan for tomorrow."

"I vote your little girlfriend is on firewood duty." Blaire spread her fingers out as if she'd just had them polished and stared up at Lane.

"Blaire, can't you ju—"

I stopped his retort with a hand in the air. "It's okay, I really don't mind. I need some time to myself anyway."

She sneered. "I'm sure this is all a lot for your little human brain to comprehend."

Letting out an exhale, I chose to turn and walk toward the woods; I wasn't stepping into her trap.

A heated breeze blew over me as I reached the tree line. I looked to my left, where the large beast made of shadows and smoke watched me, his amethyst eyes freezing my steps. He let out a low rumbling noise that I was sure was a warning by how my body reacted, urging me to step away from the wooded boundary.

"If you think I can understand growls, you're seriously mistaken," I said, placing my hands on my hips. As the last words left my mouth, Knox stood to his full, fearsome, scaled height. I gaped as I watched the shift happen. This time, I wasn't blown across a field. His massive, onyx-scaled body shimmered with a light so bright, it blinded me with the quickness of a lightning strike. The air crackled with hot energy, sending shivers over my limbs as the popping sounds of bones shifting and muscles contracting made me wince. Within moments, Knox's beastly frame shrank and contorted, and what once were scales were now smooth, muscular limbs. Smoky wings folded and receded into his back, and the long tail lined with dark, deadly spikes and fierce obsidian claws retracted as if they'd never existed. Those piercing eyes softened in color but kept their predatory qualities. The rest of his facial features reshaped into the man who had been occupying space in my mind. Knox strode toward me like he hadn't just been an entirely different creature. He was the man who twisted my thoughts, but I could still see a hint of the dragon's primal power in him.

"I could sense your body wanting to turn back, so I think you do understand me even if I'm not speaking your language." A dimple appeared as he smiled, coming to a stop just inches from me. My eyes spanned to the woods before drinking him in. The night hid many things, but I could make out the ripples of his body, my eyes skating down his torso where a black dragon flew up his chest, permanently marked onto his skin.

"I just seem to know you well enough to assume you're trying to tell me what to do," I said, looking at the tattoo. "I'm just grabbing some firewood before we all talk about tomorrow." Silence filled the thick, warm air as he watched me.

"It's to remember my father," Knox said, answering an unspoken question.

"It's stunning." He scoffed at that before I added on, "No really, I wish I had something to pay tribute to mine permanently like that. It shows how much love you have for him."

"You can trust your family will always be remembered," he said softly to me.

Clearing my throat, I said, "Okay, now go, I have firewood to collect." I waved my arms trying to shoo him.

"You can't be serious," he said. "The last time you were in the woods, alone, at night, you were almost killed."

I swallowed a lump in my throat. The reminder was not needed; the fear had already started constricting my lungs.

"What are you two whispering about over here?" Bash came jogging up to where we stood, too close to each other. I took a step back, attempting to run my hand through my knotted hair. "Lane wanted to game plan with you." His statement was directed at Knox, so I took the opportunity to continue my way into the forest, cloaked in midnight now that the sun was tucked away until morning.

"Bash, will you help Amalia collect some firewood while I speak with him?"

"Of cour—"

"I don't need a babysitter!" I shouted, cutting Bash off and only feeling slightly guilty for doing so. He threw a hand over his stomach like he'd just been stabbed.

"Damn, Mal, I didn't realize you hated me." His face contorted with frown lines and pitiful eyes as he feigned sadness. "Here I was wanting some time alone with you."

Knox's answering growl only made me want to egg this side of him on.

"Well in that case, I should have ridden you on the way here," I tossed at Bash with a wink before giving Knox a sly side-eye that his glare told me wasn't appreciated.

"Careful little temptress, you're playing with fire." He closed the small amount of distance I had put between us. "Literally," he purred before leaving us.

A frustrated groan escaped me as I stomped into the trees, swatting away branches and trampling the fallen leaves beneath my feet.

"Well, this will be fun," Bash said, sarcasm dripping from him as he followed me in, bending down to pick up a thick, half-rotted log I had stomped over in anger, not even seeing it. "You remember we're supposed to be picking this stuff up, right?"

"Yes, I remember." I scowled.

Minutes passed by as we silently collected wood, only the crunching foliage and a faraway owl making any sounds. Once my arms were full, I turned to let Bash know I was ready to head back. He leaned against a tall pine, one leg crossed over the other, his arms filled with thick logs that were sure to burn through the night, the stack piled up to his chin.

A boyish grin spread as he took me in.

"What?"

"What *is* the question here," he said. When I didn't respond, he continued, "What are you carrying?"

I glanced down at the pile in my arms. "What do you mean?"

"Mal, those are twigs at best."

I scoffed. "Well, I can't just pick them up and then throw them back, I would feel bad. They can still be used." An ache bloomed with my next words. "They can still be useful." Story used to say I was projecting, but a part of me had always believed everything had feelings in this world, even if we weren't capable of understanding how. In this moment, I knew I *was* projecting. I hadn't felt useful once since Cimmerian. I was always in need of a watcher or a savior. I may not be a mythical creature, but I'd like to think I was still important, I still had things to offer.

"Right." He drew the word out, trying to contain a laugh. "And how do you think they feel as they're thrown into a fire and burned to ash? I'm sure they really appreciate you picking them then."

I turned my arms down and let all the sticks fall to the ground in a messy pile and stole a few logs from his arms. I could still hear his hysterics as I broke the edge of the trees and shuffled into the open space where everyone was gathered.

I froze—the hair on the back of my neck rising.

"Everything okay?" Concern replaced the amusement he'd had just seconds ago.

I looked behind us, but all I could see was darkness, and I heard nothing but murmurs from the group.

"Yeah." My voice wavered, not convincing either of us.

Bash placed his hand on my shoulder and squeezed me gently. "You're safe, Mal." With a quick rub of my shoulder he said, "C'mon, we've got a lot to discuss and still need to get some rest." I spared one last glance into the darkness, unable to shake the feeling I was being watched.

"Here we go," I said, dropping the stolen logs into the pit. All Bash did was grin at me as he threw his handful onto the ground at Blaire's feet. She yanked her legs back with a yelp, trying to dodge the logs.

"What's your problem, Deckett?" Her voice was just below a shriek that grated against my brain.

"You are always a problem, Ravenake," Bash countered. This was the first time I'd heard some of their last names in a fully conscious state, and I tried to make a mental note of each one.

"Why don't you start the fire since we got the wood?" He plopped down onto his sleeping mat and brushed some wood chips from the fabric of his shirt.

"You expect me to start a fire? That's a male job. I don't do manual labor."

My brows scrunched together at Blaire's statement. "Uh, aren't you all fire-breathing beasts? Can't you just blow some sparks and start it?"

Everyone turned silent and snapped their heads in my direction. Blaire looked like she'd conjured at least twenty ways to kill me. "What? Fire and dragons kind of go together."

Blaire got to her feet and hustled over to me. "First of all, that's not how it works, human. Second of all, you are the last person here that needs to give me suggestions on what to do." My breaths quickened as her looming body radiated silent threats, her lip quirked up. She knew she was affecting me.

"Female drama is soooo boring," Kuma drawled. "Just come sit down, don't waste your time on her." She had no problems following his suggestions.

Bash grabbed a box of matchsticks from his pocket and ignited the logs. Flames grew, greedily eating up the decaying wood, and we all stayed silent while the fire grew more consuming. "We can't breathe fire while in our human form. That is a power only our dragon forms can handle. Our human forms could never withstand the heat and scorching. The only powers we can use like this are those that are derived from the elements around us."

"Speaking of elements, we will need Kuma for the first scale retrieval," Lane said, then shifted his focus to the lackadaisical slump who was still fixated on Blaire's every move. "Can you sense it?"

We all stared at him, waiting for him to recognize that there was attention on him.

"Why would he be able to sense it?" I asked.

My inquiry is what reached Kuma as he rolled his head to the side in my direction. "Because I am from the Hydra Horde." He scoffed at me like it was common knowledge.

"She was too busy fainting after finding out I was assigned to the team, she missed your announcement," Blaire chimed in, causing the pair to laugh and fall back onto their sleeping mats. Anger flared in my gut, wanting to strike out.

The flames of the fire sparked, sending embers showering the space we all sat around. I felt eyes on me from behind, but I didn't turn around; I knew who it was as the scent of oak roiled in the air.

I walked around the fire to where Lane sat cross-legged on his mat and seated myself on the one next to him. My pack was at the top, and I rustled through it to grab the extra blanket I had packed for myself before knowing he had supplies for the both of us. I fanned the blanket out over my lap and asked, "If Kuma can sense it, it should be relatively easy to get then, right?"

Kuma grunted and flung a piece of vegetation he had been fiddling with into the fire.

"Our ancestors would have made them difficult to acquire. Even if we can sense them, pinpointing their exact location and then completing whatever the scale requires is the real problem," Bash answered, his green eyes sparkling in the firelight as he looked at me.

"Whatever the *scale* requires?" He spoke like the scales were sentient.

Bash nodded. "Although they went skyward, they always planned to return. The scales are the magical markers claiming their old kingdoms. Should the time come for them to return, the scales would act as a beacon. They need a level of protection."

The smoke from the fire suffocated me as the slight breeze shifted, blowing it straight to me. I fought the attack with a wave of my hand, coughing out, "Why does King Tatum need them?" I coughed once more and swallowed, trying to coat my throat with something other than smoke. Across the fire, Knox stood beside Bash moving his hand in slow, languid movements, manipulating the smoke. The grayish, airy soot started to swirl and head in the opposite direction of me.

Four sets of shifter eyes were on me now. I pulled my blanket closer to me as shivers from their gazes ran over my skin.

"He didn't tell you?" Bash asked.

"No, it appears I am on a need-to-know basis and he felt that information wasn't something I needed to be aware of." I glanced between them, waiting for someone to answer me. "Do you not know either?"

"Lane knows," Kuma said, earning himself a murderous glare. Every turn, I found he was keeping more and more from me.

I shifted uncomfortably. "What does he need them for?" I didn't expect it, but he answered.

Peeling his glare from Kuma, he said, "All I know is that the power of each scale in combination with the fae relics has the ability to bring back what has been lost. I don't know any more than that." *Is he trying to bring the lands back?*

"But ho—"

"Can we please give the history lessons a rest for the night!" Blaire shouted, throwing her arms out as her lips pursed in annoyance. "Seriously, we haven't made one suggestion of where to start tomorrow, and I'd like to actually sleep tonight."

"I'd like to watch you sleep," Kuma retorted, giving her what I assumed he thought were seductive eyes. I tried not to visibly cringe, but I could feel my face scrunch in disgust. "Ew," she said, her mouth hanging slightly open as she narrowed her eyes. "Don't ever say that again. And move away from me." She started to push his mat as he fought to put it back.

"Here's how tomorrow is going to go." Knox stepped up to the fire, commanding attention. "Lane, Bash, and Kuma will scout the area in the morning, and try to gauge where the scale could be. Wherever Kuma's senses heighten, Bash will raise the vegetation. This will create a visual perimeter for us to search deeper in." Knox turned his attention to where Blaire and Kuma were still scuffling together. "Blaire, you will be on watch."

At the sound of her name, she quit her battle with Kuma. "Is that all, boss? You wouldn't want to take a swim to pass the time instead?" Her voice dripped with seduction as she leaned her body back, resting on her elbows. "It could be a clothing optional swim." She shot me a glance before situating her sultry, rose-colored eyes back on Knox.

"I'll pass," he said, not a fleck of temptation in his features. "Amalia and I will be occupied in the water."

Blaire's eyes could have cut me like a newly-crafted dagger, and I couldn't help but flash a smile at her as I mimicked her posture and rested back on my shoulders. *Wait.* "You and I will do what?" I said, snapping upright.

Blaire let out a dramatic *"HA"* before she responded with, "Why? So she can drown again?"

"I have to second her question," Lane added in a stern voice, ripping my heart from my chest as hurt consumed me. He sent me a sympathetic look. "I'm sorry, Mal, but you almost died *twice* in water. I don't think it's a good idea." The betrayal I felt wasn't at the fact he'd sided with Blaire. It was the knowledge he had clearly had a conversation about me with them behind my back. He wasn't the same Lane he'd been in Cimmerian. Or maybe I just didn't know him like I thought I did.

Knox pressed one hand to his heart. "I'm truly shocked," he said while covering his mouth with the other. I placed my curled index finger over my lip as my thumb tucked under my chin, trying to suppress my laugh. Lane's head swiveled in my direction, but what did he expect after that?

I addressed Knox, "I am not going into the water." After the spring incident, I was more than content never to put a single toe into any liquid death trap.

"You are." Knox looked from me to Lane. "She is." He went on, "Should this scale be underwater, you will need to be comfortable enough to retrieve it. King Tatum tasked *you* with retrieving them, there's no doubt in my mind whatever he is planning is bound to you taking the scales."

Dread filled my veins. He knew if he couldn't kill me, he could surely make my life nothing but constant suffering. "How can he bind anything to me? I thought he could only manipulate minds, binding me to something seems like it would require more magical ability than that."

"King Tatum surrounds himself with the power he needs," Bash said, and my mind went to the fae.

"Why don't you go with Bash and Kuma then? I can take the lake with Amalia," Lane said, treating my question like it was never spoken.

"I think we both know the answer to that." Knox's face turned cold as stone, the smoke billowing from the fire growing darker, casting shade over the bright flames. The air around us chilled, making me pull my blanket tighter.

"If we have the plan set, then let's get to sleep." Lane lay on his side facing me with his arms crossed, dismissing any further conversation. I said nothing, but my eyes wandered to Knox, who still held an emotionless expression, before I moved to my side facing Lane. I dragged my pack under my head to add a little bit of comfort. I tried to flash Lane a smile, but he returned it by shutting his eyes and adjusting slightly.

"Kuma, Blaire, do you understand the plan?" I didn't look over at Knox as he spoke, but I did wonder if the smoke was still reacting to the feelings he didn't show.

"Kuma already fell asleep. I'll make sure he's up to speed when he wakes up," Blaire said. I heard her breathe out a heavy sigh, then footsteps walking away from the fire.

I pulled my blanket up to my neck and glanced at where the footsteps stopped. Knox stood facing away from all of us, watching out into the darkness. I looked around at our small group. Bash on his back, his head resting on a bent arm, one knee up while the other lay against the ground. His eyes were closed, but I didn't believe he was truly asleep. Blaire lay on her stomach with an arm outstretched above her head and the other bent under her face like a bony pillow. Kuma was on her left with his legs curled into himself and one arm stretching to Blaire. The poor idiot even tried to get her attention in his sleep. I looked back at Knox, and my heart stung at how he chose to stand watch over these people instead of getting the rest I knew he needed.

I felt fingers clasp around mine; Lane was watching me.

"You'll be okay tomorrow," he said in a whisper.

"I know." I breathed out a long breath and shut my eyes. *You'll be okay tomorrow.* He said it like I was watching because I was worried... but I believed what he said. Something in me knew that if Knox was near, I would be okay. I couldn't explain it, but I let the feeling wrap around me.

Chapter 20

Bash kneeled, resting his palms on the ground, and channeled the magic that was naturally rooted within. Olive green blades erupted into tall stalks. They were full of small, vibrant, yellow-petaled flowers with slightly darker centers that reflected the color of the sun onto my skin as he plucked one and held it under my chin. I couldn't help but laugh, giving him a playful shove as I went back to reading.

The morning had been filled with tension as the seriousness of the day loomed over everyone. Lane had woken up before leaving to work with Kuma, they made scuffs in the dirt to show Bash where he needed to raise the perimeter. With everyone busy, I took the chance to slide out the book Asahi gave me. Something about the dynamic between everyone seemed off. Lane and Knox were both technically princes, but no one had challenged Knox taking control. I needed to learn more about them if I was stuck with them.

I flipped the yellowing pages until I landed on an illustration of two dragons, whose bodies made a circle as they chased one another. One snowy like Lane, and the other midnight like Knox. The text below read:

The skies have been torn between two ancient dragon riots: The Menticide Dragons, manipulators of the mind, and the Shadow Dragons, whose wisps of black shielded from the control. Menticides, with the ability to rewrite memories, fought for the spot above all others. The riot was met with backlash, and a primal instinct within each species showed the true alphas were those that drenched themselves in night.

The Shadow Riot was one of brute strength, yet compassionate hearts, their ability to protect and shield made the species into natural alphas. The Menticide Dragons slithered into thoughts, Shadow Dragons put up barriers. Menticides would weave lies, and the shadows would reveal the hidden truths.

Menticides used intrusion to gain power where the shadows used trust. While the Menticides fell in line after centuries of challenges, the battle would always rage.

By the lake's edge, Knox stood statue-still, his back turned to me as he stared off at the glistening water. The air here was crisp as I took a deep inhale, stretching my arms above my head. The boys weren't within sight, but I did see the perimeter of tall vegetation expanding around the water. The idea was rather brilliant; it showed the sections of the lake that the scale was more likely hiding within.

Closing the book and tucking it away into my pack, I joined Knox, staying quiet at first. Allowing myself the opportunity to soak in the beauty the lake offered.

"So... what's it like being a dragon?"

Knox kept his attention straight, but I noted how his cheeks perked up with the smirk gracing his face. It was a silly question, but I did really want to know.

"What's it like being a human?" He looked down at me, a dimple in his cheek making my stomach drop slightly.

"Mundane, well... actually, pretty awful lately. Turns out we can drop dead pretty easily." As soon as the words left my mouth, I could see the change in him. The humored expression turned haunted within the few seconds it took me to speak. Guilt gnawed at me, making me attach a joke onto the end. "But the big bad dragons of Santavarre have assured me I'm the safe one." I bumped into his side and smiled up at his tall frame, but my attempt was futile.

"Shall we do this?" he said, grabbing his shirt from behind his neck and pulling it over his head, tossing it to the ground at my feet. *Shit.*

Knox dove into the water without waiting for a response. His body broke the surface, and water flew in every direction, drenching my clothes. The ground beneath me turned damp as the wave he created washed ashore. I shook the excess water from my shoes as I muttered under my breath, "What a gentleman." He smirked as he came up for air, his wet, tanned skin glistening as the droplets caught the light. He whipped his head, tossing his dark strands to the side.

"Don't be afraid," he said, extending a hand to me while treading the water.

"I'm not afraid... I'm just not overly excited." I leaned over the bank. The water was so clear I could see Knox's legs moving back and forth under the surface. Small fish swam around, darting toward his legs then away in an instant. "They're going to bite you."

"They can surely try," he said, letting a grin come back. "Quit stalling, Amalia, get in the damn water." A laugh bubbled out between his words, failing miserably at trying to show sternness.

I shifted my weight from foot to foot before deciding to follow Knox's example. Crossing my arms, I grabbed my loose-fitting chemise I had slept in the night before. Hesitating, I continued with fake confidence and pulled it off, leaving me in only a silk bralette Asahi had given me. She'd swiped it from the cleaning rooms, saying how no one in that castle would notice one article missing when they owned more clothing than they could keep up with. Next, I shimmied out of my trousers. I knew better than to even *think* about looking at Knox.

Much like the spring with Lane, I started by sitting on the shore of the lake, easing one leg in and then the other. My arms trembled with thoughts of the creature. "The water is so warm!" I said, exhaling slowly, relishing in the warmth that put my mind at ease. I had mentally prepared to be struck with the ice-cold punch the spring had given me. I tilted my head back and soaked in the sensation, listening to the sounds of Knox treading water, slow and consistent—*swish, swish, swish.*

Tingles moved down my neck, my back, and over my legs as I felt his gaze on me. It beckoned me to open my eyes, instantly meeting his, now inches from me. The small ripples his movements made hit my submerged calves. Everything about him was taut and rigid. His jaw flexed and his throat bobbed as he swallowed.

"You look like the one that's afraid," I teased.

"Afraid isn't the word I would use." He propelled himself forward by making a sweeping motion with his arms, placing him directly in front of me. Space between us became nonexistent. It was my turn to swallow.

"What word would you use, then?" This was a dangerous game, but I couldn't stop myself from asking. His hands lay along the bank on either side of my exposed thighs.

"Tempted." His gaze didn't leave my face, but my knees were pressed against his chest, and my mind was screaming for his eyes to wander. My entire body felt like it was on fire just from his proximity.

"How am I supposed to get in when you're blocking me?" I asked breathlessly.

The dimple that appeared in his cheek as his mouth lifted made time stop.

"Well, since you can't swim, you'll have to start in my arms." My stomach did a backflip at his words.

"Ha-ha, you're hilarious."

I rolled my eyes while lifting my right leg and using my toes to press against the middle of his solid chest, right where the head of his tattooed dragon lay, making some space between us. The move backfired immediately as he looked down at my foot pressed against him and grabbed it with both hands, pressing into my arch with his thumbs. His eyes met mine as he said, "I'm not going to let you drown as you act like you know what you're doing." I sat firmly planted on the shore, heat rushing to my cheeks from embarrassment.

"There's no need to be embarrassed. We'll have you feeling confident in the water in no time," Knox reassured me with a voice that sounded like someone who had never been wrong. My teeth sunk into my bottom lip. Feeling his attention track the act, I nodded. Knox's hands moved from my thighs to just beneath my arms, effortlessly guiding me down into the water. The warm pool of emerald welcomed me as I sank slowly into it, my body prickling with goosebumps. Whether it was from the gentle caress of the water or from my body brushing against Knox's, I wasn't sure. We settled into the water, his presence as comforting as the gentle, shimmering ripples that surrounded us.

"Your heart is racing," he said in a low voice.

Even though he held me like a security blanket, it was like my muscles remembered my last experience and refused to loosen. "I'm fine, I think my body just needs to realize there's not an orbichor ready to kill me." I said the words unsteadily, glancing around us. My legs instinctually wrapped around Knox's torso and my arms were a vise around his neck.

"I've got you," he said simply. "Breathe."

"I know." I smiled. "So what now?" I asked, leaning back enough to look at him.

"You can start with releasing your death grip." His hands moved from my back to cradle my thighs, giving them a gentle squeeze. Everything he did was soft and sensual, I unhooked my legs from around him. He didn't let go of me, instead he placed one hand on my back and said, "Try and float, I'll support you."

"I don't know how to float," I said as my arms tightened around his neck.

"Trust is a big part of it." His hands skimmed down my spine, a whisper of hesitation as his fingers scraped over the bralette. "You need to trust your body and the water around you. Without that trust, you won't be able to get out of your head."

"So, how do I do it?"

"First," he said, "tilt your body back. I won't let go until you say."

I tried to do as he instructed, but my fingernails dug crescent moons into his skin as flashes of teeth and claws assaulted me. All I could see in my mind was falling into the depths of the water, sinking faster than Knox would be able to grab me as something swallowed me whole. I shuddered at the thought.

"So far, you're terrible at this," Knox said with a hint of amusement. "Trust me, Amalia."

Looking at him, I knew I trusted him. He'd offered me information when I asked for it. He'd protected me, challenged me, listened to what I didn't say. It was myself and this environment I didn't trust. "I-I do, it's just—"

"No just, if you trust me, then hold onto only that. Clear your mind of everything else. Every other thought that is holding you back, let them sink to the bottom of this lake."

"That's easier said than done." My mind was a cacophony of endless what-ifs. How could I just choose to silence them? He spoke, and it was almost like he could hear my question.

"You need to close your eyes."

Taking a deep breath, I did as he said and closed my eyes. I felt his hands move along my back, resting in the middle.

"Take three deep breaths and put your arms out. Just focus on me."

I reluctantly moved one arm from around him and held it out to my side, fully aware it was shaking.

"Good," he said reassuringly. "Now, your other one while you lean back."

My eyes shot open, but he shut the unspoken argument down. "Don't even try to protest. Focus on the feel of my hands. Focus on the support, not the fear."

Muscles seizing, I tried to do as he said, taking one deep breath in before letting it out and repeating it two more times. With each exhale, I felt myself calming, although I think it was Knox's hushed words of encouragement that affected me more. Lying back in the water, my ears were submerged, but I could hear muffled movements of Knox treading the water. I focused on the feel of his hand on my skin. I continued until the anxiety dwindled. Knox was my anchor. I started to smile as I realized I was doing it! Not only doing it, enjoying it.

"I've never considered these waters dull until this moment." I opened my eyes to look at Knox. He was looking down at me with a subtle lift of his mouth, his eyes scanning me in a curious way, like he was trying to figure me out.

Confused, I asked, "Why do you now?" This lake was anything but dull with the vibrant, aqua-colored waters.

"The lake has never made my heart falter like that smile of yours." Every nerve felt like it had been lit on fire. It had to be a practiced charm. There was no way he looked like this and came up with something like that so quickly.

"I bet you say that to all the women you teach to swim."

"Well, I will have to admit you're right." My smile flattened at his admission. I wasn't expecting him to be so honest, now I was wishing he hadn't been as I heard him laugh.

"What's so funny?" I jolted up and he grabbed my waist again as I sank, pulling me onto him.

"Just how easy it is to get a reaction from you." His fingers squeezed slightly against my flesh. "Your face didn't even let me finish my sentence, before it showed me how you felt about that."

My brows furrowed with the scowl I shot at him. "My face didn't show anything."

"It's doing it right now." He released one hand and used it to trace one of his fingers down from my forehead to the tip of my nose. "This area in particular has a lot to say. Even though I love to watch these features shift into glares, I was going to say that you would be right, because YOU are the only woman or female I have ever had the pleasure to teach, *Valkara*."

My face heated. I knew my cheeks were the deepest shade of pink, like the poppies that used to bloom in early spring at the base of the Godival Mountains. "You're insufferable."

"You love it," he rumbled, adjusting his grip on me.

"I actually think it's rather repulsive," I shot back.

His thumb started tracing circles against my thigh. "Lie again and I'll drop you."

I couldn't stop the lift of my cheeks. "Now who's the liar?" His answering smile sent butterflies fluttering through my stomach, forcing me to look away. *What was this male doing to me?*

"See, now your face is relaxed again. No scowl in sight." Knox's knuckles ran over my cheek before I felt his hand embrace beneath my waist once more.

"Well, so far I can float!" I blurted out, trying to change the subject.

"With support," he retorted, turning his body and leaning against the shore. You'd never know when standing on the grassy land that with just one step, you'd sink to unending depths. Just beneath the surface was what looked like a cliff face. Almost like something had cut or struck the land with immense force. There was no smooth transition from land to water. Looking out, I saw patches of green growing thick and tall—Bash.

"Can I ask you a question?"

He lost some of the playfulness in his face, bracing for what could come out of my mouth, I'm sure. "Always," he answered.

"How did you and Bash become friends? You two seem really close, I imagine you've been in each other's lives for a while." Knox swam us over to the edge of the lake and held me until I grabbed hold of the side. We rested our elbows along the blades of green as he contemplated my question.

"Bash was orphaned during the war. Our parents were close. Bash's father was trusted just as highly in the Florauna Horde as mine was in the shadows. We spent a lot of time getting into trouble while our fathers convened with the other leaders." That admission tore a laugh from me. "When his parents were killed, my mother and father took him in without question. We were inseparable, and he is the only one I consider a true brother. I trust him with my life."

I hummed in understanding. "Your friendship reminds me of my best friend. We were each other's other half. The friend equivalent of a soulmate." Sadness threatened to pull me under the glistening waters, but I snapped myself out of it. "Well, let's get back to it then. Shall we?"

The next six hours were grueling. Knox and I worked on my confidence in the water, different strokes, going under the surface while holding my breath, and he changed up how much and how little support he offered me. By the end of the last hour, I had mastered what he called dragon-paddling. I was decent at a few other strokes without any help from Knox, but the prospect of navigating this entire lake looking for a single scale... Impossible. Exhaustion had crept into every inch of me after we had made it close to a small island within the lake Knox said was named Eye Island. "I don't think I can do this for much longer," I said between breaths. "We should take a break on the island before we swim back," I whined, flipping onto my back to float. I could hear Knox's muffled words as my ears were submerged, but I couldn't make out what he said. I went to lift my head and realized I couldn't move. I was locked in place.

A deep hum started, turning into something more violent, vibrating the otherwise still waters around me until the noise penetrated my head. I could only gasp for breath at the excruciating sensation, like someone had driven a knife into my skull and proceeded to twist it slowly. I tried to scream, but I couldn't open my mouth. A tear slid from my left eye, striking the water. The second it bonded with the emerald blue, the torture ceased. Relief only lasted seconds until it was replaced with fear as I heard a melodic voice from below.

"Amalia, descendent of Mikulec the Cruel. Come, come to me and take what you seek."

My heart began to beat faster than a hummingbird's as the ancient voice spoke to me. To me, by name. Still paralyzed and unable to speak, I thought instead. *"H-How do you know who I am?"*

The voice raised to a screech. *"Don't ask such frivolous questions, girl!"*

Terror and panic ran through me. I didn't know how to end this, I didn't want to anger something that was in my mind. Knox's silhouette was a blurred shadow at the edge of my vision. *"You are distracted by the shifter,"* the voice said just before a geyser of water sent him shooting into the air. I caught only a glimpse of his body arcing into the sky. With the piercing hum gone, it allowed me to hear the impact of him hitting the water, causing my heart to drop. It wouldn't allow him near me while it had my attention.

"Clever girl. Amalia, descendent of Mikulec the Cruel. Come to me and take what you seek," the voice repeated.

Shoving what emotion I could down, I allowed myself to think. Come to me and take what you seek. The only thing that could be was the scale. *"You mean the scale? The dragon scale. I come to you, and you will allow me to take it?"*

"Yessssss, the scale of those who sought the sky. Come to me and take what you seek." The voice drifted softer as it said the repetitive phrase once more. Still unable to move, it clearly wanted something else from me.

"I will come tomorrow when the sun reaches its peak. I, Amalia, descendant of Mikulec the Cruel, will come and take what I seek." With my parting words, the hum returned, setting my brain on fire. I wanted to scream, needed to scream, to relieve the intense pressure.

Warmth wrapped around me. "Amalia! Amalia!" My name on his tongue penetrated the pain, chasing it away. Strong arms wrapped around me until I was pulled to a bare chest that radiated safety. "Shhh, shhh, you're okay. I'm so sorry." Knox shushing me was all it took for me to realize I was screaming. I could move again, no longer paralyzed by the voice beneath the surface.

Everything around me dimmed.

I wasn't sure what time it was when I woke up, but Kuma snored so loud, he almost drowned out the crackling fire. Empty bedrolls occupied the space where Lane, Bash, and Knox should have been. I looked to the lake and the forest behind me and saw no sign of them. I grimaced as I got up and walked to the edge of the lake. I didn't think I'd ever have a good experience in a body of water. My hands balled into fists at the memory of having no control over my body, at the intrusion into my mind. Blinking rapidly, I feared I must be hallucinating or suffering brain damage, because there was a glowing trail from where my feet were planted, leading to the exact spot where I had been earlier. The area pulsed with glowing aqua light, beckoning me to it. I felt it in my bones, the call to me.

"What do you think you're doing that close to the water?!" I was hauled backward, and air left my lungs from the surprise when Lane whipped me around to face him. "You could have fallen in! What were you thinking?" he said as his jaw worked.

Annoyance laced the words that came out of my mouth. "I know how to swim now, I'm not worried about falling in." Ripping my arm from his grasp, I faced the water once more. This time, the glowing trail was gone. "Did you see something in the water?" I asked, fully believing I had conjured up a hallucination.

"What? No, I only saw you making poor choices," he bit back.

Spinning on him, whatever words I was about to throw at him were swallowed as Knox and Bash made their way to us.

"Where were you guys?" I shouted.

"I see someone woke up on the wrong side of their coma," Bash said, coming up to me and wrapping his arms around me in a tight hug.

I couldn't help but melt into the gesture. "Coma?" My brows twisted in confusion.

"Yeah, that's what I called it anyways. When you get possessed, then pass out for hours. Blaire even kicked you in the ribs to wake you, and nothing," Bash explained.

My hand instinctively went to my side, where I did feel a slight pang of pain now that he said something. "How sweet of her." My eyes rolled, and I turned back to the water, squinting. Trying to catch sight of the glow.

"What happened out there, Amalia?" It was Knox this time. His tone was so different from how it usually was when he spoke to me. It sounded as if he had to force the words out.

"Yeah, there we were, finishing up the perimeter, making our way back to camp, and all I see is Knox over here flying for the first time without his wings." I looked back at them just in time to see Bash reenacting what was supposed to be Knox flailing backward before he started laughing from recalling his perspective.

Knox gave him a shove before focusing his attention back on me.

"She doesn't need to go into it tonight. This is a conversation that can be had in the morning," Lane said.

My eyes turned into moons and completed a full lunation at the fact this was one more thing he thought could be put off until another time. "You like to put a lot of important things off until *later.*" The muscles in his jaw clenched, but he didn't entertain my jab.

"Amalia?" Knox said my name like a question. It had a hint of force, but was more of an invitation to speak if I wanted.

"I know where the scale is. I have to go back into the lake and get it tomorrow when the sun is highest in the sky." What I didn't say was... that *it* was expecting me.

Chapter 21

"I don't like this," Lane said the next day. He had been pacing so much I was getting dizzy. He passed by me for what must have been the hundredth time, sighing heavily.

Contradictory to how Lane was reacting, as the sun shone brightly high in the cloudless sky, I felt a peace about what I was about to do. I'd said nothing to anyone about the voice I heard or the luminescent trail I'd seen. Not that they hadn't asked... incessantly. It wasn't that I didn't want to, it just felt like I shouldn't. Something pulled the words from my tongue every time I tried to speak about it. All night, I kept coming back to the same thought about the trail I had seen: it couldn't have been a trick of the mind. *It* was showing me the path I needed to take. The more I thought about it, the more confident I became in my conclusion. If it wanted me dead, I would be. Had it inflicted pain? Yeah, but I was certain that was the price for communicating with thought. Entering one's mind. Communicating in someone else's head couldn't be a painless task.

"I hate to say it, but I have to agree with him," Bash said.

"I will add that I'm not too happy about this either. Especially after what happened yesterday." Knox walked up to chime in his disapproval. It was the first thing he had said to me after his mood swing yesterday. He'd walked away after I had told them I knew what I had to do. He didn't even so much as look at me the rest of the night, not even when Lane came to lie beside me. Not that he should've cared, but it seemed like that would have always gotten his attention, until last night.

"Don't worry fellas, I'll watch over her." Kuma stood between Bash and Knox, giving them two rough pats on their shoulders. Neither looked convinced.

"I'll be fine." I tried to soothe their worries. I tried to let them see in the way I stood tall that I really believed the words I said.

"How are we supposed to believe that when you won't explain what happened out there? Don't you realize we could help you?" Knox's voice was almost a shout, filled with frustration. I couldn't blame him; he knew better than anyone what had happened. He'd seen me paralyzed, heard my guttural screams even when I didn't know I was making a sound, and he had been blasted away from me by an invisible force within the water. He wasn't wrong, they could help, they probably would know what it was that had entered my mind. I should have told him. I *should* tell him. I went to open my mouth, but something stopped me. Like it was a secret I didn't have permission to share yet. So instead, I asked him to do something he had asked of me.

"Trust me." I gave him a reassuring smile before looking at Kuma. "Are you ready?"

"I'm always ready, little human. I think we should start searching in the middle where the depth is greatest. That's more than likely where it will be hidden away." Kuma tugged his navy tunic off, exposing his bulbous yet taut stomach.

"Seems like she's too afraid. Why else would she be standing around hesitating?"

Kuma laughed and threw his shirt to where Blaire was now standing, her arms had been crossed except to catch the sweat-stained tunic that I was sure reeked of body odor and smoke.

"You're supposed to be on watch," Lane reminded her.

She clicked her tongue. "Aw, and miss the death of this rat?" She spat the words in my direction. "No way, I need to see this." She shot me a menacing smile that promised to enjoy whatever awful things might happen to me. I brushed off her words and gave her no reaction.

"Find a way to signal if you guys need help. Lane will be watching from the sky, but Knox and I will be here on shore, ready to jump in when needed."

"*If* needed," I corrected Bash. His disapproving look made me amend my statement. "We will." I could handle upsetting Lane and Knox, but Bash, he was too pure. "Now let's go," I said to Kuma as I stripped down into nothing but undergarments, which included my last bralette, since the previous one had burned up while drying by the fire from a rogue ember.

I sank onto the lakeshore, letting my fingers tangle in the blades of grass, until they dipped into the warm water.

"Try and keep up, human." Kuma tossed the words at me, jumping into the lake, causing water to erupt into the air as he disappeared under the surface. I watched the disturbance until the angry sloshing settled into gentle ripples. He had been under the water for at least forty-five seconds, if not longer. I looked behind me, where everyone appeared completely unbothered, so I followed suit and slipped into the lake. The water embraced my collarbone, then my neck, then my head as I dipped underwater, scanning the area for Kuma. Snapping my head down, I could barely make out a moving figure. The figure was so far away, I couldn't accurately distinguish if it was him or just a large fish.

I broke the surface, running a hand over my face to clear the water from my eyes as I said, "I think I see him, but he's insanely far. I don't know how he made it with only a breath." Worry laced the words, not because I cared for him... I'd even go as far as to say I loathed him. Nonetheless, I needed his experience and knowledge of this lake to help me retrieve the scale. Blaire snorted loudly, breaking my thought.

"He's a Water Dragon," she said, drawing out the last two words like that title explained everything. Which I supposed to them it did; however, I was still left feeling in the dark

"Yeah, we've already covered that." I could feel my face contort in agitation as I flung my hand in the air. "Hence why he's helping me." I hadn't read that far into the book on their different species, so I didn't understand the importance, other than I figured he would be able to manipulate water like Bash could nature.

"Water Dragons have the ability to breathe while submerged," Knox clarified for me.

"They can also manipulate water," Lane said, casting a look to Knox. "They can control its movements and form," he added.

"So, he just left me then?" My voice, I was starting to believe, would now always have a slight edge to it.

"What? Afraid to be in the water without someone to hold you afloat like a child?"

I inhaled deeply before exhaling my need to strike this bitch right in the nose. Anything to knock her off the high horse she believed she sat on. I didn't need Kuma. I knew where I needed to go... I thought. Following a glowing trail apparently only I was able to see, and trying to contact an invisible entity that had literally attacked my mind the day prior shouldn't be too difficult. What could go wrong?

"Good luck," I heard Lane say to me as I ducked underwater. I tried to remember the trail I'd seen the previous night, but the lake was harder to navigate beneath the surface. I had only made it a few feet when I heard a slightly muted rumble, like the ground shaking. A few forearm-length fish that had been swimming below me jolted off in various directions. Above me, I saw the shadow of large wings flying over. That sound must have been from Lane shifting. A mix of emotions fluttered through me, our...

relationship hadn't been the same since the shimmer. There was tension between us now. His personality would shift from menacing to sweet. He'd kept so many things from me, and I couldn't help but assume there was more he wasn't telling me, making me feel like I was in a constant state of being frustrated with him more than caring for him.

Air filled my lungs as I broke the surface and heard the loud bellow of Lane's call as he circled around my general vicinity. Quickly stealing a glance at the shore, I saw Bash standing rigid. Blaire was next to Knox—right next to him—with a finger trailing down his chest. I could taste the jealousy, ready to lash out, until I saw him swat her hand away, snarling something that made her storm off toward the tree line. I'd have given anything to know what was spoken. I submerged myself once more. Kuma was still as a board and his eyes beamed a deep blue, just inches from my face, wearing a horrifying smile.

Thrashing backward away from him, I breached the surface, choking on water. Lungs burning and vision disoriented from panic, I tried to get my bearings and calm myself. It was just unexpected. An overreaction. How was I supposed to face the... *thing* in the depths if I couldn't even handle Kuma suddenly near me?

"Amalia!" Bash and Knox yelled out for me in unison.

"I'm fi—" Mid-reply, I was forced downward, pulled deeper than I had been. Above me, the sunlight shrank quickly, becoming just a dot of light. I pumped my arms, kicked my feet like Knox had drilled into me, but I wasn't going anywhere. It was the orbichor all over, the panic, the descending farther into the depths, flashes of teeth and ghosts of claws scraping my skin and tormenting me.

Looking down, I could see Kuma wearing a sickening smirk, whereas I was consumed with terror. Kuma had started to shift, his lengthy tail propelling us deeper until I felt like my ears were going to explode. His arms and back were dusted with hints of scales, while his hands, which clamped my ankles, had transformed into claws. I could hear distant sounds above me—was it Knox and Bash jumping into the lake? They'd never see me. They'd never be able to get to me. Kuma's speed was shocking, yet time seemed to be slowing down the farther I was dragged. Pressure built and my ears popped painfully, sending a sharpness through my head. My lungs felt like they'd been set on fire while someone placed bricks on my chest. I needed to breathe. Just one breath. If I weren't in a lake, tears would have been streaming down my face. Anger built inside as I fought to break free of him, growing with each failed attempt.

I didn't see it, but I felt it, the moment something in the blue void stirred.

I felt Kuma release me as my body was thrown to the side. Immediately, I tried for the surface, but it was so dark at this depth, I no longer knew which way was up.

"Did you really think I wouldn't take this opportunity to make sure you wouldn't survive?"

He could fucking talk underwater.

My hands clawed at my throat as I realized I was going to die there. My mouth involuntarily opened as my body fought for its survival. I could hear Kuma laughing, and I wished more than anything that it wasn't the last sound I would hear. He wasn't the last person I would see.

The laughing stopped abruptly, and I felt a peaceful presence wash over me.

"Take a breath."

The voice consumed every part of me but sounded like it surrounded me. My body didn't hesitate to obey the command. There was no time to question and worry about the fact I might inhale water and would likely kill myself faster. The second my mind heard the words, it had to comply. I had never sucked in a breath as violently as I did then. My life literally depended on it. My lungs filled with air, but the burning stayed, as did the pressure on my chest. It took a handful of moments before those sensations dulled, leaving only slight aches.

"The one who should not have survived, fated to save them all. You have come."

I blinked rapidly, so utterly confused on what the fuck was happening.

"Whe-where are you?" I stuttered out, looking around as I stayed afloat in the depths. There was a shimmer around me, producing the slightest amount of light. Not enough to see what this thing was, but it was enough for me to see Kuma. A darkness, cruel and vengeful, that lurked inside me smiled just for a moment as I took in the sight. His body was floating just beyond me. Contorted in a forced back bend, his arms crossed behind his back and his head bent so far toward his shoulder blades I could make out the veins and tendons straining in his neck. How hadn't it broken? His legs were bent so they almost touched his head. I could see the faint shifting of flesh to scales, his body trying to shift but unable to. If I could make out much else, I would guess his skin was a blood-red shade with how much pain he looked to be in. Yet, there was no part of me that could care at that moment. He had almost killed me; he had *planned* to kill me.

The voice broke me out of my realization.

"I am everywhere and nowhere, Amalia, descendant of Mikulec the Cruel." It hissed the words out like a snake.

"That's helpful."

"You have come to take what you seek."

"I have," I said carefully, shooting Kuma a glance. Even with the conversation yesterday, no part of me thought that this was going to be easy. Now that my mind was functioning clearly again, logic was telling me to proceed with caution unless I wanted to end up like Kuma.

"I require something from you in return. I give nothing, for nothing."

"I don't know what I could possibly give you. I really have nothing." Exasperation broke free as I struggled to mentally go through everything I owned, but there was nothing I possessed that could ever make an invisible water creature feel like it made an even trade.

"A sacrifice." That was all it said to me.

"A sacrifice?" I couldn't have heard it right. Shivers raced down my back.

"A life for a life. Blood for blood."

"I'm sorry, I don't understand. I don't need a life." Confusion was making my thoughts murky. "I just need a scale that is believed to be somewhere in this lake."

Pain erupted in my head, making me cry out from the sudden attack, before I heard it scream its next words into my mind.

"The sacred scale of the Water Horde was left behind after many lives were massacred! Blood was spilled. You must give a life. Blood for blood."

My hands trembled as they floated beside me. I hadn't recognized the lack of pain during this interaction. It had taken the opportunity to remind me what this could be like, and I wanted no part of it.

"I-I need to sacrifice myself?" I couldn't do that. The only reason I was getting the scale was to make sure I survived. If I didn't get it, I'd die either way.

"A life for a life. You are not fated to die on this day."

I played its words back as they circled around me, a life for a life. If it didn't see me dying today, then... I looked over to Kuma's mangled form. "His life?" I asked warily. "You want me to sacrifice his life?"

A low, approving hiss swirled around me. Then I heard Kuma's garbled gasps as he choked out the words, "P-please... do-don't d-do thi-sss."

Could I do this? Could I truly make a choice like this? If I did, would that make me any better than King Tatum? Would it make me worse? King Tatum had given me the choice to do this or die. Kuma would have no choice.

"He has already made the choice; he tried to kill you," the voice whispered into my ears. *"He would have succeeded if not for my intervention. He will try to kill you again."*

He had tried to kill me, and I believed he would try again. Males like him didn't like failure, and everything I'd seen of him screamed cruelty. He took pleasure in others' pain.

"The choice is easy, but you must choose."

It didn't take long for the choice to settle on my soul.

I couldn't stop the words from pouring out of my mouth or the toothy smile that accompanied them. "Did you really think I wouldn't take this opportunity to make sure you wouldn't survive?"

Kuma choked out a sob, and the entity that seemed to be the water itself squeezed his body closer together. I watched as his feet surpassed his shoulders and the skin on his neck started to tear, dying the water a crimson. The deep red his body needed fading to light pink the farther from him it traveled.

"You have fulfilled what is needed," the voice said in its drawn-out way. *"Use what you must of him to reach the surface."* My brows furrowed at what that was supposed to mean. I was quickly distracted as I noticed a glowing shape about ten feet to my right, lodged between large black rocks. Was *it* the scale?

"You are capable of more than you realize. The power of all consumes you. Use it, Amalia, one who is meant to restore."

Kuma screamed out as his body contorted in on itself. The area around me that had been a veil clouding me vanished, and water intruded into my lungs once more. A panicked scream ripped from my throat, causing a slew of bubbles to break the still waters. My thoughts started to race as I was forced back into a panicked state. Air. I needed air, I needed to breathe! I moved my arms in a sweeping motion and kicked my legs with all the force I could. The only thing I cared about at that moment was breathing, surviving. *Breathe, breathe, breathe,* I screamed inside my head while my lungs felt like they were pooling with lava. The next moment felt like a miracle as I took an actual breath. I sucked in as much air as I could in the next breath. How was this possible?

Below, I spotted the scale glowing among the darkened bottom and decided I would ask questions later. I propelled myself down like Knox had shown me. It took me a few moments of struggling before I got the hang of it and grabbed hold of the closest rock. I used the rocks' faces as anchors to pull me toward the scale, and as I drew nearer, I could see that the water around the scale was rippling in consistent rings. I reached my right hand out to grab the scale, and as soon as my flesh connected with its smooth texture, I became blinded by a light that swept through the entire lake. I instantly let go to shield my eyes that had become accustomed to the midnight hues that deep. When the light shining through my hands diminished, I looked again. The scale had broken free from where it was lodged and floated in front of me. The color was a pearlescent blue I had never seen before. If this was just one scale, I couldn't fathom the beauty that would have been this entire dragon. Kuma's form had looked nothing like this. I hesitantly reached out to grab it once more and was relieved when nothing happened. Turning the scale over in my hands, I didn't see anything... out of the ordinary about it. There were no markings, there was no real weight to it. It was simply a scale. I gripped it tightly and propelled myself off the rocks below.

"Swim fast, defier of death. You are running out of time."

The voice startled me. I'd thought it had already left me. "What is your name?" I spoke aloud.

"I was once called Zarakruae, but now I have no name."

My heart ached at the thought of losing yourself, to believe you had become nothing. "Thank you, Zarakruae, you have truly saved my life." It was true, without the scale, I would have been killed, and without its interference, Kuma would have killed me. How the tables had turned for him.

"Swim fast now, so you can save them all."

I kicked my legs as if I were sprinting on land, while using my arms to gain momentum upward. I felt the water around me pushing me, closing the distance to the surface even faster. I glanced behind me just in time to see Kuma's body be completely pulled apart. He had been torn from the middle, stretched until the skin on his torso ripped apart. The fish in the area dashed to his convulsing body to eat up the bits of organs and sinew that floated in the once-pristine water. Nausea crept up quickly, and I had to force myself to look away. He'd decided his fate when he'd attacked me. My fingers reached for where I could see the sun shining once again above the lake, excitement took over until I sucked in water, no longer graced with the ability to breathe underwater.

My head broke the surface, and I choked out a few water-filled breaths before I was yanked into strong arms and pulled onto land.

"What the fuck happened, Amalia!" Knox roared the question in one ear while Bash was shouting, "What happened to the 'signal if you need help' plan?!" in my other ear.

I rolled out of Knox's suffocating hold, spread out on my stomach, and soaked in the feel of the land beneath me. Dirt, wonderful, beautiful dirt and grass. "I never want to leave land again," I whimpered, unashamed. I spread my fingers through the blades and felt a smooth surface instead. The scale. I bolted upright and held it with both hands. "I got it! I got the scale!"

"I don't give a flying fuck about the scale, Amalia!" The anger emanating from Knox killed my brief moment of excitement. He snatched the scale from my weak hands and *threw* it! My eyes widened in horror as I watched it soar through the air back toward the lake. Just before it reentered its watery tomb, Lane swooped down and grabbed it mid-air with his large, pearly claws. I slumped down in relief and watched as he flew to where the group had landed on the first night. I looked away as he shifted and set my dagger eyes on Knox.

"You asshole! Do you have any idea what I went through to get that? And you just threw it like it meant nothing!" I got to my feet and stomped toward the fire to warm up. Shivers had taken hold, whether it was because of the soaked clothes I wore or the adrenaline of what happened in the lake wearing off, I wasn't sure.

"No, I don't, because you won't answer my very simple question of what. The. Hell. Happened." Knox was on me within seconds, his eyes filled with a mix of worry and anger as he stared at me, waiting for my response.

"We saw you struggling, and then you just vanished, Mal. We tried to jump in to grab you, but you were nowhere. We didn't know what to do. You were supposed to signal if you needed help," Bash said to me with a little more empathy in his words.

I looked behind me to the landing area in the field where Lane was. He was talking with Blaire, who snapped her head in my direction. I noted the scale, now in his hand, and faced the two males interrogating me. "I'll explain everything once everyone is here. I'm going to say this once, and then I'm going to sleep." I didn't care that it was still early afternoon; I was exhausted and needed to rest at least for an hour or two.

Blaire and Lane made their way to the three of us who were sitting by the fire. I was warming my hands while Knox and Bash stared holes into my head.

"Where is Kuma?" Blaire asked sharply, raising one brow and placing her hands on her hips.

"What is that?" Lane looked out to the water, where there was a distinct section that had been tainted with a deep reddish hue.

"Well, Lane, the answer to Blaire's question is actually the answer to yours." Zero emotion filled my voice. Any care I would have had, had been erased under that lake. They both looked at me with their mouths open and eyes so wide I had to hold in an inappropriate laugh.

Blaire stepped toward me, her hands balling into fists. "You better be lying, you filthy—"

Her words were cut off as Lane put an arm out to stop her. "Let her explain," he said while visibly straining to hold her back.

"What happened out there, Amalia?" Knox's eyes were narrow and looked over me slowly, analyzing me. His head tilted to the side, and his mouth turned down as he waited for me to share the story.

Sluggishness was winning over my last ounce of energy, but I managed to fill them in.

"Kuma tried to kill me," I said flatly. "He dragged me down to the bottom of the lake, saying how I was foolish for thinking he wouldn't take the opportunity to end me."

"You're a liar!" Blaire screeched, lunging for me again, still held back by Lane, who said nothing. His hardened jaw and neutral gaze were giving me no information on how he really felt. Did he think I was lying too? Kuma and Blaire were obviously close, I had seen that, and she did deserve to know what happened to him, but I didn't have it in me to hash this out right now.

"If that's what you think, then fine. I don't care. I don't have the energy to fight with whatever feelings you're having. He did try to kill me, and he was almost successful until—" I trailed off, not sure how to explain Zarakruae to them. How do you describe something—someone?—you never saw.

I must have been silent for longer than I realized, because Bash urged me on. "Until..."

"I'm sorry." I rubbed my hands over my face and listened to the crackling of the fire for just a second longer before I continued. "I don't really know how to explain it."

"Try," Lane said flatly. It was a single word, but it told me more than his trained expression did.

"There was something else in the water. I don't know if it guarded the scale, if it is the scale, or if it just happened to live within the lake. It saved me."

"What do you mean, something else?" Lane asked, while everyone else stayed silent. Even Blaire paused her attempts to come at me.

I felt like saying its name to them would be disrespectful in some way, like no one else should hear it, so I kept that bit of information to myself. "I never saw it, only heard it. I could hear it in my mind, clear as day. It told me if I wanted the scale, I'd need to make a sacrifice."

"A sacrifice?" Blaire screamed. "You fucking sacrificed Kuma, you stupid human bitch!"

"*Drak vahr Drak,*" Knox whispered under his breath. My brows pulled together. He had said words like that I didn't understand before, it felt like I should know them. A familiarity I couldn't quite place.

Lane was struggling to keep Blaire contained, and Bash had to rush to help control her as I continued. "I didn't hesitate," I said, letting my stare harden to match Blaire's. "I don't regret it. He sealed his fate the moment he tried to kill me."

My words were her last straw.

Chapter 22

Blaire shifted right where she stood, launching Lane into the tall grass. The air grew thick as her hatred became palpable, and the ground beneath me vibrated as she transformed. I stood and faced her, taking in the sight. Even though she could easily kill me, there was no denying how captivating it was to see them change.

Her skin shimmered as the change happened, and she was surrounded in a fiery glow a much deeper red than any normal flame. Her body became elongated as her arms and feet turned into thick, scarlet-scaled legs with deadly black claws. Her eyes looked like pools of lava as she homed her sight on me. Instinct kicked in and I stepped back a few feet.

"Um, guys... pretty sure she plans to eat me," I warned the group. Lane, who was trying to crawl his way out of the grass, was muttering obscenities.

"Pretty sure you egged her on, Mal," Bash said as he moved to stand protectively next to me.

Blaire's face was now made up of a long, garnet snout, with matching spikes on top of her head. She inhaled, and I regretted how I'd handled the conversation instantly. The ground shook violently, making Bash and I share a look because Blaire hadn't moved. That's when we heard a deep snarl behind us.

Blaire lowered her neck but bared her teeth at the giant obsidian dragon standing tall, shadows taking over its wings and flowing from the tip of its tail. Knox had shifted. He didn't flinch as Blaire snapped her large jaws in his direction. They were both ginormous, but Knox stood easily five feet taller than she did, his stature much wider. The only one who rivaled his size when shifted into their dragon form was Lane. Blaire roared, motioning her head to the sky before snapping her teeth at his body. This time, she made contact, and I watched as red flowed from the top of his right hind leg. That decision cost her. Before she could draw back, Knox latched onto her neck with a sickening crunch. My ears were pierced by the sound of her pained wail before he lifted her off the ground and threw her toward the tree line. She crashed and flattened the thick trunks like they were made out of nothing, the sound of branches cracking and the trees connecting with the ground along with her body drowned out the wails. She lay limp, and no one moved for several moments.

"Did he just kill her?" I asked quietly. Knox must have heard me anyway, because he let out a huff before he headed toward her, shifting back into his human form with each step.

"No, he just reminded her of the pecking order here. She's from the Mending Horde, which means she's too valuable to lose. If any of us got seriously injured, we'd be screwed without her," Bash said, motioning me to sit down.

Instead of sitting, I decided I would lie on my makeshift bed. I feigned ignorance like I didn't have my secret book tucked away in my pack. "There's a pecking order? Aren't you all friends? Not that I'm complaining, I had no desire to be an afternoon snack."

"I wouldn't call us all friends, but to answer your question, yes. The different hordes all have different abilities, different levels of power. Some are more powerful, more dangerous than others." Bash sat on the ground next to me and pulled a nearby blanket over me, wrapping me in warmth. This was going to put me to sleep so fast, but I fought the urge to close my eyes.

"What are the different abilities?" I asked as a yawn broke up my words.

"Well, if you haven't noticed, I pull power from and can manipulate nature, any solid natural resource. Kuma can... could manipulate water, since he was a part of the Hydra Horde. He could also exist within it just like we do on land." What Bash was saying made sense in how he had been able to speak to me underwater with no adaptation needed; it was just like he would have above the water. How was I going to survive collecting the rest? Would they all demand a sacrifice?

"Do you think I'll survive this?" I looked up to see Bash looking over at where Knox must have been checking on Blaire. I didn't have the energy to move, though.

"Hm?" was his reply.

"The scales, do you really think I can do this?" I shifted to lie on my side so I could face Bash as he spoke.

"How about you get some rest. We can talk about everything once you wake up. I'll make sure to wake you in a couple of hours," Lane chimed in, walking over as he grabbed a blade of grass from out of his hair.

Another yawn broke free, making my eyes water slightly. "I don't think I can with how bright it is." I knew for a fact I could with how close sleep was to taking me right then, but I wanted to know if Bash thought I could do this. I wanted to know all of this wasn't for nothing.

"Knox is coming," Bash said.

I propped myself on an elbow and looked out at the tree line. I saw him walking up and—oh my gods! "What the hell, Bash, he's naked!" I slammed my hands over my face. "I didn't see anything... just a slight... swinging motion."

Bash laughed so hard he fell over from his sitting position while Lane shouted, "Put some damn clothes on, Knox!"

I let out a groan that lasted several seconds as I contemplated whether I should have just let Blaire swallow me whole. "Why is he naked? You guys weren't the first night we got here!"

"Knox landed farther away than we had and later. He was giving us time to get situated before you were bombarded with more than you'd care to see," Bash said through the fit of laughter he was trying to subdue. "Then he went and conducted an area check after you were on your feet. When you saw him shift, it was dark, and you were in the woods. He was definitely naked, you just didn't notice." He ran a hand through his thick brown hair, still wet from when he had jumped into the lake before adding, "Shit, I needed that laugh."

I sent the most murderous glare I could muster his way. I heard Knox approach and gather what I assumed were clothes. After a few moments, I felt a nudge to my legs, so I looked up to see him fully dressed, though I could feel my face was still painted a light shade of pink.

"What even happens to your clothes?" I said with a high-pitched voice.

Bash snorted, trying to keep from laughing again before he said, "The power it takes to shift usually disintegrates any clothing. Sometimes there are scraps found after, usually it's all just, *poof*, gone," he said, using his hands for effect.

"You need to get some rest, but is there anything else you feel we should know about what happened down there?" Knox asked me this with no pause, only a slight hint of skepticism in his voice. It put me on edge, and I could feel myself growing defensive.

"I was able to retrieve the scale..." I said slowly. "And I had to give a sacrifice in order to take it. I offered Kuma. The... whatever it was, the entity, accepted, and I took the scale." I wasn't sure what he was getting at, what answer he was looking for, and it made my nerves unsettled. That's when I remembered the blinding light. "Oh! When I touched the scale for the first time, this light flashed so brightly I had to shield my eyes. But it went away and didn't happen when I grabbed it again. It was strange, did you see it from the surface?"

"No," all the males said in unison, all of whom were now looking at me like they had even more questions.

"So, nothing else besides that, that you think you should tell us?" Knox said as he crossed his arms.

I didn't feel like dealing with this attitude of his anymore, and my response came out with force. "No, Knox, there isn't anything else. Is there something you feel like you need to ask me?"

His mouth turned up, he had been waiting for this, and I fell right into his trap. "Thanks for asking. How did you get back up?"

We stared at each other, both of our expressions cold and full of hostility, when just moments before, I had been amused by Bash's laughter and ready for a deep sleep.

I wasn't expecting that to be the question. "W—What?"

Knox moved to squat in front of me. "You were at the bottom of the lake. How did you make it back up in a single breath?"

How was I supposed to answer? That Zarakruae had helped me? It wouldn't be a lie, but... it also wasn't the full truth. *I think... I think I did something.*

My words tripped over each other. "The thing, in the lake, it told me to—" Oh my dragons. How do you tell dragon shifters that you *used* one of them? I was not even sure how I'd done it, was it because I'd been holding the scale?

"Finish your sentence, Amalia," Lane said, his attention solely on me.

"It told me to use him." The next words came out so quickly, they all blended together. "I don't even know how it happened. It was the scale, I think, but I knew I was using Kuma's abilities to make it to the surface because the second he was torn apart, I lost the ability to breathe underwater."

Lane spoke first. "What do you mean torn apart?" But then Knox said something that made me forget Lane's question.

"It wasn't the scale. It was you." His head dropped as he shook it from side to side. He rubbed his face and said, "You can channel from us; it explains so much." He stood up, scratching the back of his neck.

"What do you mean? How is that possible?" I was so confused, I couldn't channel them.

"The fire in the Forgotten Pass," Lane added. "And in the hearth when you woke up."

Bash then said, "The grass in the training field."

No, no. Those were all them, none of those were me. It couldn't have been me. "I'm not a magical creature. I can't be responsible for any of that. All of those instances were around you all, you did them and just didn't realize."

Knox threw a log into the dwindled fire. "No, Amalia, it's you. I don't know how, but it is. It could be because you survived the shimmer. It is you, though. I felt the shift in you in the training grounds. That power didn't come from Bash."

"You all are acting so calmly about this!" I shouted as my heart rate skyrocketed. "I can't be able to do these things, what does that make me?"

"An abomination." Blaire plopped down onto her bed roll, massaging her neck. She quickly cowered the second Knox let out a rumble at her comment.

"It makes you an enigma. We will figure it out," Knox said.

I threw my hands in the air. "Great, is there anything else I should know before I have a complete meltdown?"

"Yes. We are leaving for Cimmerian. In a few hours." Then he walked away like he hadn't just dropped a boulder on my chest.

Chapter 23

Cimmerian.

My home. The thought of going back sent floods of emotion into me, but I couldn't seem to separate them from each other, leaving me feeling numb above everything else. I rested for just a couple of hours, and when I woke up, everything had been packed up, everything except the blankets I was using. Blaire was even in better spirits but made a point not to even look in my direction. I'd have to remember to thank Knox when he was being less moody. I went through my packed bag and found a beige chemise and black trousers to put on. My undergarments had dried while I slept. Now they had a crunchy consistency, but there was no time to complain or dwell on things like clothes being uncomfortable.

Once changed, I headed over to where Knox and I had landed when we'd first arrived at Lake Aquasailies. Everyone was grouped together already, probably discussing the journey there. I knew if we had to walk it would take well over a week, so at that moment, I was thankful we could just fly instead.

As I joined the semicircle everyone had formed, I quickly wanted to retreat with the mixtures of facial expressions pointed at me. They ranged from pity to hatred, and right then, I thought I'd prefer the hatred. "I'll be fine," I said, already knowing what most of them were dwelling on. The fact that we'd be returning to where the only people I had ever known all lay dead where Lane and I had left them. My family. I stood taller and took a breath before confirming, more for myself than for them. "I will be fine."

"Okay, then we will head to Cimmerian. We should get there by morning. Amalia, sleep during the ride, we will be flying straight through and heading to the next scale without rest."

"Why?" I interrupted. There was no way they could fly through the night, then travel for who knows how long the next day. "We don't even know where the next scale is. You all will pass out from exhaustion."

"We aren't as weak as you," Blaire spat out before turning and leaving the group. In a matter of moments, I felt the way the ground vibrated; she had shifted. I paid her no mind and refused to look.

"What she means is, we can go a lot longer without rest. It won't be fun, but we will manage fine. Plus, we do know where the next scale is located," Bash said, throwing an arm over my shoulder.

"Where?" I threw my arm around his waist and looked up at him, waiting for his answer, but Lane interjected.

"You remember the mountains beyond the field you love so much?"

Excitement rushed through me. "We're going to my field?"

"Well, technically," Bash said, "it's my horde's field. The entire expanse of lands just past the mountains belonged to them. I believe the next scale is nestled inside what you call the Godival Mountains. I won't be able to get a better sense of it until we reach them."

A giddy squeal left me. "Let's get going then!" I looked around. "Who am I riding?"

"Woaaahh geeze, Amalia, at least take us to dinner first before a proposition like that."

I slapped Bash in the chest, pretty sure it had hurt me more than it did him, yet he faked an injury and rubbed his chest, walking away and tossing back, "Not it."

Lane spoke before Knox even tried to. "She will ride with me this time."

Knox scoffed at him. "I don't think so, little brother."

With how Knox had been acting, I didn't particularly want to be stuck an entire night with just him and I. "Actually, I would like to go with Lane." I stepped to stand beside Lane and hooked my arm in his. "You clearly have a problem with me right now, and I think we could do with some space from each other."

Lane's mouth curved up, but he said nothing. Knox just looked at me, and I swore that I could see every emotion flicker in his violet eyes. "Whatever you want, Valkara."

There was that word again. "What does that mean?"

Knox shot a wink at Lane before he turned and shifted, knocking me on my ass. I looked up to see Lane still standing, not worried about helping me off the ground as his jaw hardened.

"Hello?" I said, moving to stand up.

Lane looked back. "I'm sorry, Amalia. Here." He held a hand out for me and helped me up, brushing the dirt off the side of my leg.

"What does *Valkara* mean?"

"Nothing, c'mon, we need to get moving. Stand back until I shift, and then I'll help you up."

I nodded and did as he asked.

I was mesmerized by the process, no matter how many times I'd seen it. Lane's dragon form was such a dramatic contrast to Knox's. Where Knox was smoky and clouded with night, Lane was dazzling and pure like snow dusted in diamonds. His scales were the whitest shade I had ever witnessed, and the diamond-like, armored scales were enchanting. He lowered his body and placed his front leg out for me to climb. I felt like he was too beautiful for me to get on, like I would taint his scales somehow. As I climbed up, I grabbed hold of the various spikes protruding from his body; they all resembled clear crystals and were cold to the touch as if they had been mined from a deep cave.

As I got seated, I took in the lake for the last time. I wasn't sure if I would ever see it again, but I couldn't help but think of Zarakruae, how it was all alone in that lake. How Kuma had lost his life in the waters of his ancestors. "I'm sorry," I said in a whisper.

Lane let out a chuff and I continued, knowing that he could hear me. "For Kuma. I'm not sure how close you guys were but... I am sorry you lost him. That I was the cause for you losing him."

He didn't make any sound, but he did swing his head to look at me, his eyes no longer the ice blue but now crystalline and bright. As his head moved closer to me, the angle produced soft rainbows that I found myself hypnotized by. He held my stare for a brief moment before whipping his head back and taking off abruptly. I supposed I'd picked the wrong moment for my apology.

We ascended high above the clouds, and I watched as we slowly caught up to the others. Where Lane blended in, everyone else was visible. Blaire and her crimson scales, Bash a rich emerald, and Knox with his onyx hues impossible not to see.

We flew for a few hours, the sunset putting on quite the show in the sky, casting a golden glow across the clouds below with various pink hues fading as it dipped below the horizon. I could watch this every night for the rest of my life and never tire of it. I laid my arms out in front of me and rested my head on them as I took in the sight. I let myself drift off as the light faded beyond the horizon.

When I woke, the sun had been long gone, and there was a full moon on display among the stars, the light from the moon reflecting off of Lane's scales like a mirror.

I wished I could ask how long we had, or communicate at all. I could tell we were flying lower than we had been before due to the fact I could make out the dark shadows of trees below us. As I looked to my left, I thought I could see the Godival Mountains, but I wasn't certain. If those were the mountains, that meant we were flying over the Dival Woods. We were almost home.

I counted the scales along Lane's neck until we flew over my village, and the others started landing in the courtyard. I had counted to three thousand and eighty-two. Lane landed next, jostling me to the point I almost lost my footing, but I managed to grab onto one of the crystal-like horns just above me. He lowered himself like he had at the lake to make it easier for me to dismount. "Thank you." I patted his large leg and looked around the dark space. I could make out the structures and market shacks, but I didn't see any bodies. There had been so many the day the shimmer happened. Had they woken up like I had? A spark of hope I never thought I'd have again flared to life. I swung around to see what Lane thought and came face to face with four nude bodies.

"What the hell!" I slapped my hands over my face and abruptly turned back.

"Bet you wish you would have rode with Knox now, huh?" Bash chastised me, and I remembered him telling me how Knox made a point to hang back and wait so the others could dress, and I didn't have to witness this. It wasn't that I had a problem with nudity, but I had been brought up believing that your body shouldn't be shown to just anyone who wanted to see it. That it was special, especially in a smaller village where talk traveled fast. Dragons, however, were very comfortable in their own skin, and it didn't even seem like a thought to them, nor did they seem to pay any mind to each other. Not even to Blaire, who, laced in fading moonlight, looked ethereal. I really, really hated her.

My attention spanned to Knox, who had already gotten himself partially dressed from the waist down. Thanks to earlier... or was it yesterday, now? I could picture what was now covered. Meanwhile, Bash was the opposite and chose to throw on a white shirt first, leaving his ass exposed.

"Bet you never thought you'd see two full moons in one night." Lane dropped my pack beside me and tracked where my attention was.

I faked a gasp and threw my hand to my stomach. "Oh my dragons, did you just make a joke? Is this it? Is this the end of times?" I said teasingly, pulling a smile from him.

Lane looked more laid back and was wearing loose-fitting trousers with no tunic, exposing his muscled frame. My eyes traced each divet and line. "Careful," he warned, and my cheeks heated. I didn't have the restraint Blaire clearly did, because I couldn't help where my eyes wandered when I was surrounded by males that looked like this.

When I pulled my eyes away from him, I saw Knox staring at me, and guilt crashed over me before receding.

"The sun will be up shortly. Once everyone is dressed, we will head to the mountains," Knox said.

"Oh, I don't know, I think I like us better without clothes." Blaire's words came out as a moan, making my temper rise. "Don't you think, Knox?" she whined, winking at him before sending a smirk my way. Biting my tongue until a metallic taste filled my mouth, I gave her nothing but a blank expression. So, she kicked it up a notch. Still fully nude, she sauntered over to him, placing a delicate hand along his shoulder, slowly caressing the back of his neck as she moved around him. When she reached his other side, she pressed her body against him. Unlike Bash, he hadn't thrown on a tunic yet, so they were skin to skin. Her voluptuous breasts pressed against his biceps, his hand so close to other parts of her that if she got any closer, he could slip his fingers inside of her. My gaze went from where his hand was to his face. His jaw was clenched, and his eyes were cold and unamused. But then, he tilted his head toward her and whispered something in her ear before he smiled. My heart dropped before I could catch it, like a missed ball in a game of catch. I couldn't even explain why, but it did. I couldn't stand there and allow either of them to affect me, so I grabbed Lane's hand and walked toward the saloon. Two could play this game.

"What are we doing?" he asked.

"I need a drink," I said bitterly. "Do you want one?" I maneuvered behind the old wooden bar that had a small layer of dust coating all the burn marks and scuffs.

"Sure," he said as I grabbed the closest bottle to me without looking to see what it was. I didn't care at this moment. I just needed something to stop me from attempting to kill her, which in turn would likely end up with me dead, because as much as I'd like to think I was tough, I wasn't, and she was a fucking dragon.

I poured us both a glass of some amber-hued liquid and slid one to Lane. Holding it up to me, we clinked our glasses before we downed the contents.

I swallowed the liquid that burned my throat as it went down. "Where are all the bodies?" I blurted out.

Lane sucked air between his teeth as he swallowed his and asked, "What?"

"The bodies. When we left, they were all over the courtyard. I didn't see anyone out there besides us." I heard thunder booming as a bright light flashed in the windows of the saloon.

"I didn't notice," he said. My back hit the liquor counter from the step back I took hearing his words.

"You didn't notice that the courtyard that held the dead bodies of everyone we knew was now empty?" I couldn't keep the venom from my words, so I poured another glass, but just for myself this time.

"No, I hadn't." Lane ran a hand through his hair, which meant he was uncomfortable. I kept pushing anyway.

"What could have happened to them? Do you think they woke up like I did?" I set the newly poured drink down, waiting in anticipation for his answer.

"No, Amalia, they weren't like you. We checked them. They were dead, they couldn't have just gotten up and left." He held his glass out for me to refill, but I didn't like his answers enough to give him more. So I put the bottle on the shelf instead. He rolled his eyes and dropped the cup back on the bar with a huff.

"You really believe there isn't anyone left?" The hope I'd had was just a simmering ember now.

"I know there isn't." He said it so matter-of-factly that I wanted to change his mind. I felt like I needed to show him the possibility that I saw.

Before I could say anything else, someone yelled from outside. It was too muffled from another crack of thunder to tell who or what was said, so we decided to head out. Another conversation I needed to remember to bring back up when the timing was better. We could hear Bash laughing as we made our way back to the others. My foot snagged on one of the cobblestones, causing me to lose my balance. Knox was suddenly beside me, catching me before I met the rough ground. He had one of my arms in his hand with his other wrapped around me for support. Blaire's body pressed against him made its way to the forefront of my mind, and I ripped my arm from his grasp. "I don't need your help." I trudged the rest of the way, losing my balance once or twice but righting myself quickly.

"Are we ready?" My question was directed more to the air than to any particular person.

"Well, aren't you chipper?" Bash said with a hint of caution to his words. Which was valid, since I glared at him after he said it.

"She's had a little to drink." Lane bent down, picking up my and his packs. He handed me mine, the weight making me stumble slightly, then threw his on his back.

"That has nothing to do with anything. Are we all ready, or are we going to keep standing here doing nothing?" I snapped, like I wasn't just doing nothing in the saloon.

"Oh. Great. You're a mean drunk. This is going to be fun," Bash said.

"I'm not drunk. My nerves are just heightened. And right now, you guys are on my last one."

Bash let out a whistle as he walked past me. "I guess we should go then." His brows lifted momentarily before he headed toward the trail that led to my field.

Blaire followed, then Knox, then me. Lane stayed in the back of our single file line. No one spoke as the sky rumbled with flashes of light, illuminating the silhouette of the trees. I couldn't help but feel guilty for how my temper had sewn a blanket that surrounded us all in a warm tension.

"Maybe we will see someone," I said softly but loud enough that I noticed Knox's head turn just slightly.

"Doubtful," he said without looking back at me. He did slow his pace, though, until he was by my side. "Your village was one of the only places in this realm besides Santavarre that held life other than wildlife or creatures like the orbichor."

I stopped in my tracks, sucking in a breath. "There's no way that's possible." I breathed out.

"He's speaking the truth," Lane said as he came up to stand on my other side. "The other hordes, and the fae. They went skyward after the Kingdom End War. Working together, they took their lands above the clouds, glamouring the masses. They never wanted a repeat of history and chose to take themselves out of it. That's why all your storybooks mention dragons as mythical works of fiction. It was a way for humans to make sense of the sudden disappearance, the reason the lands had changed."

"Most humans had their memories... altered," Knox interjected, biting out the last word. "The stronger humans weren't so easily affected by the magic. While they couldn't prove the things they remembered, they had to do something to get their recollection out, hence why your storybooks were created."

"None ever returned?" I asked as another flash of lightning lit up the trail. I could have sworn there was a figure to my right, but it was gone in an instant. It was probably just Lane's shadow.

"Why would they need to?" Knox said as he flashed me a look of sorrow.

"Why are you guys here, then? Why did King Tatum stay, and those who are in the castle?" I looked to my left and then my right, waiting for one of them to speak.

"Lane, I believe you would be better suited to answer this question," Knox said before picking up his pace and jogging up to Bash, who had stayed about ten feet in front of us.

Damp leaves, wet from the dewy night, being crushed under our feet was the only sound for what felt like an eternity.

Finally, Lane answered. "My father lost a lot. *We* lost a lot in that war. He didn't believe in abandoning this realm for the sky. He thought we should fight for our rights to stay and put humans in their place, especially after the loss of his mate."

"We're almost through the woods!" Bash called from ahead, alerting us that my field was almost within reach.

"Mate? You mean like his wife? Your mother."

"Yes and no," he said as he scratched the back of his neck. "A mate isn't really the equivalent of a wife in the way that you know. A mate is a bond set by the Elysian Islands, unbreakable and stronger than anything you could fathom feeling." He laid his palm flat open for me, and I took it, hanging on to every word he was saying. "You feel a pull from the moment you meet one another, no matter what you do, and you'll always be drawn to them, by something so much greater than yourself. Some bonds have been known to be so profound, they are able to produce implausible acts."

"Implausible acts?" I said curiously. "Like what?"

"Well, now we know what happened to the bodies Amalia was talking about," Bash said at the end of the trail. My attention snapped to where he stood.

We quickened our last few steps and reached the clearing where the others were standing. My stomach dropped, and I fell to my knees, which sank in the dampened dirt. "W-What is this?" My eyes welled up with unshed tears as I took in the sight before me.

"Like bringing their mate back to life," Lane said, his tone radiating hatred.

I couldn't concentrate on what he said as I looked out at what was once a blooming field of every color imaginable, petals of various sizes and shapes dancing in the wind and reaching up to the sky. Now, the vibrant colors were ashen. My field was now desolate. Stems were wilted and decaying, the petals shriveled, gray, and lying lifeless on the ground. This had been the only place I could truly find joy, and now the air was thick with death. Everything was too still and silent. The loss of my sanctuary wasn't what brought me to my knees; it was the hundreds of graves spread throughout the scene, each marked with a thick branch most likely from the trail we had just walked. The tips of the branches marking each gravesite were lit with a flame of burning indigo that flickered into light violet at the tips.

There was something familiar about the flames, the only color in the somber expanse. I couldn't help but look at Knox, whose lavender eyes mimicked them. "You? Did this?" I choked out, trying to keep my emotions in check.

His jaw hardened, but he didn't brush me off. "The flowers were still in bloom. I did not do that. The graves, however... you said how guilty you felt for leaving everyone. I wanted you to feel at peace about it." His words trailed off.

"So you buried everyone?" I looked out at the seemingly endless burial sites, the bright flames growing dimmer the farther away they were. I couldn't believe it, even though I was seeing it with my own two eyes. It seemed so outrageous for him to do. Regret filled my heart from how I'd been acting toward him. This was the most selfless thing anyone had ever done for me. He'd barely known me when I'd confessed how I felt to him. "I don't know what to say." My hand covered my mouth as the other rested on my stomach. I rose from my knees and walked forward to where I saw four gravestones at the front of the field. My heart felt like it was being squeezed by a dragon's claw as I crept closer, noticing objects on each grave. There was an orange on one, the ink jar on another. I felt when someone came up behind me. I knew it had to be Knox.

"How did you know?" I didn't bother elaborating. He'd understand what I was asking.

"That has a difficult answer," he said, placing a hand on my back. We stood there in silence until a sob broke free from me. There was something about seeing the graves, knowing they were in there, buried, that finalized their deaths in a way I wasn't prepared for.

"Is this why we stopped in Cimmerian instead of flying straight to the mountains? For her?" Blaire seethed. "What a waste of time."

I couldn't care about her right now. This was more than I could have done on my own. I shifted my pack to my lap and rifled through the contents until I pulled out the book my sisters and I had filled out together. I ran my hand along the cover and looked at the burning flames marking their graves. Using my hands, I dug a shallow hole and placed the book within it, covering it up with the soil. They deserved to watch over it. They deserved so much more.

Chapter 24

"Thank you" was all I could manage to give him. It wasn't nearly enough. He turned to me and gave me a weak smile, and that was all it took. Crashing into him, I threw my arms around his neck in a hug, my silent tears dampening the white tunic he had thrown on. "I'm so sorry," I said, and I realized it was for so much more than just the attitude he and I had been giving each other. It was for whatever this complicated feeling was between us that had me on edge every time he was around. It was for not seeing how he had been there even when I didn't realize.

"You don't need to apologize to me. I should be the one apologizing to you, *Valkara du Zharak.*" He tucked a strand of my hair behind my ear that had been stuck to my cheek from the tears. "I told her unless she wanted a repeat from the lake, she should remove herself from my side. I shouldn't have whispered it the way I did. I'm sorry it upset you."

I wasn't expecting that at all. "It didn't." I cleared my throat.

"Your heart says otherwise," he whispered. No one had moved. They were standing at the tree line, watching us.

My eyes fluttered to meet his. "That language you keep speaking. What are you saying?"

"It's an ancient language from long before the war. The High Dragons, the original leaders, spoke it. I've always had a fondness for it. My father used to say it to my mother. She would turn into a puddle anytime he spoke to her." I could tell he was drifting into a happy memory by the curve in his lips and the fact his eyes seemed to go distant for a moment.

"What happened to them?"

I refrained from saying anything further to see if he would explain. After a deep breath, he looked up to the lightened but troubled sky and said, "My father died after the Kingdom End War. He was returning to bring Tatum back, but the spot where they were meant to meet had been laced with explosives. He never had a chance." He ran his hand down his face and scratched the stubble that had started growing along his cheeks and mouth. "After that, Tatum decided to strike out against the hordes even further by taking my mother as his."

"How is that striking out against them all?"

Knox looked over at me, and his expression was full of anger and sorrow, mimicking the sky above us. The air had become misty and dark clouds warned a severe storm was on the way. "My mother, from the Hydra Horde, and father, from the Shadow Horde, were highly respected by every horde. They were fair and just. Tatum hated the power they held so effortlessly when he had to obtain it by inciting fear and aggression."

I scoffed at that, because out of everything today, that I believed without a doubt.

"I was still pretty young when it happened, probably about the same age you are now." He sighed heavily. "She fought him every chance she could. He took her with him one day. They said they were going skyward to try and convince the hordes to come back down. When he returned, he returned alone. I don't think I'll ever know what happened to her. I hope that whatever it was, was quick, and that she's been with my father listening to her favorite words being spoken."

My face was wet with new tears for the life he'd had to endure and all the unknowns and losses he had lived through.

"Knox, I'm so sor—" My abdomen suddenly screamed with pain as I felt like I'd been struck by a spear. I looked down and saw an oily, black, curved object protruding from my stomach. I heard yelling from behind me, but it sounded so far away I couldn't understand what was being said. I grabbed the object and pulled it free from my skin. As soon as it was out, blood spurted from the wound, and I dropped to the ground. I felt no pain, I felt nothing, like I was in a dream.

"Damn it, Amalia!" Knox was yelling. "Why would you pull it out? Blaire! Blaire, get over here now!" His shouting was cut off as he seethed in pain. I looked to where he grabbed just under his shoulder; something had sliced his bicep open. A blur of vermillion passed over me as I lay on the ground, followed by a bone-chilling screech.

"W-what's h-h-happening." The words felt like weights I was too weak to carry.

"You're okay, this is going to hurt," Knox said to me, but I didn't feel anything. I tried to look at him. My vision was getting fuzzy, but he was over me, arms pressing down on my stomach. Dirt kicked up at me as someone slid to where we were.

"What do you need me to do?" That sounded like Lane.

"She was struck by an orbichor spike, the venom has already worked through her body. I need you to hold pressure, my arm is going numb from where I was grazed."

I was so sick of these damn creatures. I tried to move, to get up, but a dizzy spell hit me instead.

"How many are there?" Knox asked Lane.

"I counted six, but Bash and Blaire are making quick work of them. They should have them extinguished soon enough." Bash's bellow reverberated through me, showing just how close the creatures were to us.

"How did none of us notice they were here?" Knox growled as he sat back, letting Lane take over holding pressure. My thoughts went back to the shadowy figure I thought I'd seen in the woods while we were walking the trail. I should have said something instead of doubting myself.

Sounds of wet, sickening crunches broke the conversation as a reddish heap landed close by, shaking the ground and making me flinch. I closed my eyes and tried to focus on staying conscious.

"Blaire, we need you, now!" Knox said frantically. I didn't open my eyes. I didn't want to see the panic on his or Lane's face.

This was Blaire's chance to seek revenge, and she took it. "Oh, you need me?" she snarled at him. "Like I needed you to damn near bite my head off? Like Kuma needed to be sacrificed?" Her voice was nearing a scream, and I pictured her face just as red as her body in its dragon form. "I don't think so, she can die in this field with the rest of Cimmerian for all I care."

"I swear to the High Dragons, Blaire, if you do—"

"You'll do what, Knox? Because I guarantee I've already lived through worse than you could ever inflict upon me."

"You can't force her to heal her, Knox," Lane said, and something about his words felt like I'd been stabbed all over again. Did he not care if I died here?

"The fuck we can't!" Bash yelled. I wasn't sure when he'd gotten there. I hadn't even felt the ground tremble with his landing. If I could have smiled right then, I would have. He was primed to battle with Lane for me. Though I still stung with the knowledge that Bash wanted me alive more than the male I'd known for over a year. Maybe he did feel the same as his father, and wanted me dead for what happened to his family.

They continued arguing until I heard Knox say, "Where the hell does she think she's going?" That's when my panic set in. I'd thought she would threaten not to help, but with everyone there, I hadn't thought she'd actually fully refuse. I tried to yell out after her, but it came out as garbled sounds.

"You're gonna be okay, Amalia. BLAIRE!" I had never heard someone's voice more stricken with fear than Knox's voice in that moment. He had come to the same realization I had. She was serious. I couldn't blame her. I didn't know what she and Kuma had been to each other, but if I had to decide whether to save someone who was responsible for the death of someone I cared about, I wasn't confident I'd be able to make a different decision than she had.

My mind raced with thoughts—about Blaire's words, how I could be with my family, but I wasn't ready yet. I wanted to live. I wanted her to heal me. A scream bubbled up in my throat, but it didn't escape. *I want to be healed, I'm not ready to die!*

You are capable of more than you realize. The power of all consumes you. Use it, Amalia, one who is meant to restore.

Zarakruae's words came back to me, and I focused on what I wanted. To be healed. I put all the will I had inside me into the one singular need to survive. My anger clouded my thoughts and made it hard to concentrate. I vowed to myself that if a sacrifice ever had to be made again, it would be her who went. My veins felt like they were set on fire, the first thing I had felt since the orbichor's spike pierced me. Then I heard Blaire's screams.

"Amalia, what are you doing to her?" Lane yelled. But I didn't acknowledge his question. I stayed focused on surviving. Healing. No matter the cost. I didn't know what I was doing, but I knew what I wanted. The fire in my veins simmered with each pulse of her power, leaving just a faint ache. Blaire's shrieks became more guttural the more I pulled from her. I had been confused by Zarakruae's words in the lake, until I had been able to breathe underwater up until the point where Kuma had been killed. Something clicked then. I didn't know how I'd done it or if Zarakruae had allowed me to harness that power, but it was worth testing. Ever since the shimmer happened, I had easily shrugged off the odd things that had happened, assuming it was the others who were responsible. But as I considered what Knox and Lane had said when we all spoke about it at the lake, I realized they may be right... maybe it had been me.

My back arched off the soggy, ashen field, and I breathed in deeply, finally able to snap my eyes open.

"That's enough, Amalia!" Lane shouted, but he was the only one besides Blaire, who had been reduced to just pained moans, showing any kind of protest. I turned my head toward the trail and saw she was lying in a fetal position. I looked at Knox, who gave me a slight nod of his head, then Bash, whose expression was solid, hiding whatever he was thinking behind a trained mask.

"My stomach," I gasped, trying to point to where the wound was.

"Is relatively healed," Knox said before shooting a sideways glance at where Blaire lay.

"She was going to let me die," I breathed out, letting the connection to her loosen.

"She was." Knox confirmed what I already knew, but he said it in a way that did not convey any emotion. It was just a fact. He didn't say anything else or try to sway me to stop or to see how far me pulling on this power would go. He just met my stare and held it. The way he allowed me to choose made me let go of the invisible tether that tied her power to me. I would not be like her.

Her pained groans turned into sobs the moment I let go, and only a small part of me regretted what I had done. The rest wished I would have continued. Lane and Bash went to help her, and Knox kneeled down to help me sit up.

"*Valkara du Zharak,*" he said, grabbing one of my hands so that I had some support. I was still feeling dizzy, but otherwise, I just ached all over. "It means goddess of death."

Chapter 25

The winds picked up as the storm raged closer, whipping my hair around like clothes left out on a line. "We need to go," I yelled to Knox over the sound of the thrashing flames. "How have the fires not gone out in this wind?"

"They will stay lit no matter the weather until the day I die," he said, helping me to my feet. "The memory of all those who lived here will burn bright until my last breath."

My mouth turned up in a weak smile, because there were no words that I could say that would ever come close to expressing the gratitude I felt. There would never be a way to repay this act.

Lane ran up with Blaire in his arms, her hair in every bit of a frenzy as mine. "She's unconscious but alive."

"We need to go. Now," Knox said, taking in the relentless midnight-colored clouds advancing much faster than before. Shadows raked over the ashen land, making it more ominous than it already was. "Let's move. Bash, grab Amalia's pack!" Just as he gave the order, Knox effortlessly scooped me into his arms.

"You don't need to carry me. I can walk," I said, but I didn't protest as he held my body against his.

We headed toward the Godival Mountains which, at this distance, looked daunting. They seemed so far away. "We can't fly there?"

Knox looked at me with a smirk. "Can you sprout wings now, too?"

I leaned my head against his chest to hide my laugh as he continued speaking. "We can't fly in weather like this. Normal thunderstorms are dangerous due to the lightning, but there's something about those clouds that looks... wrong. I don't want to be in the sky when whatever those clouds are holding comes down."

"We need to move faster!" Bash yelled from behind, sending everyone into a run for the mountainous terrain.

I looked over Knox's shoulder, past Bash, to where the graves of my family were growing farther away. I focused on the flickering purple flames and serenity filled my heart knowing they were buried, with a gravesite that would have their memory preserved for years longer than they would have lived for. It made the hundreds of flames we passed a little easier to take in. I just wished this field would bloom as it once had. So that there'd be a vibrant life after all this death. Not this gothic, sinister land. Bash and I made eye contact, and he must have seen all that I was thinking, because his face contorted with pity before he slowed his pace.

"Wait, Bash," I said to have Knox slow. He turned, running backward for a few strides before also coming to a stop. "What are you doing?" he shouted.

Bash crouched down and scooped up a handful of ash before the wind dispersed it into the air violently, causing him to cough on inhaled particles. "We can't leave it like this," he said, looking at me. "Do you think you can help?" he asked.

"I don't want to hurt you." Blaire's pained screams echoed in my mind. I wouldn't be able to live with myself if I ever hurt Bash like that.

"Then don't."

"We don't have time for this!" Lane said, adjusting Blaire in his arms. "We ne—to get to the ca—ern at the base of the mou—ains!" His words came in and out as the wind howled around us. He may have been right, but that didn't stop me from tapping Knox's chest, signaling for him to put me down.

Running over to Bash took my breath away, and I was panting from the small distance that had been between us, proving I wasn't fully healed. Tremors made my hands vibrate with anxiety. "What do I do?"

"I've told you before that my powers are derived from the natural resources around me. Even though this is nothing but ash, it's still a resource. We lock into that, into the trees and the mountains around us, and we give it life again."

"Okay," I said reluctantly.

"Just trust yourself." He placed both his hands palms-down on the ground, the ash covering his fingers in a gray, powdery coating, and closed his eyes. After a moment, green sprouts burst from the gray powder between his fingers.

"It worked!" I kneeled down to look at the gorgeous, light green blades as excitement raced through me.

"I'm not wait—g around f—r this, I'm ge—ing her to the c—verns!" Lane began running in the direction of the mountains, leaving us.

My excitement was replaced with trepidation as lightning stretched clear across the furious sky, followed by a crack of thunder so loud it even had Knox and Bash pausing to gauge the storm's next move. My hands slammed against the ground as I focused on what I wanted: to use Bash's abilities without hurting him, to bring life back to my field, to see the flowers blooming above the graves to prove that life could still find a way. My body felt so exhausted, I wasn't sure I'd be able to do it. If I *should* do it. Until I felt a tickle under my palm. I lifted my hands to see dark, forest green, oval blades; then long, narrow, light green blades that seemed sharp enough to cut your skin. Bash and I exchanged a knowing look before we stood. I followed his lead as he held his hands out, turning his head up to the sky. I pictured blooming flowers of purples and reds, surrounded by stalks of tall yellows. When I opened my eyes, the growth was spreading out far past where we were standing.

I kept hold of the thoughts of how this field once looked and stood as I watched it transform back into my place of comfort, back into the field that had given me freedom from anything the day had placed on me. The flowers protruding from the ground blurred as my eyes filled with unshed tears.

Thunder shook the ground, snapping me out of the moment, the sound so loud it sent vibrations through every bone.

"We're out of time!" Knox yelled. That was all it took for us to make a mad dash for the mountains. While running, I kept my thoughts on the field, of every scrap of ash being replaced by the stems and petals that had been there before. With each step I wanted the field to come back, but it didn't work. I couldn't do anything else here.

My arms were pumping back and forth as I tried to push my legs to go faster and faster. I spotted a form crumpled on the ground to my left, and I slowed to see what it was. An orbichor. Its body was split in two, a mangled mess of black, oily organs were strewn across the ground. Its head was barely hanging on by sinew, making me gag. "Ugh, gross, what the hell." Another gag silenced me. Every inch of the pale body was covered with lifeless yellow eyes, pupils that weren't round like ours, but narrow slits. All oozing out the black, oily substance. Was that what their blood looked like?

"Amalia, go!" Bash came up behind me, pushing me forward, but I spared one more moment to see if the curved member was attached. It wasn't. This was the fucker that had impaled me. Spit flew from my mouth to the head of the creature before Bash picked me up at the waist and tossed me into the air like a ragdoll. A small squeal came out of me before I landed in Knox's arms. "There isn't time for sightseeing," he explained, and I was too overcome with the shock that they'd just tossed me around to form a rebuttal.

Lightning flashed before striking the ground thirty feet from Knox's right, making us both flinch. The air was charged and deadly, and a part of me believed we should have followed Lane when he left us. I tightened my grip around Knox's neck as he continued running at full speed, a new respect growing for their kind because I never would have made this run without stopping, not even factoring in that they hadn't rested since I retrieved the Hydra Scale. Another bolt of lightning struck the ground as something thick and hot dropped on my cheek. Droplets started to fall in slow succession. I wiped at what hit my face and noticed a substance similar to what the orbichor was covered in on my fingers. "Knox." I said his name like an alarmed question.

"I know." He was panting now from how hard he was pushing his legs to move while carrying me.

"I can run if you put me down. You're gonna collapse at this rate." Another drop landed on my arm and then his shoulder.

"Knox," Bash called out, "it's *Drakar Zynth*."

"I know!" he roared over the wind. He looked down at my quizzical expression and said, "Deadly rain."

"What do you mean deadly rain? This has never hit Cimmerian before, why now?"

His reply came in short bursts as he tried to speak while running. "It's a sign, like your dead field. T–The magic within Caligness is faltering. The balance—has shifted."

The mountains were monstrous now the closer we got. I could make out each ridgeline and the shape of foliage spotted along the terrain. *We're almost there.* Bash called out Lane's name, but we never heard an answer, so we continued forward, hoping the cave entrance would come into view. That's when all hell broke loose.

The droplets increased until it became an obsidian shower that coated every inch of us. I frantically wiped at my arms, my hair, my face, but the liquid clung to me the more it came down until I couldn't see anything left of my clothes or my skin. I could feel our pace slowing, the weight of the substance showing why it got its name. The substance created a barrier under my nose, making it harder to breathe, and every time I opened my mouth to compensate, I choked from inhaling it.

"Ah, fuck it," he growled as he placed me on the ground.

"What are yo—" My words were cut off as Bash threw his body over mine, shielding me from Knox as he shifted into his dragon form, blending in with sky and black rain. A flash of lightning was the only thing that helped me see his wings stretch before he took off into the air and circled around. I tracked the only color in the sky—his luminous violet eyes. "What is he doing?" I shouted to Bash, who was lifting himself off of me and tracking Knox the same as I was. "I thought it was too dangerous to fly in storms?" I spit out chunks of the nightmarish liquid, talking was not a smart decision in this storm.

"It is," he said. "But if he doesn't, we likely won't make it to the cave. This rain is called *Drakar Zynth* for a reason. It suffocates anything that is trapped in it. First you get weighed down to where you can no longer move or fight, then you're buried in the thick sludge and suffocate. It's an agonizing and slow death. I've never met anyone who has survived a storm like this."

"Then what are we doing? Do we run under him as he flies?"

"Not quite," Bash said, pulling me to my feet. "Just brace yourself and try not to freak out."

"What?" I yelled, noticing the stance he took like he was bracing himself to be tackled. Then I heard a low, guttural rumbling. I thought it was thunder until the sound of giant wings beating followed. Behind us, all I saw were scales and outstretched claws curling toward us. A scream erupted from me as the claws latched around us and took us into the air.

"Great job, you definitely didn't freak out!" Bash had his hands cupped around his mouth so that his voice would carry over to me, but I was paralyzed and too terrified to speak. I gripped the massive onyx claw like it was the last thing I'd ever do.

I mistakenly licked my lips, tasting the bitter bite of the deadly rain. I frantically started spitting it out, not knowing if that would also kill me. Knox let out a long, chortling bellow, before we dropped closer to the ground. This had to be challenging for him. I looked up in awe at his strength and determination. I thought back to what he'd said of his parents and couldn't help but feel like they would be so proud of their son.

"There! Ahead and to the right, do you see it?" Bash tried to yell as loud as he could to direct Knox. I had no idea what he was talking about and couldn't see anything other than the sheen of black coating everything in sight. My heart ached at the field that was probably coated in a thick layer, undoing everything Bash and I accomplished. Death always followed too closely. Knox veered to the right and began flying lower, wavering, making me grip his claw once more.

"His wings are getting too heavy with the buildup. We'll make it, though." He sounded so sure. So confident. I tried to believe it, too. The mountains were in plain view, but their usual green slopes were dripping with the sludge that had overtaken everything in its path. Knox roared, and I threw my hands over my ears to soften the sound at the same time Bash yelled, "Here we go!"

"Here we go, where?" I screamed, but it was too late. We were hurtling toward the ground that was much closer than I had anticipated. We hit the hard, cold floor of the cave and rolled a few feet before coming to a stop. Dust kicked up all around us, making us cough as it entered our lungs. Wheezing, I tried to get up but decided to just stay down when the entire cave shook like the outside had been struck by something. I turned onto my stomach and covered my head as small rocks and dust fell from the cave ceiling.

"That was Knox, he must have landed on the side of the mountain. Stay here, I'll be right back." Bash jogged to the entrance of the cave.

"Oh, trust me, I'm not going anywhere," I huffed out, raising a hand in the air. I managed to prop myself up. "Lane?" I called out his name and heard a slight echo but no response. A sinking feeling deep in my gut bloomed as I thought, did he not make it? Hacking noises came from the entrance of the cave as Bash and Knox stumbled in, both coated in black—Bash less so than Knox, who was just devoured by it. It clung to him like a thick second skin. To *every* inch of him. His dragon tattoo was barely visible; I snapped my eyes up from where the dragon's tail dipped and rushed to meet them. "What can I do?"

"Help me get him to the cave spring, hook his other arm around you," Bash said.

"Cave spring?" I questioned as I grabbed Knox's left arm and placed it over me, the fresh sludge mixing with the dust-filled sludge on me. I took some of his weight, and we headed farther in.

"Yeah, it's most likely where Lane took Blaire. It's a small hot spring said to be used for rejuvenation. While I don't really believe that, the hot water will help get the *Drakar Zynth* off of everyone."

"If we all get in one spring, won't it just turn into a black sludge pit and defeat the purpose?" I tried to imagine what the five of us in one spring trying to bathe would look like, and I wasn't convinced it would be beneficial to anyone.

Bash laughed. "It's a spring-fed system of different pools in different caverns. The water is always flowing. We won't need to worry about that."

We maneuvered around large rock formations and narrow passageways where we had to get creative in shimmying forward and still offering support for Knox, who kept grunting every time we moved too fast or made him contort his body in any fashion to get through. I kept my eyes straight ahead the whole time, trying not to look at him. After we squeezed through the third passageway, the room opened up to a sight I would have never believed was in this mountain. The room was awash with a bluish glow, pink and purple mushrooms grew in waves along the cave walls, some mushrooms flat with wavy edges, others were little puffs of glowing white. The air was chilly and damp, small dewdrops covered the ceiling and trickled down long formations that grew toward the cave floor. It was magical. "Wow," I breathed. At the back of the room, Lane and Blaire were lying close together, both sleeping like a death storm wasn't raging outside.

"They obviously weren't very worried about us," I said under my breath, making Knox snort.

"The springs are this way." Bash motioned his head to the left, where I could see a shadowy alcove. I fixed Knox's arm around my neck, and we headed for it. "We will go to the second spring, it's a little bigger," Bash said as we entered the first spring. Heat radiated off the surface of the turquoise water, which felt welcoming after the chill of the main cavern. The walls surrounding the springs were also adorned with mushrooms of various glowing hues. This place felt like it held so much magic and wonder. We entered into a short tunnel that opened to the second room, which, besides the bigger size, was very similar to the first, except this one had a shallow ledge where you could walk into the water without being fully immersed.

"I think I'm in love with a cave," I said in complete awe. If I could have seen myself, I'm sure my eyes would have been as wide as an owl's. They were my best friend's favorite bird. She'd loved how they would sleep all day to then be a top predator at night. We would even mimic their call when we wanted to signal it was time to sneak away from our daily chore duties. I smiled at the memory and wondered what grave she was in back at the field, which reminded me of the sludge and how her grave—if she had one—would be completely covered by it anyway now. My smile faded just as quickly as it came.

"It's intriguing," Knox said between coughs.

Bash started easing into the water, so I did the same. "What is?" I asked while coaxing him onto the shallow ledge. The water was just below being too hot, and I wanted to lie down and soak in it, but we needed to tend to Knox first. He'd been hit much worse by the storm. After what he'd done for me, after all that he'd done and probably would do, I would delay scrubbing this gunk off me for as long as I had to.

"How often your mind flips through thoughts. Your face is constantly twisting into new facial expressions." He coughed again, only this time, it sounded like it came from deep within his chest. He turned his head and spat out a glob of putrid black, then sighed. "That feels a shit ton better."

"That can't be good." I looked at Bash, who just shrugged. "And my face doesn't twist," I said defensively.

"Tell that to your twisted face." Knox lifted one side of his mouth up as he unhooked his arm from Bash and poked my nose at the tip.

I let go of his arm and let him drop into the water.

"Amalia, what the hell?" Bash said, kneeling down to where Knox was propped up on an elbow, lying on his side in the water.

I rolled my eyes. "Oh, he's fine. And deserved it," I said, crossing my arms.

"He literally just saved your life," Bash reminded me sternly, causing Knox to start laughing.

"He still deserved it." Bash rubbed his face like he wasn't sure what to do with either of us.

"Can you just help get this off of him? There's moss by those rocks," he said, pointing to a group of damp rocks to the side. "Grab a few handfuls and we'll use them to scrub him clean."

I did as requested and grabbed as many handfuls as I could carry, since we were all disgusting, and brought them back. I laid them along the edge just before the shallow ledge, so they would stay dry until we needed them. I kneeled in the water and took a second to relish the feeling of the heat against my legs and waist. "Mmm," I sighed. "This feels so good."

"I'm gonna need you to refrain from saying things like that while sighing," Knox said with a predatory look in his eyes.

"Why?"

"Because I don't need to be replaying those words, or sounds in my head as you give me a moss bath while I'm naked."

"Oh my dragons." My cheeks heated as I understood his meaning, my eyes darting down to where, luckily, his leg was positioned to hide certain parts of him, and I quickly looked backed up.

"That's it, I'm out," Bash said, throwing the handful of moss into the water behind Knox.

"What? You can't leave!" I shouted, then regretted it as it echoed around us.

"I'll be in the first spring if you need me... which is doubtful." Then he got out of the water and left us.

Knox was smirking at me, probably studying my "twisting" expressions, and I was alone with him, in a hot spring, while he was naked.

Chapter 26

Watching Bash leave, I clicked my tongue, rolling my head to the side to look at Knox. I stifled a laugh at the fact I still couldn't make out much of him at all besides his striking gaze. "You look ridiculous," I said, grabbing the moss floating in the water.

"Do you think you look any different?" he shot back playfully. I hadn't thought about how I looked, but it couldn't be good. It had been days since the last time I was able to brush my hair, and I hadn't properly bathed with soap. We had brought supplies to do all the necessary hygienic acts, but there'd been no down time where I was not fully exhausted. None of those acts were given the time they needed.

"Can I?" I asked, holding up the moss.

He nodded and moved to a sitting position, leaning his back against the edge of the spring. I took a subtle breath and chose to start on his face, so he'd look less crazy. He closed his eyes as I brought the moss up and gently rubbed it down the length of his cheek. A glob of black covering it, I swished it around in the water and repeated the process until the left side of his face was visible again. "Well, I almost forgot what you looked like under all that." I used my free hand to grasp his chin and turn his face toward me, so I could get the other side. His eyes met mine with a burning heat that rivaled the temperature of the water. "Are you okay?" I asked him, not able to keep eye contact for long, and switched the moss to my other hand.

"I have nothing to complain about right now," he said in a gravelly whisper.

My eyes flickered to his before refocusing on the spot I was raking the moss over. "Other than the fact you are covered in an inch-thick layer of cloud goo?"

"If I wasn't, I wouldn't be sitting in this hot spring with *the goddess of death*. So no, not even that will pull a complaint from me." The name sent tingles over my body.

I started to work on his forehead and nose, when he grabbed his own handful of moss, dunking it into the water. "Am I going too slow for you?" I said, doing the last pass on his forehead. I looked at his hair and decided he would need to soak it and I'd have to scrub it out with my hands.

"You're perfect. I just thought it would be nice if I helped you while you were helping me." He brought his moss up over my shoulder, letting the hot water drip onto me, running down my arm before he rubbed a layer of grime off.

"Oh." I cleared my throat. "That, um, that would be efficient." I moved my hand down to his neck and worked as he continued running the excess water over me before placing the moss against my skin. Every part of me was on alert. We worked in silence for a while, stealing glances at one another. I was able to clear his neck and work my way down to his chest. He cleaned off most of my arm before making a disapproving sound. "What is it?" I asked.

"It's hard to get the spots I need to with the way you're sitting," he said to me, cleaning the moss in the water.

My face contorted. "You can reach me perfectly fine, what are you talking about?"

"It must be that my arm is just too tired from the weight of the *Drakar Zynth* and carrying you and Bash to safety." He dramatically dropped his arm into the water, causing it to splash us both.

I rolled my eyes. "You're such a liar." I went to adjust my position—my knees had started to ache from kneeling for so long—and when I did, Knox grabbed me at the waist and planted me so that I was straddling him. My entire body froze. No part of me wanted to get off, but every part was screaming. "Um... can you reach better now?"

Knox simply uttered an, "Mhm." His white teeth flashed as he smiled wide; I loved his smile. His teeth were near perfect, his lips framing them like a pristine picture. He didn't show this smile often, but when he did, it was breathtaking. "What is going through that head of yours?" he asked.

"Just thinking about how filthy you still are." I brought the moss back to his chest and started nervously scrubbing. He tilted my chin up with his hand and brought the moss to my cheek, using it to rub away the caked-on mess.

"Four." He stated the number like it was a fact.

Was I supposed to understand the relevance of that number? "I have noticed you like saying random, incomplete sentences to confuse me," I said, a bit frustrated.

He chuckled, dipping the moss into the water and swirling it around some before speaking. "Four is the number of colors in your eyes."

My hand stilled on his chest, and my gaze met his. "What?" The question came out quiet and breathless.

"Your eyes are a dynamic green, but there's also browns, amber, and yellow around your pupil. They're beautiful." He used his thumb to caress my cheek, and I couldn't help but look at his mouth. It was parted slightly, just like mine was. Everything in me was yelling at me to lean in and kiss him, it was so intense it felt like a need. His hand moved from my cheek. His fingers threaded in my hair just below my ear. I could feel him growing, becoming hard beneath me, and it made me ache for something to happen that much more. I shifted slightly and then put all my weight onto his lap, causing him to inhale through his teeth. "Amalia." When he said my name, it broke my control. With my hands on either side of his face, I pulled him to me, our mouths just centimeters apart—

"Amalia?" Lane called out for me. "Amalia? Bash said you'd be back here. Where are you?"

I exhaled deeply and pressed my forehead against Knox's. "I'm going to kill him for this," he said through clenched teeth. He pressed his nose to mine, and I felt tears welling up, which was ridiculous.

"I'm sorry, I should go let him know I'm okay." I didn't move until he nodded. I moved my face away from his just a little before he grabbed me and pulled me back in to kiss my forehead. It wasn't a quick peck, it was long and meaningful, making one of the tears escape and roll down my cheek. When he parted from me, he used his thumb to wipe it away without asking why it was there. I wasn't sure I could explain even if he did.

I lifted myself out of the water and looked down at the pants I was wearing. They were completely soaked and disgusting. I walked out of the spring, leaving Knox sitting there as his hands fell to the water. He didn't look back at me as I left the cavern, but I couldn't help but look at him with every couple of feet that I walked away.

"You were calling for me?" I said to Lane, who was standing by the first spring, which Bash no longer occupied. I wondered how much easier it was to clean yourself up when there were no distractions.

"Yeah, I was going to see if you wanted to get washed up. I brought your pack. It has clean clothes, and a few other things like a brush, soap, toothpaste." All of that sounded like heaven right now. "I can help get you cleaned up—" He stopped mid-sentence and actually looked at me. "Were you already washing up?"

"Yeah, uh, Bash and I had to help Knox into the spring. He was in rough shape. He had to shift to get us here before the storm trapped us."

Lane's face became stone as I told him what had happened. "Listen, Mal, I know you're friends with him, but he can't be trusted."

"That's your brother," I whisper-shouted.

"By marriage, not by blood," he said matter-of-factly. "You should stay clear of him unless you absolutely have to be near him. He's bad news. You're too innocent to get tangled in any of his messes." He went to caress my cheek, but I pulled away from him. His words hit a trigger, and I became so enraged I could barely look at his face.

"He's not the one who was more worried about Blaire being in pain than the woman lying half dead on the ground in front of you. He's not the one who left me while I was trying to make something that was so special to me full of life again!" This time, my voice definitely came out as a shout. "He is the one who buried my entire kingdom because of a passing comment I made about feeling guilty. He is the one who stayed by my side during the storm, ensuring I was safe, while I was bleeding out and venom was eating away at me, so I wasn't alone, even though he was injured. He is the one who would rather train me for a day than let me come on this suicide mission strictly depending on a group where most of them want me dead." I shoved my finger hard into his chest. "Maybe you should stay clear of me for a while." I grabbed my pack from his grasp and stomped back toward the spring, back toward Knox.

Lane didn't call after me or chase me; he let me leave. Hopefully that meant what I said had hit a nerve. He'd barely been there for me, had talked about us being together at random times, treated me like I was helpless, but yet Knox was the problem? As I stomped into the second cavern, I didn't see Knox. My heart dropped. There must have been another way out. Echoes sounded in the cavern as I walked up to the edge and knelt to rummage through my pack. I grimaced as the black goop covered the material, despite my best efforts to only touch the unaffected parts, it clung to my skin. I grabbed the soap first and set it on the ground while I looked around, seeing no one but the empty pool of water. The cavern was empty so I lifted my chemise over my head. It felt glued to me from the sludge seeping through the material and onto my body. Then I wriggled out of the trousers I had on—they weren't as bad since I had just been sitting in the water, they'd had time to soften, making getting them off easier—then stripped my undergarments off.

I sank onto the shallow ledge and pulled my clothes into the water with me, lathering some soap onto the fabrics and using the moss that was left to scrub away the events of the day. I started to hum a song my father used to sing to me when I would become too numb to be active during the day. There wasn't always a reason. Sometimes my body would feel like it'd shut down on itself, so he'd created a song to sing to me to remind me it was okay to not always be okay.

"*Hmm hm hm hm hmm oh, baby girl, you'll be okay eventually, you survive every day and hide away in the silence. Hmm hm hm hold onto the ones that love you, and remember even when your mind takes you miles away, they will always be with you.*" I dunked the soapy clothes under the water and swirled them around. "*You'll be okay eventually, suffering leads to strength, and baby girl, you'll be the strongest to ever be. Hmm hmmm hmm.*"

"Where did you learn that song?" I jumped clear out of my skin as Knox's voice filled the cavern. I slammed a hand to my chest at the sudden intrusion and looked around, trying to spot him, glancing behind me and around to the entrance I'd come in. I didn't see him. His laugh surrounded me as I heard movement in the water, and at the far end of the spring, covered in shadows, was Knox.

"Have you been there the whole time?" I shrieked, thinking about what a show I must have put on getting into the spring. I was perched on the shallow ledge where only up to my waist was covered. My hands flew to my exposed breasts, and I made quick work of sinking farther into the water, holding tight to the ledge as I kept myself afloat.

"If you answer my question, I'll answer yours," he said, moving closer to me, the shadows behind him dissipating.

I swallowed. "My father used to sing it to me when I would go through numbing spells." I ran a hand over my now-wet hair. "He said it was to remind me that he was there. He made it up while lying with me one day. He struggled trying to rhyme but said it didn't matter because it came from the heart." A short laugh escaped me. "It ended up being my favorite song."

"It sounds like you had a great father," Knox said, resting his arms on the ledge next to me.

"Hm, yeah, I did. He was hard on us growing up, but he and I were so alike, we always had a strong bond. Even when times were tough." I felt a lump lodge in my throat, and I dipped my head underwater, then came back up to disguise any emotion that may show.

I think he knew my ability to speak about it was over, because he changed the subject. "Yes, I was there the whole time, yes. I watched as you angrily got undressed and then as you sank in the water." His eyes roamed over me and stopped where my chest broke the water's surface. Nothing was visible right now except for the swells of my breasts, but with everything he had seen, he was probably imagining what was concealed.

"That's extremely inappropriate." I shoved water toward him, and he ducked beneath the surface to avoid it.

When he came up again, he said, "What's inappropriate is coming back to a spring you knew I was in and acting like you were alone just to tease me."

My mouth dropped open; there was no way he was serious right now. "I was not *teasing* you," I said. "I looked for you, I thought maybe you had known of another way out and had left, not wanting to see Lane."

He hummed, grinning at me. "I'm serious!" I shouted.

He threw his hands up in a mock surrender and said, "Okay, okay, I believe you," through chuckles.

An aggravated scream left me. "You're the one lurking in the shadows spying on me."

"Spying? It's not spying when I hadn't moved except to swim in the spring, and you gallivanted in here and stripped before I could announce myself."

"You had plenty of time to announce yourself," I shot back at him.

"We will have to agree to disagree," he said, the grin still plastered on his face.

"I agree to nothing." I turned my body toward the ledge and used my arms as a pillow, resting my head on them as I looked at him beside me. I tried to fight the smile that was fighting to break free at this childish argument.

"So, why did you come back?" His tone had shifted, turning the conversation more serious.

I looked away from him and stared at where my pack lay on the ground. "Because Lane is an idiot and pissed me off," I said, exhaling a deep breath, knowing what his next question was going to be.

"What did he do to piss you off?"

I could see from the corner of my eye that he had turned to fully face me, waiting for my response. Ready to react in any way he needed to.

I dipped my mouth under the water and blew anxious bubbles, trying to avoid having to answer this. How could I tell him I was pissed off at the fact Lane was warning me against being near him, and that, in turn, made me run straight to him? "He was saying things about you that I didn't agree with... then I kind of lost my temper with him... and then I wanted to see you after."

Knox didn't say anything, and he usually had something to say. I looked over, and he seemed to be in disbelief. His brows were raised, and his mouth was open as his wide eyes just stared at me.

"What?" I said nervously.

"You wanted to come back to me?" he said slowly as he moved closer to me.

I moved slightly back, unsure of what was happening right now. "Y-yes, I just, I don't know how to explain it. I just needed to see you." When I looked back at him, his eyes were trained on my lips.

"Knox," I whispered. And then he was on me. He moved so fast, I barely registered his movement. His hands grabbed my face, and he consumed me. His mouth devoured me and sent stars shooting behind my eyelids. I felt his kiss down to my core. Tingles swept through my entire body, and I felt ignited. A moan escaped me, and it made him more feral. His hands left my face and grabbed my waist, hoisting me up onto the ledge. I squealed at the sudden change, pressing my fingers against my still-tingling lips. "What the hell just happened?"

"Fate," was all he said before he kissed me again. His lips were soft and aggressive as they commanded mine. His tongue slipped in, and he tasted of midnight. Like the fresh air you breathe when the moon is at its peak and you're the only one outside. I broke free and cupped his face, relishing in the hunger I felt for him. It was enthralling to feel the need for his touch in my soul.

He moved slower now, kissing down my neck, my back arching on instinct. A pleased groan rumbled from him as my peaked nipples pressed against his chest, an invitation. He didn't hesitate as the kisses trailed from my collarbone to my breasts. He sucked my nipple into his mouth while teasing the other between his fingers. His breath was hot and made me ache down to my core. I needed more. I was desperate for more.

I grabbed his hair, and his name came out as a moan, "Knox."

He pulled away, excitement churning in his violet eyes. My heart felt like it was going to beat out of my chest, thunderous like the storm outside. "Why'd you stop?" I whimpered.

"Even in this water, I bet if I were to touch you right now, I'd be able to feel you slick with desire for me." His hands caressed my thighs as his fingers trailed up slowly and gently until he reached my sex. He didn't go further, no, he just trailed along the flesh reaching my other thigh. My legs tried to tighten at the feel, but he was between them, keeping them open, unable to get relief. "Am I right, *Thy Valkara?* My goddess," he amended.

I didn't dare answer him, fearing my voice would come out as nothing but a shaky, inaudible whisper. Instead, I whined and used my legs to press him closer.

"If you need more, you need to say it. Tell me what you need," he whispered, his voice full of the shadows that had surrounded him before.

"I need you," I said, my body begging silently for him to take me. I didn't need him to touch me and prove I wanted him; I felt it in every nerve. I knew without touching myself this was the wettest any male had ever made me, and I wanted him to claim me.

A growl escaped him as he grabbed my waist and hoisted me further onto the ledge before he pulled himself up. His body was glistening, steam rolling off his tanned skin. Every inch of him was sculpted to otherworldly guidelines. I couldn't breathe as I looked at him, took him in. My gaze trailed from the curves of his abs down to the defined V that led to a thick, hard length. My eyes bulged as I took in the sheer size. "That is not going to fit inside me," I said, gasping.

"Don't worry, you can take it." He lowered himself over me and pushed my legs so that my knees were bent. "But first, I have been dying to taste you." As he said the last word, his tongue flicked over my lips, causing a jolt through me. The second lick was slower, and I felt as his tongue parted me on his way up to my clit.

"Holy High Dragons," I cried. He blew a hot breath down the path he licked, and goosebumps spread over my body and went straight to my nipples, hardening them further. He used one hand to spread my lips, then the other to run his fingers up the exposed, pulsing, slick slit. I could have sworn the lightning was cracking inside me at the intense pressure building within me. He slid one, then two fingers inside me, curving them upward, slipping them in and out, in and out, while his thumb rubbed the sensitive flesh. I tried to grasp something, anything, but the ground was flat and hard. I tried to close my legs, to stop the buildup that was happening. It would be too much. This was too much. I wanted to scream his name, to yell out, but I was fighting for my life to try and stay quiet. I didn't need the echoes to reach everyone else. But gods, this, this was beyond anything I had ever experienced. "Knox, stop, you're gonna make me cum," I whined, restlessly moving what I could.

A rumble of approval came from him as he said, "I want nothing more than to watch you cum all over my hand." That statement sent me over the edge, and I erupted. Tremors took over as my legs shook, my back came off the ground as I yelled his name. I threw my hands over my mouth as a guttural moan filled the cavern, echoing off the walls.

"You're so damn beautiful." Knox pulled his hand from inside me, sending another wave of pleasure through me, before he devoured me again. My pussy was so sensitive I could barely breathe with his mouth sucking and licking after what he had done. I lifted my back, trying to relieve the sensitivity, and his hands went under and cupped my ass, pulling me back to his mouth. "You taste so fucking good," he said, inhaling the scent of me.

Gasping, I groaned in a sultry voice I had *never* made before. "Oh gods, Knox, yes." I needed him more than I could comprehend. I no longer wanted his mouth, or his hands, I wanted *him*. "Please," I begged. "I need to feel you, all of you."

"You never need to beg me. I am yours to take." He adjusted so he was over me, his cock brushing my entrance, making me whimper. "Are you sure you want this?" he asked.

"I have never wanted anyone more than I want you," I said, breathless. I spoke the truth. What I felt in that moment was out of this realm; it took over every thought and feeling. He was everything. He leaned down, planting a sensual kiss on my lips, letting me taste what he had. As his lips left mine, his cock stretched me open. He pulled out slowly, the loss of him felt in every inch of me, before he grabbed his cock and rubbed the tip against my clit, creating endless shockwaves before he thrust into me. "Knox!" I screamed. He leaned down and kissed me so fervently. With each thrust, I felt as though I was having an out-of-body experience. His mouth claimed me, his tongue teasing mine before he tugged on my bottom lip.

"You will be the ruin of me," he groaned, moving a strand of hair from my face. "I would burn the realm for you if you asked." My heart lurched, because I truly believed his words. He had already done so much for me, I didn't think there were any limits to how he'd show he cared. I reached between us and cupped his balls in my hand, giving them a squeeze as he thrust into me harder.

"Fuck!" he groaned. "Fuck, Amalia." His thrusts grew more frantic, and he kissed along the side of my breast, making me moan at the light caress.

I pushed against his chest, making him straighten so I could admire his physique. "Let me show you how much I wanted this," I said to him, motioning for him to lie on his back. He obliged with a fire in his eyes. I straddled his body, hovering my entrance over him before lowering down onto the head of his dick. I dropped my head back, running my hand through my hair, teasing my nipples with the other.

"Damn it, woman, you're perfect," Knox said, placing his hands on my hips, guiding me up and down. I placed a finger in my mouth, sucking it before I slipped it between my thighs, circling my clit as I rode him. The sensation of being filled with the electricity shooting from my sensitive bundle of nerves sent shockwaves through me. It wouldn't be long before another orgasm claimed me.

"I can feel you tightening around my dick, are you going to cum for me again, *Valka-ra*?" he said with a rumble in his throat. My thighs burned from the repetitive motions of bouncing up and down on his hard length. I wanted this to last forever, while my body was screaming for a release.

"Together?" I asked in a moan as my climax neared its peak.

His fingers dug into my hips as he brought me down hard. The sounds of our bodies coming together echoed through the cavern. Fulfilled screams tore from me as I lost the ability to help, but he didn't miss a beat. Using his strength, he continued to lift my quaking body before bringing me back down again. "Knox!" I yelled, when he plunged into me once more, as deep as he could manage, and I felt him release into me as I spiraled out of control. His eyes squeezed shut as he pushed even deeper before slowly lifting me, jerking every few inches until he was completely out of me.

I wiped the sweat that had beaded along my forehead. "Was that real?" I said in disbelief.

He shifted me to lie next to him, putting his arm under my head. "If it wasn't, I don't ever want to wake up."

My sex pulsed as aftershocks shot through me, making me moan softly. I stretched out, basking in the pleasure it provided, and he rested his other arm over my stomach, tracing the deep red scar from not one but two orbichor attacks.

"Death comes for you at every turn, yet you defy it each time." He sounded in awe, like it was some ability that made me untouchable.

I rubbed his forearm and said, "Usually, death will find a way to right when he's been wronged. He will come for me again."

"And I will stand by you, should that day come again."

Chapter 27

Knox spent the next twenty minutes washing my hair, lathered and massaged the soap into my scalp so well I almost fell asleep. The things this male could do with his hands. After he rinsed it, he placed a kiss on my forehead before I got dressed. While he soaked a bit longer, I took some time to brush my hair for the first time in days. It would likely dry in wavy locks, not staying the darkened, straight strands they were now. But at least it was given some attention. "I'll go grab your pack," I said, putting my supplies back into my own bag. I still felt unexpected rushes that heated my core, and I wondered if that would always be the case with someone like him.

"Don't worry about it. I'll just walk out there," he said nonchalantly.

"You're naked," I reminded him. "Everyone is out there, they'll see you."

He glided out of the water, the droplets giving his skin a speckled sheen. "They have all seen me naked plenty of times. I can guarantee no one will react the way you did for me." He placed his hand under my chin and kissed me. Wetness burst from the seams in an instant, ready for more. He broke the kiss but stayed just an inch away from my mouth as he added, "Plus, I think it's better you don't walk out there alone, sound tends to travel in cave systems." He tapped his thumb on my chin and chuckled as my face turned bright red.

"I will live here for the rest of my life, then. There's no way I'm going out there."

"We have a scale to get, little goddess. Come on."

As we entered the main cavernous room, everyone was dressed and sitting on various rocks. Lane looked up at me with a murderous glint in his eyes. He didn't move or speak, and that made me more uneasy. I'd rather him just voice his displeasure with me than spiral over what he planned to do. Would he try to hurt Knox? Bash tossed Knox some clothes, and I stood there awkwardly, not knowing what to say or how to act. "Toss me everything," Knox said to Bash, who raised an eyebrow at him.

Bash looked over me and must have sensed my unease. "Want to hear a joke I've been working on?" he asked, flipping a dagger in the air before catching the wooden hilt.

"Sure," I said, trying to sound chipper.

"What do you call a melon that's committed a crime?" He looked at me expectantly with his eyes wide and a huge grin on his face.

"I'm not sure... what?" I asked.

Behind me, Blaire groaned. "Please don't fucking say it."

"A water-felon." Bash slapped his knee and started laughing like he truly thought he had crafted the joke of all jokes.

"Wow." I dragged the word out. "That was... definitely something." I could feel knives being thrown in the back of my head, so I turned around to see Lane glaring at me. I needed to have a conversation with him, but where was I supposed to start? I walked over and sat next to him, waiting to see if he would speak first. He didn't. "Lane, I—"

"Don't," he bit out, clasping his hands together. "Am I really just the other brother to you? The one you must pity. We had something together. I've known you longer, better. I warned you against him and instead you jumped on his dick." He was standing now, towering over me. Shock overwhelmed me. I hadn't expected this kind of reaction from him. He'd given Blaire more attention than he'd given me, but I somehow was the villain here? I'd expected hurt feelings, but this, this was over the top. "You tell me to give you space just so you have room to move in on him!" He threw his hand back in the general direction of Knox, who was standing dead still, Bash next to him, looking from him to Lane.

"I'm sorry," I choked out, leaning back trying to create space as he moved closer to me.

"You're sorry!" Lane's spit struck my cheek like the deadly rain had, hot and searing. "Were you sorry when you were fucking my bro—" His last word was cut off as a whistle cut through the air and a crack sounded above my head. I flinched, my back hitting the cave wall as I looked up and saw the hilt of the dagger Bash was just tossing sticking out of the cave wall above me. I looked at him. Stunned, he immediately pointed a finger at Knox, who stood facing us with his legs shoulder-width apart and his arms crossed.

"The only thing she was sorry for during our time together," Knox drawled, "was your interruption the first time." He stepped closer. "Don't worry, we made up for that slight delay."

My eyes grew three sizes. Bash just shook his head, letting out a weary sigh, like this wasn't the first time he'd witnessed these two in this state of dominance. I spared a glance up at Lane, who was still staring at me, and he lifted a hand to his left ear then pulled it away, exposing fresh blood on his fingers. *My fault. It's always my fault. I should have never gone back.*

Knox had cut him. Lane looked at his bloody fingers for a moment before looking back at me and smiling. There was nothing heartfelt about it. It was full of a threatening promise, and for the first time, I was scared of him. He'd never looked at me like this before. Guilt washed over me.

"Good luck getting the scale, Mal. We will talk when you come back." He placed his bloody hand along my jaw, smearing the sticky substance on my skin. I didn't move until he turned and walked away. I sucked in air. My lungs burned—I hadn't breathed since the dagger flew, hadn't dared—as his bloodied palm cupped my face. *I did this. I unraveled him.*

"Hey man, sometimes we should react on the inside before reacting on the outside. Yeah?" Bash said as Lane passed by him and Knox.

"Always so full of wisdom, Bash. It would be a shame if she had to sacrifice you for this next scale." He launched his shoulder into Knox, who barely moved from the impact, before he disappeared into the narrow passageway. The tension in the room didn't lessen with Lane's absence.

Knox walked over to me and placed his hands on my shoulder as he kneeled on the ground in front of me. "Are you okay?"

I nodded, but didn't speak out loud just yet. With my fingers trembling, I balled my hands into fists. I wanted to make sure there were no traces of fear in my voice. I didn't want anyone to have that kind of power over me. He rubbed my shoulders gently but didn't push. Instead, he looked over his shoulder. "Bash, are you ready?"

"Ready, boss!" he said as he walked over and pulled his blade from the wall. "That is definitely going to dull the blade." He shot an unamused look at Knox, who shrugged. Bash ran his finger over the engraved teeth that were at the tip and bottom of the hilt, like the opened mouth of a dragon. In the center was a carved circle with the head of a dragon inside. There were words carved around the circle, but I couldn't decipher them, they must have been the ancient language they spoke from time to time.

Bash placed his hand out and I took it, letting him guide me to a wall on the right that was draped in glowing mushrooms. He stood and faced the wall and then did... nothing.

"Do you think it'll just materialize there for you, Deckett?" Blaire chimed in, apparently finding this worthy of her attention.

Bash said nothing. With his eyes closed, he placed his open palm against the wall and said, *"Kralthar Vornak."* Once he spoke the ancient language, the glowing dimmed and then brightened in pulses, the wall dissolving before us.

"What did you say?"

"Open the tunnel," he replied as he stepped over the still-dissolving wall into a tunnel that was lit by glowing blue worms that hung from the ceiling.

"Are those worms?" Trepidation made me pause following him in. "Yeah... not my favorite, is there another dissolving wall we can use?"

"They're caterpillars, not worms," he said, sounding offended. "If we're lucky, there may even be dragonflies somewhere in here."

"Worms, caterpillars, they're practically the same thing, but I'm pretty sure dragonflies don't evolve from a caterpillar." I said.

Bash smiled at that and kept walking, forcing me to follow.

The wall reformed once we were both through. I kept my sights on the ceiling to make sure none of those globs fell on me. "Do you know where we're going?" I asked.

"Yes and no," he responded, walking around one of the caterpillars trying to squirm its way across the walkway. "I can feel the pull to it, but I can't exactly pinpoint where it is.

I'm surprised you can't feel it since you can absorb our abilities, which, by the way, isn't normal."

I laughed. "I don't think anything that's happened since the shimmer is normal." I contemplated telling Bash about what I'd seen and heard in the lake. Some of it seemed relevant now. "When I was standing by the lake, I saw a glowing aqua trail leading to one spot. After everything that happened, I don't know if that's where I retrieved the scale or not, but it had to have meant something, right?"

"I don't know, I never saw it. But you are a wild card. You may be able to see things we can't. No one knows or even wants to broach the subject of what you are. You could be capable of anything with the ability to channel magic."

The path opened up into a fork, both pathways looking identical. Bash went to take the right, and I paused before following. I attempted to listen to the cave, to try and feel for the scale. I wasn't sure what exactly I was supposed to be doing, but something urged me to go left. "I think I should go left," I said.

"We. You think *we* should go left." Bash ran his hand along the cave wall as he walked over to where I stood. "Is it speaking to you or something?"

I couldn't help but giggle. "Or something," I said. I looked down the path that was lacking the glow of the one we stood in currently. It felt ominous, and that was exactly why I thought I should take it.

Bash whistled before saying, "Yeah, I don't know, Mal, this path or the one that is lit like the main pathway. I'm gonna have to recommend not going down the path of doom."

"I don't think you should come with me. I think you should take the right and see where it leads," I said, fear coursing through me at the thought of having to decide between myself or him surviving. I wouldn't be able to choose myself.

"Respectfully"—he paused—"that's not going to fucking happen."

"What if—" My question was interrupted within seconds.

"You won't need to. Whatever needs to be done, we will do it together," Bash said, extending his elbow out for me to take. We took our first steps into the tunnel shrouded in nothing but night.

We walked silently and slowly with one hand on the tunnel wall to help guide us, only accompanied by the sounds of our nervous breaths and soft-footed steps. I started to hear faint whispers around my head and looked over at Bash before remembering I couldn't see a single thing. I squeezed where I held his arm. "Do you hear anything?" I asked quietly.

"No... should I?" he said, placing his other hand on top of mine. "You are the only thing I have heard so far, and frankly I've been focused on how I couldn't tell you up from down right now. It's not my favorite experience," he said dryly, making me smile.

"I keep hearing whispers, but they aren't words, just whispered sounds I think? I don't know, it's hard to make out. I could have imagined it. Weird things happen in the dark." He let go of my hand, and I heard the sound of dirt being brushed away to the floor as we moved, indicating he had resumed running his hand along the tunnel wall. Murmurs filled the quiet once more, only this time, I could grasp at snippets before they became inaudible.

"Not alive... need air... KILLS me! What am I? What am I? What am I!"

The words made me stop in my tracks, halting Bash in the process. "What's going on, Amalia? You hear something again, don't you?"

"They sound like they need help... something terrible has happened, I think. I couldn't hear everything, they still sound jumbled. I only heard a few words." I desperately wished there was a light source in here, the pitch black was making me panic. My breaths became shallow as my heart thumped erratically.

"C'mon, let's keep moving. It'll have to open up somewhere, and when it does, there's bound to be some sort of light," Bash said, picking up on my heightened anxiety. Could he hear my heart like Knox could?

We made it twenty more steps before more voices started speaking all at once. They were in my head and around me, they were everywhere but nowhere. I released Bash's arm and threw my hands over my ears, dropping to my knees in submission. It wasn't painful like Zarakruae had made it, but it was terrifying and unnerving, testing my mental stability. "Ahhh, please stop. I can't understand you when you're all saying different things at the same time." My words came out as a plea, but they seemed to have listened. The voices quieted, and I started hearing them one at a time.

"You came to take, but you must prove yourself worthy."

"I'll do whatever you need," I said with relief.

"What is happening?" Bash said, touching my shoulder in unsure taps, reminding me that when I'd dropped, he wasn't able to see I was still next to him.

"They said I have to prove I'm worthy." I reached out and pulled his hand closer to me.

"Um... hello, voices... I would just like to go on record and say, I think I'm a pretty decent guy, and while I agree she should prove herself, please don't make her sacrifice me.

It's been a pretty shit day already. Ugh... thank you for your time." I felt pressure where his hand was on my shoulder and his breath by my face.

"Are you bowing?" I asked.

"Hush, it's a show of respect, and I'd rather not be sacrificed in a tunnel no one will ever find me in."

The voices laughed in unison, filling my ears with the sounds of giggling and making me think back to when I was young and in school. All the girls would whisper about the boys they liked, leading us into a fit of laughter when one walked by saying hi. I grinned at the reaction he evoked from them.

"Did they say anything?" Bash asked, giving me a nudge.

"They're just laughing at you," I said, shrugging. He couldn't see it, but he should've felt it.

"Is that a good thing?" he asked, dragging the words out.

"I think so." I moved to stand back up and felt his arm. In a place where you couldn't see, it was good to have something that grounded you. "How can I prove myself worthy?" I said into the dark.

"You must answer three simple questions to pass through."

"That's it?" That seemed too easy. "All I have to do is answer three questions and we can get the scale?" I repeated what they said so Bash knew what was going on.

"Answer three questions, and you may pass through," they said in a unified sing-song voice.

Okay, maybe it really would be that simple. "What is the first question?"

They all talked at the same time, but their voices blended together in a perfect harmony; it wasn't as overwhelming as the chaos before.

"I am never alive, yet I can grow, overtaking the tallest trees; I do not breathe, but need air to fuel my growth; I can be unstoppable, but water will end me." The voices split from each other and repeated, *"What am I? What am I? What am I?"*

I went over the question again in my head. I mumbled the words as I thought through the underlying meanings.

"Are you going to tell me what the question is?" Bash asked with little patience.

"I'm sorry, I keep forgetting you can't hear them." I went to repeat the riddle and decided to ask them first. "Is Bash allowed to know the riddles, or must I do it on my own?"

The only reply I got back was a fit of giggles. "I'm taking that as a yes."

"The first part is I am never alive, yet I can grow, overtaking the tallest trees."

"Well, that doesn't even make sense. How can you grow if you're not alive?" Bash said.

I rubbed my temple, knowing I was going to do this on my own. "That was very helpful Bash, thank you." I repeated the rest to him anyway. My brain stuck to the conundrum of how it wasn't alive but grew, and I became frustrated that I couldn't think past it.

"Are the next two questions similar to this?" I asked into the void.

Laughter filled the space before a meek *"yes"* surrounded me. "Oh my dragons," I groaned. More fits of laughter followed.

"Well, the only things I've ever seen water kill are people, animals, and fire," Bash said. The sound of his foot kicking the ground followed.

"Yeah, but all of those things are alive." More laughter. These things were going to drive me crazy with their amusement.

Wait.

"Bash, you're a genius!" I went to grab his arms and shake him but missed, so I said the answer aloud. "Is the answer a fire? It can take over an entire forest of trees. It's not technically alive, but it grows with fuel, which would be air, and when you pour water on it, it dies!" Excitement laced every word.

"She got it! She got it!" the voices murmured in glee, and I let myself take a moment to appreciate Bash not leaving me.

Are you ready for the second question, Defier of Death?

"Uh, yes," I said hesitantly. "Bash, I'm going to try something. Don't freak out."

I could hear his footsteps move away from me. "Yeah, I'm not sure I like that phrasing you used. I will need more context than that."

"I'm going to try and connect us to see if you can hear them too." When I'd absorbed Blaire's abilities, it felt like I had formed some type of tie to her at that moment. I couldn't help but wonder if I would be able to do the same with Bash, but allow him to use me. I placed my hand in his and focused on what I wanted: For us to have a painless connection. For him to hear the voices that spoke to me. I put everything I had into that thought. "Do you hear them?" I asked.

"I don't hear anything except you," Bash said. Why wasn't it working? When I had channeled Kuma and Blaire, it was in extreme situations. Maybe I couldn't syphon their magic unless it was dire?

"Tell me what you're trying to do and maybe I can help you," he said.

I exhaled and explained, "I thought I could connect us somehow so you could hear the voices talking, but it's not working. I don't know what I'm doing. It came so easily before." I felt defeated, like I should be able to do it with only a thought and I was failing at something so simple. *Thinking.*

"You're putting too much pressure on yourself," he said. "Where are you?" I could feel the light swooshes of air as he waved his arm out trying to find me. Laughing, I stretched mine out and clasped his hand. "Now, just feel our skin touching. Think about how our hands are connected. Don't focus on making the connection—it's already made."

I followed his instruction and just focused on the way his calloused palms felt against mine. How our hands were the connection we needed. I relaxed my shoulders and thought about his friendship and only stopped when I heard Bash suck in a breath.

"Why do they keep laughing?" he asked, confirming it had worked. "Good job, Mal. I'm proud of you."

That one affirmation went straight to my heart. "I think some of them have a crush on you," I snickered, and they gasped. "We are ready for the second question." I squeezed Bash's hand and waited for the next riddle.

"Very well. Very well. It is not harder than the first, but is important for you to remember," they said before the riddle came. *"I can travel the skies without wings. I shed flooding tears with no eyes. Wherever I roam, darkness follows below. What am I?"*

"Did you hear that?" I questioned, still not sure how the connection worked or if it held during the time they'd spoken.

"How many are there?" His question answered mine, but there was no way to know.

"I think I know what this is," I said confidently. "I used to lie in my field staring up at the sky for endless hours. I would watch shadows dance across the blooms, water rain down and soak them during rain showers." Today had shown with no doubt in my mind that where they roamed, nothing but darkness followed.

"Then say it," Bash pushed.

"It's clouds. Clouds travel across the sky but don't have wings. They rain down droplets of water that, in a way, are their own tears. The clouds outside are bringing darkness to the mountain, even if it wasn't the deadly rain, shadows would cover the grounds as they passed. The answer is clouds."

"Yes! Yes!" they shouted in a wild flurry of voices. *"Never linger when the darkness comes. It takes, it takes, she wants to take, but she does not look like the darkness. No, no, she is the defier, the evader of darkness."*

The voices seemed to be arguing with themselves, getting sidetracked in what they thought of me, of the storm outside that they called the darkness.

"I can't listen to this, it's nonsense," Bash said, breaking my concentration on their words. "Can we hear the final question, please?" he said into the nothingness. "I'd really appreciate being able to see myself again."

The voices hissed in disapproval.

"I don't think they liked your interruption."

"I would have to say you're probably right," he agreed.

"Impatient! Such impatience. I thought he liked us. He wanted to leave us! Shhhh, give them the last riddle. They must pass through. They must go on."

Anxiety crept in as thoughts that we may not get the answer taunted me.

"The final question you must answer is: the more you take, the more you leave behind. What am I? What am I!" The voices started to shriek the question as the excitement of reaching the end filled the darkness.

The more you take, the more you leave behind. "That could be so many things," I said, aggravated. I was ready to be done with this. I was over not being able to see, being surrounded by voices that felt like they were inside and outside of my body.

"So name them, and we will see what clicks," Bash said.

"... I can't name them," I said defensively.

"What do you mean? You just said it could be so many things, what things could it be?"

Both of our nerves were shot from being in the pitch black for so long; it was starting to affect us, and not in a good way.

"That's just something you say when you know it could be multiple things, it doesn't mean those things actually came to mind," I explained. "And even if I had thought of some, you putting me on the spot is going to make them *poof*, disappear from my brain." I made motions with my hands to add emphasis, but it was lost since he couldn't see it.

"Humans say too many useless phrases." He let out an aggravated sigh. "What about trail mix? People take it, then leave it behind so they don't get lost."

I cleared my throat. "I'm going to say that one doesn't click for me."

We spent at least five minutes throwing possibilities back and forth, to the point where I really didn't think either of us wanted to hear the other's voice. "How about we just be silent for a minute and think." I put my hands out, searching for the dusty wall. When I reached it, I slid down and sat, leaning my back against it. With my knees bent, I set my elbows on them, resting my head in my hands. I tried to think about the words, two sentences. Two sentences were going to be what stood between the scale and I. It was so simple. I knew I was overthinking it, but I couldn't stop. I heard Bash's footsteps going back and forth, and I truly thought he was trying to make me psychotic.

"Would you stop pacing?" I growled at him.

"Walking helps me think. For every step I take, my mind clears a little more. Leaving behind the stress and thoughts. So, if you want to solve this, I will take as many steps as I need to."

"What did you just say?"

"Listen, I don't want to pull the species card, but I'm a dragon. I am not in the mood for spicy Amalia right now."

"No, Bash. Really, repeat like the last ten words you said." I rushed to my feet. Dragons be damned, he may have just actually solved this.

"That I will take as many steps as I want?"

"YES!" I squealed and went to run but quickly stopped, not knowing where I was going. "Steps! Steps is the answer. The more steps you take, the more you leave behind. You could take one step forward just to look back and see hundreds that you've taken."

"You may pass, you may pass! Just like you evaded death, you have beaten the odds. You were able to think through the riddles while your mental state was tested. You have proven yourself worthy, Amalia of Cimmerian. Remember the words said here, you will need them."

As they said my name, the tunnel lit up with the bioluminescent caterpillars that hung from the ceiling. Only these were cocoons and not wriggling, worm-like noodles. This I could deal with. Bash and I looked at each other for the first time since we'd entered this path, and we ran to hug each other tight.

"I couldn't have done that without you," I said softly. "Thank you for not leaving me." I gave him an extra squeeze before I let go.

"If I had, Knox would have killed me," he said. "But like him, I would never leave you." He brushed my cheek before he took my hand.

We walked to where we could see the opening into the next room. As we approached, I wished we could go back to the darkness. In front of us was a creature that put the size of the dragons to shame. It was a mountain within one.

Chapter 28

Sitting on the other side of the empty cavern was a colossal, jagged, stony form that hunched over most of the ceiling. Petrified limbs clung to the surface of its body, seeming to be holding it against the cavernous space. Olive gray moss protruded from the cracks where each stone making up its body joined. A deep, slow intake and exhale of air could be heard as if the form was sleeping.

"Remind me to never follow you down a dark path again," Bash whispered to me in a tense tone.

"Remind me to never be threatened by a murderous king with serious grudge-holding issues forcing me to go down dark paths," I whispered back. "What do we do?" I questioned, not sure if we should enter just yet.

"Wake it up, I guess," he said before I felt his elbow go into my ribs. "Go on."

"What!?" I silently shrieked. "Why do I have to wake it up?"

"I'm not doing it, so that leaves you," he stated.

I let out an exasperated sigh. "Such a gentleman." Accepting that this *was* my responsibility, I cleared my throat, then waited a few seconds before speaking, to see if that would grab its attention. The deep snoring continued, and I knew I had to make much more noise. Who knew how long this thing had been dormant—days, years, centuries? How would you wake something from that deep of sleep? I inspected the giant and focused on the petrified vines holding it upright. *Maybe if I...* "Hey, Bash." I drew his name out innocently.

"No," he said flatly.

"You didn't even let me ask anything."

"I didn't like your tone. It was full of the words 'I'm up to something and it probably won't be good.'" He held his hands up as he spoke, mocking me.

"I was just going to ask if I could channel from you." I gave him a slight shove. The giant let out a garbled sound but didn't wake.

"Oh," he said, narrowing his eyes at me. "Sure." His face said he still didn't quite believe that was all, but I took his consent and put my plan to work.

Focusing on Bash, I pictured our hands clasped, forming a connection between us, and I looked up at the vines snaking around the giant's chest and arms. Vines were natural, so I should be able to manipulate them. I thought about what I wanted: the vines to fall away from its body. If I could loosen some of them, maybe the feeling of slightly falling would wake the giant up? We watched as the vines crumbled into dust, first from the giant's chest, then from the left arm and the right. In my head, I'd pictured an immediate waking as he slipped forward, and if not, the rest of the vines would hold him in place. That was not what happened.

As the vines turned to nothing but specks of dust floating in the air, the giant's weight made quick work of snapping the remaining brittle binding. The giant plummeted face-first into the cave floor, causing the entire space to rumble, knocking loose debris from the walls and ceiling. Bash placed his upper body over me to shield me from the falling pieces before yelling, "THAT was your plan? You used me to piss off the giant rock!"

"That's not what was supposed to happen," I bit back at him in annoyance. "He was supposed to wake up before he hit the ground," I corrected. "I don't know how to control this ability, so it kinda just did its own thing."

"Yeah, great plan. His face just became part of the floor. I'm sure he will be really joyful when he wakes up."

I chose to ignore his retort, coughing as the dust invaded my lungs.

The ground shook as the giant let out a bone-chilling screech.

"I don't think it's very happy!" Bash shouted over the noise.

What had I done?

I looked beyond the heap of stone and saw the other side of the walkway. The giant was strung up to guard the path, and we had to get past it.

"Hi?" I squeaked out. "My name is Amalia. This is my friend, Bash. We would like to pass."

The walls shook as the giant spoke. "Pass? Pass to take what I protect."

"I wish to collect the Florauna Horde's scale. Is that what you're protecting?" I stepped a few feet in as the giant pushed up from the ground, balancing its weight with its arms and staying in that position, now having to prop itself up without the support of the vines. The large stone head rolled up from where it faced the ground, and I saw that it had gem-like amber eyes surrounded by sparkling onyx.

"To pass, you must—"

"Prove herself?" Bash interrupted.

The giant rolled its head to face him, the amber gems seeming to narrow in agitation. "Yes," it grumbled.

"What do I need to do?" I asked. I didn't think this creature wanted to ask me riddles.

Particles fell all around us as the giant shifted its weight and looked at me. "Long ago, I was taken from my home across the sea, a land called Lanark that was covered in what we called *Vyr* moss."

"What does that mean, that word *Vyr?*" I asked.

The giant's body groaned as it shifted once more. "You must be in so much pain," I said. Noticing the stiffness and uncomfortable position it'd been forced into, crammed in this chamber.

"It means many things, but we understood the term to mean essence." Its voice was gravelly and deep, commanding attention. "The moss was full of life and magic, granting us the ability to survive. Our *Vyr* was harvested from our lands and used for something unnatural. The Vyr is the heart of all like me, the moss lives within." The giant lifted one massive, jagged hand and placed it on its chest before returning to support itself. "Restore the heart of me, and you shall pass."

"How can I do that?" I asked, feeling like this was an impossible task. How was I meant to restore the heart of a creature I knew nothing about? "What is your name?"

"I am called Brythos." It leaned its head down before looking at me once more. "Our essence was dimmed when Lanark was pillaged. The *Vyr* thrived off of connection to the land, to us. It thrived off of powerful emotion and bonds. That is all I can give you."

"They say love is the most powerful emotion there is. That it conquers all," Bash said, thinking out loud.

"I have loved so many things." I smiled thinking about the first boy I ever loved at an early seven years old. My favorite stuffed animal I had named Toby. It was just a stuffed golden dog, but it'd made me so happy. I'd carried it around everywhere until it was lost. My field, my family, Cimmerian.

"I loved my father," I said to Brythos. "He was a strong and stubborn man, but his heart was so full of love and care for those around him, sometimes he couldn't accurately express it. When some thought he was harsh, I could see the cracks showing that he cared too deeply."

The moss embedded in the joints of each rock that made up Brythos produced a dim glow as it absorbed the words of love. "Where is your father now?" Brythos rumbled.

"He died not long ago, in something I call the shimmer. It killed everyone in my village." My heart ached saying it aloud, and I couldn't keep the sorrow from my voice. No sooner than I said it, the moss dimmed as quickly as it had glowed.

"You're trying to restore its heart, Amalia, not break it further," Bash seethed. I winced and realized I needed to be more careful with the truth that I said.

"I'm sorry, that probably didn't help." The laugh I forced out tasted like the dust filling the cavern. "It's heartbreaking, the loss. It could have crippled me. It almost did. Still could—if I let it." I took a step closer as those amber eyes watched me. "Screams of pain are constant in my head, wondering why I am the one who survived, why I had to lose everything, why even after all of that, I'm still dealt with the worst circumstances." Anger fueled my words as I spoke.

"Amalia—" Bash tried to reach out to me, but I put a hand up.

"Through all of the pain I've endured, I still got up each day. I found reasons to laugh, to smile. I have found others who fill the void of ones I've lost." I looked at Bash, his emerald eyes glossed over as he watched me. I thought about Knox and how he'd made me feel the most alive.

"When I'm lost in the nothingness, when I feel like I can't take anymore," I said, quiet as a whisper, "they become my anchors. Showing me I can go on." I exhaled the emotion.

"Everyone equates the heart with love, but I think strength is what really fuels it. Love fills the soul while strength builds the heart."

Bash placed his hand on my shoulder as I looked up at the giant, whose amber and onyx eyes glimmered like wet river rocks. The giant rumbled as it started to step to the side, which proved difficult as it had to stay hunched over, taking up most of the cave space. The moss glowed vibrantly and began to stretch and grow around each stone of Brythos. Until the entire surface of the giant was covered.

"What did you do, Amalia?" Bash asked, nervousness bouncing off of him.

"I don't know, I changed my tactic. I didn't think talking about all the people I loved who are now dead would help."

"But you thought talking about how you've been dragged through hell would?"

I hushed him with an aggravated "shh" as we watched the giant get enveloped in an illuminated cocoon. The moss grew tighter, and as it did, we could hear the sound of the strings snapping and tightening. The cocoon seemed to be shrinking slowly as the glow pulsed, and the moss started to throb in and out like a heaving chest. Before our eyes, the giant began to decrease in size until it was standing tall without hunching over the span of the cave. The moss started to unravel, receding back to its original place in the crevices where the rocks joined together.

His body was still made of stone, yet his amber eyes were more human, his face oval with sharp, pointed, stone ears, similar to the fae within Santavarre.

"You have succeeded in your task," Brythos rumbled, only now it was no longer threatening or shaking the space around us. "You have proven yourself wise and strong. Seeing the importance of emotion and will together."

"T-thank you," I said, stunned at the transformation.

Brythos stepped to the side and bowed as Bash and I walked through the chamber. The moss around his body was bright and pulsing with life. "What will you do now?" I asked.

"I will return to Lanark. I will do what I can to try and restore it. Maybe even find I am not the last of my kind."

I nodded at him, knowing all too well how he felt to be the last. It was something I hadn't allowed myself to dwell on just yet. It was there in the back of my mind, always. I was the last human in the realm of Caligness. Goosebumps pricked my skin as I gave validation to the claim.

"Will we have to face anything else in there?" Bash's voice sounded drained; he had been awake for longer than anyone should be. He needed rest; we all did.

Brythos stood tall. "No, this path leads to a dead-end alcove, there you will find what you seek. Protect it at all costs. I have no need to know your plans with it, but in the wrong hands, the scales of those who left for the sky would lead to realm-ending consequences. Be strong, Defier of Death, no matter who you face. Let the *Vyr* give you strength."

I flinched at the name. This was not the first to refer to me as Defier of Death. It sounded eerie and foreboding. I knew it was meant to be a title that showed perseverance, but it felt more like a promise of retribution. We headed into the tunnel, which was lined with the same moss that covered Brythos. It stretched farther as we walked, and I looked back to see the parts we had passed had disappeared. The dead end was up ahead, and as we reached the small, carved-out room no bigger than the height of me, the moss swirled around, lighting up the entire space. On the floor, nestled in luminescent mushrooms of greens and yellows, sat the Florauna Horde Scale. It shimmered with a shade of metallic-like jade. We both stood there, taking it in. A part of me felt like it was wrong for us to be here, like we shouldn't have been removing these scales. If I didn't, King Tatum would kill me. I looked to Bash to see if he wanted to be the one—it did belong to his horde, after all.

"Go on," he said, nudging me in.

"Are you sure? It technically belongs to you." I felt like he needed to be reminded.

"You are connected to nature now as much as I am. Go ahead," he reassured me.

I stepped closer and held my hand out before pulling away.

"It's not a whole dragon, Mal. It's not going to bite you."

I shot him a scowl. "I know that," I seethed. "When I touched the Hydra Scale, it blasted me with a blinding light. It wasn't the most pleasant experience."

"Just take it," he said, unamused with my fear.

I flipped him my middle finger and said, "I don't like sleep-deprived Bash."

I held my hand out again and poked the scale, testing to see what it did. Nothing. Absolutely nothing happened. I gripped it with both hands and carefully lifted it to hold it against my chest. I waited... still no sign of any repercussions. "Nothing happened," I said, smiling over at Bash.

"I wouldn't exactly say nothing," he replied, looking at the ground.

My eyes snapped to my feet, where thorny vines with scarlet and indigo flowers bloomed. The vines stretched over the ground, covering a thick blanket of dark, lush grass. A laugh bubbled up from me, and Bash extended a hand to help me maneuver through the prickly floor.

"We got it," I said excitedly. "We actually got it, and we're both alive!"

"I think that's in part because I didn't try to kill you," he said, laughing. "C'mon, let's get back.

Chapter 29

When we emerged from the alcove, Brythos and the voices were gone. There was no trace of them, making me feel like we'd imagined the whole thing. I kept the scale close to my chest the entire walk and only released it once we passed through the dissolving cave wall.

"I'll take it now," Bash said to me.

I passed it to him, releasing it when both of his hands covered it. "Where is the Hydra Scale?" I had no recollection of what had happened to it after Knox chucked it out of my hand. I knew Lane had grabbed it, but what had come of it after that?

"Knox has it in his pack," he whispered in my ear. "They have to be kept safe."

I simply nodded in return. I sighed, exhausted. But there was Knox, sitting on a makeshift bed, with his eyes on me. There were three other beds made up along the cave floor; however, Lane and Blaire were nowhere to be seen. My feet dragged toward Knox, I collapsed onto the blanket that was spread out beside him, assuming it was meant for me.

"That's mine," Bash said, placing the scale into Knox's pack.

I groaned, not wanting to get up again, which caused Knox to make a low chuckle.

"Move over," Bash said, pushing me closer to Knox before he joined *his* blanket. He lay on his back with one hand behind his head and the other on his chest. "The storm must still be going." His eyes were closed, so I wasn't sure if he was stating a general fact or asking. I moved to lie on my right side facing Knox and mimicked Bash by using my arm as a pillow.

"It is. We will get some rest here and head out when it clears, probably won't be until morning," Knox answered with a yawn.

"I still don't understand what that storm is." It wasn't a regular storm, that was certain. "Nothing like that has ever hit Cimmerian before, so why now?"

Knox shifted, propping his head on a hand as he faced me. "That storm used to only hit the Lands of Stygian. It started when Tak—King Tatum killed my father," he said, sounding like he meant to say something else. "The death was against nature, an ultimate act of hatred, intent to kill. It caused a shift in the balance." He rubbed my arm as he spoke. "When magic, life, becomes unbalanced, it creates fractures. From those fractures, events like the deadly rain happen, or the death of your field. They are all signs that the realm is breaking." His gaze looked haunted as dread filled his words.

"What do you mean the realm is breaking?" I popped up at the seriousness of the statement. That sounded... final.

"If King Tatum continues the path he's on, it will shift the realm to where there is no possibility of it being righted. I don't know what the end looks like, but if he's not stopped, we will all find out."

Here I was collecting scales for some plan of his. If I gave them over, would that lead to the breaking point? Would I be the reason Caligness fell? All to save myself?

"We will figure it out," Knox said as he pulled me to him, tucking me into his body.

Warmth spread through me as I felt Knox's hand rest over me. "How did it go?" he whispered. I was thankful for the change of topic, and I was excited to tell him.

For the next twenty minutes, I told him everything that had happened—the voices, Brythos, the vines that grew after the scale was moved. When I finished, I yawned wide and sat up to rub my eyes.

When I opened them, I saw Blaire's naked body walking out from the open path that led to the springs. She strode into the room with her back arched slightly, puffing her chest out, flaunting her erect breasts. Her body was toned and taut, with no sign of any body part jiggling from the impact of her walking, unlike mine. A shadow hid her lower parts until she walked to the blanket across from where we sat. She spread her legs out as she stood above the blanket, looking back in mine and Knox's direction before bending over, exposing herself to us.

"I'll take the first watch while you guys get some sleep. Maybe you'll have some exquisite dreams," she said seductively. And I knew she was directing that to Knox, who said nothing. I heard him lie back, but I couldn't look away. Fury fueled me.

Everything was on full display. Anger filled my veins as she attempted to get under my skin by flaunting herself so deliberately in front of Knox. He'd made no commitment to me, nor I to him, but he still felt like... *mine*. Every inch of me went on the defensive. She had done nothing but harass me since the moment she knew of me.

Black tendrils made their way over me and across the room to where Blaire was still bent over. They curled over her calves, growing thicker and wider until they shielded the intimate parts of her. I looked at Knox, who had his head back and eyes closed, a smirk lifting his right cheek. "You don't need to worry, Valkara, I only have eyes for you."

The moment Blaire noticed, she shrieked and jumped back, falling onto the floor.

"You bitch, you did this!"

Knox went to speak up, but I stopped him. She could think it was me all she wanted. She'd love to know Knox was behind it. She'd use it for the rest of her miserable life.

"I urge you to think carefully before you purposefully try to piss me off. Next time you want to walk out in front of others who have no desire for you, consider putting clothes on." I stood up and brushed myself off. "I know there must be a lot of resentment and self-hatred locked up in that body of yours, but I'm way past tired of dealing with you."

"You will regret this, I promise you," she fumed.

"Maybe." Grabbing my pack, I placed a hand on Knox's chest and kissed his cheek. A silent thank you for what he had done. I needed to head to the spring and wash the dust off. I got to the first cavern and set my stuff down, scooping my hands under the water's surface and pouring it over my face. The warm water felt soothing against my skin, and I splashed another handful on me. I did a quick rinse of my arms and neck, listening to the sounds of the cave. I moved my pack over and stretched out, laying my head against it. My eyes felt heavy, so I let them close as I thought about what was to come.

A bloodied woman choked back a sob. "I don't want to go yet, I don't want to leave you," she cried out, squeezing her eyes shut. After a few seconds, her eyes snapped open. A look of determination in them before both arms extended, reaching like she was summoning something to come to her.

"It's the only way." Heat radiated below me, but my gaze didn't leave the woman. I watched helplessly as fire flowed from either side of where I stood in long rivers of flaming orange and red hues, heading toward each of her arms.

The fire reached her hands, and as the flames licked at her skin, before they devoured her blood-coated body, turning her into nothing but ash, she looked straight at me and said, "Death must become you in order to bring balance." A shiver ran down my spine as she tilted her head up to the sky and screamed, a blood-curdling howl like she was letting out all the pain from a thousand lifetimes. The world around me trembled as I heard a bellow so powerful I felt it in my bones, infecting me with the emotions behind the horror-stricken scream. Heartbreak, anger, and disbelief ricocheted through me until a shockwave made my vision go black.

My eyes flickered open, back aching from falling asleep on the cave floor.

I really needed that rest. The sound of any water had always been a weakness when it came to putting me to sleep quickly. I stretched out and winced as pain shot through my lower abdomen. I used my arms to prop myself up and looked to see the pants I had put on were covered in blood around my pelvis. I quickly stripped off the pants and underwear I had on and dunked them into the water, scrubbing them with my nails. I frantically rummaged through my pack, grabbing the soap and the last change of clothes I had. I snatched the soaked fabric and rushed to the second spring, where there was a shallow ledge. As I entered the water, I crouched, easing myself in. The water numbed the stabbing pain just enough as my mind raced. What day was it? When was the last time I had my monthly bleeding? It didn't feel like that long ago, but time had gotten away from me. I took the soap and lathered myself and the clothes, scrubbing as hard as I could, but it didn't seem to be helping. After a few minutes of tackling it, I gave up. Soaking the clothes once more underwater, I wrung them out and threw them on the ground. I washed the blood from my thighs and other delicate parts and winced at the contact.

I heard footsteps drawing closer, and I slinked into the deeper water to finish scrubbing myself so no one would see. Knox came through, and I let out a breath of relief. He had my pack in his hand as he approached and set it down next to the pile of clothes. He paused, looking at the reddish hues that coated them.

"What happened to you?" he asked, his head snapping to me. Humiliation washed over me.

"I... uh... started my monthly bleeding. I fell asleep, and when I woke up, I noticed. I thought I could wash it off, but..." The words trailed off as my cheeks heated, not wanting to be having this conversation.

"Are you sure that's what it is?" he asked incredulously.

My brows furrowed together at his question. "What do you mean, what else could it be from?"

He let his head fall, looking at the blood-stained clothes again before looking at me, sadness or worry filling his eyes. I couldn't decide which I was seeing, maybe both.

"Are you sure I didn't hurt you when—"

"Oh my gods, no, Knox. No. That would have happened instantly, not hours later." I tried to reassure him, but it didn't seem to work. I pulled myself onto the ledge and stood, walking over to him so he could see that I was fine. Though it did the exact opposite. His jaw hardened as his eyes focused on my lower body. I looked down and saw the bruises on my thighs that must have been covered by the blood before. "I didn't see those before," I said calmly. "It's okay. I loved what happened, it didn't hurt. I promise you." I grabbed hold of his bicep and he pulled it away.

"You should get dressed, we're headed to Anamnesis Cave." He looked at me with so much regret in his eyes. I didn't want him blaming himself; I would trade a thousand bruises for what happened between us.

Chapter 30

I threw on my clothes and shoved the spoiled ones inside my pack, telling myself I would deal with it later.

"What is Anamnesis Cave?" I called out, trying to catch up to Knox, who was practically sprinting out of the spring chambers.

"It's where the Menticide Scale is," he said, not bothering to look at me. I grabbed his arm and turned him to face me. He let out an aggravated growl and glanced at the ceiling.

"Knox, please don't do this. The two things are not related. And pain is not at all what I felt during or after our time together. It wasn't until I just woke up. I swear to you. It could very well have been from the orbichor in the field." The mention of the creature was the only thing that brought him back to me. "I didn't fully heal myself."

"You swear I didn't hurt you?" Those violet irises danced as he tried to find a sign that I was lying. He placed his palm against my cheek, and I melted into it. "I swear," I whispered. He moved his hand to the back of my neck and pulled me against his chest.

"If I ever—"

"You won't," I interrupted.

"But if I do..."

"I will," I said, knowing what he was inferring. He would never hurt me, and I knew that to my soul.

He wrapped me in his arms and inhaled deeply, then pulled away. "C'mon."

The entrance to the cave was slick with a black sheen; it had to be a few inches thick. I was nervous to see what Cimmerian had been reduced to.

"Where is everyone?" I questioned. I hadn't seen the others on our way here, nor were they at the entrance.

"They're outside, already shifted. I told them I would find you." He tucked a piece of hair behind my ear that was half wet from where the bottom of my strands had gone in the water. "You'll ride with me. It's a much longer ride, and we will have to go over Lake Aquasailies again. I'll let you know when we're about to pass over in case you don't want to see it after what happened."

He was talking about Kuma. I should have been bothered by it, but I was more intrigued by whether I'd hear Zarakruae speak as we passed by—if they lived in the lake or just happened to have been there at the time. "I'll be okay, I want to see it."

"We will be in the air for about three days. I'll fly ahead of the others and stop when you need to, otherwise it'll be a nonstop trip."

"You guys can't keep up this pace for much longer. There's time for you guys to rest, you don't need to kill yourselves for me." I felt like the weak link holding the pack back.

"We will be fine. After we get the scale from Anamnesis Cave, we will have to go to the Barren Lands for the Mending Scale and Air Scale. Blaire can help locate the Mending one, but we have no way of knowing where the Air Scale could be. We will need all the time we can get for it. Lastly, we will head to the Lands of Stygian to get the Shadow Scale. I will help you with that one." He shot me a wink. "Are you ready?"

The weight of all that we still had left weighed on me. I'd thought at the rate and ease in which we had acquired the first two, they'd all be similar. I hadn't thought about the Air Scale, or how difficult it may be to locate something with no known whereabouts or shifter to sense it. This was far from over.

We left the cave, and I was taken aback at the blanket of obsidian covering every part of the ground, stringy droplets hanging from the top of the opening stretching down toward the ground. Bash's scales were the only green in sight, even though this once used to be nothing but foliage and life. Lane's color was pristine comparatively, the black sheen blanketed his diamond claws up to the middle of his legs, tainting his pearly scales. Blaire could suffocate in it for all I cared. Knox stepped out and shifted when he cleared the cave, a gust of wind blowing my hair back. I turned away as the goop was forced toward me and shielded my face with my hand.

A fluttering sound whirled around my head, and my gaze snapped side to side, trying to locate the source. A flicker of molten gold and twilight-purple hues caught my eye—wings that blended so beautifully together with hints of lake blues and sunset oranges. The wings were outlined in obsidian and held flecks of saffron. Scales covered the small body with razor-sharp horns that dotted its head and raced along its back.

Dragonfly? Bash's previous words echoed in my mind; these were not what I'd been expecting to come out of those glowing cocoons. Where I had been expecting a mundane insect, there was a small, armored work of art. Holding a finger out to it, I stayed as still as I could, hoping it would land on me. The wings were larger than its body, making small gusts as it lowered itself onto me.

The little dragonfly gripped my pointer finger with sharp, coal-colored claws and perched itself there, its tail lashing, letting out a little chirp. I could hardly contain my excitement; I forced myself not to jump up and down in pure joy.

"I'm going to call you Star."

Star chirped at the name, and I took it to mean it approved, not exactly sure how to tell what gender it was.

"Would you like to come with us?"

Star's wings fluttered before it lifted off my finger to curl up on my shoulder, where its wings lay back against its body. It nibbled at a few locks of my hair before resting its head in the curve of my neck.

"I'm taking that as a yes."

Becoming off-balanced in the slick substance coating the ground, I carefully made my way to where Knox was waiting. His slitted eyes narrowed at the miniature being on my shoulder.

"I'm keeping it. Its name is Star, and this is not negotiable." I took a second to enjoy that he couldn't communicate back to me at this moment, but prepared for when he could.

"*It* is a female."

What the fuck? My steps faltered, because I could have sworn I just heard Knox's voice. I eyed the beast suspiciously. "Did you just—"

"Yes," he replied.

There was no way this was real. I was still sleeping by the spring. "I—I heard you, how is that possible?"

"It can happen when... fated come together," he said hesitantly.

My brows knitted. "Fated?" Star clamped her sharp teeth on my earlobe, "Ow! Not nice!" I scolded her. She huffed at me, blowing little puffs of smoke out of her nostrils. "So we can talk now? That will make this ride more entertaining," I said as I climbed up to sit along Knox's shoulder blades. His shadows gripped around my waist to hold me in place.

"It will only last a short period, *Valkara.*" My lips turned down. I would have loved to have a connection like that to him forever.

His massive wings beat like thunder from the deadly rain, letting the others know it was time to go. Star's claws sank into skin as we ascended. I pulled my pack around, grimacing at the dried, ink-like substance still caked on the fabric, and opened it to usher Star inside.

The aerial view as Knox's wings carved through the sky shattered my heart, and the stench of decay infected the air even from the clouds. Cimmerian was nothing but a wasteland, rivaling the blackened ground found in the Lands of Stygian. The forest trail was nothing more than onyx-soaked pillars. I looked behind us, beyond the others stood the Godival Mountains, their faces glazed black, the hardened substance creating a new layer of unnatural stone.

"It's all destroyed. There's nothing left." The words cracked as tears filled my eyes. "Everything is really gone."

Knox's rumble shook the tears loose, and they fell in streams down my cheeks. "Not everything is gone," he said. His shadows surrounded me before swirling below his right wing. I grabbed hold of the spike in front of me and leaned to see what he was showing to me. Violet flames flickered, the graves marking those who hadn't survived still alight. The flames burned like he claimed, forever remembered while he lived and breathed. I placed a hand over my mouth as we flew over the only flecks of color in the midnight field. It would never be the same, the image slowly replacing the memories I had of it. The joy I remembered was stolen, like everything else I'd lost.

"Surviving will never be easy, Amalia. Don't let this taint your heart," Knox said before banking to the right.

We flew in silence as I mourned what I would never have again. As distance grew between Cimmerian and us, the black blanket of death dissipated and trees started to open up, exposing the green leaves they held until there was no longer a trace of the rain.

Time went by as we passed over thousands of trees, and they started to blur together into one giant sage expanse. I could feel my lids getting heavy with grief-fueled exhaustion as I heard Knox say, "We will be coming near Santavarre soon."

His voice wasn't a sound. It was a presence around me. "How many scales have you acquired?"

King Tatum's voice echoed in my thoughts, thinning before Lane's spoke. "Two, Father."

"Show me," King Tatum demanded. "I trust you have them in your possession."

Lane's voice sounded so near, like it were my own speaking. "They react to her, Father, I've seen it."

It felt like a knife was jabbed into my skull. "You think I don't know that?" King Tatum's voice seethed.

"She's different, Father, the cleansing changed her." Lane's voice wrapped around me. "Why can't we just take what has been found, kill her, and gather the rest?"

King Tatum's laugh bellowed. "It wasn't the cleansing, boy." Irritation filled his words. "You know she must be the one to bind them; her blood is key."

Lane scoffed. "He will guard her."

"She will sacrifice herself, begging for his death not to come," Tatum said. "If we want her, we will break him."

Star was nudging the bottom of my chin, making a small whimpering sound as I tried to discern what was reality and the strange dream I had just had. King Tatum's voice still felt coiled around my throat as Lane's lurked in my thoughts. Tears pricked my eyes from the phantom stab of betrayal. *It wasn't real.*

I stretched and brushed my palms against Knox's scales, grounding myself. Star whimpered once more. I used a finger to rub her snout, assuring her I was okay.

Knox's familiar rumble came before he said, "What just happened to you?"

"What do you mean?" I asked. Leaning back against one of his onyx spikes, I spread my fingers in and out of the shadows binding me to him.

Knox banked left slightly before righting himself. "Your heart was beating erratically. I tried to call to you, but you were blocked from me."

"I'm fine, it was just a bad dream," I said. I still felt like I was in a haze, it had been so real.

Knox's massive head turned back toward me. "Like your nightmares?"

Was it like that? Those felt like a memory, where this... this felt like it was happening to me. "I'm not sure," I said. My eyes went wide. "Look out, Knox!" I shouted as a flock of geese flew straight toward us. His jaws opened as he snatched two mid-flight, gulping them down easily.

"Are you serious!" I didn't want to witness the death of geese or watch him eat them feathers and all. His chuckle was the only response I received.

Lake Aquasailies came into view. It was still light out, and I wasn't distracted with thoughts of seeing Cimmerian, so I was able to appreciate the beauty of the lake from the air. It was shaped much like a dragon in its own abstract way. I wondered if Zarakruae was there, looking above the depths, if it could see us flying over. The water glistened with the fading sun. "Wow," I said to no one in particular. "Star, look at that, isn't it beautiful?" Her little form pranced along my arm to perch on the back of my hand, little chirps getting lost to the wind.

Knox dipped until we were level with the surface of the water, dipping the tips of his wings in until a light spray cast rainbows in the air. They were so similar to what Star's wings reminded me of. A spectrum of beautiful colors. I couldn't help but hold my arms out, laughing as the mist wet my skin. He always knew how to bring me back to life. I was glad this place hadn't lost its beauty. It deserved to be left untouched by death.

Other than Kuma's.

Night passed. Dawn came and went. By midday, the air turned frigid.

"Raeganarde is ahead on the right." Knox spoke, startling me from playing with Star, who was gnawing at my pinky finger as my other fingers tickled her armored stomach.

I looked off into the distance and saw the snow-capped peaks of the Stiriacus Mountains. Did those mountains hold the remains of my brother? The entire field forces? How many bodies were hidden under feet of snow?

"When we finish this, I want to go look for my brother. He deserves to be buried," I said to Knox, who craned his neck. "I don't want his soul to wander alone, looking for them in the Elysian Islands." I didn't know if souls found each other once they crossed or not. If I could help him find our family, I would. Knox hadn't said anything, so I rested my forehead against one of his spikes. "Did you hear me?" A chuff answered me. Our connection had finally been severed, and I felt the deep ache of loss I had grown accustomed to. Another thing taken. I looked out longingly at the peaks, the icy landscape that promised to preserve whatever lay below the surface. Frozen lakes reflected the sunlight like beacons calling us to them. "I'll come back for you," I whispered. "I'll come back for you."

Chapter 31

The past three days had been challenging. I'd never thought about how uncomfortable sitting on scales, in between large, spiky horns would be for an extended amount of time. Now, I was fully aware of what it was like. The views were unbeatable, but my butt and thighs had been screaming since night one. Knox only stopped when I needed to relieve myself. After our connection was lost, the flight was mostly silent, besides listening to them speak to each other in grunts and huffs. Star slept when she wasn't nibbling on something on me or attached to me. They'd all been flying nonstop, and it was inspiring seeing their strength and resilience.

Knox started to descend, which meant we must be nearing the cave. I shifted my body to his left side and looked over the spiked horn supporting me, feeling his shadows tighten around me so I didn't fall off. Large, glass-like crystals protruded from the glittering landscape. The ground glistened, creating small, iridescent rainbows where the sunlight struck. There were thousands of crushed crystals making up what would have been soil anywhere else. I felt Star's claws making their way to the top of my shoulder as she strained to look where my focus was. The wind from Knox's speed blew her wings and little face backward, yet she tried to hold on through the struggle. I held my breath to quell my laughter, but it was no use. It came out loud and gasping, making Star snap her jaws at me before retreating to my pack.

There was a large, gaping hole in the ground with various-sized geodes and gems surrounding all but one side. They poked out in different directions and cast light prisms over everything that was near.

Knox's shadowed wings began a steady beat as we approached. Everything about this area was mesmerizing. *Thud, thud, thud, thud.* Every dragon touched down in the dirt in front of the cavern entrance. The only spot not covered in the glass-like shards. They all tucked their wings close to their bodies so as to not scrape them against any of the protruding glimmering rocks.

I slid down Knox's front left leg with my pack carefully in my lap. When I hit the ground, I made sure to turn my body away, and I felt the breeze brush against my back from their shifts. I smelled amber and oak and knew Knox was close to me.

"You know, you've seen all of us before, you don't need to turn around," he whispered into my ear, the feel of his lips lightly grazing against it sent goosebumps over my skin.

"That doesn't mean I want to keep seeing it... Well, it doesn't mean I want to keep seeing everyone," I replied, giving him a wink.

I heard his low chuckle get farther away from me, so I bent down and opened my pack up to see Star nestled in a soiled shirt. There was no way that could smell good. "C'mon," I said as if I were speaking to a child, holding my palm out. Star took no time hopping into my hand and running the length of my arm up to my shoulder.

"Is everyone decent?" I asked no one in particular. "Are we going straight in or are you guys resting?"

"Whoa now, I know I said we don't have a lot of time, but we," Knox said, motioning to the other three, "do need to rest some."

"What should I do?" For the first time on this trip, I actually felt rested, not needing to take this time to catch up.

"Use the time to brainstorm how to find the Air Horde Scale, and we will talk it out when we wake up. Stay close to me, wake me if anything happens."

As everyone found a spot to stretch out and close their eyes, I stood there for a few minutes, watching their chests move up and down, up and down. I looked back to the cave entrance, wondering how far into it the scale was hidden.

"Do not go into the cave alone," Knox said, scolding me like a toddler.

"I wasn't going to." Crossing my arms, I stomped over to my pack and sat until I knew they were all asleep.

I stepped into the opening of the cave, choosing to ignore Knox's request to stay put if they were going to rest. I didn't need to constantly be under surveillance. I could at least try to find the scale, and if I did by the time they woke up, we could move on to the next, and I would have saved us all a lot of time. The king had given me a deal which he thought would end in my death. He thought he knew I wouldn't be able to handle this. The others knew their abilities made everything easier; this wasn't hard or tasking for them. I needed to prove I was able to do something. I could be useful, an asset. My life was worth preserving.

The air inside the cave was similar to the Godival Mountains, cool and damp. That's where the similarities ended. The walls of the cave were naturally decorated with gemstones and crystals that shone like diamonds or stars in the night sky. Knox's admiration of the dress I'd worn during the celebration re-entered my mind, bringing a bashful smile to my face. The deeper I went into the cave, the more minerals I saw. Each one caught the dimming light wholly, reflecting it into a medley of colors. It was beautiful, but disorienting.

My head spun as my eyes tried to track all the colors and crystals around me, some reflecting my image, turning me around. I needed to focus on the path I was taking. This was the Menticide Scale, which meant this place was meant to alter your mind, play with reality.

I turned back toward the entrance and scuffed a mark into the ground with my foot. For every five steps I took, I'd place a fresh scuff to help leave a trail for me to follow back or know what paths I'd already taken. The back of my neck tingled as a shiver of awareness ran down my spine. Unease filled the colorful space. "Hello?"

Metallic wings fluttered in, and I breathed a sigh of relief as the little scaled creature made its way to me. "You almost gave me a heart attack." Star nudged my cheek, placing her tail around my neck. Her scales were cool and smooth, wrapping around me like a cloak. Star let out a chirping sound before I moved deeper into the cave.

This place seemed eerily alive, as if every step I took was examined, my moves studied to see how I could be tested. I felt like I was being watched, like every angle held eyes within the stones. The longer I was inside, the more cautious I became. Every sense was heightened and on alert. Even Star had stood up, lowering her head, like she sensed something as well. I passed by a large, lilac-colored crystal that emerged from the ground and came just feet away from embedding itself into the cave ceiling. A shadow moved within it, and suddenly, all my senses zoned into one important truth: I wasn't alone in here.

Star let out a soft rumble, confirming I was right. Heart racing like I had just run for miles, I said, "You followed me." I didn't know who would answer, but I knew stating that fact would get them to speak.

"Amalia," he said my name so softly, emerging from behind a large stone. His voice echoed around us. I turned to face him, trying to keep my expression neutral. After our last cave interaction, I wasn't going to show any fear. "I know you're wary of me, but I need to apologize. I haven't had a chance to explain myself."

Those words were not what I'd braced for, and it made me hesitate. He could have waited to have this conversation after they'd all rested. Instead, he'd waited, followed me in when everyone else was asleep, and didn't announce himself until I made him aware I knew I wasn't alone. I nodded. "You didn't have to secretly follow me. You could have just joined me," I said reluctantly. He was blocking the way out, and if I tried to leave, I wasn't sure he would let me. There was no part of me that thought continuing farther was a good idea.

"I wanted to speak, without prying eyes and ears. Without interruption or other opinions." Lane's voice was laced with charm as he gave me a boyish grin. It didn't ease my nerves; my body was still telling me to run.

"Let's talk on the way out then, I'm starting to feel a little crazy being in here." As I passed him, Star snapped her teeth at him with a snarl, tucking her wings back close to her body. My eyes danced from Star to Lane. I had never seen her act like that before. She'd been playfully nippy, but that was not intended to be playful. She meant to draw blood. "Sorry." I tried to laugh it off. "I told you we were going a bit crazy, even dragonflies aren't immune." I squeezed past him in the narrow entryway, the sharpened point of a crystal gliding over my lower back.

He grabbed my arm in the crook of my elbow, halting me. The sting from the point of the crystal pressed against my spine. "I truly am sorry. You are the survivor of a cleansing my father orchestrated. I should hate you. I should want you dead. But every time I look at you, I feel as though you are a lesson I'm to learn about looking past what is expected and listening to my heart instead."

Confusion and wariness took hold as I tried to understand what he'd just said. "What do you mean, survivor of a cleansing your father orchestrated?" I yanked my arm back, the jolt from the movement making the crystal dig deeper into my skin.

I watched silently as Lane's jaw hardened, his throat bobbed on a nervous swallow.

"What do you mean, Lane?!" I shouted at him. "What do you mean?" A scream burned up my throat at the reality. Was this real? Or was this the cave playing with my mind?

I saw shadowed movement in my peripheral vision, making me glance toward where Knox stood. His eyes flickered between Lane and I, a mixture of concern and agitation danced on his face. Star squeaked, lifting off my shoulder and flying straight to Knox.

"What's going on?" Knox asked, his voice full of suspicion. Something in me knew it wasn't from us just being alone together. He walked toward us slowly, until he was close enough to touch. I went to move for him, but Lane grabbed my arm again. "That's not what I meant, Amalia!" He tried to backtrack, but the words were already said.

Instinctively, Knox grabbed hold of my other arm, pulling me to him, the sound of fabric tearing echoing through the cave as my shirt ripped against the crystal. Anger boiled in me at being pulled like a toy.

Images materialized like a fuzzy illustration. I saw myself twirling in the flowers of the field, a gold shimmer dropping down—I hadn't noticed it yet, though. There was a shadow in the shape of a dragon cast over me, and then the image changed as I heard the call of my name, a voice so familiar. Forms were all around me as I lay in my bed. Vague pieces of blue and red shifted, and someone set a glass of amber liquid on the bedside table, beads of sweat on the outside of the glass. The moment turned into a haze before clearing into a new scenario. I was falling off the dais, someone took me into their arms as screams filled the room. The haze returned, and I was sleeping by the spring within the mountain. A hand ran along my arm, then down my torso. Crimson filled the image as I heard my name muddled in a groan, one I didn't recognize. Whispers of words drifted in and out. *"Not all lessons are gentle. Your suffering will never be enough retribution."*

What felt like a punch to the gut snapped me out of the illusion. Knox's eyes widened in shock, his expression shifting from confusion to anger as he went absolutely still, no longer pulling but still holding me tight, squeezing, like he was frozen in place. Lane staggered back, as if he had been struck in the chest and knocked off balance, releasing my arm from his grip.

Unsure of what had happened, I quickly withdrew my hand, my heart pounding at the sudden turn of events. "Did anyone else see that?" I asked, voice a little shaky. I went to cup Knox's face, but he pulled away from me. Shadows licked at his back, and his eyes were burning brighter than I had ever seen.

The tension in the air was palpable as Lane, Knox, and I stood staring at each other. "What was that?" I pressed.

"It's just the cave, it's messing with our heads," Lane said.

Anger exploded as his previous words fought through the tricks of the cave. "Don't you say another word to me!" I spat the words at him before whirling to Knox. "Lane said his father orchestrated the shimmer... the *cleansing*. His father is the reason my entire village is dead!" My voice was bordering on becoming manic as I repeated the words Lane had so carelessly thrown around. "I—I knew he wanted me dead, my family, but every human within Caligness? He wiped out an entire species!" I shouted, my throat stinging with the force.

Knox didn't say a word. He just looked at me—he looked at me in a way that told me this wasn't news to him. He had no reaction besides an expression that looked filled with pity, with regret, for what? Not telling me himself? "You knew," I whispered. "You've all known... all this time. You've let me believe you were my friends. You're all behind the fact that everyone I have ever loved is gone."

"No, Amalia, you don't have all the facts," Knox raced to say before I could go on.

"No, of course I don't, because all of you have been lying to me! Using me to get whatever these scales are for!"

"I don't give a fuck about the scales!" Knox growled.

My resolve hardened as I looked at him, knowing Lane was watching and listening. "Then the both of you should stop giving a fuck about me, because after I get your father," I said, turning to speak directly to Lane, "his precious scales, his precious relics. I never want to see your faces again." I slammed my feet as I headed deeper into the cave, away from the males who'd just destroyed my whole world.

Chapter 32

Despite the unspoken animosity between us all now, we were stuck together for one single purpose: retrieving the Menticide Scale. I could feel the weight of my words, and whatever happened, pressing down on us, a silent current of resentment that threatened to drown us. But there was no time to dwell on it. I needed to get this over with, now more than ever.

As we ventured deeper into the cave, the mesmerizing glint of gemstones and crystals surrounded us, their light refracting into a kaleidoscope of colors. As we weaved silently between them, the path before us shifted and twisted, and soft rumblings came from farther in the distance.

The first words spoken since my earlier slash: "It's a maze," Lane said carefully.

I couldn't help but question if that was more knowledge he chose not to share earlier, or if he was just figuring it out at the same time as us.

We stood and evaluated the scene before us. It did look to be a maze, designed to disorient us with the shifting pathways made up of clear quartz. The crystals moved of their own accord, sliding and producing low rumbles across the cavern floor, creating new pathways and sealing off others. How would we ever get through this? This required memory, communication, and a functioning team. We had none of those things in our current state.

"We'll have to stay vigilant if we're going to reach the center," Knox said, his jaw set in determination. Despite the tension and my current hatred for both of their betrayals, we had to work together to navigate the maze and retrieve the scale. There was no other option.

Step by step we weaved through the endless paths, constantly having to adjust course as the crystals lunged and moved. The air was filled with the sound of grinding stone, jagged amethyst spikes jutted up like jaws trying to devour us, forcing our path to shift in a different direction. As time went on, frustrations and tempers rose, and the maze grew more complex, each turn a potential dead end.

"We should mark the paths we've already taken," Lane said, drawing in the dirt with his finger.

"You should know how to get through this since your kind are the ones that created it," Knox growled to Lane, speaking his first words to him since the cave had cast a hallucination which silently affected us all.

"I'm not the one who created it," Lane said. "I'm just as turned around as you two are."

Did his father create it? Why couldn't he get it himself?

Knox's chuckle rivaled the shifting masses. "What's the matter? Don't like it when something is fucking with your head?"

"Enough!" I snapped. "This is draining enough as it is; I don't need to listen to the two of you bickering."

Lane pressed his palms into his temple. "You got something to say, Knox? Say it." His question was a challenge, and by the predatory look coming over Knox, Lane was about to regret it. Knox prowled ahead, slow and comminatory. The air heated as Knox closed in, his shadows vibrating and stretching around his footsteps.

A corridor of black obsidian erupted from the ground, surrounding the three of us. A scream escaped me as Knox pulled me closer to him. The midnight stones lifted and whirled around us like leaves in a thunderstorm, growing in speed and intensity as my hair started lifting with the wind. "What are you trying to accomplish here?" Lane shouted at Knox.

"This isn't me." Knox's arms pulled me closer as Lane moved toward us, placing a hand on my shoulder. My head jerked up toward the top of the cave, where hundreds of transparent quartz laced the ceiling. Images flashed within them, my eyes flicking between them all, seeing moments and glimpses. I couldn't take in a whole breath. Star whimpered. I felt her tuck under my hair along my neck, but I was frozen.

A gasp, Lane was on top of me, sprawled out on the bed in Santavarre. His hands pinning down my body.

A sob broke free, conversations played like a poisonous melody. Kuma's admission, his wish to kill me once alone. Agreements from Lane and Blaire that he must wait until he got me alone.

My mouth opened on a silent scream. King Tatum and Lane spoke. Tatum's frustrated shouts were about no longer having the ability to shift; he had angered the fates of Elysian. Lane agreed to avenge their family. Agreed to make the bloodline suffer, even if it was in silence.

A tear dropped, cascading down my cheek. Lane was pressed against the dining hall door. Whispers of the training grounds. My voice said, "We do not tell Lane." His cheeks lifted in a promising smirk.

A growl shook me to my core. The obsidian stones dropped to the ground in a heap and my lungs filled with air, sucking in like I had never breathed it before. "What just happened?" I said, winded.

Knox moved with such brutal force—unstoppable. One moment Lane was standing just feet from me, the next Knox's hands had his shirt in a tight grip, lifting Lane's body from the ground. "I knew you were a coward, but this?" He slammed Lane's body against the blackened stone. "I'll make sure you choke on every lie you've told as I rip your fucking throat out." Tendrils of onyx surrounded them, clouding my view of what was going on.

I lunged for the males, trying to unfurl Knox's grip. "What are you doing?" I screeched. His eyes shot to me, and they were no longer human. His pupils were slits, irises burning like the violet flames he'd left in Cimmerian.

"Are you blind, Amalia? You can't tell me you didn't see the same things I did." His grip only tightened as he hoisted Lane up before slamming him back against the stone with a sickening crack.

Lane's feet were fighting for purchase. "It's—agh, fuck—it's not real, Knox!" His words wavered as his legs connected with Knox's ribs. "The cave is screwing with your head. It's trying to manipulate us." His face was turning red as he struggled to gain control. He was no match for Knox in his enraged state.

I'd known this wouldn't be easy, but I hadn't thought it would try bending our minds until we tore each other apart. "Please, Knox," I cried. "None of it is real. You can't let it in." The crystals had seen my anger, my hurt, the betrayal from them, and they were twisting it until it warped all of our minds. We had to push through. We had to be stronger.

The smoke around him coiled tighter as his eyes dimmed, a look of sadness taking root. "I haven't, Amalia," Knox said to me. He had, though. He'd let those visions affect him, trick him. His grip loosened as he dropped Lane to the ground.

Coughing, Lane said, "Thank fuck you saw some reason." He struggled to his feet.

Knox looked at Lane like a squashed insect. "You forget the shadows see truth. They can see what lurks in the darkness." They moved, snaking around Lane's ankles, up his torso, and around his throat. "When the moment comes, they'll expose every secret you've kept buried." The shadows tightened. "Then I'll watch as you drown in them."

"Stop it!" I yelled. Their attention snapped toward me. "Can we please focus on retrieving the scale? You've both been full of secrets, and here I am, still existing in the same space as you." I took a breath. "So I think you guys can suck it up and get over yourselves. Let's get on with it."

We continued in relative silence. I had Star fly above and help guide us through the shifting stones. They affected her the same as us, so it took time to maneuver through, but we needed to do whatever we could to limit our interactions between the three of us.

Finally, after what felt like an eternity, after two meltdowns, pulled hair, and one unsuccessful attempt at turning around, we reached the center of the maze. The Menticide Scale had done its job. It made me question every thought and memory I'd had while trying to get here. It had tested us all more than I'd expected or wanted.

The scale shimmered with a diamond-like light, making me think of Lane's scaled armor in his dragon form. It wasn't nestled in any rocky area or hidden in the depths like the others; this scale hovered mid-air in the center of the cavern, casting a luminescent glow across the space. I could feel my eyes fill with wetness as everything it had taken to get there pressed on my chest. The lies weighed the heaviest.

I stepped forward, my heart pounding with anticipation. As I reached out, the crystals around us shifted once more, forming a protective barrier. I paused for a moment, hesitated, aware of the weight of Lane's and Knox's gazes on me. Pulling my hand back, I asked, "What does your father *really* want these for?" This was a pivotal moment. Would he tell me the truth, or lie to my face? More importantly, how would I know?

"He plans to use them to kill Mikulec." Knox spoke up after Lane's lapse in reply. "He wants him and his bloodline dead for what happened during the war."

"Why does he need the scales? The runes? Can't he just kill him?" I asked, not yet believing a word coming out of his mouth.

"No. Mikulec is no longer human..." Knox said cautiously. Star flew around the Menticide Scale, hovering just before it, gazing at its reflection.

"What do you mean... no longer human?"

"Mikulec," Lane spat, "drank the essence, the blood of the dragons lost during the war. It gave him eternal life. A dragon's blood is sacred, with more magic than one can comprehend, and he took it. Creating an unnatural life for himself."

"It wasn't just the consumption of dragon blood, he worked with the fae, somehow persuaded them to sacrifice one of their own so he could consume their blood. The two essences together, it's a power never seen before. The only way to stop it is to combine them again," Knox explained deeper.

"So we have to combine the relics and the scales to have a chance at killing Mikulec." My instinct said there was more that wasn't being said. The other parts of me liked to believe they wouldn't lie to me again. Words circled back to me. "I thought you said he wanted them to bring something back that was lost?" I directed the question to Lane.

He stared at me, his jaw working. "It brings back the chance for him to get his revenge."

With a deep breath, I extended my hand once more, feeling the energy of the scale pulse through me. The moment the scale was in my grasp, the cave fell silent, the shifting crystals coming to a halt. *I know there are truths yet to be revealed. I won't allow lies to infect my mind.* I thought the words to myself with a resolve to be more guarded, to listen to the things that weren't said. My fingers closed around the scale, and with a final surge of strength, I pulled it to me. I turned to Lane and Knox, the scale radiating a soft white glow in my hands. Despite the new state of our relationships and the tension that lingered between us, we'd retrieved it.

Chapter 33

The crystals retreated as we walked our way back to the opening of the cave. The air was thick and heavy with emotions. The light from outside shone in as we neared the entrance. A shadow appeared, and I looked at Knox. He gave me a simple shake of his head, relaying it wasn't him. My steps slowed in caution. What appeared as a shadow formed into the silhouette of a man as we neared, and the light casting inward showed him standing with an impatient authority.

"Who is that?" I questioned, refraining from looking at anyone, eyes trained on this new presence. He was tall and lanky, yet intimidating, dressed in the regal white and gold uniform of King Tatum's court. His eyes were sharp and calculating, moving over me until his rat-like stare saw the scale. A slight lift to his lip curved his mouth up on the right side.

"His name is Alaric, one of my father's most trusted advisors," Lane answered, extending a hand out to greet this *Alaric*.

Alaric took Lane's hand, giving a firm shake before crossing his arms, that smirk staying permanently affixed to his sunken face. "Well, well," he drawled, his voice smooth, but I knew better. "What a delight to see you here, Amalia. The king is curious about the success of your task so far. How many scales have you managed to collect? I see at least one," he said, nodding to the one I held in my hands. I clutched it tighter to my body. Knox moved toward where Bash and Blaire were standing, observing the interaction. "He has sent me to relieve you of the ones currently in your possession."

"Over my dead body," I replied." How did you even find us?" I didn't know this man, and no part of me trusted that I really knew the intention behind why I was collecting the scales.

My eyes darted to Lane, his jaw tensed before answering the question meant for Alaric. "The deal binds you to my father. All he has to do is focus on the thought of you, where you are, and he will know at least the vicinity of your location." He waved a hand toward Alaric and said, "It's okay, you can give them to him."

"She said no," Knox said. His voice was deadly, dripping with anger.

Lane dropped his hand and scoffed, rolling his head toward Knox. "This doesn't concern you."

"Everything happening here concerns me." Knox's hardened gaze flicked to me, his violet eyes glowing, the dragon within wanting to come out. "Especially when it threatens *her*."

Alaric's booming laugh only added to the already too-tight tension surrounding me. "He was hoping you would say something like that." Alaric wiped a joyous tear from his eye and sniffled lightly, composing himself. "You see, Amalia, you don't disobey the king without severe consequences." He cracked his knuckles as he took a step toward me. "The king gave me explicit instructions to take them at whatever cost—shy of killing you, of course." I saw Bash step forward until he looked at the cloud of black growing behind the unsuspecting man.

Knox moved with predatory precision, his steps silent as he raised the sword his shadows had slipped from the man's sheath along his back. His eyes tracked the movements of his prey. He circled behind Alaric, who bent his neck from side to side. "This will only hurt a little." I stepped away from his advance, and Knox, in a swift motion, raised his sword. Within a heartbeat, it met its target with deadly accuracy; the blade met flesh. Alaric's eyes widened in shock, looking down at the bloodied steel protruding from his chest before his body crumpled to the ground.

"I'm sure that only hurt a little," Knox said as he slowly removed the sword from Alaric's back.

Instinct guided my next move, and my hand reached out for something to hold onto as the shock of what had just happened sent my heart into overdrive. I grabbed hold of Lane's hand before I could think about what I was doing. Knox turned his gaze to Lane, his sights locking in on our joined hands, his expression cold. "*You* will never touch *her* again," he declared in a voice lacking all emotion. Knox took a slow, measured breath before his eyes went dark like a starless midnight sky. I felt Lane's hand spasm. I looked down, then felt warm liquid hit my face, my neck, and chest. I wiped at my exposed skin and saw crimson. Blaire's screams tore through my head. I turned to tell her to shut the fuck up when the world seemed to stop. I noted a slow movement to my left.

Lane.

His head tilted only slightly. Blood had reached him as well, covering his neck. I watched as it dripped, then as his head slid sideways, I met his eyes. Those glacier-like irises, looking back but seeing nothing. His head hit the ground with a wet thud before rolling, leaving trails of shining crimson in its wake until coming to a stop farther inside the mouth of the cave.

I should move.

I should speak.

I should...

I turned to stone, unmoving. Unfeeling.

Lane's hand turned limp in my tightened grasp.

I fell with him as his body crumpled, my knees cracking against the ground. I could feel that I was screaming, but I couldn't hear it. I knew people were rushing around me, pulling me, but all I saw was Lane's hand, all I felt was the heat of his blood on my skin.

Blaire's screams fused with mine, drowning out the shouts of Bash and Knox over what had just happened.

Knox was walking away; he tossed the bloody sword to the side and didn't look back.

Just walked away.

Just left.

Chapter 34

I stayed motionless at the cave's entrance, listening to the fight that ensued between the three shifters that were left. I could feel the supportive nudges of Star against my hands that lay weightless beside me. My gaze locked on the no-longer-bleeding body of Alaric, knowing if I looked just over my shoulder, I would see Lane's head. Those eyes full of shards and secrets were nothing more than a blank canvas. Numbly, I peeled my hand from Lane's motionless one, finger by finger, slowly, as if disarming a bomb. My mind told me it could come back to life at any moment.

"He will send someone else. What have you done?" Bash asked Knox.

"What I had to do to keep her safe," Knox replied. Those words, *to keep her safe,* were all that I needed to snap out of the state I was in. A laugh burst from my throat, startling everyone. All eyes snapped to me in confusion as I slapped my hands on my thighs and continued the fit of laughter, gripping my stomach from the tightness.

"This?" I motioned to where Lane's body had collapsed beside me. "This was to keep me safe? From what, his jealousy?" I exhaled a long breath. "Wow, Knox, that was so incredibly thoughtful of you."

"You don't understand, Amalia. You were not safe with him around." Knox's jaw rolled as he stepped closer to me.

"Don't!" I yelled. Tears welled up in my eyes, cascading over my lids like a waterfall. "Why did you do this?" I said, choking on the words. My fingers gripped the roots of my hair as I tried to understand what had happened.

Knox walked up to me then, bending down to be on my level. "I know you want me to tell you the reason, but I promise you, it will only hurt you more. You don't deserve to bear the burden of the truth, and I am terrified it will destroy you. Please, just trust that I was protecting you."

"Trust you? I just found out *ALL* of you"—I looked to where Bash and Blaire were standing, Bash's brows pulled in with his mouth turned down—"have been lying to me, keeping secrets from me, then you killed the only reason I am even here!" I was blown away by how he could ever think I could trust them again.

Standing up, Knox said, "You can think whatever you want of me—hate me, ignore me, fight me, choose to trust another, but I hope you can hear and keep the knowledge that there is no version of you that I do not think is beautiful. That I wouldn't protect. If you want to be sad, be sad. If you want to be angry, be it. Be whatever you need to be to sort your shit out. I will be here whether you like it or not, admiring the woman that you are. Admiring the battles of your life and how you handle them. Even now. I will be here thinking with every breath I breathe that I am the luckiest male alive to be in your life." He breathed in deeply as he bent down and slid a strand of my hair away from my cheek. I didn't budge, my breathing quickening when he then said, "Amalia, because of that... I can never hurt you the way I would if I were to tell you what you're asking. I would rather you hate me."

"Then I hate you. You broke me—you broke the parts of me that were barely keeping me pieced together. Now? Now I'm nothing but a shell. There is nothing more to me besides skin and bone. That will forever be on your shoulders." His hand dropped, and he gave me a small, sad smile that didn't reach his eyes, then turned and started to walk away from me. I wasn't done speaking, though.

"He saved me! He is the only reason I am alive. No matter what he said or what truths he held back from me, he saved me, and you killed him for it!"

"I SAVED YOU!" he snapped, his body whipping back faster than lightning. "I am the reason you woke up in that field. I am the one who dove into the icy waters that night to get you after the attack. Lane, your *savior*," he said with venom, "slept peacefully while you were losing your life!" Bash started walking up behind Knox, a hand extended to place on his shoulder.

"I don't need saving, I never asked to be saved!" My stubbornness, my anger and hurt trumped any other emotion I could have right now, the heightened emotions blocking the full weight of his words to me.

"I will protect you, whether you need it or not, until my last breath, my last moment. Even on your darkest days, I've been by your side, whether you knew I was there or not.

I will always be there for you." He gave me one last look, scanning my features like it was the last time he'd be able to fully take me in before he walked off.

This couldn't all be real. This was all an illusion; I never got the scale. This was all a test. I roared into another fit of laughter, my body keeling over, unable to stop. "This isn't real." I turned to the cave. "THIS ISN'T REAL." More giggles tickled my throat. "I solved it!" I spun, looking at the shifters. "This is a test, this isn't real! Ha-ha, I just have to figure out how to pass the test." My mind spiraled, their faces contorted into pity, confusion, and grief.

Knox shook his head, and as he passed Blaire he said, "Take care of Lane's body, throw it in the cave for all I care. Just deal with it." His words made her spiral into tears again, and sent me into hysteria.

"I don't know why you're crying," Bash threw to her. "You should be happy about this after everything they've done to you." That sentence made my delirium fade momentarily. Interest sparked, another secret I wasn't privy to.

"I'll help you," I said softly to Blaire. The last thing I wanted to do was show her any comfort or sympathy, but I did want to know what Bash meant. Maybe this was part of the test?

"I'll pass." She wiped her nose and trudged past me. "You've clearly lost your mind."

I heard her audible gasp from behind me, and I didn't need to look to know what had caused it. "Are you still going to pass, or can you get over yourself for one minute and let me help you?" When I faced her, I saw her fingers intertwined in golden locks, her tears falling onto an ashen face. She was holding Lane's head, her body trembling from the suppressed emotion.

I chose to keep quiet as I grabbed hold of the shirt he had on. Pulling it, it slipped halfway off, having only his arms as an obstacle. I grasped the hands that could no longer return the gesture. All of the times he held his hand out for me, for comfort, when was the last time? The emotions that swelled as I struggled to remember were squashed like a roach. Tightening my grip, I pulled them, dragging his body into the cave.

"How are you being so calm about this?" Blaire asked, eyeing me like I was from a different realm.

"It isn't real," I stated simply.

She pulled on my arm, stopping me, and looked in my eyes for the first time without disgust. "It's real, Amalia. This isn't an illusion." She pointed to the scale that had ended up on the ground. "You already have the scale. Lane is gone."

Blood roared in my ears. No. This—this had to be an illusion. I was angry with him. The relationship we'd had was erased into lies and deceit. We weren't given time to fix things. He died truly believing I hated him... and I didn't fully know if I did. Tears threatened to flow, but I couldn't keep crying. I couldn't keep feeling all of these useless emotions that wouldn't keep me alive. So I shoved them down. I hid them so deep, they wouldn't be able to find the surface. I let the darkness take over, numbing me. Like Lane would always say, like he'd never say again: it could be handled later.

I stopped for a breath, laying Lane's arms on his chest, resting my hands on my hips. I composed myself. "Are you going to help or not?" I asked. She looked at me with eyes full of disbelief before she arched her arm back and threw Lane's head into the cave. It made contact with a loud *thwack* against an emerging crystal.

"What the fuck is wrong with you?" I shouted, watching as it rolled behind a stone out of view. Blaire clapped her hands together and started walking back to her bedroll in the grass. Completely flabbergasted, I had no idea how to respond. It didn't make any sense. How do you go from shedding tears to chucking a severed head?

I pulled Lane's body back and stopped where his head lay, deciding it was as good a spot as any. I'd rather he be buried, show respect, but clearly his kind didn't seem interested in that. Eyeing Blaire as I walked out, I set up my own bed, Star making herself comfortable the moment I did. I took a seat. "I thought you and Lane were close? What the hell was that back there?"

Scoffing, she started picking at loose threads on her blanket. "I don't believe he ever actually cared for me. I'm more valuable alive, so he made sure I was kept that way." Her eyes shifted to me. "I guess we have that in common." She exhaled deeply. "His father will send someone else when his advisor doesn't return. He will come for you," she promised, not in a threatening way, more of a warning. I nodded, because she wasn't saying anything I hadn't already assumed. "Why did Knox do it?" she asked, her features turning calculated. "What finally triggered him enough to kill Lane?"

"What did Bash mean when he said you should be happy about his death after everything they had done to you?" I answered her question with a question of my own. She may have been curious, but I had my own agenda. I was not going to be the one person trapped in the dark anymore.

"Why do you care?" she asked, pausing her monotonous task of messing with the threads to focus her attention on me and eyeing me wearily.

"I don't; however, I've learned there have been many secrets swirling around me, and I'm over it. Clearly, this is something everyone seems to know but me."

Blaire studied me, her reddened eyes boring into my soul. I had a feeling she was contemplating whether she wanted to expend the energy to tell me or not. Honestly? If I was her, I wouldn't tell me a damn thing. She liked for the attention to be on her, though, so she just might open up.

"All of you knew King Tatum created the shimmer, you all knew the cleansing was an orchestrated attack based on a hundred-year-old revenge scheme. No one has had the decency to tell me my entire species was wiped out on purpose. So I think the one thing you could do is answer this simple question." More venom seeped into my words than I had intended, but it proved to do the trick as Blaire sighed and spoke.

"The Mending Horde is known for their ability to heal. What many don't know is that our tears are deadly." Lying on her back, she propped her arms under her head. The tears I'd seen that had fallen on Lane as she held his head, would those have killed him if he wasn't already dead?

"King Tatum took me from my family when I was young. I used to be skyward." She pointed a finger into the evening sky. How unbelievable to think there were kingdoms up there, invisible to all that were below. I couldn't help but imagine what those lands looked like among the clouds. "I lost everything, too," she said solemnly.

"That's what Bash meant when he said that? Because they took you away from your home?"

She laughed and it was a rich sound, pure but with pain behind it. "No. I believe Bash was referring to the fact King Tatum kept me locked up in chains in a cell in the Lands of Stygian. He would torture me until I broke. Until I shed those precious tears for him." She turned her head toward me then. "King Tatum used my tears to help create the cleansing, or what you call the shimmer. So I guess I am one of the reasons your entire civilization is gone."

My breathing was heavy, and she seemed out of focus now as I let her words resonate with me. "I'm sorry," I said, and I truly meant that, despite everything.

She peered at me. "I don't need your pity," she snarled, her ruby eyes flaring to life.

"It's not pity. Even you don't deserve what happened to you. I think if he hadn't taken you, tortured you, you'd be a different kind of person." I smiled weakly. "Maybe even a tolerable one." Her expression was one of disbelief. She had probably never heard those words before, and they may not have meant much coming from me, but she deserved to know that no one deserved that type of life.

A yawn broke free. She looked away, and I knew she wasn't going to say anything else. I turned and nestled into my blanket, expecting to go to sleep, but it was wishful thinking. Star walked over to the crook of my neck, pulling the scale I had forgotten about. I placed it within my pack and thought about what this scale had cost, what all of the scales had cost me. Tomorrow, we would head to the Barren Lands. I would be traveling with people I no longer really knew to collect items that, deep in my gut, I knew could never get into the hands of King Tatum.

Chapter 35

The three of us stood on the riverbank facing the Barren Lands, the rush of the water ringing in the air. Star zipped around our heads, doing loops and sharp turns.

"We can just fly over," Bash said, looking at the churning waters.

Rapids sent harsh water thrashing against submerged rocks. The thought of getting on Knox right now pushed me to say, "I'll swim over." There was a moment of hesitation, a silence thick with unspoken words. I knew at least two of them had arguments, but we all knew any trust between us had been shattered like broken glass yesterday.

"This is my last pair of clothes anyways. We can just swim it," Blaire chimed in, surprising me. "They could do with a good cleaning in the river." She wasn't wrong, though. We were all running out of supplies.

"Amalia, you learned to swim *very* recently, I don't think you should be crossing a river. We have no idea how strong the currents are. This isn't safe," Bash said, reaching out to touch my arm, but I pulled away before he could make contact. The idea of relying on them, even for a moment, was too much for me right now.

"What's not safe is me being with three dragons, who all knew my entire race was cleansed by the male who sent me on a suicide scavenger mission and never felt the need to tell me." I shoved my pack into his chest and headed to get in.

Knox grabbed my arm. "Don't be stupid just because you're angry," he snarled. Star banked toward him, nipping at his hand.

A grudge? That's what he thought this was?

"It's not a grudge. It's hatred after a betrayal. After murder." Yanking my arm back, I faced the river. My pulse thrummed in my ears. I could see how the Barren Lands stretched out ahead. The land was harsh and unforgiving, nothing but copper sand and large formations in the distance. It wasn't the sight of the Barren Lands or even the river that promised to swallow me whole; something else ate away at the back of my mind, the recent events were just a harbinger.

Irritation bled over his words. "The Barren Lands are known for their unpredictability. It's a place where everything resists life. Once across, don't go far. Your life is worth more than your hatred." Knox took off the sheath he had taken from Alaric's body and held it in one hand before jumping into the water feetfirst. When he came up, he held his sword over his head and started for the other side of the river.

It was my turn next, and I found myself hesitating. "Go ahead and fly over. I'll meet you on the other side," I said to Star, who chortled in response. She'd enjoy the short flight and most likely find insects to gobble up once she made it. I glanced at Blaire, who let out a huff before walking up to the bank. She jumped in, albeit not as gracefully as Knox, but quickly enough that I mustered up the courage to jump in behind her. The icy waters stole my breath in an instant. Bash entered after me, no doubt to make sure I made it.

The current tugged at my legs with a relentless pull, making it hard to kick myself across. My breath came in ragged gasps as I fought to keep my head above water, the roar of the rapids filling my ears.

This may not have been a good idea.

Knox reached the opposite bank, his hands clawed at the soil, hauling himself up. The effort of fighting the water burned my lungs, but I drove my legs to kick harder. Blaire, ahead of me, looked like she was struggling worse than I was, the churning water lapping over her head every chance it had. I could hear her spitting up water each time she was forced under. "Blaire!" I yelled as the seconds stretched before she resurfaced, her fingers splayed out, desperate to find anything to grasp.

She had been through so much, turning her into something bitter and vengeful. Some would say this was what happened when your actions caught up to you. One more glance toward the bank along the Barren Lands. Knox was catching his breath. I chanced a look behind me, where Bash was straining as he fought the current, his biggest problem was having to stay behind our slower pace. I was the closest to Blaire.

He wouldn't reach her in time. "Amalia, don't you fucking dare!" Bash warned as he saw determination set in my eyes.

Too late.

My muscles screamed as my arms propelled me forward just like Knox had shown me. Her red hair was the only thing I saw as she went under once again, the water dousing her flame. I dove for her. Blind under the water's surface, my body tumbled from the force of the current, slamming against the riverbed. The air was knocked from me. Stretching my hands out, I searched for her, for anything of hers to grab onto. I felt flesh and wrenched her to me. The added weight of her body made it nearly impossible to get back to the surface, and panic made me desperate trying to push off from the rocky bottom. She started thrashing, her legs kicked out, and we pushed together as the stirred-up sediment circled around us.

We broke the surface with frantic gasps of air. "Are you okay?" I coughed up.

"You saved me?" Her voice was full of tremors as her teeth chattered, breaking up the words.

"We're not. Going to talk. About it." The words came out ragged as I fought to get us to the bank. Bash reached us with a growl and helped push us along while keeping himself afloat. Knox, on the bank, reached his hands out and grasped Blaire under her armpits, yanking her onto the now-muddy shore.

Bash helped guide me up next, his hands clamped my waist and hoisted me up before he pulled himself out. Blaire was crouched, retching up remnants of sediment and water. Our eyes met, and for the first time, I thought I saw gratitude in hers.

Chapter 36

"Are you okay?" Knox was at my side, fixing the mangled hair that had overtaken my face. I pulled my face from his hands and looked to the ground, afraid that if I allowed myself to see him, allowed him to provide even an ounce of comfort, I'd forget the betrayal.

"It doesn't bother me that you try to push me away," he said, backing away. "It's just you, how you handle things you can't process. I see you, Amalia. I will wait for a chance to make it right with you, when you're ready."

I kept my gaze away from him as I felt his hand caress my cheek. "I don't know how many times I'll need to say it, but I'm sorry."

"I don't need your apologies, I just need to know why," I said, finally looking at him. His mouth turned down, letting me know he wasn't going to tell me. If that was the case, he could apologize every hour of every day, and it still would mean nothing unless he allowed me the opportunity to understand.

Blaire's voice, normally tinged with a hard edge, softened. "I know where the Mending Scale is," she announced. "It's at the Temple of Thalvyr."

"Lead the way," Knox said with distrust in his voice. I wasn't sure I blamed him. Blaire had never been one to offer assistance. She was showing how easy it is to change when you're offered kindness. I smiled at her in a quiet thanks, and she returned a weak one back, not meeting my eyes. It was better than the usual looks we gave each other. I wouldn't say we were on the verge of being friends by any means, but I did think we had come to a truce at the very least.

Several hours went by as we trudged through the barren landscape. Sand swirled in the air, feeling like needles puncturing our skin and coating our lungs as we traveled. The sand was consuming, making every step a fight to break free. Large copper rock formations grew higher than six dragons. It was desolate, as the name suggested, but it also held its own unique beauty, a clean, blank slate. Brythos would probably have liked it here.

The temple started to come into view. It was made of cream-colored stone with marks that bore darker coloration from its age. Much like the vines that covered Brythos's body, the temple was shrouded in petrified plants, showing that these lands had once been bountiful with life and now had been forgotten. There was a large opening at the top of a wide staircase. The sense of unease returned as we drew closer. With each step, my mind screamed at me to turn around.

I came to a stop midway up the staircase and looked around us. *Something is wrong.*

"What is it?" Bash said as he came to stand next to me, my cautious gaze making him check out the area. "Do you see something?" he asked.

"No, I—"

A blood-curdling scream rang out, and I slapped my hands over my ears, crouching to get away from the noise. Bash's hands flew over me protectively, and Knox jolted upright, his face turning pale like he had seen a ghost. Without a word, Knox sprinted toward the opening of the temple, Blaire running after him, calling his name.

Knox whirled around to her. "That was my mother's scream!"

"What?" I yelled at him. "I thought she was dead, King Tatum—"

"He couldn't have..." As the thoughts spiraled, his body reacted, propelling him into the darkness of the temple. Blaire followed like a child not wanting to separate from their parents.

Bash went to chase after them, but as he reached the last step, a large, cream-colored stone matching the rest of the temple rose, the ground trembling in its wake. He ran to get through before it closed, but five figures fell from the top of the temple, landing with thuds against the stone. They were all dressed in pure white with glittering gold masks covering their faces. Even without seeing their identities, it was evident these were the king's men.

I was still in the same place, the middle of the staircase, when I remembered the Menticide Scale in my pack. He couldn't have it. I ran down the steps, leaving Bash. A sharp pang of guilt went through me, but this was above everything. I didn't know what the king wanted with the scales, but I knew with certainty it would only bring more death.

I slid in the copper sand, tucking myself into the protected corner where the staircase and temple foundation met. I used my hands to dig furiously without making myself known. I could hear Bash fighting, the grunts and smacks of weapons clashing together. I had to hurry. I had to help him. Star was suddenly next to me, using her little claws to dig into the sand as well. I grabbed my pack and threw it into the hole. Covering it up as quickly as I'd made it. I whispered to Star, "You need to stay here where it's safe. No matter what happens, don't come out." She flew up and snapped her teeth at me, clearly unhappy with my order, so I switched tactics as I heard Bash yell out in an agonizing shout. "Protect the scale for me." I touched my finger to her snout and ran up the staircase, only glancing back to make sure she wasn't following.

As I reached the top, I saw multiple strangers sprawled lifelessly on the ground. Bash was down on one knee with some sort of vial sticking out of his neck. Blood ran down his bent leg. Panic surged through me. He noticed my arrival and slurred, "Remember your training."

"It was a fucking day, Bash! One day!" I shouted. How could I help him?

One of the assailants raised a sword to him, the intention clear. The act was reminiscent of Knox with Alaric as the stranger stood behind Bash.

"Noo!" I screamed, tears welling up in my eyes. Bash was good, he was funny and kind. "Stop!" I pleaded. "Take me! I'll go with you, but please don't kill him."

"Amalia, Run!" Bash said, twisting to me, his panicked eyes meeting mine. The moment he spoke, a burlap bag was forced over my face from behind in tandem with a sickening *crack*. The last thing I saw was Bash's body hitting the ground, unmoving.

Chapter 37
Knox

The temple's door rose from the ground, and moss dropped from the grinding of stone against stone. Instinct took over and I moved to jump over the closing entrance, but Blaire pulled me back, causing me to stumble backward onto my ass. "What the hell are you doing?" I growled. Then, a scream. Raw, ragged, the same scream that had haunted my nightmares, the scream I'd heard night after night that she'd been stuck with King Tatum after my father had been killed. The door crashed shut behind me, shaking me from the memory.

"I'm sorry," whispered a voice. *Blaire.*

The words sank into my gut as what was going on became clear.

"*You,*" I snarled. "What have you done?" She flinched when my fire ignited, purple flames illuminating the tears streaking her face. I was the only species that could use their flame when in their human form. This wasn't information others remembered, since King Tatum had worked hard to erase my horde from memories. Judging by the way Blaire was quaking in fear, she had forgotten like the rest.

Outside, I could hear the faint sound of steel clashing. Bash's roar cut through the stone: "Amalia! Ambush—!"

I lunged at Blaire, pinning her to the wall. "What have you *done*?!" I said again with every ounce of rage I had in me.

Her breath came in panicked gasps. "I'm so sorry, Knox. He made me do it." The tears streamed down her face now, leaving trails of crimson in their wake. "He—he had me for years. Tortured me. Took my tears, every last drop."

My fury didn't simmer as she spoke words I already knew.

"The shimmer... it's *me*. My pain. My fear." She lifted her pale hair to show a single scar on her neck, one I had never noticed despite having known her our whole lives. Her healing ability could completely erase wounds, making it as if they were never there... if she chose to show that kindness, which she rarely did. So why hadn't she healed this fully?

"This was the first and deepest cut. I keep it as a reminder of what I went through." She sucked in a breath, trying to collect herself. "But so much more than that, he used the essences of the fae. Combined them together. He and Folsom, t—they figured out how to alter the magic, make it dark. Deadly." That was information I hadn't known. "I couldn't... I couldn't do it again. The screaming—" A sob broke free from her.

My rage faltered.

"He promised to stop. Swore it. If I lured you here." She gagged on a sob.

Pulling her from the wall a mere few inches, I slammed her against it again. "For what?" My eyes scanned the room. "Is the scale even here?" I shook her, needing her to answer. "Lured me here for what?"

"Please, Knox, please understand." The words came out garbled as she spoke through choked sobs. "He only wants her."

Bash's battle cries grew desperate. Metal screeched. Silence fell. Somewhere beyond the temple, Amalia's voice vanished mid-shout.

"You made a deal to give up Amalia?" Dread hit me like a gut punch. "Do you have any idea what he will do to her?" Spit flew from my mouth as I screamed the words at her.

Blaire lifted her chin in defiance. "I know all too well."

My hand found the hilt of my stolen sword as I unsheathed it and pressed it against her throat. "You won't ever have to worry about King Tatum again. This betrayal? It's the last thing you will ever do," I seethed, pressing the blade harder against her skin. I would cut down every last person who chose the king's dark will over what was right.

"The scream!" Blaire rushed out. "It wasn't a trick. Your mother... She's alive. Or she was while I was in the Stygian prison. She was there with me, locked away. They liked to keep women together, to have them watch each other's torture." Her words came out quick and desperate. "They said it made the essence, t—the tears more potent. That cry was hers. Tatum traded her to Mikulec's men for a female fae he used to make the shimmer."

The dark rushed in. The nightmares that had haunted me, the things I'd conjured up thinking about what could have happened to her becoming reality. I released some of the pressure from my blade.

"How can we hear it? How are her screams within the temple?"

Blaire slid to the floor. I followed her down, not ready to completely release her yet. "I-It's just an enchantment, magic."

Rage and reason warred in my mind. Blaire was a wild card, yes. But she had information I couldn't let die with her. I crouched, tilting her chin to meet my eyes. "You'll live. For now."

She shuddered. "Thank you."

"Don't say those words to me." I stood, disgust dripping from me, shadows coiling around my fists. "When Amalia is safe..."

I leaned close, crouching once more. "You'll tell me *everything*. About the king. About my mother."

Blaire nodded, trembling. "I'll tell you everything you want to know."

I turned to face the dark room we were trapped in. The shadows welcomed me. "First, you'll show me how to get out of here." I looked down at her body, still crumpled in a teary heap against the stone wall. "Then you'll tell me where to find Amalia."

As we walked through the never-ending darkness, Blaire's whispered words stabbed into me, forever leaving a mark. "She cried out for you. Your mother, every night. She would yell out your and your father's name."

I didn't say anything. I couldn't. My throat had swollen shut at the thought that her cries had been left unanswered for so long. The one I'd heard just a short time ago now too real in mind to ever fade.

Amalia's cries would not go unanswered. *I will save her.*

Chapter 38

They tied a burlap sack around my head, taking my sight before dragging me away. There was no way to know where we were going or what they would do with me. King Tatum would want me alive; he needed me alive.

Right?

The one leading held my hands behind my back with one of theirs, before a stringy material replaced their grip, binding mine together.

Fingers dug into my arms, my hips, my breasts as they yanked me upward. Air rushed from my lungs as my stomach slammed against a ridged surface. Someone was next to me? In front of me? No, no, behind me. They shifted my body so I was draped over the object, then rested one hand on my lower back. A deafening screech sounded, causing me to jump, and the sound of wingbeats followed shortly after with a steady rush of wind whipping around me. My stomach swam. I had to be on the back of a dragon.

My thoughts were on Bash. The sound of the blow he'd taken ricocheted in my ears. I should have done something, anything.

"Remember your training."

The words haunted me. What had he expected me to do? *Oh my dragons.* Was he telling me to channel from him? Why hadn't I thought of that? I *could* have helped him. He'd tried to tell me how! Silent tears streamed down my cheeks. I'd failed him when he'd tried to ask for help. I'd caused the end of us all. Nothing they did to me now could hurt worse than knowing my mistake took him. The consequences from my lack of action terrorized me more than the thought of what I was heading toward.

Coarse burlap fibers scratched at my face as darkness held a firm veil over me. I clenched my jaw tight, fighting the urge to throw up from my stomach being draped over the hard scales.My insides squirmed with every rise and weightless fall in altitude. My heart never stopped racing. I was never able to calm myself like I could on the back of Knox. That three-day flight was the Elysian Islands compared to this.

How much time had gone by? Surely people would see me when we arrived in Santavarre—they couldn't keep me like this. Whatever time passed, it passed slowly. The air grew thicker with heat, like when you over-boil water. The scent of sulfur and ash soaked through the burlap and stayed trapped inside, suffocating me.

"Would you like to see your new residence?" a man's caustic voice said before the burlap was ripped off my head, the string that had tied it shut ripping my skin away from under my chin. I hissed at the pain, but the sensation muted as I took in what lay below—nothing but hues of red and orange bubbling up from blackened mountains.

"Welcome to the Lands of Stygian."

I had heard of this place. It was said to be made of darkness and liquid fire. It was forbidden, and no one who sought it out to go looking there ever came back. Rumor said its protectors enjoyed feasting on trespassers. After the tales of Stygian spread far enough and people had remained missing, others had stopped trying to see it for themselves. It became another forgotten land.

The blackened ground came closer as we descended to an enormous crater. Inside were... homes. It looked like a town. People stopped to look up as we glided by, faces wearing stony expressions. There were even children running around, bumping into adults who were distracted with our arrival. "I-I don't understand, I thought everyone was skyward except for those who reside in Santavarre and Cimmerian?" I said, not actually thinking the man would provide any further explanation.

His voice was rough. "The people who live here were created, or exiled from the sky for deeds that showed they were unfit to remain."

"What would make children unfit?" I said, not being able to think of how a child could get exiled.

"They weren't. The children grew up here; their parents were exiled. Many for acts of treason such as killing or stealing. Others for not following *Mikulec*," he said the name with disgust, but the hatred in his eyes was turned on me.

My ears perked up. Mikulec was skyward and had the authority to exile people? He had power over the creatures that brought their lands to the sky? I tried to sit up, but it was a failure with my hands tied behind my back. There was no way for me to move more than an inch, and even then, it was more of a wiggling motion. "He sounds like a powerful man to have that kind of influence over magical beings."

The man shoved my face down, *hard*. My cheek slammed against the gray scales beneath us.

"Shut your fucking mouth! The king knows you're working with him. We will kill him and you, the last human of Caligness. This realm will belong to us again." At the conclusion of his words the dragon slid to a stop, and rough hands yanked me from where I lay, throwing me off the back of the beast. The impact reverberated through every bone in my body, making me gasp for air. The man hopped off with elegance, the white suit blowing slightly in the heated breeze. He grabbed the back of my shirt, ripping me off the ground, onto my feet, and dragging me around the large creature I'd thought was a dragon.

It had a dragon's face, but instead of horns, there were wispy, red tendrils coming from its gray scales. Its eyes were that of the liquid fire we'd passed over. There were no limbs on this creature, I noted, as my own tripped over rocks. Its body was long and curled like a snake, and the end of its tail had a puff of red fur that grew to a point from a wide base. "What is this thing?" I wondered aloud. The beast's eyes locked on me like it understood I'd referred to it as a *thing*.

King Tatum emerged from the stone entrance beyond the beast. His attire is still a stark white with gold accessories making him the focal point. Two guards followed close behind, their stares beyond me, like they weren't aware of their surroundings. King Tatum's voice boomed with confidence and pride. "They are called Sky Gliders; they are my most successful creation to date. They are faster than any dragon and can outmaneuver any creature in this realm."

"Lovely," I said to him, breaths still heavy.

King Tatum looked at me, his eyes gleaming with a cruel satisfaction, like he'd just hunted the most valuable prey. I stood as tall as I could, jutting my chin in defiance. *I will not show weakness. I will not show weakness.*

"I've been waiting for you, Amalia," he said, slow and menacing.

"I can't say the same for you." A sharp pain shot through my side as the man holding me landed a punch to my rib cage. King Tatum howled with laughter. "What do you want with me?" I demanded, coughing out the last word.

"Information," he drawled, before turning on his heel and moving toward a towering gray-stone fortress. A palm cracked my spine between my shoulder blades, rocking me forward, but I pushed back. I wasn't going to make this easy, and I wouldn't just walk into their prison willingly. They would have to drag me as I kicked and screamed.

The man seemed delighted by my resistance. He grabbed me by the back of the head with a fistful of my hair and yanked me to the floor, where he used the strands as a makeshift rope, pulling me where he wanted.

"I won't give you what you want!" I screamed, thrashing against the hold. I could hear chunks of my hair ripping from my scalp.

King Tatum chuckled, a low, unnerving laugh. "We shall see, Amalia. Everyone has a breaking point."

I let his words hang between us. This was different from the things I'd had to do for the scales. This was true danger, and as much as I wanted to fight, King Tatum was not one to show mercy. Everything about him proved he enjoyed the struggle, the fight.

King Tatum walked ahead as we went through pathways of jagged rocks within the walls. The man finally allowed me to walk after I stopped kicking and thrashing around. My scalp pulsed with my heartbeat from the trauma. Inside, the walls inside were obsidian with lava flowing down cracks into gutters along the pathway, providing low light for the walk. My throat burned from the heat. I couldn't remember the last time I'd had a drink of water.

Some of the pathways had barred, window-like cutouts. I chanced glances through them every time I could to see what lay beyond the walls—tall watchtowers sculpted from the natural formations that grew from the earth. Who would they be watching for? Mikulec? My boots struck heavy on the ground, making King Tatum stop and turn to me. His eyes glazed over my body in an unimpressed manner until he looked at my feet.

"Take those off of her," he commanded.

"Yes, sir." The man dipped into a bow before bending down and attempting to unlace my boots. He'd tied my hands, not my feet. Shifting my weight, I rammed my booted foot into the man's chest. He wheezed, toppling backward in shock. I turned and ran. I had no plan, but I knew I needed to *run*. King Tatum's laughter filled the space before I created too much distance, and his tone changed to one of anger. "Get her, you idiot!"

I could hear grunting over my hard footfalls as I pushed myself to go faster, faster. I felt the man grab for me and miss. He was too close. I needed to—

The man tackled me to the ground, both of us tumbling farther down the scorched floor, my face stopping mere inches from the lava stream. Parts of my hair fell in, hissing as they singed before I moved away, groaning. With my hands tied, the force of the fall was excruciating; my shoulders felt like they were being ripped from my body. As I rolled over, the man attempted to get up, but his hand touched one of the cracks in the wall oozing the red-hot liquid, and he hissed in pain.

I shot to my feet and pressed my hands against the wall, smiling as the twine that bound them went slack against the lava. With my hands now free, I ran once more.

"Oh no you don't, you little bitch," the man said, grabbing me hard on the upper arm and swinging me back down to the ground. My head cracked against the stone and lights dotted my eyes. Blinking rapidly, I tried to focus on staying awake as a whimper left my mouth.

"Lorcan, stop screwing around, bring her back to me!" King Tatum bellowed. Lorcan didn't seem to hear him. His eyes were cold and threatening as he looked at me.

"You shouldn't have done that," he said in a low voice. He'd pinned my hands over my head, and pressed his lower body on mine to keep me down. I was entirely helpless and not strong enough to fight whatever he was—his ears were pointed, but his eyes were black against his pale skin. He grabbed my shirt near the buttons and ripped the fabric open, exposing my breasts. "Now what should we do here, little human? Do you think you'll be good now?" He took a small blade from his belt and scraped the tip over the curve of my breast down to my stomach, stopping where my pants sat.

"Lorcan!" King Tatum boomed, demanding to be heard. My entire body was trembling. Lorcans's eyes went milky white before he released my hands and removed himself from me. I went to close my shirt, but he'd destroyed it. Only one button remained, and it was a useless bottom button.

King Tatum stepped up, offering me a hand. I hesitated for a moment, not wanting to take it. I looked at Lorcan, whose eyes were still covered in that milky gloss. "He will not bother you again," King Tatum said. "I apologize for his behavior. He's not used to women who... don't go easily."

I took his hand, slowly getting to my feet, feeling dizzy and a bit nauseous from the hit to my head. King Tatum motioned his hand out, urging me forward. "Here, you will understand what happens when you choose defiance and deceit."

"What have I done that's deceitful?" I said, knowing very well every choice I had made could be considered defiance.

King Tatum's voice rose, "You are working with Mikulec even after what I shared with you," before he collected himself mid-sentence. "After I showed vulnerability to you about the loss of my family. You still chose to go to him."

My brows furrowed in confusion, making me pause mid-step. "I have no idea what you're talking about. I haven't seen Mikulec—I wouldn't even know who to look for. I've been collecting the scales like YOU requested."

King Tatum grabbed me by the throat, throwing me against the wall. Pain and frustration made tears fall from my eyes. "Don't lie to me!" he spat in my face.

"I'm not!" I cried out. *Do not show weakness, do not show weakness.*

I couldn't wear the mask of bravery anymore; no part of me thought this was going to end well for me. He threw me into a room made of the same black, stony material. There were no windows, only chains strung up on the walls and a side table holding various tools.

"You may have heard of this room before," Tatum stated flatly as he took my hands and placed them in the cuffs, locking them with a key before moving to cuff my ankles. "It's used to extract the things that I want, and what I want from you is the truth. Some may think it is beneath me to waste time with you." The click of the engaged cuffs sent goosebumps over my skin. "But you may have noticed, I can't exactly trust others to do what's needed... and I want to be the one who pulls the truth from your mind."

Tatum moved to shut the barred metal door with a loud *clank*. I took a deep breath and righted myself after wobbling. This was going to test me to my soul, and I needed to remember strength. The information he wanted, I didn't have. He would eventually realize I wasn't lying; I just had to make it until then.

So quickly, that morning's problems seemed so minute. The anger I held toward Knox, Bash, and Blaire meant nothing compared to this. I wanted nothing more than to have Knox bust through that door and save me.

King Tatum turned to face me. Whatever he saw in my expression pleased him, because his eyes lit up before he said, "Let's begin."

Chapter 39

A muscle twitched in my jaw as I silently inventoried every poor life choice that had led to this moment. I held my breath as King Tatum walked to me, a calculating gaze and a cruel smile shown proudly on his face. The cuffs bit into my wrists as my body hung forward. He moved to the side table, surveying the tools he had, deciding which ones he wanted to use on me.

"You hold many secrets, Amalia," he said, still wearing a cruel smile. "I am eager to see what it takes to make you spill them."

"I don't know anything about Mikulec," I pleaded, my voice growing hoarse. My father had always said *"The truth will set you free."* I'd like to take this moment to say that was utter bullshit.

King Tatum tsked under his breath as he picked up a stone painted with swirls around a dragon's eye. "I was hoping you'd lie to me again. Now, let me show you what happens when you do." His fingers held the stone up to his eyeline as he whispered words I couldn't understand. It lit in an aqua hue before a pulse of energy blasted the room. Agony seared into my skull and lit every nerve on fire. I held back my scream and bit down on my cheek, tasting blood.

The invisible attack was much like Zarakruae's had been, and I tried to breathe through it. King Tatum's smile thinned as I held back my reactions, not giving him the show he had wished for.

"I see. You think you can overcome this. Let me be frank. You cannot."

King Tatum continued on for what felt like an eternity. Each rune he used inflicted pain somewhere else within my body. He used them in tandem with each other to elicit screams and pleas from me for him to stop. He grew more and more frustrated the longer it went on. I didn't tell him what he wanted. I couldn't. If I were working with Mikulec, I might have broken long ago, but how do you break when you have no information to break over? The room was stifling as the fiery liquid seeped in through the cracks, pooling in the carved-out spaces on the floor.

"I will admit, you surprise me, child. You have lasted longer and proven much stronger than Blaire. I am not easily impressed, but you—" he said, pointing a finger at me. "You have impressed me." He stripped his pearlescent cloak off as the temperature rose and rolled up his sleeves. He wore the same suit from when we'd first spoken in Santavarre.

"We will see how you do against me." His words were like ice in my veins. "Call this vengeance for what your bloodline did to my world," he seethed. I knew what his kind were capable of, and I did not want to experience him inside my mind. Would he alter it? Would he dig deep looking for the truth and realize I was never lying? Would he see everything, Lane's death? Fear grabbed hold of me, and it felt like Tatum had hold of my throat again as I thought about what he would do to Knox if he ever found out about what happened to his son. The only family he had left.

King Tatum stood before me, placing his hands on either side of my head. "I will make sure this hurts," he said before his eyes went diamond-like. I fought against the fingers that tried to pry into my mind. I could feel him trying to inch his way into my memories, and a strangled yell tore from me as I fought against him, his face contorting in confusion.

I could feel my body trying to channel and I let it. I let in all the power he was using to invade my mind, and I turned it on him, without even having to touch him. His mind was a swirling, black pit of anger and longing. Flashes of his life played in front of me, moments of love and yearning for a woman with long, golden hair and striking blue eyes, of their mating bond forging into place with a silver, glimmering wing on the inside of their wrists. Then, memories of an attack, the dragons and fae working together. His rage became my rage, his sorrow, my sorrow. I felt the pain as a group of fae bled him while he was strung up, runes in a circle below him. An illusion of his dragon form being chained, never to transform again, his soul changed irrevocably at the loss of what made him whole for a second time. I felt *everything* that had led him to this point.

I broke, and a scream tore through me, out of me. The power erupted, sending the lava around the room into the air in chaos.

King Tatum staggered back, panting and clutching his head like he'd just realized what had happened. He was visibly shaken. Beads of sweat clung to his forehead above his wide eyes. He ignored the fiery rain falling around us. My cuffs heated, burning my tender skin.

"That's enough for now," he said, composing himself, adjusting his suit, and running his hands through his hair, reminding me of Lane. He wouldn't look at me. He was unmoving, like he was stuck in a trance. "You will wake up in a different cell. This is not the last time we will see each other," he promised with slow words.

"Wake u—"

Chapter 40

My hands were chained above my head once more, shoulder-width apart, aching with a pain so deep I knew what had woken me. I had no relief, since my now-bare feet were barely touching the ground, my entire body weighing my hands down into the cuffs. Dried blood left darkened streaks down to my shoulders and raced to the front of my chest. I looked up at the damp, stone-covered ceiling, trying to hold back my tears.

"Tears do not show strength; facing the struggle with fierceness does." My father's voice echoed in my mind, bringing an entirely different type of pain. Growing up in a family made up of mostly women, he'd always tried to encourage our strength in ways that didn't involve what he'd considered the weaker emotions. I closed my eyes and took three deep breaths, shoving down my feelings with each exhale to the deepest parts of me, locking them away like I had been taught.

My head snapped to the metal door as I heard the loud clanging of the lock being disengaged. I jutted my chin and narrowed my eyes, ready to face whoever walked through that door. My resolve disintegrated as I saw a familiar figure walk in with beautiful, glossy black hair pulled into a ponytail.

"A-Akira?" I said, voice breaking from the screams that had come out during my time with King Tatum. She was carrying a tray of food. What looked like a biscuit and some liquidy substance. It was hard to see in this room; the only light radiated from a single torch on the opposite side. She didn't speak as she came closer; her features were dull and void of any emotion. Like I was nothing to her. "Akira!" I tried to say louder, looking for a sign my friend saw me, heard me, wouldn't leave me like this, wouldn't DO this to me.

"Please, Akira, say something," I choked out, my voice a rasp.

She said nothing as she approached. She stood before me, face blank. That's when I saw her eyes. Once full of chocolate, they were now a pale white—there was no life in them. *She* wasn't in them.

"Wha—"

"Eat," she demanded.

I pulled on my chains. "What happened to you?" I struggled to get the words out. She didn't respond. "I'm not eating any of that." Channeling the strength I had left, I stared at her face, into the blank-canvas eyes that used to hold stubbornness and spice. One of her hands left the tray and went behind her back. When she brought it back, she was holding a knife.

I said nothing.

"Eat," she demanded again. I'd never heard her voice so menacing before, but I kept quiet and looked to the side, away from this imposter.

"Very well." She dragged the words out, and then I felt a stinging in my forearm as she used the knife to slice open my skin. I clenched my jaw and slammed my eyes shut, breathing hard through my nose, refusing to make a sound. Once I felt the blade leave my skin, I looked back at my friend and saw a tear running from one milky eye.

"Eat, or bleed," she said, only this time there was a quaver to her voice.

Realization hit. Lorcan's eyes had gone white before finally obeying King Tatum. I knew he had the ability to alter minds, erase or add memories—but could he control minds as well? If King Tatum had control over Akira now. Had Lane ever controlled me? The tears were a sign she was still there. Another slice in my skin, only this time, on my right rib cage. She sliced deeper and longer, until the cut stopped at my belly button. A whimper escaped from us both, and I saw her hand trembling.

"Drop the knife, it's me, it's your friend," I pleaded. "I know you really didn't consider me your friend, but you are mine. Please don't do this." A warmth spread across my stomach as blood soaked into my tattered top. "How are you here?" My voice quavered. Was this why she had gone missing? What could she have done to deserve this? Did Asahi know?

"Eat, or bleed," she repeated as her eyes grew glossy with unshed tears, lips trembling just slightly as she said the words.

"Okay, okay, I'll eat," I said, panting.

If she didn't have control, then the only thing I could do was not make it any harder for her. We both didn't need to be tortured.

"They will make you bleed either way," a frail voice said from the darkness.

I strained to see who spoke, not realizing anyone was in this cell with me. "Hello?" I said cautiously. "What do you mean?"

Akira lifted a spoonful of the liquid up to my mouth, and I opened for her. She tipped the spoon in, and my tongue was assaulted by a vile taste, so bitter I instantly spit it out, coughing. Akira took her blade and pressed against my collarbone, sliding it from my left side to my right. A throaty scream burst from me as stars danced behind my eyes at the pain. "Stop!" I screamed. "Please." Sobs broke my words now as I couldn't hold them back any longer. "Please, Akira, don't do this." She brought her blade to my right elbow and pressed the very tip of the blade into my skin, dragging it down the length of my arm, stopping just before my armpit. Another scream escaped me.

"Eat, or bleed," she seethed, her white, cloudy eyes narrowing as she bared her teeth at me.

"I tried," I wailed, sucking in pained breaths. I could barely speak with my sniveling. I pulled at the cuffs, trying to rip my hands free, but all it did was increase the unbearable pain. Blood flowed readily from the pressure on my wrists, and I was forced to stop as I started to get lightheaded. Akira broke out into a fit of laughter, but tears were streaming down her face. My heart broke at the thought of what was going on in her mind, the battle she must have been fighting.

"She will leave now," that frail, feminine voice stated.

The cell quieted as Akira's laughter came to a halt. Metal against stone reverberated through the small space as she dropped the tray of food to the ground. The bowl tipped over, spilling the liquid contents. Akira reached to the back of her white linen dress, now spotted with my blood, and pulled the keys to my cuffs from the band that kept the dress fitted to her form. Her mouth was scrunched and her brows pulled in, making it look like she was in pain, before she dropped the keys to the ground.

"I will save you," I promised her. Her face went back to expressionless as she looked up at me, before turning and walking away, closing the now-unlocked cell door. She was still in there. Another sob broke free, and spit dripped down my bottom lip as the weight of what she had just managed to do hit me. The power it had to have taken. I felt so much pride in her. She was a force to be reckoned with, and I needed to be the same.

"She's lost, girl. There ain't no saving her," the voice said.

"She's still in there!" I shouted, pulling against the chains. "You know nothing about her!" She was tough. She could make it through this.

"I know I have watched many come and go, and they all go the same. Their minds melt and they start going insane, end up killin' themselves. All the same. She's lost, girl."

A frustrated growl left me, and the force of me pulling against the chains made the wound on my arm gush even more. "Let me out!" I screamed, my throat burning from the force.

"Shhhh, girl, you'll make him come in here, then you'll really have something to scream about." I heard the chains that must have been holding her clang, like they were dragging along the floor. There was a small, open-but-barred window at the top of the cell to my left, directly in front of the cell door. She seemed to be chained to the opposite corner I was.

"Who are you? What are you doing here?" I bit out while trying to use my bare foot to grab the dropped keys, which were just out of reach.

"My name is Zara. I was traded to Takae many years ago," she said as she came into view in the limited light shining in from the moon. The night breeze trickled in, chilling the back of my neck. That all-too-familiar feeling urging me to remember.

I hadn't allowed myself to let the memories in. Recalling my mother's voice brought so much pain. It played like an old song, the last story she'd ever told me and my sisters before she died. We had almost lost Brantley along with her. The mention of King Tatum's full name after everything I'd gone through broke through all the barriers I'd worked so hard to place. *He* was the one from the Kingdom End Chronicles. It had never been just a story; it was all true. Would my life be the next story children heard but would never believe?

"What got you placed in a cell?" I asked. She had to be about eighty years old. I couldn't imagine what she could have done to be sent to such a hostile place.

"This is the only place he could put me where he could extract what he wanted. I've tried to leave many times," she said flatly. "As you can see, I wasn't very successful at escaping."

I breathed out in surprise. "Extract what? Why?" A low creak broke the silence as the breeze reached the slightly open cell door.

"I believe you already know. I can feel my essence within you," she said curiously.

"I have no idea what you're talking about." I tried to adjust myself, but it was no use. There was no way to get relief, and I had already lost so much blood. My eyes were getting heavy.

"You are different from the others they bring," Zara stated, snapping me back into the moment. "He needs you."

I said nothing.

"I have been in this cell for many long years, girl. Never has he been so riled up about a prisoner. Not even the ones who tried to end him." Zara coughed relentlessly. They sounded like they came from deep within her chest, causing her to wheeze once the fit was over.

"I will not allow myself to be here for two years, not even two weeks. We will get out. My friends, they will come for me."

Zara's strained laugh startled me. "Oh, girl. I will die here. My fate has already been decided; there is nothing left for me beyond this cell. And you." Her voice dropped lower. "You will die here with me." Her manic, tortured laughter continued, and I screamed again, flailing against the chains that held me.

Zara's laugh ended with the start of my screams as she shrank back into the shadows. "Shhh, girl, he'll come for you!" she shouted. But I didn't care. I wanted him to come. I wanted him to face me. "C'mon Tatum, I'm waiting for you! I'm right here!" I kicked off the wall and slammed back against it, pulling at the chains, an aggravated scream belting out of me. "Come face me, you coward!"

BAM! A faraway slam sounded, and I stopped. Loud footsteps echoed down the corridor. From the sound of it, it must have been stone, just like it was in here. The door to our cell flew open, slamming against the wall, extinguishing the burning torch.

"My dear, why are you causing such a scene? You're giving me a headache, and I tend to get angry when I have a headache." Tatum walked in, wearing his white suit adorned with gold embellishments.

"I don't give a fuck about your headache," I seethed.

He landed a blow so brutal to my face, I saw memories of a dream. Of a village burning. Then he slammed his fist into my stomach, then my ribs. Unable to cower or fight back because of the chains that held me, I just had to endure.

"I will break your mind until you feel it in your soul, until you feel as though your body is crumbling from the inside. You will be nothing but a shell when I am finished. A mere afterthought in the minds of everyone you think loves you. Of everyone I allow to remember you," King Tatum said, walking around my exhausted body.

"Then this is ironic," I said as I felt and tasted the blood that seeped from every inch of my face.

"Is it? Please enlighten me, Amalia, while you are able. I must say, you have me interested," King Tatum said, sneering at me.

I raised my head as much as I could to show he had not broken me like he believed, I would not cower. I met his eyes. "My soul has always been broken. I've lived every day in pain you can't imagine. So, this?" I spat out a mouthful of blood to the side. "This is only the physical representation of what my body feels on the inside. Every. Single. Day. From the moment I woke up in that field. So, Takae Tatum, do your worst. It will be nothing compared to what I have already lived through."

It was taking every ounce of strength I had to keep my head held high as I stared at his expressionless face. Slowly, the right side of his mouth quirked up into a vile smile. He walked out of the cell and out of my line of sight as he went down the hallway. When he came back, he had a lit torch in his hand. "I only needed your blood, my dear. I'm certain Lane has retrieved the scales you've found. I can handle the rest."

My heart started to race as images of him burning me alive flashed through my mind. He walked into the icy cell and to the corner beside me, where a pile of wood sat unused. He turned to me and said, "You are no longer of any use to me; I'll enjoy knowing you've suffered." Then, he dropped the torch, igniting the wood. He moved to stand in front of me, and before I could register what was coming, he slammed his fist into my skull. And my world went black.

Chapter 41

I woke to Zara's shouts.

"Wake up, you stupid girl, wake up!" She shrieked so loud I felt it in my jaw as my teeth clenched from the onslaught.

"Yes, yes, that's it, wake up!"

My head drooped down the moment I attempted to raise it. It felt like someone was pushing against it, keeping it down. My eyelids lazily opened, and I couldn't see anything past a gray haze. I blinked, but my vision wasn't clearing.

"Girl, you must get out!" Zara's voice cracked as she began coughing. The sound quickly turned to a strained wheeze.

Thumps clambered against the stone floor. I tried to lift my head again and could make out the bottom of a white gown. Akira.

"A-ki—" My voice broke, the haze invading my throat. I coughed, and red liquid came spilling from my mouth. I spit it on the floor and tried again. "Akira!" My voice was hoarse, but there was a slight pause in her movement. "What are you doing?" I squinted, trying to see her. I could make out movement, but not much else. All I saw were her arms making a throwing motion before thuds rang through the cell.

"What is she doing?" I wheezed.

Zara's words sounded strained as she said, "She's fueling the flames, girl. While you've been out, thanks to your own doing—" Her words were interrupted by another coughing fit before she continued. "She has been instructed to continuously throw wood in, until the cell is filled. He wants you to burn."

A deafening roar rumbled the cell walls, and in my soul, I knew it was *him*. Knox. Even after everything I had said, my attempts at creating distance, he still came for me. I yanked on my chains and screamed, but my voice was so damaged from the smoke that it was barely audible. Tears streamed down my face as reality set in—I was going to die here with an angry old woman while I listened to Knox search for me just outside. He was so close.

I wasn't ready to give up. I didn't want to die here. He bellowed again before a red glow lit the small, barred window. It lasted for several seconds before it began again. Akira threw more wood into the cell. This time it landed below my feet. The flames from King Tatum's fire had spread down the middle of the cell, creating a barrier between Zara and I, effectively choking us both out with smoke. It lapped up the fresh kindling, and more flames began to flicker at my toes. I screamed, more from terror than pain, and tried to bend my legs up. The shift in weight pulled my wrists against the cuffs, a blinding light flashing through my eyes as the pain erupted in my nerves.

"Akira, please don't do this." I was sobbing now, hoping she could somehow break through whatever connection he had with her. The fiery glow from outside grew closer, the crackling harmonizing with the fire burning inside the cell.

"You will die now," was all she said before closing the cell door. There was no sound of a lock being engaged, but I guessed it didn't matter when the people inside were bound and burning.

"Akira!" My throat burned from the way I tried to scream her name, hoping that the urgency, the cry, would make her come back. But it didn't. I strained to keep my legs above the flames that had already grown bigger. Blood pooled down my arms, and I knew that if I didn't burn alive, I would likely soon bleed to death.

"Zara…" I croaked out. "What horde are you from?" I asked, praying she'd say Mending.

Her voice was so weak I could barely hear her. "I'm no dragon, girl. I'm from Orcalorne, a fae kingdom."

Disappointment clouded the wonder I would have felt being in the presence of an older fae. From what I knew, they could live exceptionally long lives, which meant she was millennia old.

Fluttering sounds filled my ears, and I struggled to lift my head. When I did, there was only the blur of vibrant hues against a smoky backdrop. Sharp prickles told me Star had pressed her horned head against my cheek. "Star!" I choked out. "You're here." I smiled and felt the dried blood crack along my lips. "You shouldn't be here, Star, you could be hurt!"

"Stupid girl—the keys!" Zara wheezed out.

"The keys on the ground, can you get them?" I pleaded to Star. She gave a few chirps before flying down to the floor. The keys were now between chunks of wood that Akira had thrown in. I held my breath, not wanting the flames to harm her delicate wings. She chomped at the metal ring but had to let go as an ember flew down near her wing, almost searing through it. "Star!" I screeched, my anxiety running rampant. I may not have known her long, but the little dragonfly had quickly sewn herself to my heart.

Star grabbed at the loop holding the keys once more, this time clamping on with her little but mighty jaws. She dragged the keys backward before trying to fly upward. The first attempt failed as she tried to maneuver around the shape of the keys; the second, she seemed to struggle with the weight of them. I was tempted to instruct her to drop them where I could grab them with my feet, but I wasn't strong enough to bend my legs up toward my mouth, and even then, how would I get the key into the cuff? Everything depended on this little creature. Her third attempt, her wings were rapidly beating, and her golden eyes were scrunched tight as she lifted the keys off the ground.

"Yes, yes, Star, you're doing it!" I could jump for joy if I weren't chained and half dead.

Zara spoke in gasping breaths. "Have the little dragonfly go to your chain, girl, I will do the rest." The smoke had completely blocked my view of her, turning the once-dark, musky stone room into an airless, choking sauna.

"You've got it, Star. You are doing such a good job." I started choking, my lungs struggling to find clean air. Star stopped, and the weight of the keys almost took her down, but she quickly righted herself and hovered just above my cuff.

"She's there!" I said to Zara. There was no reply. "Zara!" I tried again, still nothing. I stifled a sob, hoping she hadn't succumbed to the smoke. She was a grumpy woman, but this was not a death I would wish on anyone... Well, there were a few, but she wasn't on that list.

Star let out a low growl, a sound I had only heard from her once. She was usually a playful, lovable little thing. I lifted my head as much as I could, the pull of unconsciousness becoming overwhelming. The keys were tugging against Star's grip, toward my cuff. Star pulled back like they were trying to get away. The more the keys pulled, the more Star tugged back, using all the might her body could muster, sending her wings into overdrive. "I-It's okay, S-S-Star, I-it's okay S-S-Star," I choked out, eyes watering. "Y-ou can l-let them go." I was putting all my faith in the assumption Zara was behind this.

Once Star let go of the keys, they moved on their own to the keyhole in the cuff holding my right hand. The key slipped into the lock and turned, making an audible *click*. The cuff opened and tingles rushed through my limbs from my arms being dropped, a painful, bone-deep throb shooting up to my shoulder from the blood loss and how long my body had hung against it. I painstakingly grabbed the keys and unlocked my other cuff. My body crumpled to the ground, feet burning on the ignited wood below with embers flying in all directions.

"Go, Star. Star, go outside now." I pointed to the barred window that I knew the dragonfly could easily fit through. She protested and made an attempt to bite my finger. "Find safety, I will come for you when I'm out. You saved me." I kissed her snout and ushered her out of the cell. She perched next to one of the bars, watching me from above.

Knox's roar sounded again, only this time, it was full of sorrow and fury. I had to get to him. No matter what we'd been through, I knew that he was safe.

"Even in your darkest days, I was there to protect you."

I needed to push past all that I was feeling and get to him. I shoved the engulfed wood away from me, not caring about the smell of burnt hair and skin. Using the strength I had left, I dragged myself to the middle of the cell. There was a small section where the wood didn't cover the entirety of the ground, which meant it became my path through. "I'm coming, Zara." The words barely left my dry lips. A sharp burning pain trailed up my arms as I used them to shove the blackened logs away. This low to the ground, it was easier to make out my surroundings. I spotted Zara slumped on her side, and unlike me, her chain was attached to the ground and hooked around her ankles. There were no bruises or marks where the cuffs met skin. She'd stopped fighting long ago. I made my way to her and used her clothes as grips to pull myself up before shaking her. Her head wobbled back and forth with the force of my shakes. "Zara! Zara! Wake up, I have the key, I'm going to get you out," I said frantically. Her eyes opened just enough for her to see it was me.

"Stupid girl," she said with a cough.

"You're welcome," I bit out. As I took the keys and went to put them in her cuff, the key missed the hole as she slid her foot away. My brows furrowed with a sting. "What are you doing?"

"Get out of here, girl. I made peace with death a long time ago; there is nothing for me out there."

"That's not true, Zara, please come with me." I shook her once more when her eyes began to close again. "Come with me!" I shouted, my voice barely breaking above a whisper. "I'm not leaving you here to burn!" Tears welled up in my eyes, and I was surprised there was any moisture left in my body to produce tears.

"Stop it!" Her body jerked up, and her eyes were wide, staring at me. "You will go, girl. You will go now! Take this and guard it with your life. You have proven yourself to be loyal and empathetic today. Strong, and stupid." Her last words, I felt, weren't necessary, but my attention had gone to where she held her pale, veiny hands in front of her chest. A white light burst from her as her head tilted up toward the smoke. "Use this wisely, girl. Death must become you for there to be balance. This will lead the way." The light started to dissipate, and floating between her hands was a translucent stone with swirls moving in tandem within. Silvers and blues created the likeness of an evening sky. "This is Monsteralafe's moonstone; it is meant to be brought back to Raeganarde, where our lands once were. It has magical properties my people believed sacred. Hold it up toward the moon, and it will help you. It will give you strength." She gasped once, sounding so strained it must have been painful. "The one you seek is in the sky." She spoke to the stone next in a hushed whisper. "He will not have what's left of me. I give my life to the moon."

My fingertips brushed hers as I took the stone—her fingers were colder than any winter I had experienced. I could feel the stone's magic pulsing, much like my racing heartbeat. I held it close to my chest as I whispered, "Thank you."

Zara's mouth moved slowly into a sad smile. I wasn't sure she'd heard me. Her eyes were dull and lacking. Her body had gone gray, cracking from the cuff on her ankle and splintering all over her body, like a spider had woven a dark web over her skin. As the cracks spread and consumed each limb, Zara broke apart, her body crumbling, turning to dust, becoming indistinguishable in the smoky air.

My ribs ached at the loss of someone I'd barely known, one of my hands holding the moonstone, the other filled with her ashes.

Chapter 42
Knox

The scent of her fear was like a thorned vine wrapping around my heart, threatening to destroy me. I tasted it beneath the ash I left in my wake—Amalia's terror, sour and metallic, threading through the walls of King Tatum's fortress. *I have to get to her.* My body was already full of adrenaline from finding Bash unconscious. His body had been hauntingly still, and I had thought he was dead until I'd seen the vial embedded in his neck. Blaire assured me he was alive, that the vial stopped his ability to shift. King Tatum had used it on her during their sessions. Bash had a blunt head wound, which was bleeding more than I had ever seen, but I'd left them, putting his life in Blaire's hands. If she betrayed me again, I didn't care what information she had. She would not live long enough to stab me in the back a third time.

My claws shredded stone as I scaled the watchtowers, devouring the guards as if they were nothing but insects. The ones too far for my mouth to snap over were engulfed by my shadows, their bones crunching like dry twigs. *Faster. Faster. I have to get to her.* Her heartbeat thundered in my ears, the only sound I could hear over the roar of my own anger. The only thing fueling me. *She's alive.* I held onto that with everything I had.

Tatum's flags, portraying a dragon coiled around a diamond, whipped in the windy night air. The sight sent a surge of wrath into my veins like a dam that had broken free. I exhaled flames of deep purples and watched as the fabric ignited. I'd let this whole damned forgotten kingdom burn.

The courtyard stone fractured under my weight as I landed, shaking the ground. Soldiers swarmed, blades already in the air. Idiots. They were weighed down in blackened armor, a stark contrast to the guards within Santavarre who sported lightweight white armor. *Find her. Kill him. Burn the rest.*

I didn't bother shifting; my fire did the talking. My shadows ruined whatever the flames didn't decimate. A sweep of my head, mouth gaping to expel the fire, and flames devoured the soldiers mid-warcry. Their ashes stuck to my scales. I didn't blink. I didn't think of anything past finding her.

"Show yourself, coward!" My roar shook the ground beneath me. Even in my dragon form, I knew he heard me. I allowed my mind to stay unshielded from the shadows. The moment I was within range, he'd be reading it—it put me at risk, but it was worth it if it meant it would draw him away from her.

My mate.

She may hate me, but that didn't change the fact that she was mine.

More guards came at me, more cautious this time. Something wasn't right. My shadows surrounded me in defense of something I couldn't see. The guards laced in black metal smirked at me, their teeth sharpened like mine when I started to shift. These didn't feel like dragons. They weren't human, but they weren't my kind. Her scent distracted me—orange blossoms and blood. A new wave of anger fueled a roar. "Fight me, Tatum! Unless you're too afraid and have to send your abominable pets to do it." My jaws snapped at the creatures inching closer, their feet rippling with gray-green scales. There was something unnatural and evil about them.

All at once, they shifted fully in a shrieking rampage, their gray-green scales glistening like infected wounds as their snake-like bodies hurtled toward me. I expanded my wings to their full width and felt my shadows ready themselves to obey my will. This was the first time in longer than I could remember that I'd used them for battle. After the death of my father, I'd made it a point not to announce that I was the last from the Shadow Horde. Most within Santavarre believed the rest of the horde was skyward. Only Tatum knew the truth.

The first creature, the one who had eyed me from the moment they approached, flew fast, its jaws unhinging to spew a stream of bile-green acid. Nightshade venom, deadly to most dragon species. I was not most species. It would cause hallucinations, but I'd survive. My shadows swallowed the venom, evaporating it before it even got close. My tail lashed, crumbling the walls before I launched into the air. *They wanted to fight a dragon? I'd put up one hell of a fight.*

Shadows pooled around me as I circled the courtyard, the creatures using the smoke and night sky as shields. I had my own. My shadows exploded outward in smoky tendrils. I focused on the scent of death and nightshade and drove the shadows there; they pierced two creatures through their bellies. I felt them writhe against my attack, shrieking, as my darkness claimed them.

Another creature dove from above, claws outstretched, as the shrieks from the other two died along with their now-falling bodies. I rolled, my spines shredding its underbelly. The scales were much softer there; its entrails rained down on me. *No mercy.*

Three more surrounded me, a mixture of claws and spiked tails. One latched onto my hind leg, its teeth sinking deep, slicing through my hardened scales with ease. I roared, the sound creating a shockwave, destroying the last remaining watchtower. I torched the creature trying to rip my leg apart in an eruption of purple flame. A shriek sounded as the pain of its teeth and claws receded. I let out a starving shadow that wrapped itself around a creature's throat and midsection. Once it was in the shadow's grasp, I willed it to slam the creature to the ground. It did, violently, with a wet smack as the creature's skull burst open upon impact.

The final creature hovered, its milky eyes darting over the carnage. I advanced, shadows coiling around its neck like a vise. The creature hissed, spraying venom in panicked arcs. My tail whipped out, impaling it through its chest. I yanked it close, our faces inches apart. The creature, critically wounded, shifted back into its human form just in time to hear my words. "Tell Tatum," I rumbled, "his kingdom is falling, and I will burn it to the ground if he does not give me *her.*"

I let his body go, relishing the thud when the body hit the ground. Somewhere, Tatum was laughing.

Let him.

My shadows craved his bones.

Footsteps echoed through the rubble of ruined cobblestone.

"Ah, how proud your father would be if he were still alive," he crooned. "It's a shame he couldn't see the potential of our species so long ago."

"Where is she?" The words cut my throat. My self-control dwindled every second I was in his presence, fixated on the image of ripping his head from his body. *Find her, then kill him.*

He smiled. "Alive. For now. But you'll have to be... *precise.* She doesn't have much longer," Tatum purred.

"Give her to me!" I bellowed as I let my fire erupt, engulfing him in a burning violet flame. It did nothing. As the flames receded, he was no longer standing there. Instead, it was Amalia's lifeless body blackened by my blind rage. "Amalia!" The thorns constricting around my heart penetrated the organ as I gasped her name once more. Then she was gone. She was never there. I could no longer hear her heartbeat or smell her citrusy scent.

"One heartbeat left before the flames take her," Tatum said, his voice echoing around me. Tatum was no longer within sight, his laughter circling me, taunting me. I didn't care. Let him run. Let him *burn in this place.*

I reacted.

Fire erupted.

Then I saw her again. Her strawberry blonde locks blowing around, mixing with the ash in the air.

She stood at the edge of a fiery stream, its molten liquid bubbling and flowing through the newly formed cracks. Relief flooded through me as I shifted into my human form and ran to her.

No.

She turned. Her skin was full of angry pink blisters, peeling and expanding. Her beautiful hazel eyes were dull and depleted of life, of energy.

"Knox..." she whispered, so much pain in the attempt to speak. *Did I do this?*

I reached for her, but her eyes rolled toward the sky. She fell back into the red river of heat, igniting her instantly.

"NO!" Every part of me felt the moment she was gone. My soul screamed as it tore in two with the loss of its fated mate.

"Now you know how I felt." Tatum sighed. "When she took away everything I've ever loved. Did you truly think I'd dirty my hands? You were always the weapon, boy."

"She did nothing to you!" I screamed, the words lost in the emptiness I felt. I kneeled in her ashes. They stuck to my face, my clothes. *I can taste her death.*

Tatum's boot nudged my kneeling body. "She took everything from me. Her blood is the reason I have become who I am."

"You'll only ever be known as the dragon who destroyed the world for ghosts of his past." I lifted my head to meet his gaze, a single tear falling for *her.*

He laughed at my words, and I soaked in the sound as I readied to kill him.

Chapter 43

Ash clung to my lashes as I surveyed the scene before me, seeing for the first time the damage Knox had caused while I was trapped in that cell.

His rage, his fury, had sculpted this town into a wasteland.

Everything was either burned or still actively burning. Nothing survived, destroyed in his feral rage. My throat tightened. *All this... to find me?* I carefully trudged through rubble, still hot with burning embers that heated my ankles, my shadow dancing along as I walked, the flames flickering beside me. I could hear Tatum's laughter echoing through the wind that swept the smell of death around me.

King Tatum tried to end me, tried to erase my existence, the human existence. Each step I took played as a reminder of what he'd done. Yet, here I was, Defier of Death. Coming for him. "Tatum!" I shouted.

Ahead, King Tatum stood, his expression turned from humorous to a mix of shock and disbelief. He thought he'd won, maybe he even thought I was a ghost. But if I'd learned anything since the shimmer had taken my entire world from me, it was that I was not so easily extinguished. I walked toward him slowly, making sure he saw the promise of revenge in my eyes.

I still clutched the moonstone in my hand, its power had only grown stronger since I'd emerged from that stony dungeon. Thoughts of Akira slammed into my chest. Zara's body breaking down around me. All the lies and secrets from those I thought cared for me, swirled in my mind. Raising the stone to the sky, that bright light washed over me like a caress. If I ever had to wonder what moonlight felt like, this would be the only thing close enough to explain it. The light flitted over my arms and down to my still-bare, burned feet, mending each physical and invisible wound with a gentle kneading. The pain slowly went away with each trace of light that touched my skin, replaced by a surge of strength and resolve. I would do what needed to be done. King Tatum had proven he was not capable of peace, so fueled by hate he was willing to decimate an entire species.

"Amalia," Tatum seethed, his voice faltering as he took me in. He tried to take a few steps back but lost his balance on a plank of burning wood. The fear that broke through for a flickering moment was quickly replaced with arrogance. He still thought he would win. Still thought he could see his plan succeed.

I stopped just before him. The moonstone illuminating the both of us as the light still danced around my skin.

"You thought you could destroy me," I said, my voice steady for the first time. "You thought you could break me. Burn me," I said louder, harnessing the power of the moonstone. "But you have only made me stronger. I have walked through your fire, risen from it like a phoenix, proven humans are not always so easy to erase." My eyes flicked to where Knox was on his knees, wet trails along his cheeks. I couldn't allow emotion to cloud my judgment right now. I needed to keep my promise. I needed to end this.

King Tatum's mask wavered as I set my sights on him. Every emotion, all the hatred I felt, I channeled into this gaze. "You think you can defeat me?" he sneered, though his voice told me all I needed to know. He was actually afraid.

I smiled. "I don't think, Tatum. I know." The moonstone pulsed, the waves of energy coursed through every inch of my body, the power was fueling me. It gave me strength and as long as I had it, I was capable of so much *more*.

Clutching the moonstone in my right hand, I slammed my left into King Tatum's chest. His gasps were a sweet melody as my hand went through him like butter. My fingers glided through flesh and bone as if he weren't real. I wrapped my fingers around his erratically beating heart and squeezed.

Flashes of images flowed into my mind, and our conversation at the castle played like I was a bystander in the room. The conversation was all wrong; he was congratulating me on surviving, welcoming me into his family with the promise of an engagement soon to happen. The scene changed. Lane and I were laughing under a willow tree, snuggled up together as he kissed my lips.

No, no, no, this was wrong, this was all wrong. He was trying to make me doubt what I knew, doubt what fueled me. "We could achieve so much together, you and I, Amalia. We are not so different after all." He choked on his words as blood spilled from his lips.

"No!" I screamed, using his tactic against him. I thought of the courtyard, how Lane and I had seen everyone lying lifeless, and shoved my emotions and the images into him, not sure how to do it but remembering the brief glimpses I'd seen when I'd touched Lane and Knox. I saw the moment it reached him, his face slackened slightly and his eyes glazed over as if he was seeing a different world. I thought of the orbichor attack and made him feel the pain I had felt that day, the agony of the teeth biting through my flesh. His body jolted as if he had just been struck. I grabbed hold of his shoulder, making sure he couldn't move or accidentally kill himself before I was ready. I wanted him to experience all the hurt that he had caused. I thought of flames flickering over the field that now held bodies instead of the flowers I had loved so much. Although I didn't know what the horrors of Blaire's past looked like, I showed him her face as she told me her story, even if brief, and I watched his face as a tear slid from his right eye. Just a single one. Finally, I showed him his son. Lane. My heart lurched and I almost stopped pulled back. He needed to know, though. He needed to take in the knowledge that his decision, his life fueled by revenge, was what led to all of this. It was what led to his end. I allowed the memory to shuffle through and watched his eyes go wide as he saw Lane standing beside me, seeing Knox slice his blade through his flesh. King Tatum yelled out a sorrow-filled groan the moment Lane's head hit the ground.

King Tatum grabbed my arms with a grip so powerful it broke the connection, then suddenly, I was under his control. Seeing what he wanted *me* to see. "I may be the villain in your story, my dear." He coughed and splattered blood along my face. "But I was avenging the family the villain in mine destroyed." Images of a beautiful, diamond-encrusted dragon filled my vision. Its tail wrapped around three hatchlings, white as snow, within a nest cowered in fear. *This must be his mate.* She lowered her head and nudged the younglings, trying to comfort them. Little yips sounded from them as they all looked at something I couldn't see. The image changed to a tall, broad-shouldered man with reddish hair, laughing as smoke billowed behind him. The sound sent chills down my spine. The image spanned to the nest I had seen moments before. My breath caught as the flames devoured the creatures, the long neck of his mate reaching for the sky with a last cry that received an answer somewhere in the distance. A promise to save them, but it was too late. My heart felt like it was being torn apart one piece at a time.

Suddenly the scene changed, and I was in King Tatum's summoning room. He and Lane were talking about the scales. About a rumor of promised life. I couldn't make out all the words; he was holding me back from hearing it, only showing me what he wanted. "We will get them back," he said to Lane.

"You ask too much of me, Father. I won't be able to be around her. My hate is too strong. Her blood, her life, is at the cost of everything we lost."

"Do whatever you must to survive being around her, but we will need her when the time comes. Her blood will be the key. This is not a request."

The scene flashed back to the burning nest, where only two young bodies lay, still tucked within their mother. My grip loosened around his heart, something telling me he had information I needed. My instincts screaming that he didn't deserve this.

Then he smiled, seeing my doubt. I was no longer allowing my own hate and need for revenge to fuel my actions. "I'm sorry for what he's done to you," I said, voice breaking. "I am not *him.*" I tried to bring my arm back, but his hands tightened even more.

"Everything I am is already gone. You will not survive this, my dear." His mouth spread in a blood-filled smile. "The realm is dying. The balance was broken long ago. Your mate," he bit out with a cough, "should have never brought you back. One must die. It will never be Mikulec." With his final words, he forced my arm out of his chest, his eyes going slack.

I looked down to see his heart cradled in my fingers. I turned the no-longer-beating organ over in my hand. Its warmth and thick smooth surface jarred me. I had never seen a heart outside a body before, a numbness washed over me before Tatum's body crumpled to the ground, and I looked at Knox. The second I did, I broke. Ash matted his hair, dried blood crusted his face, his knuckles. I joined him on my knees, and he reached for me like I wasn't real, as if he were seeing me in the Elysian Islands. "Are you really alive?" he said, so low I might have misheard him. I looked into his eyes. No rage burned in them. They were focused, analyzing me. I touched his face to show I was really there. That I was sorry. His skin was rough with dirt and ash, but the moment we touched, I saw it register in his bulging eyes before he pulled me to him and kissed me so violently I could hardly keep up. We both gasped for breath while trying to deepen the kiss.

Knox whispered in a pained, cracked voice, "I thought I had lost you. I thought I—" He pressed his head to mine as his voice broke, and we both shuddered.

"I thought I was lost, but you came for me. You always come for me." The roars I'd heard while in the cell would be ingrained into my memory for a lifetime. "You saved me." In more ways than just this moment. *He brought me back.* That would need to be discussed when we both could think straight. For now, I'd keep the questions surrounding that knowledge to myself.

Star chortled before landing on my shoulder, nudging her head into mine, snapping her teeth at Knox's nose. I smiled for the first time in a while, and it felt good, even surrounded by destruction. My heart warmed knowing she was safe.

"What now, *Valkara?*" Knox asked, lifting my chin up so that I was looking at him. The remnants of what he'd done stuck to him like ink. Soot smeared his face. Drops of blood seeped from a cut on his eyebrow. I lifted my hand to wipe it away, but he deflected it in favor of pulling my hand to his chest. The act brought a sliver of light into his shadowed eyes.

"We need to collect the rest of the scales, find the relics, and..." Determination laced my words as King Tatum's plan for the scales sparks my own. *I could bring everyone back.* "We go skyward. We find Mikulec."

To be continued...

Acknowledgements

First and foremost, thank you dad. You'll never have the ability to read this. Leaving us all too soon. As I write this it's been officially one year since you've been gone. The illogical part of my brain will always blame the beginning of this book for your passing. Little did I know then, that a week later you'd be gone. You shaped me into the person I am today and I am so grateful for you and your ability to fight through everything life has thrown at you. Amalia's perseverance is based on you. Her ability to get the shit end of the stick at every turn and still be able to grow and allow it to build her character instead of break it is based on you. You may not be able to read this story, and see yourself within the pages but I'd like to think that you are proud of me wherever you may be. I love you more than could ever be expressed, you are missed every day.

There are a few main people I have to thank for championing not only this story, but me.

Sir William, the man who has allowed me the time and space to pursue this project. Who got up early to feed the cats when I was dead to the world from staying up so late trying to hit self-made deadlines. You've allowed me the opportunity to go after a dream without attempting to discredit it or complain (that much) about the time it took away from us. Thank you for everything you've done for me, I love you bunches adventure buddy.

Sam~may~may. My soulmate in friend form. You have been through so many stages of my life, we have been on so many wild adventures, and I wouldn't trade them for the world. I know that we will be in each others corners for a lifetime. You will always be my best friend. Thank you for being a constant in my life, even during times it was hard for me to even exist. You always stayed with me until I found the light again. You have saved my life more times than you know.

Jenny, the support, kindness, love, and validation you give is priceless. Thank you for being in my life. You're always checking in and supporting me in all my crazy phases. You come and set up at events with me, just so I'm not alone. You have been an absolute blessing in my life, you are the kind of person that everyone deserves to experience a friendship with. I would have been lost so many times in the past few years without you.

Katie you are a supportive queen! I wonder if our one shared brain cell is telling you I'm writing this... You throw so much love and inspiration into everyone around you, ensuring they know they are capable of anything, and that they have someone in their corner. You deserve everything in the world and there isn't one soul who has met you that hasn't walked away with their darkness being dimmed by your light.

Brittany, you care so deeply about everyone and I feel incredibly lucky that I have been on the receiving end. I don't check in nearly enough as I should but I know that our friendship will always be there. I love you so much and it has been so amazing to see the positive direction your life has gone, in the time we've known each other. Also thank you for traumatizing me on your birthday... I'll never be able to look at your feet the same ever again.

To my editor, Kayleigh. You have been such an incredible human. Not only are you obviously great at what you do, you were able to dive into the ROUGH manuscript and help me believe in myself that this story was worth it. You took the time to explain the "why" behind each edit to ensure I never felt like I wasn't good enough. You worked through me figuring out how the heck to even do all of this which I'm not sure a lot of editors would. Finding you was the best thing that could have happened to this story. Thank you for supporting me through it all and understanding that there were moments I had to work through mentally before I was ready to let this go. You are forever stuck with me and I wouldn't want to be google doc trauma bonded with anyone else but you.

Thank you to my wonderful community of people who have blindly supported me before you even knew how you felt about the book. I will never be able to express what that means to me and to have such an amazing group hyping me up, validating and helping me navigate any concerns or issues, offering excitement, it all just helped fuel my passion to finish this story. So here's to my street team Chantelle, Nikki, Sheena, Whitney, Laken, Katelyn, Donna, Mel, Valerie, Erica, Emma, Savanna (also the best graphic maker I have ever seen), Macee my forever hype queen, Kimberly, Nicole, Reharn, and Amara.

To my Beta readers, you literally received shit and somehow found the hidden potential underneath! I don't believe any Beta's ever receive a first draft but you guys took it and really helped mold this story and show me all the places I was overlooking or didn't give enough attention. You helped me believe there was a reason for continuing forward. Thank you Nicole, Sarah W., Sarah D., Gulcan, Angie, Marci, Clarissa, Melisa, Arianna, Sarah H., and Matt.

Nicole W. thank you for being the FIRST fan of A Dragon So Savage. For emailing me all those Kickstarters and just fully embracing the story even in its most raw format. The excitement you had was shocking and gave me a glimpse at what this story could do for others. You said this story came to you in a moment when you needed it, and I truly believe I was lucky enough to find you in a moment of need. I was second guessing everything, I had just received a pretty brutal email from another reader and felt like I should quit while I was ahead. YOU gave me confidence and reminded me some may hate it but others may love it. Every author deserves to have someone like you in their corner.

To all my readers, you took a chance on me and this story. For that I am eternally grateful. I hope you found strength within the pages while reading, like I did while writing. You are literally making my dreams come true. I will never be able to express how it feels to know people around the world are supporting me.

www.ingramcontent.com/pod-product-compliance
Lightning Source LLC
Chambersburg PA
CBHW020545120726
47903CB00001B/142